GOLDIE

A NIGHT REBELS MC ROMANCE

CHIAH WILDER

I love hearing from my readers. You can email me at chiahwilder@gmail.com.

Make sure you sign up for my newsletter so you can keep up with my new releases, special sales, free short stories, and other treats only available to newsletter readers. When you sign up, you will receive a FREE hot and steamy novella. Sign up at: http://eepurl.com/bACCL1.

Visit me on facebook at facebook.com/AuthorChiahWilder.

Chapter One

THE TATTOO SHOP bustled as young men and women filed in to make a statement on their skin. The weekends at Get Inked were crazy since it was the only tattoo and piercing shop that looked decent. Bent Needles, the shop's competitor, had been cited for health violations numerous times by the county. The Night Rebels owned Get Inked, and customers felt comfortable in the clean, professional-looking establishment. The ochre-yellow walls and dark brown laminate floors had a calming effect on people who paid to have needles pierce their designs into their skin.

"Did Flora ever call?" Tattoo Mike asked Goldie as he slipped a wad of cash into the cash register.

"Nope. I tried calling and texting her a bunch of times. It'd be a big help if we had a receptionist tonight. It sucks to have to run the counter and do the ink. We should fire her ass. This is the second Saturday she's pulled this shit." Goldie ran his hand through his short hair.

"I already have an ad online and in the paper. She's history." Tattoo Mike glanced over the appointment book. "We gotta start limiting walk-ins on the weekends. You got any appointments for tonight?"

"I just finished with my last one. You?"

"I got two, and both of them are pretty intense in design. Looks like you, Skull, and Jimmy are gonna have to handle the walk-ins."

"No problem. I'm going to get a club girl over here to handle the front desk." Goldie picked up his phone and dialed one of his brothers. "Dude. We need one of the girls to help out tonight. That bitch Flora was a no-show again. We're slammed and it's just gonna get worse. Seems like everyone wants a tat or a piercing after downing a few shots."

Goldie chuckled.

"I'll bring one of the girls over. The bitch just lost her job," Paco said.

"Tattoo Mike's already got an ad out. Thanks, dude. See you in a few." Goldie set his phone down and looked up as Skull approached.

"Jimmy's sick as shit. There's no way he can work on anyone." Skull pulled out a bottle of root beer from the mini fridge behind the counter.

"Fuck! Tattoo Mike's got two customs." Goldie clasped the back of his neck and rubbed it hard.

Jimmy was the only citizen tattoo artist who worked at Get Inked. He'd been working there for over five years and his work was impeccable. The club had talked about taking on another citizen artist part-time, but they hadn't found anyone they thought was good enough and fit into the overall vibe of the shop. The tattoo parlor didn't just have customers from Alina; citizens from the outlying county and as far away as Durango came to the shop. Their reputation for having top-notched tattoo artists was known throughout the southwestern part of Colorado.

"Looks like we'll be hustling our asses in about another hour." Skull looked at the wall clock that was surrounded by framed pictures of tattooed men and women. The clock read eleven; soon people would be leaving the bars. "I hope I don't have to kick anyone's ass tonight. We don't have time for that shit." Skull guzzled the root beer.

Goldie nodded. The road captain for the Night Rebels usually loved a good fight, but not when he was working and needed to concentrate on what the hell he was doing. Many people staggered in drunk and loud, demanding to have a tattoo or a piercing. The policy was to turn them away. Sometimes they had to get tough and throw them out, and there was always someone who thought he could fight them. It really got under Goldie's skin.

"Hey, guys," Kelly said as she walked through the door. She was the club girl who usually offered to help out at the club's businesses if they needed backup.

"Hey. You're the receptionist for the next three hours." Goldie moved aside as she squeezed in behind the counter, rubbing her behind against him.

"You owe me. I was right in the middle of getting real cozy with one of the Fallen Slayers. He was cute too."

The Fallen Slayers MC was a club the Night Rebels were friendly with. They lived about an hour away in Silverado and would come to the club's weekend parties. Once in a while, the Night Rebels would go to Silverado to shoot some pool with them or hang at one of their parties.

"You guys need anything else?" Paco asked.

Goldie smiled. "No. You anxious to get back to the party? How's the citizen turnout tonight?"

"Fucking awesome." Paco lifted his eyebrows.

"Damn. We need to be there." Skull came out from behind the counter and sank down onto one of the black leather couches against the wall.

"They'll still be there when we get off," Goldie said.

Paco nodded. "If you don't need anything else, I'm outta here."

Goldie lifted his chin. "Catch you later, dude."

Two guys walked in and approached the counter. "We'd like to get a tattoo," the taller one said to Kelly.

She turned to Goldie. "You available?"

He eyed the two guys. "How old are you?"

The shorter one turned red and looked at the floor, but the tall one said, "Eighteen."

"Bullshit. You guys don't even look sixteen. Show me some ID."

"I left my license at home," the tall one said; the short one kept staring at the floor.

"No ID, no tattoo. Pretty simple."

The tall one shifted from one foot to another. "We heard you guys were cool here. That this was owned by the Night Rebels."

"It is owned by the Night Rebels, and we're cool as fuck. I still need to see your IDs. If you're eighteen, you'll go back to one of the rooms. It you don't have any IDs, then you'll have to come back when you do."

"But we have the money and are ready—"

Goldie held up his hands. "Now you're just pissing me off, kid. I'm not negotiating with you. I'm telling you that you're not getting a fuckin' tattoo without any ID telling me you're eighteen. So hit the pavement."

The shorter teenager moved away from the counter. "Let's go, Tyler."

"We'll just go to Bent Needles." Tyler glared at Goldie.

"Do whatever you want, but you're not getting tatted in this shop."

"I'm not going there. My cousin went there and got a massive infection in his leg. Let's just go home. My mom will be pissed if I'm late again tonight." The shorter guy moved toward the door.

"Just shut the fuck up, Brandon." Tyler clenched his fists and stormed out.

Goldie, Skull, and Kelly laughed.

"I'm so glad I'm not a teenager anymore. Those years were hell," Kelly said as she wiggled on the stool.

"You're not kidding," Skull said as he glanced at two men who'd just come in.

Soon Skull was in a room with one guy and Goldie was with the other. Thankful his customer wanted a simple design, Goldie stood and stretched forty-five minutes later while the man slipped on his shirt. "Remember to keep the bandage on until the morning. No sun for at least three weeks. Follow everything on this sheet of paper and you should be good. It you have problems or questions, give us a call." He handed the aftercare list to the customer, who paid Kelly and handed a twenty to Goldie. "Appreciate it, man."

The client nodded and walked out.

"Why'd you shave off your beard? I thought Army bet you couldn't grow it longer than Diablo's."

"I couldn't fuckin' stand it. It itched, and I was scratching my face all the time. I gladly gave Army his winnings." He ran his hand over his smooth face.

"I like you either way, sweetie. Skull's still working on his guy. I've gotta pee." Kelly slid off the stool and scratched Goldie's back with her fingernails. "I like your muscles. They make me horny." She winked at him and leaned in. "You wanna fool around?"

Her body was soft against his, and the scent of orange blossom invaded his nostrils. He wasn't fond of overbearing fragrances, and many of the club girls bathed themselves in it, including this one. He stepped back. "I thought you had to pee."

"I do. Just thinking about when I get back." She squirmed in place, then rushed to the bathroom at the end of the hall.

He watched her go. Normally he'd be all over it, but right then he wasn't feeling it. He was restless and had been for a couple of months. What he was restless about, he couldn't say; he just wanted something different from what he had. Of course, he had his pick of women, and he was the first to admit unabashedly that he was a player. What could he say? He loved women—all types. But for the past couple of months, he hadn't felt that energized when he'd been screwing the club girls. It'd begun to seem routine.

He perched on the edge of the stool, pulled out a copy of *Easyriders*, and thumbed through it. As he was reading an article, the door opened and loud giggling filled his ears. He looked up and saw three women, but the one in the middle made his blood pump. She kept covering her full pink lips with her hand as if to suppress her snigger. Her chestnut hair had blonde streaks in it as though the sun had kissed it, and it cascaded past her shoulders, which were bare.

Then she looked at him. Her eyes were seriously blue—field of cornflower, summer desert sky at noon. Perfect. Her hand dropped down to her side and her lips parted. Goldie watched every movement, wishing he could slip his tongue into her mouth for a quick taste.

"I really had to go." Kelly's voice broke through the intensity of the moment. The woman turned away, and her friend whispered something to her. A peal of laughter erupted from them.

Kelly came behind the counter and he stood away from the stool so she sat once more.

"Can I help you ladies?" he said. *I hope she wants a clit piercing. I bet her pussy is as pink as her mouth.*

The two women next to her shoved her forward, saying, "She wants a tattoo." They laughed. She shooed their hands away from her and shook her head, then looked at him again.

He groaned inwardly and his cock stirred as she skimmed the tip of her tongue over the contours of her lips, lips that were made for sinning.

"Is it a yes or no?" He threw her the smile that melted most women's panties. She shrugged. "Have you been thinking about this for a while, or did you have a couple of drinks and come over here?"

Laughter burst from all three of them and it made him grin more. *She's fucking sweet.*

Kelly tapped her fingers on the counter. "Do you want a tat or not?" The women quieted down.

Anxious not to break their jovial mood, he turned to Kelly. "I'll handle this." She rolled her eyes, then looked down at the magazine Goldie had on the counter.

"Hay's been thinking about it for a while. That's all she talks about," the dark-haired woman said.

"Especially when she's had a couple of White Russians," the other woman chimed in. That made them start laughing again.

Goldie moved in front of the counter. "Are you drunk?" His voice was low and gravelly.

She darted her eyes to his and their gazes locked. The laughing hyenas, Kelly's aggravated sighs, the whir of the needles all faded out; there was nothing in the room but him and her. Heat stirred within him as his hungry gaze devoured her rounded hips and long shapely legs. Her cheeks burned brightly as she shifted in place.

"So are you?" he asked.

"Am I what?" she breathed.

His eyes climbed slowly from her pretty sandaled feet to her bright red face. "Drunk?"

"Hay's not drunk, but we are," the dark-haired woman said between sniggers.

"So, Hay's getting the tattoo?" He locked gazes with her again. She nodded. "Where do you want it?"

"On her butt." Her friends giggled.

He raised his eyebrow. "Your friends seem to be doing all the talking. Is that where you want it?"

"Uh… yeah. I've been thinking about it for a while now. I'm also not drunk. I've had a couple of drinks but I'm good."

"Do you know what design you want?"

She nodded. "It's nothing too big or anything." She pointed to Kelly, whose head was buried in the magazine. "Is she the one who's going to do the tattoo?"

He shook his head. "She's the receptionist. I'm going to do it." She gasped as her hand covered her pretty mouth. He chuckled. "You seem to have a problem with that."

"Oh, go on, Hay. I'm sure he's seen a lot of asses before. It's like a doctor. After a while, all asses and boobs look alike." Her blonde-haired friend pushed her forward a bit.

"Stop it, Claudia. You and Rory are starting to get on my nerves."

Mine too. "You're not going to find a woman artist in Alina, or the county for that matter. If you go to a bigger city you'll find them there." *I bet she has a gorgeous ass.*

"Is it like Claudia said? I mean, you must do a ton of these. It's probably like no big deal."

He pressed his lips and ran his eyes over her face. "Yeah. I do a ton of these, but it's up to you. I don't want you to feel uncomfortable."

Snickering, she threw her shoulders back. "What the hell. Let's do it."

A celebration complete with horns and streamers broke out inside him. "Yeah. What the hell. Follow me."

"Can my friends come too?"

The last thing he wanted was the giggling duo, but he was afraid if he said no she'd back out. He nodded and walked down the hallway, the clacking of high heels echoing behind him.

He opened the door to a room that had a padded massage table. The walls were adorned with drawings of tattoos, and there was a small black leather love seat against one wall, a built-in desk with a computer, and several bookcases stuffed with black binders and books on various designs.

"Do you have a design in mind?" Goldie asked as he gestured for Hay to sit on the table. "I want a standing trunk with a bunch of flowers wrapped around it. I don't want the trunk real thick, and I want the flowers to look like they're in watercolor."

Standing in front of the bookcase, he pulled out a thick binder and leafed through it. Then he walked over to her, pointing to a floral design. "Something like this?"

A smile spread across her face. "That's exactly what I want. It's beautiful. Is it your design?"

He nodded, then went over to the sink in the corner of the room and washed and dried his hands. "What's your pain tolerance?"

"I'm not sure. Is it going to hurt?"

"A little. Everyone is different. I can put a numbing cream on the area. I usually don't do that except for areas that can be extra sensitive, which the buttocks can be."

"Really? I wouldn't think that since there's so much flesh there."

Yeah. I bet she's got a soft, squeezable ass. "Doesn't seem to matter. Some people breeze right through it. Others squirm a lot. It's up to you." Reaching down, he pulled a bottled water from the small fridge near the sink and gave it to her. "Drink up. I want to make sure you're hydrated."

"If I do the numbing thing, how long will it take?"

"Usually about thirty minutes to an hour for it to take effect."

"Let's just go without it. I'll be brave. I promise." Her bright smile pulled him in, and he craved to press his mouth on her full lips.

"Okay. Slip off your panties and lie on your stomach. You allergic to latex?"

"No. Why?"

"Just wondering what type of gloves to use." As he watched her wiggle out of her lacey panties, his dick pulsed. He hadn't even seen her ass and his cock was already misbehaving. He shook his head and came over to her, waiting for her to get comfortable. Lifting her skirt, he sucked in his breath as two rounded ass cheeks came into view. They were perfection. *Damn. I gotta concentrate on what I'm doing, not on how badly I want to bite and smack her ass.*

"Can we see the design?" Rory said. Grateful for the intrusion, Goldie nodded and handed her the binder. "Oh wow. It's beautiful. I may just have to get me one of these." She smiled and caught his look.

Diverting his gaze back to the most beautiful ass he'd ever seen, he began to adorn it.

An hour later, he secured the bandage over the tattoo and helped her up. Claudia handed Hay her panties, and she giggled as she began to slip them on.

"Make sure you follow all the instructions on this sheet. Since you got your tat higher up on your cheek, it should be easier to sit. Just make sure you keep it clean and moist. You don't want to wear anything too tight, and you may want to reconsider wearing panties for a couple of weeks."

His lips twitched when crimson streaked her face.

"Thanks," she mumbled as she took the sheet from his hands before she rushed to the door and walked down the hall with her two friends in tow.

"You forgot to sign in." Kelly's voice bounced off the walls. "And put down your phone number."

"Why?" Hay asked.

"That's the rule."

Kelly's nails scraping against the counter grated on his nerves. He went into the reception area.

"We ask for customers' phone numbers to check up on them and make sure they're not having any problems," he said.

"Do I have to?" She looked everywhere but at him.

"No. It's optional." Goldie watched as she hesitated, then quickly wrote something down.

"Let's go." She and her friends went through the front door, nearly colliding with a couple of guys as they came into the shop.

Goldie watched the three women disappear into the night. *If she left her number, I'll give her a call tomorrow to see how she's doing.* He walked over to the front counter and glanced at the sign-in sheet. He jerked his head back and a sudden coldness spread through him as he read the name "Hailey Shilley." *What the fuck?*

"Goldie, did you hear me? Are you zoning out?" Kelly's voice pierced through his veil of shock.

"What do you want?"

"These guys want tats. Are you available?"

He nodded slowly. "I can do one and Skull can do the other. Buzz him." He turned to the twentysomethings. "Where do you want the tats?" They both said their upper arms. "Okay. Give me a minute while I set things up."

Walking to one of the rooms that had a black leather chair that resembled a barber's chair, he gripped the counter and shook his head. He still couldn't believe the woman he'd had a hard-on for, the one whose ass he'd seen and touched, was Hailey Shilley.

Is it possible that this is just some fucked-up coincidence? But he knew it wasn't. He only knew one Hailey Shilley, and she was the little sister of his best buddy, Ryan. But when he'd last seen Hailey, she'd just turned fourteen. Their dad was transferred to New Mexico and that was the last time he saw or thought of her.

She grew up real nice. He shook his head forcefully. *Damnit! This is Ryan's little sister.* He couldn't go there. Even though he was drawn to her, and he suspected she was to him, he couldn't start anything with her. *Ryan would kill me. I just have to forget about her.*

He prepared his room, then went to the front. Only one of the guys was sitting on the couch. "My buddy went with the other dude," he said.

Goldie nodded and motioned him to follow. *I always call my customers after they get a tattoo. I'll give her a quick call tomorrow and then it'll be done. What's one call going to hurt?*

Resolute in his decision, he motioned for the guy to sit in the chair, and then he closed the door.

Chapter Two

HAILEY GROANED WHEN she turned on her back in bed. Rolling to her left side, she glanced at her digital clock and grimaced: five thirty. The area where she got her tattoo throbbed, so she pushed herself out of bed and padded to the bathroom to take two Tylenols. *I can't believe I got a tattoo on my butt. I can't believe I let that gorgeous guy* see *my butt, and* touch *it*. She silently swore she'd never drink White Russians again. She'd lost her head the previous night. And Rory and Claudia were just as much to blame as she was. *They pushed me into doing it*. But she knew she was more than willing. She'd wanted one for such a long time but never had the nerve to do it, especially when she'd been living with her parents in Albuquerque.

After filling the glass with water, she downed the Tylenol, then went back to bed. It was Sunday morning and she wanted to sleep in. It was the only day she had off from the flower shop she was running for her aunt Patty. It'd been eight months since she'd come back to Alina—her hometown. She wasn't sure how she'd feel about it, but she had to admit it was great being back with her two best friends, Rory and Claudia. The three of them had known each other since they were old enough to walk, and even though they'd kept up with each other through social media, it wasn't the same as being together again in the same town.

Closing her eyes, she hoped sleep would come, but the handsome face of the tattoo artist stayed in her mind. He was definitely hot, with his muscled chest and his tight, sculpted biceps. She was a sucker for a man's biceps, and the cutie from the previous night had the best pair of arms she'd seen in a very long time. Maybe even the best ever.

But it hadn't stopped there. His face was smooth and clean-shaven, just the way she liked it. So many men had scruff, but she loved to run her fingers over a freshly shaved face. When she'd first seen him, his blue eyes pierced her like shards of ice on a wintry day. It was like he was trying to see inside her core, her essence. It both unnerved and excited her at the same time. He had a nice sprinkling of tattoos on his built arms, and she found herself sneaking peeks at him whenever he wasn't looking. His jaw was square and his cheekbones high, but it was his full lips that beckoned her. *I bet they're soft but firm.* He struck her as a man who would know how to please a woman.

Tingles skated across her skin as she imagined being in his arms, his mouth pressed against hers, her body fused to his. She licked her lips. *I really need to get laid. I've been here for eight months and haven't even kissed a guy.* The problem was that she was so busy at the flower shop, and the men who did approach her just didn't do it for her. They didn't spark anything in her to make it worth her while. No one really had except for the rough, sexy tattoo artist. Just thinking about him made her shiver all over.

He probably has a girlfriend. And he's probably a cheat. A guy that good-looking never has a shortage of women.

The vibration of her phone startled her. *Who in the hell is calling me at this hour?* Warmth flooded her when she saw Ryan's name flash on her screen.

"Do you know what time it is?" She tried to sound pissed but failed miserably.

"It's a quarter to three in the afternoon in Bahrain." His chuckle rumbled over the phone.

She winced when she rolled onto her back and quickly turned back to her side. "You're in Bahrain? Are you on leave?"

"Yeah. A few of us are here for four days. I'd rather be in Alina though. You getting used to being back?"

"I am. I'm just so busy all the time with Aunt Patty's shop. She didn't listen to the doctor and went back to work, and then she had to get another operation. I told her I could take care of everything and for her to relax and stay off her leg."

"Aunt Patty was always stubborn. She kinda reminds me of a sister of mine." Ryan laughed.

She giggled. "I would've at least listened to the doctor. Anyway, she's in rehab for about nine months and she's climbing the walls. When are you going to come home for a visit?" Hailey hated thinking of him fighting overseas. She was just as upset as their mother when he'd enlisted in the Army when he turned twenty. Even though he'd tell her not to worry, she couldn't help it; he was always in the back of her mind. She wished he hadn't reenlisted a couple of years before, but he did and she just had to deal with it.

"I may be able to take two weeks off this summer. I'll let you know."

"Summer is just around the corner. That'd be awesome! I miss you so much, and so do Mom and Dad." She blinked rapidly to stave off the tears.

"I know. I'd love to come to Alina and see some old faces. It's been a long time since I was there."

"I've been meaning to ask you for Garth's phone number. I keep forgetting to get it every time we text or e-mail."

"You don't want to look him up. He's in a biker club now. A badass one, as in dangerous and doing all sorts of illegal shit."

"But you're still friends with him."

"Of course. We've been buds since we were in first grade. I'm just saying there's no reason for you to look him up. He's got a ton of women around him all the time, and he's busy as hell with his club."

She laughed. "I wouldn't be looking him up to date. I just thought it'd be nice to connect with someone who knows you and can talk about you. It'd be like you were here. I know that sounds silly."

"It does. I have to go. Don't work too hard. You've got to have some fun too."

"I know. I loved talking to you. Take care of yourself."

After she placed the phone on the nightstand, she grabbed a tissue and blew her nose, then wiped her wet eyes. She and Ryan were close even though there was a four year difference between them. When she was younger, he used to take her to get ice cream, to Overland Lake to swim, and all the other things a teenage brother wouldn't be caught dead doing with his little sister.

Smiling at the memories of their childhood, she pulled out another tissue and dabbed the corners of her eyes.

Then the face of Garth Saner floated through her head. She'd had the worst crush on him, starting when she was eleven years old up until the time they had to move to Albuquerque. She'd thought he was the best-looking boy in the neighborhood. He'd always been nice to her, especially when she'd started growing breasts. When she turned thirteen, she caught him glancing at her chest more times than she could count. It used to make her feel funny, and a fluttery feeling in her stomach made her turn away from him when he'd come over to hang out with Ryan. When she'd entered Jefferson High School, she'd get a burning sensation in her chest every time she saw him with his arm around a girl or caught them kissing near the bleachers. She didn't know why she cared, but she did, so she avoided him as best she could. Then halfway through her freshman year, her father was transferred to Albuquerque.

I wonder what he looks like now. He's probably still a player, breaking all the girls' hearts like he did in high school. Picturing him in a biker gang was easy because he'd had a bad-boy edge about him when they were growing up. He got in trouble a lot at school because of fighting, mouthing off to teachers, and smoking on school grounds. He was a definite rebel. Part of her wanted to ignore Ryan's warnings and try to locate Garth, but she knew she wouldn't.

As her thoughts slowed down, she felt drowsy. Pulling the sheets over her shoulder, she closed her eyes and let sleep settle in.

WHEN SHE HEARD the vibration, she sat up in bed, the late spring sunlight beating against her window shades. For a few seconds she was disoriented and thought a bee was in her room. As she swatted at the air, the vibrating sounded muffled and she looked under her covers, petrified that a bee had somehow ended up trapped in her Martha Stewart lilac sheets. When she saw her phone, peals of laughter burst from her.

"Hello?" She giggled.

"Do you always sound this cheerful in the morning after having a tattoo?"

A rush of adrenaline surged through her. *The tattoo guy. Fuck.* "It's the only way to deal with the pain." *What a stupid lame answer.*

He chuckled. "How're you doing? Do you still have the bandage on?"

"Uh… yeah. I was sorta sleeping when you called."

"Sorry. I should've figured you would be after your night out. You and your friends definitely had a party going on."

"Last time I drink White Russians. They make me do crazy things, like have my butt tattooed." *I can't believe he called me. Wait. Don't jump to conclusions. It's his job to see how his customers are doing. This is routine.*

"Sometimes doing crazy things is the spark we need in our lives to keep on going. Anyway, if having some flowers tatted on your ass is the craziest thing you do, then you need to get out more." His voice, low and gravelly, stroked her senses like velvet.

"I haven't been in Alina very long. I'd love to have someone show me the hot spots in town." She held her breath. When he didn't answer, her heart sank. *Could you sound any more desperate? He only called to ask how you are. It's routine. I made an ass out of myself.* "I have to go."

"Sure. If you have any questions or issues, just give us a call." His smooth baritone sounded strained.

"Okay," she mumbled and hung up. *"Just give us a call."* He didn't *tell me to give* him *a call.* She buried her face in her pillow as the blood rushed to her head. If she decided to get another tattoo, she'd never go back there. How could she ever show her face in that shop again? Even if she had to drive to Durango to get a tattoo, she'd do it before she went back there.

I so need to go out with a man. Maybe I should go out with Rory's coworker. What was his name? Blake, or Blaine? Maybe it was Brandon. Anyway, he seemed nice, and he wasn't super-hot so I wouldn't make an ass out of myself. One thing was for sure: she *did* need to get out more.

She picked up her phone and sent a text to Rory, asking her to arrange a double date with her coworker. When Rory responded with a series of happy faces and exclamation points, Hailey groaned and buried her face in the pillow.

Chapter Three

G OLDIE SAT AT the table, his legs stretched out in front of him, and watched Brutus and Jigger play pool. He curled his fingers around a large can of Coors, then brought it to his lips and took a long drink.

"What's happenin', dude?" Army asked as he slid a chair out from the table and sat down.

"Not much. Just chillin' until I have to go to work. What're you up to?"

"I got a hot date for later tonight. She's a real looker. She's got big hair, big tits, and a big ass. She's really something. The tats on her are awesome. It looks like your work. She said she had them done at Get Inked. Do you remember her?" Army picked up his glass of whiskey.

"Not offhand. I've worked on a lot of chicks who fit that description."

"You'd remember her. Anyway, I was thinking that after you get off work, you could join us. She's got a friend who's got the right curves. I know you'd like her. What do you say?"

"Not tonight. Tattoo Mike's gotta cut out early. His old lady's having an anniversary party for her folks and he's gotta be there. That just leaves me and Skull. I'll probably be there past closing."

"When have you ever passed up a sure thing? The chick's friend doesn't care what time you get to their apartment. She just wants you to get there." Army smiled widely and leaned back in the chair.

"They roommates?"

"Yeah. It could get real fun." Army chuckled.

Goldie wasn't in the mood for hooking up with a citizen. His head was still reeling from the fact that the beautiful woman with the luscious ass was Hailey Shilley. His thoughts rolled back to when he and Ryan used to hang out and Hailey always wanted to tag along. Even when they'd climb up to their treehouse, she would stand at the base of the tree and call up to Ryan. He sniggered. *She knew how to manipulate us. We always gave in and I'd scramble down and help her climb up.*

"What's so funny?" Army asked.

The memories scurried away as Army's voice and the clack of the pool balls brought him back to the present. "Nothing. I'm going to pass for tonight. Ask Chains. He's been itching for someone new. You know how he gets after being with the club girls for too long—he's ready for some fresh game."

Army busted out laughing. "Perfect way of putting it. Okay, I'll ask him. It's your loss." He moved his chair around so he could watch the pool game.

Goldie stared at the players, but they were just fuzzy silhouettes as his mind brought back pictures of Hailey. When he was a teen, it'd seemed to him that she'd grown breasts and curves overnight. He remembered the first time he'd seen her in a tight-fitting sweater. His pants had grown tight and he'd beaten himself up over what a douche-bag he was for getting hard at the sight of her. He'd realized in that moment that he'd like to hang out with her more, but he hadn't dared to. How could he? She'd been his best friend's sister, and her fourteen years were a little too young to his eighteen. But it didn't stop him from glancing her way from time to time, and he'd caught her sneaking peeks at him when she'd thought he wasn't looking.

But she was all grown up now and had a killer body. One he'd love to roam his hands all over. *Fuck. Stop. Ryan's still your best friend.* The fact that Hailey was living in Alina and didn't look him up told Goldie that Ryan must've told her not to. Hailey and Ryan were very tight and she'd respect what he'd asked her to do. Knowing that Ryan purposely didn't give her his phone number told Goldie that his best friend wouldn't be pleased if he hooked up with his sister. *He'd kill me.*

Of course, that was if he found out. If he didn't tell Ryan, and Hailey didn't know it was him, there'd be no problem. He ran his hand through his hair. *Only problem is that I can't do that shit to Ryan.* It wasn't in his character to do things behind his friends' or his brothers' backs.

"Brutus is killing you. Hope you got a shitload of dough to pay him," Army said to Jigger as he looked behind his shoulder at Goldie. "What the fuck's wrong with you?"

"What're you talking about?" Goldie crushed his can in his hand.

"You looked pissed off."

"I am pissed off, but it's about something personal."

"It's better to turn that shit off in your brain. When I think about shit from my past it always pisses me off." Army turned back to the game when a few cheers filled the air.

And she was definitely flirting with me on the phone. She practically asked me out. She doesn't have a clue it's me. It was real tempting to call her back and make a date with her for later that night. He knew she'd jump at the chance.

Shaking his head, he sat up straight. He just couldn't get her out of his mind. If she weren't Ryan's sister, he'd be all over her already. He'd love to get to know her as a woman and see if the sparks they felt at the tattoo parlor the night before were real.

She's not just some chick with a pretty face and perfect ass. She's Hailey, and I've got to stay away. Fuck. He pushed away from the table and jumped up, the force of it knocking over Army's drink. He threw his two crushed cans across the room.

"What the fuck?" Army yelled as he rose, the amber liquid dripping off the table.

Goldie shrugged and glared at Kelly, who whispered something to the club girls. "You wanna tell me what the hell you're saying?" He started to walk toward them.

Army pulled him back. "Leave it be, dude. They're not doing shit. What's gotten into you?"

Goldie thrust off Army's hand. "Fuck you," he growled, then looked directly at the club girls. "And fuck all of you."

"No one's doin' shit around here except you. Take your damn problem outta here." Army glared at him.

Without answering, Goldie stormed out, slamming the door behind him. He marched over to his Harley and took out his sunglasses before he straddled his bike. As he grasped the handlebars, Chains rode in and parked. "Hey, I need to talk to you," Goldie said.

Chains came over and bumped fists with him. "What's up?"

"Can you get some info on someone for me?"

Chains was the computer whiz of the club and could locate and dig up just about everything on a person. He nodded. "Is this club business?"

Shaking his head, Goldie wiped the corners of his mouth. "It's personal."

"What do you want to find out?"

"The address of someone in Alina."

Chains raised his eyebrows. "That's it? Too fuckin' easy, dude."

"I can text you her name."

"*Her*?" He chuckled.

"This is between us, okay? I don't want any of the brothers knowing."

"No worries. Once I get the name, I can send you her address in minutes."

He grasped Chains's forearm. "Thanks. I owe you." As Chains walked away, Goldie remembered the chick Army was trying set him up with. "Chains. Talk to Army. The way he talks, he's got a chick who's a sure thing and looking for some fun tonight."

A wide smile cracked his face. "If she's so great, why aren't you in?"

"I have to work. Talk to him about it. Later." He switched on his Harley and rode out of the lot. He had no idea what he was going to do with Hailey's address once he got it, but it made him feel better to know where she lived. *I'm acting like a goddamn teenager.* He pushed the throttle harder, aiming his bike for the back road that cut through the great expanse of the desert.

The road was straight and one of his favorite rides in the county. He loved the way the San Juan Mountains rose up from the flatness of the desert. In the background, the blue-tinted mountains bursting with color were a vibrant contrast to the brownness of the sand, rocks, and brush. Springtime in the desert was beautiful in a harsh and desolate way. Since the early spring months had brought a lot of rain, pops of color from some of the flowers on the green bushes kept the landscape from appearing so monochrome.

Being the lone rider on the road added to the experience of being one with nature. It was like he was the only one in the world surrounded by such beauty. The wind, the earthy scent, the cloudless sky all engulfed him, swallowing him and fusing with him until he surrendered to them. It was at that moment that he achieved his nirvana: head cleared, senses acute, weightless.

After a couple hours, he looped back and headed to Cherry Vale, the nursing facility where his grandmother resided. She'd been living there for the past two years after she fell and broke her hip. She should've been able to rehab and come home, but Alzheimer's made sure that would never happen. Since the disease had crept into her brain a few years before, she no longer understood how to follow the physical therapy instructions, so she ended up a permanent resident at the facility. Goldie paid for her care, which gave her a single room on the rehab floor, not the skilled nursing floor. It was a minor thing, but Goldie didn't want to think about his grandma living in a nursing home.

The double sliding doors opened into a lobby that looked like a living room on a movie set. A large aviary stood in the corner of the room, and several residents sat staring at the canaries and finches as they flitted. A few smiled and cocked their heads as the canaries' songs filtered into the area. Goldie turned the corner and entered the first door on his right.

He stood in the doorway taking in his grandma, who sat in her forest-green recliner watching the images flickering on her television set.

She looks so frail and small. Even though Goldie came by several times a week to spend time with her, he was always blown away when he first entered her room. He wasn't sure he'd ever get used to how much her appearance had changed. In his mind, he still saw her as the robust, energetic woman who'd raised him, his two brothers, and his sister when their parents had crashed into a mountain during a storm. His father had been an avid pilot, having been in the Air Force. His mother was scared to death to fly in the twin-engine plane his father had bought, but she'd grit her teeth and do it knowing it made his dad happy.

His parents had gone to an old friend's birthday party in California, and when they were coming back to Colorado, a storm came up and their plane went off course. Goldie had always held on to the thought that they didn't see the mountain before they slammed into it. His maternal grandparents immediately took them in and raised them. They had taken them in on and off for a few years before his parents crashed. His mom had bailed on them and took off, and his father couldn't handle four young kids, so his grandma stepped up to the plate.

Then his mom had come back, and his parents had reconciled and family life had been back on track. Then they died. At first, Goldie's world seemed like a bad nightmare where everything was the same but it wasn't. But for a ten-year-old, life kept moving rapidly, distractions came up daily, and soon his parents became a memory. There were times when he'd think of them, but it was his grandparents who'd put up with him during his teen years and after.

"Hey, Grandma," Goldie said loudly.

Her pale blue eyes looked at him and a smile lit her lined face. "Garth," she said softly.

He went over and bent down, kissing her cheek. "How are you?"

She stared at him, the small twinkle of recognition replaced by a vacant look. He sighed and pulled up a chair next to her, grasped her bony hand in his, and watched the television. He hated the look of disconnection that had become more pronounced in the last few months.

"Your grandma's doing great," Shelly, the nurse, said as she came into the room with a small cup of applesauce.

"She looks too thin. Is she eating okay?" Goldie glanced at his grandma who didn't divert her gaze from the screen.

"She's up and down. Sometimes she'll eat real well and other times she won't take anything. We give her a protein drink on those days. How've you been?" She ran her eyes over his arms.

"Good." He knew she had the hots for him. Whenever she was on shift when he was there, she'd come into the room dozens of times. She told him she had a bike, a rice burner, and she often asked if he'd like to go riding together. Shelly was cute enough with her shapely legs, brown hair and eyes, but he wasn't interested. He knew she was the clingy type, and if he had a fling with her, she'd cause all kinds of problems. And he didn't want a pissed-off chick taking care of his grandma.

"You're looking real good. You been riding much?" She licked her lips, the applesauce still in her hand.

"I'm a biker. That's what I do. Is that for my grandma?" He pointed to the Dixie cup.

She laughed dryly. "Of course. Uh… yeah. This is your grandma's medication." She went in front of the elderly woman and brought the spoon to her lips.

His grandmother opened up, then smiled. She craned her neck to Goldie. "Are you going to eat any? You and Chad used to love it when I made it. Homemade. None of that pre-made stuff." She smacked her lips as she took a few more spoonfuls.

Goldie laughed. "You made the best applesauce in town. Hell, you were the best cook in town. Remember how many blue ribbons you won in all those cook-offs?"

She nodded, smiling, and then the smile faded and the dementia pushed the slice of lucidity away. She stopped opening her mouth, and her gaze returned to the pictures on the screen.

"You just got to take them when they come," Shelly said softly as she ran her fingers through his grandmother's white hair.

"I do," he said in a low voice.

"I'll call in the aides to put Helen on her bed. She's been sitting too long." Shelly walked toward the door, then looked over her shoulder. "If you ever want to go out and get a cup of coffee, I'm available. I know how hard this is, and I understand what you're going through. Just reaching out to you."

"Thanks. I'll keep that in mind." Goldie turned back to his grandmother and wrapped his arm around her thin shoulders, resting his cheek against her head.

Two muscled men came in a few minutes later. One of the CNAs, Hendricks, told Goldie all about the Harley he'd just bought. Goldie welcomed the distraction, and he was always game for motorcycle talk. Kingsley, the other one, told Goldie he was thinking about buying a Honda bike, and Goldie decided it was his duty to talk him out of it.

A couple hours later, his phone pinged and he opened Chains's text.

Chains: *5605 Linda Vista Rd*

Fuck yeah. He tipped his head back as a jolt of adrenaline coursed through him, and then he tightened up. *What the fuck's the matter with me? I'm acting like an ass, and for what? A chick?* But he knew it wasn't just for a chick. It was for Hailey, and he had to stop that shit pronto. *I haven't seen or thought about her in years. This is fuckin' lame.*

Well, that wasn't exactly true. He *had* thought about her, wondering how she was doing and how she looked. Ryan rarely talked about her, and if he did it was just in passing. Whenever Goldie would ask how she was doing, Ryan would just say she was fine and change the subject.

Glancing at his grandmother, he saw she was sleeping; she looked so peaceful. Leaning over, he stroked her cheek, then kissed it. "I'll see you soon," he whispered. He took out a CD from her drawer and placed it into the small player on the nightstand. "Moon River" was one of his grandma's favorite songs, so he hit the Play button and the piano and harp strains floated in the air. With one last look at her, he walked out the door.

Goldie jumped on his bike and glanced at the time. He had to be at Get Inked soon. He left the parking lot and headed in the direction of Hailey's address. As he waited for the light to change, a car with a couple of women pulled alongside him.

"I love your Harley," the passenger said as she stared at him.

He gave her a chin lift.

"Do you want to come to a party?" She ran her fingers right about her ample cleavage.

He shook his head.

"That's too bad, because me and my friend can be a lot of fun."

Normally, Goldie would take the busty redhead up on her offer, but he wasn't interested. He wanted something different from the same old thing.

He wanted Hailey, but he knew that was fucked.

When the light changed, he swung a U-turn.

Fuck it. I'm done with this.

He headed to the tattoo shop.

Chapter Four

"BRENT IS SO excited about going out tonight. He really is a nice guy," Rory said as she nestled further into the massage chair at the nail salon.

"Don't make this into something big. We're just going out for dinner. And don't be pushy tonight." Hailey stared at her toes as the nail tech painted them. "I'm not so sure about this color. The blue seems too dark."

"I love the color. Do you like mine?"

Hailey looked at her friend's cotton candy pink color. "I do. It's perfect for the warm weather we've been having. This summer we've got to do a barbecue together. Wouldn't that be fun to have one around the pool?"

"You're so lucky that your aunt has a pool. It gets so hot here in the summer. I hate it." Rory picked up her bottled water.

"You're welcome to come over and hang by the pool anytime. I told Claudia the same thing." She studied the nail color again. "I really wanted a blue that looked like denim."

"Would you like me to bring you some other blue polishes?" the manicurist asked.

"That'd be great." Hailey watched as the woman hurried over to a large display filled with nail polishes. "What did you think of the artist from that tattoo parlor?"

"The one who gave you the ink job? He did an awesome job. Are you loving your tat?"

"Yeah. He was so gorgeous. And did you see all the ink on his arms? Did you see his *arms*? They were delicious."

Rory laughed. "You and biceps. The guy was great-looking, and he had a real badass vibe about him. I know that's what you're picking up on. You've always had a thing about bad boys. I can't understand it. Me, I'll take a nice guy every time. They're usually so eager to please, so loyal, and they treat women like goddesses."

Hailey giggled. "I wouldn't say that Sage was any catch. He was acting like such the attentive gentleman and he was banging that woman in his office the whole time he was with you."

"A nice guy in bad boy's clothing." Rory laughed.

The nail tech handed Hailey a denim blue polish. "Do you like this one?"

"Yes, that's perfect. Thanks." She picked up her iced tea and took a sip. "Anyway, I thought he was seriously sexy. I wish he was the one I was going out to dinner with tonight. Don't give me that look, I'm just saying."

"I can guarantee Brent can run circles around that tattoo guy. He may not be as good-looking or have a ripped body like that guy has, but Brent is a nice, decent man. You have to give him a chance. Ever since I can remember, you've always drifted toward the bad boys. Like that friend of Ryan's. What was his name?"

"Garth?"

"Yeah, that's it. You had such a crush on him."

"I wouldn't say he was a bad boy."

Rory's eyes widened. "Are you joking? He was always fighting and getting into trouble. And remember when he bought a motorcycle? He used to ride around the neighborhood purposely making as much noise as he could. Remember how it pissed off Mrs. Glover?"

Hailey laughed. "I forgot about that. I guess he was a badass. I didn't see him that way because I knew him as Ryan's friend for such a long time. He was pretty cute on his bike though." A flutter of shivers tickled her as she recalled Garth and how he used to look at her when she was in high school.

"I wonder whatever happened to him."

"Ryan told me he joined a biker gang."

"Is it the Night Rebels?"

Hailey shrugged. "I don't think he told me the name of it. I just know he told me he was in it, and that he was a major womanizer."

"I bet it is. That's the only motorcycle club around here. They're like totally scary. If I see them on the street, I don't even look at them." Rory ran her hands up and down her arms as if she'd been seized by a sudden chill.

"I guess that's why Ryan told me not to look him up."

"If he's a member of the Night Rebels, you definitely don't want to reconnect. And I'm not surprised to find out he's a player. He was that way when we were in high school. He was always with a new girl and had a line of them waiting to go out with him. That's what I mean about bad boys. Give me a nice guy any time."

"I do like a guy with a rough edge, but a motorcycle gang is too rough. Although, I'm still curious as to how he looks now that he's a man."

"Take Ryan's advice and let it go. Now, tell me what you're going to wear tonight. I hope you guys hit it off so you can double-date with me and Troy. This is going to be such a fun summer."

After they were done with their pedicures, they stepped out into the bright sun and firmed up their plans for that evening. A bemused smile played on Hailey's lips until she slid into her car. Rory was so excited about her and Brent hitting it off that she already had her whole year planned out with him. *Pretty soon she'll be leafing through bridal magazines to find the perfect wedding dress for me.* Of the three of them, Rory was the romantic, Claudia was the skeptic, and Hailey was the realist.

She made a right turn at the light and headed up Santa Nella Street. It was in the opposite direction of where she lived, but the perfect way to go to the tattoo shop. *I just want to see if I can spot him. Rory would be so disappointed.* She snickered and turned on Saguro Street. Five blocks on each side of the street housed restaurants, bars, some funky boutiques, and Get Inked. She slowed down as she passed by the yellow storefront, hoping to catch a glimpse of him. Nothing. She went around the block. *You're totally crazy. He dissed you. Why the hell are you making a fool of yourself?*

Again she slowed in front of the shop. That time she saw a man with a muscular build, blond hair, full inked sleeves, and several facial piercings, but it wasn't the blond she was dying to see. She pursed her lips; she couldn't go by again. Shaking her head, she turned off Saguro and made her way to her aunt's house.

Her aunt lived in a three-bedroom, two-bath Victorian in the historic district of Alina. She'd always loved Patty's house when she and Ryan used to come over after school. Her aunt always had fresh-baked cookies or cheese and apple slices waiting for them when they arrived. But what she'd loved most about the house was all the nooks and crannies: a small room under the stairs, corner cupboards, many bay windows, and a hidden staircase behind the wall in the library.

Since coming back to Alina, she'd stayed with her aunt, and now that Patty was in the rehab center, Hailey lived in the wonderful house all alone. She smiled when she entered the sitting room and saw prisms of light from the beveled glass windows dancing on the mosaic-tiled floor. As a child, she'd been fascinated by the small chunky rainbows. She slumped down on one of the cushy chairs and thumbed through the mail.

I hope tonight turns out well. The last blind date she had several months before was a disaster. One of the customers at the floral shop had insisted that Hailey go out on a date with her nephew. When she'd finally relented, she'd found herself fighting him off most of the night.

I wonder if the tattoo guy was at the shop working on someone. I bet he sees a lot of pretty women. Her cheeks heated when she recalled his hands on her butt. She still couldn't believe she let him see her ass. *Why do I keep thinking about him? Even if he were interested in me, he'd turn out to be an asshole. I just know it. Most men are, and you take his good looks and raw sexiness, and he just spells trouble.*

Her phone pinged. She looked at the screen. *Rory. Why did I think it might have been him? I don't even know his name. Crazy.*

Rory: *I think ur white skirt is better than ur black. U always wear black. U don't want Brent to think u're goth.* ☺

Hailey shook her head.

Hailey: *If he thinks I'm goth just bc I wear black, he's an idiot. See u soon. :)*

She slipped her phone into her pocket and went to get ready for her night out.

WITH ITS WINDOW boxes of trailing sweet potato vines, orange and yellow marigolds, and red miniature roses, Chianti's had a homey feel to it. Spread around the front patio were wrought iron tables and chairs under earth-toned umbrellas. Inside, the eatery's walls were covered by watercolors of Italy. The bar had fancy bottles housing liqueurs and brandies from around the world.

There was always a crowd at Chianti's, as the family-owned restaurant boasted some of the best Italian food in the county. Hailey, Brent, Rory, and Troy sat at one of the outside tables.

"Isn't it nice out here?" Rory asked.

"I think it's too hot. We should sit inside," Troy replied.

"I'm okay. It's cold most of the year, so when I can sit out and eat, I enjoy it." Rory tossed her hair over her shoulder.

"I think it's perfect," Hailey said as she reached for the glass of water the busser placed in front of her.

"Works for me." Brent smiled broadly at Hailey.

"I guess the majority wins on this one." Hailey chuckled when Troy stared sourly at her.

After they placed their orders, they chatted about the restaurant and the upcoming summer; there was an excitement in the town since the winter had been so bitterly cold.

"It'll probably rain and ruin most of the summer," Troy said as he placed a generous portion of the antipasto on his plate.

Rory's face fell. "Oh don't say that. It has to be a perfect summer. I was so cold all winter that the only thing that kept me going was knowing summer was coming."

"Just saying. You know how it goes around here. Remember a few summers ago when it rained and hailed most of the time?"

Changing the subject, Hailey interjected, "Rory and I are planning to have a pool party."

"You have a pool?" Brent asked.

"My aunt does. I'm staying at her house while she rehabs."

"If it's lightning, we may all fry in your pool," Troy said.

"Troy!" Rory poked his arm.

"If we go swimming while it's lightning, then we deserve to be torched," Hailey said. Brent guffawed and Troy glared at her.

Halfway through her pasta carbonara, Hailey excused herself to go to the ladies' room. The truth was she had to take a break from the doomsayer. Troy was driving her crazy. She fluffed her hair and reapplied her apricot lipstick. Rory always saw the world through rose-colored glasses, so how she put up with Mr. Downer was beyond Hailey's comprehension. She knew her snippy remarks to Troy's doom and gloom were starting to irritate him big-time. Rory had thrown her "the look" several times, and she was trying to be good, but Troy was grating on her nerves big time.

The way Brent was playing the peacemaker was also picking at her. She had to admit that, other than his conciliatory gestures, he was an okay date. He was considerate, attentive, and agreeable—in other words, vapid as hell. He didn't excite her one iota.

Cringing when she anticipated Rory's chagrin over her assessment of Brent, Hailey pulled down her black skirt and headed to the door. *Brent seems like Rory's type. I'm surprised they're not going out.*

She stepped into the hallway and slammed right into someone. "I'm so sorry," she gushed as she stepped back.

"That's okay. How are you?"

That voice. I know it. She looked up into the eyes of the tattoo artist. Her stomach turned over, her pulse raced, and the hallway became a lot smaller. "It's you."

His smile revealed white, straight teeth, making him more handsome. "Yeah. It's me."

"Are you here with a date?" The minute the question spilled out of her mouth she wanted to take it back. *Why the fuck did I ask that? I sound like a desperate moron.*

"No. Are you?" He leaned in to her as a woman came down the hall.

"I am. Blind date." Her lips twitched and she looked away. The scent of soap, leather, and fine whiskey looped around her, making her light-headed. Heat radiated from him as he pressed closer to her. She leaned against the wall and he placed his hand on it, his toned arm inches from her. Glancing sideways, she saw his tattoos curling and twisting around his magnificent bicep. Tempted to run her tongue over his taut skin, she bit on the inside of her bottom lip.

"And how's that going?" His tone was low, velvety in its richness. It slid over her, landing right between her legs.

She shifted to her position. "Okay."

"That's good. How's your tattoo doing?" His warm breath fanned over her face.

"Good."

For a few seconds, their gazes locked with each other's; then he turned his head and bent down further. Parting her lips, she raised her head slightly. Her heart beat wildly and everything around her disappeared except for him. Raw, male sex exuded from him and, without thinking, she placed her hand on his hip. He came closer and she felt her lips sparking in anticipation of his kiss.

"What're you doing, Hay?" Rory's voice came crashing in, shattering the moment.

He pulled away and stepped back, and she groaned in frustration.

He threw her a half smile and winked at her, then sauntered away.

"Wasn't that the guy who gave you the tattoo? What were you doing with him?" Hailey watched as he disappeared around the corner. "Brent was wondering what was taking you so long, so I came to find you. You *do* know you're on a date with Brent, right?"

Hailey focused her attention on Rory. "Don't lecture me, okay? I just bumped into him, literally, when I came out of the bathroom. No big deal. Let's go back to the table."

"It looked like you guys were going to kiss." Rory walked behind her.

"Well, looks can be deceiving." Hailey made her way through the restaurant, her gaze darting around, but she didn't see him.

For the rest of the night, she couldn't rid him from her mind. Every time Brent would brush against her or place his hand over hers, she wished he were the tattoo artist. The blond-haired man with the drool-worthy body tempted her, teased her, and made her want him. She'd never had a reaction to a man like she had with him. She wanted to rip his clothes off, kiss and touch every inch of him, climb on top of him and ride him to ecstasy. She wanted his lips on her skin, licking her and making her come over and over. Hailey crossed her legs and shifted in the chair; just thinking about him aroused her.

After paying their bill, Rory suggested they go to a bar to continue the evening. Brent readily agreed, while Troy grumbled about it, and Hailey wished she could go home.

"Let's go to Rocky Top. They always have great drink specials," Brent suggested.

"That's a good idea," Rory said as she grasped Troy's arm and snuggled next to him.

"We can't stay too late because I have an early morning meeting," Troy said with a frown.

Rory smiled. "It's still early. We'll only have a couple of drinks."

The quartet walked down the block and entered the bar. It wasn't very crowded and they found a booth by the window. Pop songs played overhead as they placed their order with the waitress.

After a few minutes, Brent scooted closer to Hailey and put his arm around her. "You doing good? You've been quiet ever since you came back from the ladies' room," Brent said.

Rory threw her a warning stare. Hailey stirred her drink. "I guess I'm just tired. The shop's been so busy."

Taking her hand in his, he squeezed it. "I know how that goes."

"And it's the damn heat. You probably got overheated at the restaurant, and now it's freezing cold in this bar. It's not good for your body to go from one drastic temperature change to the next." Troy brought his bourbon and seven to his lips.

"I don't think that's it. Hailey's been running the floral shop and going back and forth to the rehab center to see her aunt. That can be exhausting. And she's at the shop six days a week," Rory said.

Hailey nodded, but her mind wasn't on the conversation—it was on the sexy guy's mouth sucking her nipples while his fingers dove into her. "Oh." The small moan escaped through her lips, and heat rose up her neck as all three of them stared at her. If she wasn't so mortified, she'd have busted out laughing over Rory's tight-assed expression. She gulped her vodka tonic, then picked up her purse.

"Ladies' room?" Rory said tensely.

She shook her head. "Home. I'm really tired, and I have to open the shop in the morning." She pushed her chair back. "I had a really nice time. Thanks." Smiling at Brent, she stood up.

He jumped to his feet. "Are you sure you don't want to stay out a little longer?"

"I'm sure. Thanks for dinner."

"I'll walk you to your car."

Ignoring Rory's disapproving look, she walked out of the bar with Brent at her heels. When she got to her car, he gently turned her around. Staring into her eyes, he said, "I had a great time. I'd like to see you again."

Dread weaved up her spine. *I hate this part. He's a nice-enough guy.*

"I'm so busy right now."

"Lunch, coffee, a quick drink. We can even agree that we'll only go out for an hour. I'm pretty flexible. I just want to see you again."

Shit. "Okay. Give me a call and I can see what my schedule looks like." *Chicken.*

Brent's eyes lit up. "Great. I will." He leaned in for a kiss, but she turned away and his lips landed on her cheek.

She pulled away and opened her door. "I've gotta go. Thanks again."

"I'll call you," he said as she pulled away, and she didn't doubt for a minute that he would.

On the way home, she took a detour past the tattoo shop. As she approached the parlor, she saw three men standing outside. Slowing down, her breath caught when she saw him. Without thinking, she pulled into a parking space and shut off the engine. Gripping the steering wheel, she took several deep breaths. *This is insane. I need to go home. Right now.* Looking in her rearview mirror, she saw him talking with two other buffed men who were dressed similarly in jeans and leather vests. He took a drag on what she thought was a joint and exhaled, wisps of smoke floating around him. As if sensing something, he turned in her direction.

With her insides quivering, she switched on the ignition and drove away.

By the time she arrived at her house, she'd calmed down. Grateful that she hadn't made an ass of herself, she parked in the garage off the alley and walked through the yard. Inside, she changed into her cotton nightshirt, poured a glass of wine, and curled up in one of the cushy chairs in the sun-room.

There was a full, bright moon, and glimmering stars freckled the ebony sky. As she sipped her wine, images of him played out in her mind. She knew she wouldn't get much sleep that night, her mind too active with thoughts of him. *I should stop all this nonsense and try to find someone best suited for me.* Brent wasn't her type, but she figured there must be someone in Alina who was and wouldn't be a heartbreaker.

Maybe I need to just forget all this and concentrate on the shop and Aunt Patty. If someone is meant for me, we'll find each other. She laughed. *Now I'm beginning to sound like Rory.*

The truth was things didn't turn out like the storybooks. Many jerks had confirmed that for her.

She took another sip of wine.

Yeah. It was going to be a long night.

Chapter Five

S ITTING IN HIS pickup truck a couple houses down from where Hailey lived, Goldie lit a joint and took a long drag. He'd been parked watching her house for the past half hour. It pissed him off to no end that he was doing it, yet he was still there. What he hoped to see was beyond him. *I'm nothing but a damn stalker wanting a glimpse of Hailey. This is so fucked.*

Ever since the previous night when he'd almost kissed her in the hallway at Chianti's, he'd been obsessing over her. She hadn't made it easy on him when she drove by his shop and parked nearby. He'd thought for sure she was going to change her mind as he watched her sitting in her Buick, but when she'd pulled away, he regretted not going over to her. He wanted just one taste of her lips, then he'd move on and forget about her. He could do that. He'd done it with all the women in his life. Some of the chicks made an impression on him, but not enough for him to stick around too long. Leaving women didn't even make him break out in a sweat, so he had no doubt he could forget Hailey in the sweet embrace of another chick with chestnut brown hair.

Scrubbing a hand down his face, he dragged his fingers to the back of his neck and rubbed it hard. *I'm done with this shit.* He sat up straight and grabbed the key in the ignition. Just before he turned it, Hailey walked down the porch stairs, beyond sexy in her shorts and halter top. Staring at the way her hips swayed while she walked across the grass, he readjusted his jeans and leaned his head back against the head rest.

Hailey bent over and her shorts rode up a bit, showing the crease right below her butt cheeks. *How well I know your ass.* Straightening up, Goldie saw a bunch of weeds clutched in her hand. She walked over to the sidewalk and picked up the newspaper, then went back into the house.

He'd sat out in his truck for forty minutes in the hot sun for a five-minute glimpse of her. *The brothers would be all over me about this. And they'd be right. I'm acting like a goddamn pussy. This shit stops now.* Turning the key in the ignition, the blue pickup growled as Goldie pulled away from the curb, heading back to the clubhouse.

When he walked inside, a blast of cool air hit him. He went straight to the bar where a frothy glass of beer waited for him. Tilting his head back, he guzzled it down.

"Damn hot out there," Army said as he wiped the sweat dripping down his face. The prospect behind the bar placed a mug of beer in front of him.

"Damn straight. What's going on at Lust?"

"Not much. Good crowds on the weekends. Lately we've been getting the suit-and-tie rush around four on Wednesdays and Thursdays. Guess all the suits want to get their stripper fix before they go home to their wives."

"Does Fiona still work there?"

"Yeah. She was asking about you. What happened? You had a major boner for her, but I haven't seen you around for a while."

"I've been busy. Steel had me helping out at Skid Marks for a while, which was a major pain in the ass. I was busting my ass between the bike shop and the tattoo parlor. Glad that shit's done." Goldie picked up the new beer Ruger put in front of him.

"Maybe you can come by this weekend. We got a few new strippers who are real hot. Fiona's working on Saturday."

"Saturday's a bitch at Get Inked. Besides, we can't fuck the help. Steel and Paco remind us of that at least once a month."

"Looking's good too. Fiona has a new number that's driving all the guys crazy. How're the women who come into the shop to get inked? Any hot ones you've hooked up with?"

"I don't really look at them that way. If I did, I'd fuck up their ink."

"Bullshit. You're always checking out women. You're giving me a load of shit, which probably means you've either fucked a customer or are getting ready to do it."

"Neither, dude. I don't like to mix business with pleasure. So, how'd the double date turn out with your squeeze and her roommate? Did the chick go for Chains?"

"Better than I could've imagined. The two women ended up being totally down for a foursome, and we had a shitload of fun. Chains is eager to do a repeat performance. I'm arranging something for next week. You really blew that one. Those women are so fuckin' into the dark shit. Love it."

"Yeah, well, you know I prefer it solo with a chick. Glad it worked out."

"Do we got church?" Eagle asked as he joined the men at the bar.

Goldie glanced at the clock on the back wall. "In about fifteen minutes."

"Enough time for a few beers," Eagle said as he held up three fingers to Ruger, who promptly placed the requested bottles in front of Eagle. He picked one up and drank it in one long swallow. "Nothing better than ice-cold beer on a scorching day."

The brothers chatted for a while, then headed to the meeting room in the back of the clubhouse. The room filled up with more jean-clad members, the scraping of metal and wood against concrete echoing as the brothers sat down at the large table. Steel and Paco were standing in front waiting for everyone to quiet down. A wooden gavel brought the meeting to order.

"We're helping the Fallen Slayers procure arms. They've been getting some shit from a local gang in Silverado that seems better equipped than they are. These punks have been starting all kinds of shit, so Roughneck's asked us to help them out. Told him about Liam and how great he's worked out for the Insurgents and now us on that last deal."

Fallen Slayers were a smaller MC with only ten members. Roughneck was the president and Patriot was the vice president, both good friends with Steel. They'd all known each other even before the clubs were started. Most of the Night Rebels got along with the Fallen Slayers, although the way they treated their club girls didn't sit too well. But the club girls wore the Fallen Slayers' property patch voluntarily, and they chose to go through initiation to become part of the club. Even so, the Night Rebels respected and treated their club women as part of their club, never pushing them to work at Lust or go out and prostitute to make money for the club.

"Are we gonna help them with their punk problem?" Sangre asked.

"Is it an established gang or a wannabe?" Eagle said.

"For now we're just helping with the arms deal. Roughneck will let us know if he needs more help. We'll open it up for discussion if that time comes."

Steel nodded to Paco, who stood up. "The gang is an affiliate to Los Malos in Colorado Springs and Pueblo. Los Malos started as a neighborhood gang, but they've evolved into an organized, dominant, and criminally successful one. This smaller one in Silverado helps Los Malos out in some of the counties with selling drugs and stealing. They have a fuckin' attitude and think they can just set up shop and establish the area as their turf."

"Sounds like what the fuckin' Skull Crushers and Satan's Pistons were trying to do," Goldie said.

"Exactly, except these assholes aren't bikers. They have backup from Los Malos and maybe some fuckers higher up. I spoke to Hawk and he's looking into it, since he's the one who keeps up with that for the Insurgents and their affiliates. He told me the Insurgents are looking real close at Los Malos and their affiliates. They want to nip whatever shit these fuckers are trying to sneak in before it becomes a worse problem. I told them we're ready to jump in and lend a hand if it comes to that. I know the other MCs that we and the Insurgents are on friendly terms with would join forces with us too. But for now, we're gonna help Roughneck get his gun supply way up." Paco crossed his arms and leaned against the wall.

"What do these jerks call themselves?" Muerto asked.

Paco smiled. "Los Malitos."

"Wonder how long it took them to come up with that name." Muerto laughed.

"We don't give a shit how these fuckin' street gangs make their money or what the hell they do as long as they don't do shit in biker territory. Banger is beyond pissed," Steel stated.

"I'm sure he is," Rooster said. He, Tattoo Mike, and Shotgun knew Banger, Hawk, and Throttle well. Being the oldest of the Night Rebels brothers, they went way back with the Insurgents, even before the Night Rebels was formed.

"These punks never fuckin' learn. We oughta annihilate them and be done with it." Diablo slammed his fist on the table.

The members voiced their agreement. Steel looked at Diablo. "I want you to get together with Knuckles and see if he needs any help."

"Already did that. I'm going to Silverado tomorrow to go over some stuff with him." At first, the Fallen Slayers' sergeant-at-arms and Diablo, the sergeant-at-arms for the Night Rebels, didn't get along with each other. But since they'd done a couple of charity poker runs together, they'd become brothers and friends.

"When's the deal going down?" Chains asked.

"Next week," Steel replied.

"Moving on, Steel and I have been talking about doing a biker rally this summer. As you know, we normally do one in October and one in spring, but since most of the spring was shitty weather and we couldn't have our rally, we thought it'd be a good idea to have it in July," Paco said.

The idea was given to the membership, who unanimously voted for it, and the date was set for the last weekend in July. The Night Rebels motorcycle rallies attracted many biker enthusiasts, and they were held on private land owned by an ex–Night Rebels member who made a fortune in the marijuana-growing business. The rallies usually began on a Thursday and went through the weekend. There was a campground on the land, motorcycle contests, live music from local bands, bike washes from the scantily clad club girls, wet T-shirt contests, and a Saturday barbecue. Strewn around the area were vendor booths selling mostly motorcycle-related items. The club made a lot of money at their rallies and gave fifty percent of it to their favorite charity—Bikers Against Child Abuse.

"Is Raven going to have a booth?" Goldie asked Muerto as they walked out of the adjourned meeting.

"Yeah. She's already making a bunch of jewelry with some biker charms. They look pretty cool. You going to Cuervos tonight?"

"Fuck, I forgot about it. It's Tattoo Mike's anniversary party."

Muerto laughed. "You have been working too hard, dude. This is the first time I've ever known you to forget a party where there'll be a lot of available women."

Goldie grinned. "You're right. What's up with that shit?"

"Hell if I know."

"I'll be there. Jimmy will be handling the shop tonight with the new guy we just hired. It should be good."

Paco walked up to Goldie. "Did you ever find a replacement for Flora?"

"Yeah. She catches on fast. We'll see if she works out long term. You going to Cuervos tonight?"

Paco nodded. "I'm pretty sure everyone's gonna be there."

Tattoo Mike and his old lady, Sam, had tied the knot twelve years before. That night, the anniversary party was a family event, meaning club girls weren't included, only old ladies. Old ladies and club girls didn't mix. The club women knew to keep out of their way, and if they happened to be in the same room, the club girls would immediately leave the room out of respect. Of the old ladies, only Sam and Shannon had the biggest problem with them since their husbands tended to occasionally have sex with the club women. The old ladies had come to terms with their husbands' dalliances, but it didn't mean they liked them. The way Sam and Shannon figured it was that their men always came home to them, and that the club sluts were bitches with holes.

"I better get over to the shop to make sure all is good. Friday nights can be a bitch." Goldie slipped his hand in his pocket and took out his keys.

"I'm right behind you," Tattoo Mike said.

"Let's roll." Goldie walked out of the cool clubhouse into the dry heat. Swinging his leg over his bike, he made a mental note to hit up a high school buddy about his band playing at the rally in July. He adjusted his sunglasses and rode away from the clubhouse.

WHEN GOLDIE WALKED into Cuervos, the party was underway. Scanning the room, he saw all the familiar faces of the brotherhood, as well as many citizens glancing nervously at the group of men as they chugged bottles of beer. Several women smiled at him as he made his way to the bar.

"Didn't think you'd make it," Chains said as he bumped fists with Goldie.

"I stopped by to see my grandma. There're some hot-looking chicks in here."

"Tell me about it. I have my eyes on a few of them."

"What're you drinking?" Jorge, the owner of the bar, asked.

"I'll start with a bottle of Coors. How've you been?" Goldie said.

"Not bad. Business is back to where it should be. It took a long time after the shooting last year to get people to come back in."

"That's good. Time makes most things pass. You gonna put Steel to work tonight?"

"I'll let him enjoy the night. Maybe I'll recruit Breanna." Jorge laughed as he handed Goldie his beer.

"Give me another one, dude," Army said from behind Goldie.

Goldie half turned. "You down for a game of pool? I need to make some money."

Chains guffawed and Army shook his head. "I'm down for it, and

I'm gonna beat your losing ass."

"Anyone want to play Raven?" Muerto interjected as he came up to the bar to place his order.

"I wanna win some money tonight, not lose." Goldie brought the bottle of beer to his lips.

"Looks like you're gonna have to be the one to play. Brutus told me he's taking a break. He's yet to beat her." Army chuckled.

"Didn't know you were all a bunch of pussies," Muerto joked as he walked away with two drinks in his hands.

A shapely redhead edged in between Goldie and Chains and leaned against the bar. She cocked her head and a sultry smile formed on her shiny red lips. "Am I crowding you?" She ran her painted fingernail down his forearm.

"Nah." From the seductive look in her eyes, he knew where she wanted this to go.

"What're you drinking?" Jorge asked, leaning forward to get a better look at her cleavage in her low-cut halter top.

"Whiskey sour." She fixed her attention back on Goldie, the tip of her tongue outlining the contours of her lips. "You're an officer with the Night Rebels," she said, her fingernail running over the raised lettering "Road Captain" on his cut.

He nodded and took another pull of his beer.

"You do all the runs and rallies, right?"

"And other stuff that involves bikes."

"I bet you have a big Harley. I love Harleys. They're such powerful machines. Just like the guys who ride them." She leaned in to him, the side of her thigh pressed against his.

All he had to do was tell her to follow him to the back room and she'd be down on her knees with her red lips wrapped around his cock, sucking the hell out of him. He didn't doubt that she'd give him a damn good blow job, but he wasn't feeling it, and that surprised the hell out of him.

"She's practically drooling, dude. Give the chick a break and take her in the back," Army said from behind.

Goldie craned his neck. "You want her?"

Army jerked his head back. "You don't? What the fuck? She's a sweet piece of ass."

The woman giggled and smiled at Army.

"Go for it," Goldie replied.

Army scrubbed his face with his fist, then came in closer behind the woman. "My brother here is a fuckin' idiot. You're a gorgeous, sexy woman who needs a biker's touch."

She whirled around and pushed out her ample chest. "Are you an officer too?" Her brown eyes scanned his cut.

"Yeah."

Goldie and Chains laughed.

"How come I don't see your patch?" She ran her finger over his cut.

"Just got appointed today. I'm in charge of finding prime pussy for the brothers. We have a lot of parties, and we need only the best in Alina."

"I didn't know you guys did that, but it makes sense. You want to weed out the skanks, right?"

"Right."

"He works real hard at his job," Chains said as he leaned closer to the woman.

She glanced at Goldie. "I was hoping you and I could get friendly."

"Army's position is way higher than mine. We take pussy very seriously. He's the one to impress." Goldie picked up his beer bottle.

Her gaze lingering on Goldie's, she said, "Do you want to audition me?"

Army held out his hand. "I wanna find out what your pretty mouth can do besides talking." He threw back his shot and placed the empty glass on the bar next to Goldie.

"Then let me show you." She pushed away from the bar, gave Goldie's arm a squeeze, then placed her hand in Army's and walked away.

"I can't fuckin' believe you let that hot one go," Chains said.

"I can find ten more just like her if I want to. I'm sure someone in here will pique my interest before the night's over." He scanned the crowd and made a mental note of a few women he wouldn't mind getting to know between the sheets.

Twenty minutes later, Army came back over with the redhead in tow. She brushed against Goldie as she reached for her drink that was still on the bar. "You doing okay?" she said in a low voice. He nodded.

"All right, baby. Why don't you join your friends? I'm gonna hang with my brothers." Army winked at her, then smacked her butt when she walked by.

When she was out of earshot, Chains asked, "How was she?"

"Okay. She's worth having at one of our parties. I told her to come around the club next Friday night. She acted like I gave her the winning lottery ticket." Army laughed. It always amazed the brothers how many women wanted to fuck them just because they were in an outlaw club.

As the evening went on, more people filed in. Food, drinks, and good conversation flowed amongst the brothers, and the old ladies sat at a table near their men, laughing and talking as the night went on.

Goldie, Brutus, Army, Chains, and Skull were throwing back shots and shooting the breeze when Eagle approached them. "Do any of you have a joint?"

Goldie pulled one out and handed it to him.

"Thanks, dude. Can you spare another one? I saw this hot-as-fuck chick and want to have a spare in case she wants one. This babe is so fuck-worthy."

Army turned around and looked out at the crowd. "Really? I bet it's the chick who sucked my cock earlier. She's a hot one. Is she a redhead?"

"No. She's got light brown hair and the most fuckin' blue eyes I've ever seen. I gotta have this one."

"Where's she at?" Goldie asked.

"Right over there." Eagle pointed to a table toward the front of the bar. "The one with the four chicks."

Goldie glanced over and a jolt of desire tore through him. *Hailey.*

"You talking about the one with the black top?"

"Yeah. The tight-as-hell black top that shows off her tits real well."

Army whistled under his breath. "She's definitely hot. I wonder if we can get her to come to our parties. And she can bring her friends. They're good too."

"Definitely prime piece of ass," Brutus said as Chains and Skull nodded.

"I'm gonna see if she's into bikers." Eagle started to move away but Goldie pulled him back. "What the fuck?" Anger darkened his brown eyes.

"You're not going to get near her." Goldie's tone was matter-of-fact.

"Why the hell not? I saw her first, so you gotta find some other chick to fuck." Eagle jerked away from him.

Body tensing, Goldie crossed his arms and glared at Eagle. "I know her. Pick another pussy."

Eagle widened his eyes. "You're fuckin' bullshitting because you want her."

"When have you known me to bullshit?" Goldie's jaw twitched.

"He's got a point there," Brutus said.

"Goldie always tells it straight," Skull added.

Eagle and Goldie stood breathing noisily, their gazes boring into each other's. Finally, Eagle broke eye contact and stepped back. "She's all yours, dude. No sense in getting pissed over pussy. Where's the redhead you mentioned?" he asked, turning to Army.

Their conversation became muffled in Goldie's ears as he lit a joint and watched Hailey. After a few minutes, he tossed it to the floor, grinding it out with the toe of his boot. Reaching behind him, he grabbed his glass of Jack Daniels, threw it back, then made his way over to Hailey's table.

As he approached, he recognized one of the blonde women as the one who was with her at the tattoo parlor the weekend before. The blonde glanced up and smiled at him. *She probably thinks I'm hitting on her.* Then she said something to Hailey, who looked over her shoulder just as he reached their table.

"Hey," he said in her ear as he bent down low.

"Hi." Her cheeks rose with her grin and her eyes shimmered.

"Can I join you?" He pulled out a chair and sat down before she answered.

Hailey pointed to the three women. "This is Claudia. She was with me when I came into your shop. And this is Sera and Aubree." Pointing to him, she said, "And this is…." She giggled. "I don't know your name."

"Goldie." He pushed his chair closer to hers. She smelled like the beach: sandy, sunny, and a briny tang. It washed over him like a cool breeze and reminded him of when his grandparents had taken him and his siblings to Disneyland and Laguna Beach one summer long ago.

"I'm Hailey."

He smiled. *I know who you are, sweet girl.* "Can I get you ladies a round of drinks?" They all nodded and he called the waitress over.

"I'm pretty tipsy," Hailey said in his ear. Her warm breath made his dick wake up. "It's funny that I ran into you again. First at Chianti's and now here. I wonder if the universe is trying to tell us something." She held his gaze with those beautiful eyes. "Maybe we should do something about it."

Lust surged through him. "Like what?" He placed his hand on hers.

"I dunno. Maybe go out on a date? Do you date?"

He chuckled. "Not often. Depends on whether the woman's worth the time."

"Am I?"

"Oh yeah… you're absolutely worth the time." *Remember Ryan. Fuck, this shit is hard.*

"So…?" Her glossy pink lips parted.

Ryan, in full battle gear, floated in front of him. His best buddy was in Afghanistan fighting in one-hundred-plus degrees and he was here in an air-conditioned bar, hitting on his bud's sister. Ryan trusted him. *Fuck!*

Sliding his hand off hers, he pulled away, then stood up. "I gotta get back to my party, ladies. Have a good time." He ignored Hailey's fallen face and walked back over to his brothers.

"Struck out with the hottie?" Army asked.

"Leave it alone." Goldie threw him a hard look. He felt her staring at him, but he made himself ignore her as he talked with Steel and Paco. Out of the corner of his eye, he saw her walk down the hallway to the bathrooms. He watched Sangre's hungry eyes devour her as she'd passed. When Sangre headed in the same direction she had, he cursed under his breath before he went after him.

"It's a fuckin' good party. This place is teeming with hot chicks. I just saw a sweet piece of ass and I'm gonna see if she's as willing as I am to party." Sangre chuckled.

"The one who just came down here?" Goldie asked. Sangre nodded. "She's with me."

"Really? I didn't know that. You've been hangin' out with the brothers most of the time."

"That doesn't mean shit. I told you she's with me. That's all you fuckin' need to know."

"Don't talk shit to me or we're gonna have a problem." Sangre flexed his muscles and took a step toward Goldie.

Goldie clenched his fists as the adrenaline began to pump through him. And then he saw her coming out of the ladies' room. "Just chill, okay. I'm just pissed about shit. Nothing with you. I let it spill over. She's really with me. I know her."

Sangre glanced down the hall as she came toward them. He clasped Goldie's shoulder. "No worries. Later." Then he sauntered off.

Hailey turned her head away from him and brushed past him, but he reached out and grabbed her arm, bringing her crashing against him.

"What the fuck is your problem?" she said.

"I left the table kinda fast. I don't want you to think I'm some kind of jerk."

"Too late. I already think you are." She yanked her arm back, but he held her firmly, pulling her with him as he walked down the hall.

"Where are you taking me?" Fear laced her voice.

"I'm not gonna hurt you. We can't talk with all the noise."

"There's nothing to talk about. It's obvious you aren't interested in me. I made a fool of myself. End of story. Nice knowing you."

He kicked open one of the doors and pulled her inside. Swinging her around, he pushed her back against the wall. Cupping her chin, he tilted her head back, his gaze searching hers. "Not interested? Fuck that."

He tilted his head down and pressed his lips against hers. They were smooth, soft, and silky as shit, and he knew he was a goner—one taste would never be enough. Hungrily, he slipped her bottom lip between his teeth and sucked hard, knowing he was leaving his mark. A guttural moan escaped from deep in her throat, and it went straight to his cock that was punching to get out.

She wrapped her arms around his neck and drew him closer to her, and he pressed into her softness, loving the way she felt in his arms, the way her scent wound around him, tangling around his dick. As her lips parted more, he slipped his tongue inside to taste and feel her. Her fast breathing filled his ears, and he ran his hand over her hips and glided it over that perfect ass of hers. Cupping the cheek, he gripped hard, careful not to touch the one he'd recently tattooed. Hailey rubbed herself against his throbbing cock and he thought he'd lose it. His cock was so hard that it hurt. He wanted nothing more than to have her full lips around it, sucking the shit out of it as he pumped fast and hard.

The door swung open and, out of instinct, he jumped to attention, reaching for the knife in his cut's inside pocket. One of the waitresses smiled at him. "Sorry. We're out of napkins." After grabbing two large packs, she said over her shoulder, "Go back to what you were doing." The door closed behind her.

Goldie looked at Hailey, who was still against the wall. Her hair was disheveled and her lips were a bit swollen and glossy from his kiss. Raising her hand, she brushed the strands of hair away from her face, then looked down at her fingers.

Way to go, asshole. "I gotta get back out there." His voice filled the space between them.

"Sure. Me too. I'm sure my friends are wondering where I am." She moved away from the wall and walked to the door.

He looped his arms around her waist from behind. "About the kiss, I—"

A nervous laugh spilled out. "No worries. We've both had a lot to drink. Well, I mean, I did. Gotta go." She untangled his arms from her, opened the door, and disappeared into the hallway.

Goldie slammed the door and rested his forehead on it. *Fuck!*

The kiss was so good. He wished it would've been shitty, lukewarm at most, but it wasn't. It was raw intensity. The type of kiss that stayed with you, scorched your insides, and invaded your thoughts.

The type of kiss that couldn't just stop at one.

He was so fucked.

Chapter Six

Turning into the parking lot of Cherry Vale, the rehab center, Hailey shut off the radio and pulled the visor down. Swiping a bright fuchsia pink on her lips, her stomach fluttered when she thought of Goldie's mouth on hers. She'd never been kissed that way by any man, and she could only imagine what his sexy mouth could do to her body.

She leaned back in the seat and closed her eyes. Their stolen kiss in the back room had been more than hot. If the waitress hadn't come in, Hailey didn't doubt that she probably would've ended up doing something decadent and totally out of character. She wasn't one to rush sex or act on her emotions when it came to men, but the way he held her, rubbed against her, and kissed her was beyond awesome. Whenever she thought about it, her lips tingled and her body shivered.

The only snag was that he acted like the whole thing had been a mistake. She'd told him it was no big deal only to save herself the humiliation of him dissing her, but the truth was she'd felt a connection to him, one so strong that she'd chided herself about it the whole way home. *What's the matter with me? So he was a good kisser, and he probably knows how to screw real well. So the fuck what.*

As if on cue, her phone rang and Brent's name flashed. Making a face, she shoved her phone in her purse and exited the car.

Her aunt Patty was propped up on a straight-backed chair in front of the large window overlooking a courtyard. The flowering crabapple trees around the small pond gave off the ambiance of calmness. Her aunt's roommate wasn't in the room, and Hailey smiled as she saw a half-made afghan. Josephine, the roommate, was either crocheting or knitting, and afghans, scarves, and baby hats were her favorite projects to make. Hailey reckoned she'd be taking home the red, green, and yellow striped afghan she saw on Josephine's bed when she'd completed it.

"Hi, Aunt Patty." Hailey went over and gave her aunt a soft squeeze.

Patty shifted her body around. "How's the shop?"

"Doing great. We've got so many weddings for the next three months. It's going to be wildly busy. How're you doing?"

"The same. Stuck in this damn room and bored out of my mind. Some of my friends came by yesterday and snuck in a bottle of champagne. That was fun. You should've seen the way Josephine guzzled it down. I don't think she'd ever had any. She was out cold for the rest of the night." Patty laughed.

Hailey placed a box of chocolates on the table next to her aunt. "I didn't forget."

Patty's eyes lit up. "Did you get the mixed variety?"

Hailey nodded. "What does the doctor say about your progress?"

"He tells me everything's going as it should be. I still can't put weight on this damn leg."

"Just keep listening to him. You don't want to end up coming back here like the last time when you rushed it." She glanced outside and then back to her aunt. "It's a beautiful day. Do you want me to take you for a walk so you can get some fresh air?"

"Not today. I'm feeling kind of tired. Let's just talk. Tell me all about the weddings and the flowers we'll have to order."

For the next two hours, Hailey and Patty talked, laughed, and reminisced. Her aunt loved talking about the business as much as Hailey did, so she filled her in on all the goings-on at the store.

When the physical therapist came in, Hailey stood up and said her goodbyes. Promising to see her soon, Hailey left the room and walked down the hallway.

During the day, Cherry Vale was a flurry of activity with the nurses, aides, doctors, and techs bustling about. Residents congregated in the lobby either watching the birds flit in the aviary or the traffic whiz by on the street in front of the center. Hailey walked slowly and looked at the names posted on the residents' doors.

When she reached the end of the hall before the lobby, she glanced at the name on the door by the entrance. On a gold background in black lettering, she read "Helen Humphries." The name sounded familiar. Then she remembered it was Garth's grandmother's name. A tickle rode up her spine. *Can there be two Helen Humphries in Alina?* She supposed it was possible, but it seemed like too much of a coincidence. She stopped at the doorway, then went in quietly.

The early afternoon sun beat against the closed drapes, making the room not quite so dim. A woman in her early eighties with white hair dozed on a dark green recliner as the images on the television screen blinked. Padding over to the woman, Hailey glanced around the room and noticed several framed pictures. She paused and looked at one on the wall. Standing beside the Helen she remembered were Garth, his sister, Monica, and his brothers, Chad and Dylan. She smiled when she saw Garth's smartass smirk and his blue eyes full of devilishness. *He must be about thirteen in this picture.* "I had such a crush on you," she said out loud.

Helen moaned, and Hailey darted her gaze to her. The woman's eyes fluttered open, and a vacant look searched Hailey's face. She went over to her, bending down in front of her.

"Mrs. Humphries? I don't know if you remember me, but I'm Hailey Shilley. Ryan's sister. It's been a long time."

"Is that you, Susan? Where's your father? Did he come home from work yet?" she asked in a feeble voice.

"My name's Hailey, not Susan. Susan was your daughter. Garth's mother."

"Is Garth here? Where's your father? Why won't you answer me, Susan?" Helen's face contorted into a mask of distress as her tear-filled voice crushed Hailey.

"I shouldn't have come in. I'm sorry if I've upset you."

Helen tried to push herself out of the chair, wincing when she fell back against the cushion. Wringing her hands, her gaze darted around the room.

"Are you family?" a woman's voice asked.

Hailey spun around and saw a pretty woman in pink scrubs walking into the room. "No. My aunt's rehabbing here. Patty Manning. I just stopped in when I saw Mrs. Humphries's name on the door. I used to live in Alina, and I knew the Humphries and their grandchildren. My brother and one of her grandsons were best friends. I just wanted to say hi, but I'm afraid I've confused and upset her."

The woman ran her eyes over Hailey. "Don't sweat it. She's confused a lot. I know your aunt. She's a very funny lady. I'm surprised I've never seen you before." She extended her hand. "I'm Shelly. I'm the day-shift nurse five days a week."

"Hailey. I usually come after work, or on Sundays."

"That explains it, since I have Sundays off. I'll be back in a few minutes. Helen's too agitated to take her meds right now. It was good meeting you."

Shelly dashed out of the room and Hailey hung her head down, pivoting around to face Helen. "I feel terrible about upsetting you, Mrs. Humphries."

"What did you do?" a deep voice asked from behind.

Jerking her head up, she spun around and gasped: Goldie stood looming in the doorway. *What the hell is he doing in Mrs. Humphries's room?*

He walked into the room and went over to the woman. Bending down, he kissed her cheek and a huge grin spread over her face when she saw him. He hugged her. "How're you doing, Grandma?"

Grandma? This is Goldie's grandmother? Confusion flitted through her. *What the fuck's going on?* Then she looked at his leather vest, the one he wore the night before. She remembered he'd had a lot of patches, but she hadn't seen the back of it. Now, looking at the back, the words "Night Rebels MC" stared at her in red lettering. *Night Rebels. I know that name. Wait, Rory said it's that biker gang. The one Ryan told me*

Garth joined. Goldie must be Garth's friend. "Do you know Garth?" she said.

He raised his head and his eyes boldly ran over her body, making her feel conspicuous in her jean shorts and blue T-shirt. She crossed her arms over her chest. He laughed.

"Do you?" She stepped back.

"Why do you ask?"

"Because my brother told me he's in a motorcycle gang, and this is his grandmother. I knew him when we were younger."

"Night Rebels is a motorcycle *club*, not a gang. Gangs are for fuckin' losers." He leaned back on his boot heels.

"Garth! Your language," Helen said in a strong, clear voice.

He guffawed, leaned down, and hugged her tightly. "Awesome." The elderly woman laughed, but then her bright eyes turned dull and the vacant veil came back.

"She's got Alzheimer's," he said softly as he ran his fingers through her snowy white hair.

Hailey darted her gaze from Goldie to Helen, then back to Goldie. "I'm sorry. She thinks you're Garth."

He leaned against the windowsill behind the recliner. "I am, or at least I was. No one calls me Garth except for my grandma." He pursed his lips.

A hand flew over her mouth as she took him in, her stomach twisting in knots. *Goldie's Garth? The guy I kissed last night is Garth!* "I had no idea. You've really changed."

"I fuckin' hope so. You grew up nicely." His gaze dropped from her eyes to her shoulders, then to her breasts.

An unwelcome surge of excitement coursed through her, and she moved farther away from him. "I can't believe you're Garth. I mean, you gave me a tattoo."

"On your ass. And an incredible kiss on your lips."

She groaned and threw her head back. "I can't believe this. Did you know it was me?"

"When you came into the tattoo parlor, I had no clue it was you. I thought you were just another hot-looking chick. Ryan never mentioned you moved back to Alina. When did you get here?"

"About eight months ago. My aunt Patty shattered her left femur and needed help with the shop. She's here for rehab. That's why I'm here. I was visiting her earlier. I just happened to see your grandma's name on the door. I don't know why I didn't notice it before."

"They just put them on the door. Before, they were just on the charts inside the rooms. This is a small world. I wonder why Ryan didn't tell me you're in town."

"I think he was trying to protect me. He did tell me you joined a biker gang—I mean club. I don't know. Sometimes he acts like I'm still a child."

Cocking his head to the side, he slid his gaze over her again. "He knows me too well."

"This is kinda awkward." Hailey rubbed the back of her neck.

"Why's that?"

"Because of last night and the tattoo and all that."

"I bet you wouldn't have done any of that if you knew it was me."

"No, I wouldn't have."

"But you were attracted to me."

"Yeah, but I didn't know it was you, Garth. I mean, the whole thing is weird. You're my brother's best friend. We've known each other since I can remember."

His face hardened. "You're right. Ryan would be pissed, and we can't do that shit to him. We'll forget last night ever happened, and I'll try to forget your cute ass."

Before she could answer, several personnel ran past. She poked her head out into the hallway and saw a bunch of people go into one of the rooms. A few residents stood in the hall trying to peek inside.

"I wonder what's going on," she said.

He came up behind her, pressing against her back as he looked over her head and down the hallway. Static charges jumped through her as the heat radiating from him hugged her. Her body became alert and she felt his heat radiating off him. When he placed his hand on her shoulder, it set off an inferno inside her, and she leaned back against his solid chest. A subtle scent of leather, pine, and earth infused her senses, and her arousal screamed for his touch, for his lips on her skin.

"Looks like a problem in Mrs. Heller's room." His breath fanned over her shoulders and she fell farther back into him. His finger caressed her cheek. "Be careful what you're doing. You might wake the beast in me, and he doesn't play nice." The way he ground his hips forward, rubbing his hard dick against her, made her want to wake up the beast and more.

Shelly ran by, then stopped and came back to the door. Tension etched her face, and she glared at Hailey before looking at Goldie. "I didn't know you'd come in."

"What's going on down there?"

"Mrs. Heller's passed."

"Damn. That's too bad."

"Yeah. She was old. When you get past eighty, you never know."

"Age doesn't matter to her family. It still fuckin' sucks." Goldie's hand slipped under Hailey's hair and he swept his fingers over the base of her neck. Goose bumps freckled her skin as she shivered from desire.

"True." Shelly looked back down the hall. "I have to go. Are you going to stick around for a while?" She smiled widely at him.

She's got the hots for him. Hell, I've got the hots for him. I can't believe how sexy he turned out to be. But he's a womanizer. Remember, Ryan told you that. You're so out of his league.

"I'll be here for a bit."

"Sweet." Shelly scampered down the hall as the administrator of the facility tried to move the residents away from Mrs. Heller's room.

The exchange with Shelly must have brought him back to reality, because he stepped back from Hailey and cool air replaced his warmth as he went back over to his grandmother. Hailey pivoted around and watched him wipe Helen's nose. That single act made her heart melt.

She wanted to tell him that she'd always had a huge crush on him, that the kiss they'd shared the night before was the best one she'd ever had. That he did something to her—always had—and that she wanted to get to know Garth the man. But she just stood mutely in the doorway, watching him share a tender moment with his grandmother.

He threw the tissue in the trash, then went into the connecting bathroom and turned on the water. When he came back out, drying his hands with a paper towel, he gave her a half smile. All of a sudden, she felt like an intruder. She smiled back and went over to the chair to pick up her purse.

"I better get back to the shop," she said.

"Okay." There was a spark of some indefinable emotion in his eyes.

She spun around and walked out of the room. Outside, the hot, dry air bore down on her as she cut across the parking lot. It was an inferno inside her car, and she turned up the air conditioning to high and rolled down the windows to let the heat escape. Her mind was still spinning over the discovery that the man she'd been lusting after since he'd given her a tattoo was Garth. What were the chances of that? She didn't think he'd contact her again. Since he was a player, he probably figured he could fuck her a couple times and then move on. Discovering who she was must have put a major kink in his plans of seduction.

Her phone vibrated and she hoped it was him. With slumping shoulders, she read Rory's text.

Rory: *What's going on? Brent said u haven't returned his call.*

With a heavy sigh, she frowned while she shook her head slowly. *Not in the mood for this, Rory.*

Hailey: *Been 2 busy 2 think. Slammed @ the shop.*

Rory: *I feel 4 u, but u have 2 get out. What about Sat?*

Hailey: *Not sure. Brent doesn't do anything 4 me.*

In anticipation of Rory's response, she pressed her lips together and looked out the window. In front of her, a silver metallic motorcycle shone under the glaring sun. The artwork on the bike drew her in—a zombie apocalypse. She'd never seen anything like it, and her gut told her it was Goldie's bike.

Rory: *Y not? Please don't tell me u're into the tattoo guy.*

Hailey: *K, I won't.*

Rory: *R u serious? Brent's handsome, smart, witty, and a NICE GUY.*

Hailey: *Then u go out with him. Gotta run. Later.*

She chuckled as she started the engine. What could she say? Brent just didn't do it for her. She was serious about Rory going out with him. He was a million times better than that pessimist Troy. Anyway, she was seriously attracted to Goldie. The funny thing was that she saw the sexy tattoo artist as Goldie, not Garth. Garth was still a teenager locked in her memory. Plus, thinking of him as Goldie made her not mind so much that he was Ryan's best friend.

The tires squealed as she turned too sharply onto the main road. Maybe she'd come back the following day and see if she happened to run into Goldie. Maybe she'd turn into a stalker or something. One thing she knew for sure: she would see him again, even if it meant her seeking him out.

She wanted to get to know him all over again. Ryan wouldn't be happy about it, but he was halfway across the world. Goldie was just across town. Besides, people were always running into each other in small towns. It was inevitable.

She'd make sure to make the unavoidable happen.

Chapter Seven

WHEN GOLDIE ENTERED the clubhouse, he saw Steel sitting at a table with Paco and Sangre. He walked over to the table and Patches placed a bottle of Coors on it, then went back to the bar.

"Hey," he said to his brothers as he sat down.

"How's the poker run coming along?" Steel asked.

"Good. I've got all the travel routes set up, and I'm planning the club's basic itinerary. A lot of the brothers signed up for it, and I got a bunch of other bikers who are down. It should pull in some bucks." Being the club's road captain, he was responsible for organizing all the runs and tours, leading the formation on rides, and enforcing rules and procedures for group rides. Goldie also had to supervise the maintenance of all club vehicles, but he usually designated that to Shotgun, who ran the club's bike and auto repair shop.

"We could use some pocket change for the upcoming rally," Sangre said. He was the treasurer of the club and always looking for ways to bring in more money. The club's businesses brought in a steady stream of income, but it was the marijuana dispensary that was killing it for the Night Rebels.

"You gonna go on the ride with the Fallen Slayers this weekend? Afterward they're gonna have a helluva hog fest. They're even having women wrestling in barbecue sauce. I gotta fuckin' see that." Paco laughed.

"My ass will be there. I'm craving some new pussy," Sangre said.

"You guys will have a good time. I'm passing. Breanna wants to go to the Wildlife Museum in Durango. We're gonna make a day of it." Steel pulled his black hair into a ponytail.

"Sweet pussy or a museum. Damn, that's a hard choice," Paco joked.

"Not for me. I get both. I wouldn't want it any other way," Steel replied.

"You down?" Sangre asked Goldie.

"I think I'm going to pass. I don't feel comfortable leaving the shop for the weekend."

"Tattoo Mike's not going. There's no way his old lady's gonna let him spend a weekend with a shitload of chicks," Paco said.

"What the fuck's up with that? He's the man. If he wants to go, he should go." Sangre frowned.

"He could do that, but he probably wants to have some peace for the next few months," Steel replied.

"And some lovin'," Paco added.

"That's why I'm aiming to stay single. No way am I having a chick tell me what the fuck I can and can't do. That's bullshit." Sangre motioned the prospect to bring him another beer as the brothers laughed.

"There's definitely something to be said about the single life. I'm not planning on changing that either." Paco took the beer from the prospect's hand.

"Me neither. There're plenty of chicks around. Who needs one to mess with your head and life? Just because she's fuckin' hot doesn't mean shit. There're plenty of hotties who're more than willing to spread for biker cock." Goldie stretched out his legs and looked at his brothers, who just stared at him. "What? I'm right, you know."

"Who's the chick who has your cock?" Paco asked as he scooped up a handful of pretzels the prospect had just brought over.

Red spots clouded Goldie's view. "No woman's got my cock. No way that shit's happening."

"Really? You sure are making a lot of fuckin' noise about it." Steel's blue eyes twinkled.

Goldie's jaw tightened. He turned to Sangre. "You know what I'm saying."

"I guess. But it does seem like you got someone's pussy on your mind."

"No fuckin' way. Pass the goddamn pretzels."

Paco pushed the bowl to Goldie, and Skull and Army came over. Soon the brothers were talking about their favorite topic—Harleys. As they conversed, Goldie's mind drifted to Hailey, as it seemed to be doing far too often. It pissed him off that he couldn't forget her and just take up with another chick. He'd thought that once he'd kissed her, he'd be done, but it'd only gotten worse.

When he'd seen her in his grandma's room, he'd almost left before she spotted him, but he couldn't. Watching her bent down, her shapely legs looking damn good in her shorts, he'd been rooted to the floor. All he'd wanted to do was watch her big tits sway as he took her from behind. He groaned at the visual in his head and quickly looked at his brothers to make sure no one heard. They were still enthralled with motorcycle talk.

He blew out a deep breath. *What the fuck's up with me? Hailey's just a chick. A fucking hot, tempting one, but a chick nevertheless. There're a ton of them. I could call Kelly over right now and have her suck me good. Easy.* But he didn't want Kelly down on her knees; he wanted Hailey's pink full lips wrapped around his hardness, her mouth gliding up and down it.

"Fuck," he muttered under his breath. He'd never been as attracted to a woman as he was to Hailey. And it wasn't just the "forbidden fruit" crap—although that was a huge plus. No, he'd felt a spark between them the night she'd come into the ink shop. Before he'd known it was her. When he'd seen her on her stomach, her cute ass waiting for him to design it, it'd taken all his strength to not run his finger between her folds. "Damnit!" he hissed as his cock throbbed, punching against his fly. *I gotta stop this shit.*

Goldie had to get his control back. As far back as he could remember, he'd never let a chick bother him. Even when he'd been attracted to Hailey back in high school, he hadn't acted on it. But it'd been different back then. She'd only been fourteen and he'd just turned eighteen, and she was Ryan's sister. *She still is.* Nothing had really changed except that she was a woman now and had needs he was dying to fill. When he was standing behind her in his grandmother's room, desire ribboned through him as the subtle scent of her perfume lured him closer. He'd almost dropped his head down near the curve of her shoulder and nuzzled her creamy flesh, just below her ear. It was a good thing Shelly had come by.

"Sign me up for the poker run." Jigger's hand on his shoulder pushed Goldie's thoughts backstage.

He looked up. "Sure. Bring your bike to Skid Marks and Diablo will check it out. He's putting a priority on all bikes that are going on the run next week." Jigger nodded and joined the growing number of brothers at the table.

Goldie's phone rang and he slipped it out of his cut. *Ryan. Fuck.* He jumped up and to the back porch.

"Hey, dude," Ryan said.

"Is your ass hot enough over there?" Goldie asked.

Ryan chuckled. "You can't believe how fuckin' hot it is. What laws have you broken since we last spoke?"

"Too many to tell you."

"I gotta ask a favor of you. Hailey's moved back to Alina. Our aunt Pat's laid up and needed her help in the flower shop," Ryan's voice crackled.

"We got a shitty connection here." Goldie sucked in his breath.

"Can you hear me better?"

"Yeah."

"Anyway, I just found out that her fuckin' ex-boyfriend's found out she moved to Alina. This guy was obsessed with her to the point that she had to take out a restraining order. It's times like this that I wish I were home so I could bust the fucker's face. The asshole hit her and she got out of there real quick, but he started stalking her."

Picturing Hailey with bruises on her from some sonofabitch made his blood boil. "You want me to watch out for him?"

"Yeah. It'd make me feel a lot better if I knew you had your eye on her. I'm not sure this asshole will come there, but he still tells people they're together."

"I got this. You gonna tell Hailey?"

"Not sure. She's been in Alina for eight months. I didn't tell you because I know what a wolf you are." His laugh broke up.

"It's hard hearing you, dude. I'll take care of it."

"Yeah, I can't hear you very well either. Watch Hailey."

"What's the fucker's name?"

"Nolan Colley. Fuck! I gotta go. Later."

"Ryan?" Silence. Goldie took out a joint, lit it, and inhaled deeply as he watched the leaves from the trees sway in the warm breeze. Ryan wanted *him* to protect Hailey from some asshole. He could do it, no problem. But who was going to protect Hailey from him?

You gotta get a grip on all this. Ryan was his best friend and needed him to help out his sister. Easy. All he had to do was remember he was there to watch out for Hailey and nothing more.

Nothing. More.

Right.

Fuck.

Chapter Eight

SHERIFF WEXLER CHOMPED on his gum as he looked at Terri Crews, Mrs. Heller's daughter. The blonde lady leaned over his desk, her charm necklace clanking against it, and said, "Someone killed my mother. What're you going to do about it?"

He cleared his throat. "We have to first establish that your mother didn't die of natural causes. I spoke to your brother yesterday and he doesn't agree with you."

"He doesn't want any delays that will tie up his inheritance. He's only ever cared about the money since our mother became ill. He came by to see her maybe two times in the six months she was at Cherry Vale. I know my mom. I know how she was right before she died. I spent most of the day with her. She ate well, she was laughing, and she told me if she kept feeling better, she'd be home soon. Then she died? No. Something's wrong here."

"Your mother was eighty-three years old. Sometimes a person feels great right before they die. It happened to my grandfather. I'm just saying that, according to the medical reports, your mom was a very sick lady."

"Is that what Dr. Daniels told you?"

"I'm just going by the medical reports I reviewed at Cherry Vale."

"Well, talk to Dr. Daniels. He's as surprised as I am that my mom died. He told me she was doing well."

Wexler sighed and leaned back in his chair. He knew how hard it was to lose a parent. He'd buried his mother the previous Christmas, and it still made him choke up when he thought about her. Mrs. Crews was understandably upset over the death of her mother and was trying to make sense of it. Death slipped in when people least expected it, and for those who couldn't handle the shock, they tried to find ways of showing that the loss of a loved one happened too soon. *Hell, whenever someone you love dies, it's too soon. We're never prepared.*

"So are you going to look into this? I insist on an autopsy." Mrs. Crews rummaged through her purse, smiling wanly when he pushed the tissue box closer to her.

"Let me do some digging. If it looks like an autopsy is warranted, I'll order it. At this point, that's the best I can promise you."

Nodding, she wiped her nose and took another tissue. "Don't let this sit on your desk. I have to bury my mother." Her voice cracked at the end.

"I won't. I've got your number. I'll call you." He rose to his feet and extended his hand. "Again, I'm very sorry for your loss." He watched her walk away, her shoulders drooped as she took small, hesitant steps. After she was out of earshot, he went over to Deputy Miles Carmody. "Go over to Cherry Vale and ask some questions about Mrs. Heller. Find out who was on shift when she died."

"The old lady? Is there something suspicious with her death?"

"That's what I'm trying to figure out. Her daughter's adamant that there's foul play. I said we'd look into it."

Miles jumped up from his chair and tucked his shirt into his pants. "I'm on it."

"Let me know what you find out when you get back. I'll be here for a while." Wexler went back to his office.

The truth was he had nowhere else to be. He'd never married after his divorce ten years before. It wasn't that he lacked female attention; plenty of women in the county found the forty-six-year-old, six-foot sheriff handsome even though his blond hair was thinning at the sides. Being a cop was what broke up his marriage, and he couldn't go through that again. Maybe when he retired he'd find a permanent companion. His daughter's two kids kept him entertained, and he and his son still went fishing when Wexler could get away. Since both of his kids were out of town for a few weeks, he'd been passing his nights at the office.

There was something about the way Terri Crews insisted that her mother had been killed that made him send Miles to Cherry Vale. If nothing turned up, at least it would appease his mind, and hopefully Mrs. Crews's.

He took a sip of his cold coffee and pulled out a stack of paperwork that needed to be turned in to the city council. He could always count on the county to fill his time. Picking up a calculator, he began plugging in figures.

Chapter Nine

AILEY HAD WALKED past Helen's room several times hoping to see Goldie, but he was never there during the times she went to visit her aunt. Glancing at the clock in her car, she realized she had some time to kill before she met with customers for their upcoming wedding. Without thinking, she turned down Saguro Street and snapped up a parking space a few storefronts away from Get Inked.

Gripping the steering wheel, she tried to talk herself out of going inside the shop, but it didn't work. It seemed that whenever Goldie was involved, her reasoning couldn't compete with her desire. Sighing, she locked her doors and headed toward the tattoo parlor.

When she walked in, the pervasive scent of medicinal soap mixed with the sweet aroma of weed hit her full-on. A blue-haired woman with tattoos on her arms and several facial piercings smiled at her.

"Welcome. Do you have an appointment?" she asked.

"No." Hailey pulled on the strap of her purse. *What the hell do I say? That I want to see Goldie? What if he's working on someone? I shouldn't have come.*

"So you're a walk-in?" The young woman tapped an open notebook with her finger. "You need to sign in."

"Sign in?" She'd forgotten she'd signed the book the night she'd stumbled into the shop for her ink job; she thought she'd just given her phone number. *Wait a sec. I wonder if Goldie saw my name. He called me the next day, but—*

"Did you change your mind?" The receptionist's high-pitched voice broke in on Hailey's thoughts.

"I came here about three weeks ago. Is there any way I can see if I signed the book then?"

"Sure. Do you remember the date and time you were in here?"

After Hailey gave her name and the rest of the information, the woman said, "I found it. Here you are. You had a tattoo with Goldie."

"How did you know the name of the tattoo artist?"

"His initials are there, meaning he signed off on it."

He saw my name. Heat stole onto her face, but her embarrassment quickly turned to raw anger. *That asshole! He's been playing me all along. When he kissed me, he* knew *it was me. He didn't even tell me! I'm sure he got a kick out of me making an ass of myself.*

Hailey stumbled away from the reception desk. "I've changed my mind," she mumbled. She spun around and bumped into a broad, muscled chest. Her hands splayed out over the skintight T-shirt. "I'm so sorry," she said, then looked up. Goldie's blue eyes sparkled and an amused smile tugged at the corner of his lips.

"You!" Her voice was cold and lashing. She punched his rock-solid belly.

"What the fuck?" His lips thinned, and the sparkle in his gaze turned ominous.

"You've known all along who I am. How could you do that?" She threw another punch at him. Grabbing her fist, he pulled her behind him. "Stop it! Let me go."

He stopped abruptly, which made her crash into him. In a low, dark voice, he said, "You're making a fuckin' scene. We'll talk about this in my room." Without waiting for her to answer, he pulled her along until he opened a door and shoved her inside. With his back against the door, he glared at her.

"Don't even think of giving me that look. I'm the one who has good reason to be pissed. You've known since I came into the shop who I was. You jerk!"

Staring at her, he ran his gaze over her while he shook his head. "I found out after I tatted your ass." His words felt like needle pricks.

"So why didn't you tell me that the next day when you called? You made me practically ask you out. You made me act like an idiot."

"That was entirely your doing. Anyway, I figured if I told you, you'd be embarrassed considering I spent an hour looking at your ass. By the way, you've got a nice one."

She shook her head. "You *are* a player. Ryan and Rory warned me about you. Was your plan to seduce me and walk away?"

"I don't need to do much seducing. Women pretty much come to me." She rolled her eyes. "You're no exception. Why the hell are you here?"

"It's none of your business. You kissed me and you didn't tell me you were Garth. That's misrepresentation."

He laughed. "You gonna sue me? As I remember, you were enjoying the kiss."

"Unbelievable. You don't even think you did anything wrong."

"The only thing I did wrong was kiss you. I shouldn't have done that. Ryan's my best bud, and I should've respected him."

"What about respecting me? Were you ever going to tell me that you knew?" Hailey asked.

He shrugged. "Don't know."

"Just great. Move away from the door. I can't stand being in the same room with you."

"That's too bad, because Ryan called me a couple hours ago and asked me to keep an eye on you."

"You can stop lying now. Move on to the next woman."

His body stiffened and his face grew dark. The boy she'd known as a child was nowhere to be found in this tall, menacing man. Momentarily losing her balance, she stumbled as she took a few steps backward.

"Don't ever fuckin' call me a liar again," he gritted.

"Then play it straight. Ryan specifically told me not to look you up. Now you're telling me he called you to keep an eye on me. How damn convenient." She knew she was playing with fire, but she didn't care.

"Never did know when to shut your bossy mouth. Remember how many times it got you in trouble when we were kids?" His icy eyes narrowed.

"Whatever. I have to go meet some clients." She took two tentative steps, but he didn't budge an inch.

"Ryan said you've got a crazy ass stalking you. An ex by the name of Nolan Colley."

She suddenly felt foolish and very small. *Maybe I'm making a bigger deal than it is because I felt stupid about how I acted with him when I thought I didn't know him.*

"What's the deal with him?" Goldie asked in a low voice.

"He's a stupid, abusive jerk who never had a girl say no to him. He comes from a good family in Albuquerque. We started dating and he seemed cool. Then the closer we got the more possessive and controlling he became. After we slept together, he acted like he owned me. He was always accusing me of cheating on him. I never did, but he had it in his mind that I did. One night we had a huge fight and he hit me for the first time. The next day while he was at work, I packed up my stuff and went back to my parents'. He never forgave me. He doesn't know I'm in Alina."

"Ryan seems to think he does. He wants me to make sure you stay safe." He ran his gaze over her.

"By the way you're looking at me, I'm thinking I have to find someone to make sure I'm safe from you."

He flashed her a boyish grin, the kind that made women go weak at the knees. "What can I say? You're a very pretty woman."

A funny feeling fluttered inside her. "You're a handsome man."

He pushed away from the door and came close to her. "Seems like a shame not to do something about our mutual attraction." He slowly ran his finger from her cheek down to her collarbone.

Sucking in her breath, her heart beating wildly against her rib cage, she hooked her arms around his neck, pressing her body next to his. "Then let's do something." For a few seconds, sparking desire zinged between them, filling the spaces and making time stand still. And then he stepped back and scrubbed his face.

"Don't you have clients to meet?"

Blood began to pound in her temples and she quickly looked away, her pride bruised. Brushing past him, she opened the door. Before leaving, she looked over her shoulder and said, "I'd rather not see you again. And you don't need to babysit me. I can take care of myself." Without waiting for his reply, she shut the door and marched out of the shop.

When she got into her car, she rested her forehead against the steering wheel and tears trickled down her cheeks. *I've got to meet this happy-in-love couple in fifteen minutes and I'm going to look like a mess.* She raised her head and dug out a few tissues from her purse. Looking in the rearview mirror, she dabbed at her eyes, then saw him coming toward her car. She threw down the tissues and started the car. He picked up his pace and she pulled away from the curb, slamming on her brakes when a horn blared at her. Regaining her composure, she made sure the way was clear and drove away.

I'm so done with him. And what's Ryan's deal? There's no way Nolan's coming to Alina to find me. I wish he'd stop treating me like a baby. She switched on the radio and turned up the volume, getting lost in the beats of Maroon 5's "Cold." But as hard as she concentrated on the song, she couldn't get him out of her mind. She could still smell his scent, feel his closeness, and hear his deep-whiskey voice. And the way he'd kissed her was forever burned into her lips and her memory.

What am I going to do?

Chapter Ten

FRESH PERFUMED FLOWERS made Rose Higgins's room beautiful at Cherry Vale. All of her friends, children, and grandchildren had made sure she had plenty of flowers and cards to decorate her room. Since the doctor had told her she had to be there for a few months, she was glad she had the bed by the window because there was a view of the mountains.

The stroke had felled her all at once; one moment she was baking her special chocolate mocha cake for the charity bake sale, and the next she was hooked up to tubes in a stark white room at St. Joseph's Hospital. That'd been a month ago, and she'd just come to Cherry Vale less than two weeks before. Her roommate, Marge, had been discharged the previous day, and the facility hadn't placed a new patient in her room.

The hum of the machines filled the room, and the sedatives in the IV fluids dripping into her veins made her groggy. Outside, the stars were masked by the dark clouds that change shape as they move across the inky sky. There was little light in Rose's room but for the digital numbers on the machine next to her bed. Since it was after ten at night, the overhead hallway lights were switched off, so only the floor lights cast any sort of illumination in her room.

She inhaled the sweet scent of the bouquet her son and granddaughter had brought her earlier in the evening when they'd come to visit, then closed her eyes.

A shuffle across the linoleum woke her and she turned her head to the doorway. A dark silhouette leaned against the doorframe. She couldn't make out any features to tell who it was as the figure stood there immobile. Had she been able to speak, she would have asked who it was, but she lay in her bed watching the figure. *Maybe it's one of the aides. Is it already time to turn me on my side?* Having the pain medication in her system didn't help Rose think or remember clearly.

The figure came farther into the room, but it was so dark and her vision was so blurry from the medications she was taking that all she could see was a shadow approaching her. She wished she could smile, but the doctor told her that would come in time with physical therapy. Rose was positive it was the aide, and she braced her body for the turn. She hated being turned on her side because she couldn't tell the personnel whether she was comfortable or not, and if she wasn't, she'd have to stay in that position until they'd come back to turn her again in two hours. *I hate being helpless!* But she had to focus on getting better, on the positive. She'd already made tremendous progress in the short time she'd been there.

The shadowy figure came over and stroked her forehead. Its hand was cool and soothing while the movement was hypnotizing. *Am I dreaming? Is this an angel?* Rose's thoughts were all jumbled, mixing and bumping into each other. Then the shadow bent down and whispered in her ear, "I'm setting you free." His voice was deep and his icy breath tickled the hair on the back of her neck. *Who are you?* The voice was vaguely familiar, but she couldn't place it.

He straightened and pulled something out of his pocket. *A syringe. It's one of the nurses. It must be time for my shot.* But the doctor hadn't ordered any shots; all of her medicine was being dripped into her bloodstream by the IV. The shadow fussed with her IV, then rushed out of her room. Her drooping eyelids closed as sleep began to claim her.

Then Rose's eyes flew open and she gasped. Her heart pounded wildly and she feared it would burst through her skin. Frantically her eyes searched for the call button. She could still move her left hand, but she couldn't remember which side of the bed the button was on. A searing pain tore through her chest and she clutched at it in a vain attempt to soothe it. Black filled the edges of her vision and her heartbeat flooded her ears as her breath came in ragged, shallow gasps.

Wetness leaked from her eyes as she realized there would be no more walks in the park, no more gardening or baking, nor would she see the snow again. She'd never see her children or grandchildren.

A suffocating sadness choked her as her fragile heart beat one last time.

Chapter Eleven

"**Y**OU SURE ARE gentle with your hands," the brunette said as she stood up from the chair. "I bet you get a lot of repeat customers." She winked at Goldie.

"Once a person gets a tattoo, they get addicted. Just make sure you follow the instructions on the aftercare sheet. If you have any problems, let me know."

She brushed against him, her hand skimming the waistband of his jeans. "Does feeling nasty qualify as a problem?"

He stepped away from her and shook his head. "I'd say it's more of an asset." He opened the door to the room, then moved away. "Just keep the tat moist and don't scratch or pick at it."

She stopped at the doorway. "In case I have any problems, do you have a number I can call you at?"

"The number's on the instruction sheet. Just ask for me. I have to prep the room for the next customer." He turned away and smiled when he heard her heels tapping on the hallway floor. Having female customers come on to him went along with the job. Usually he'd have some fun with it either by flirting or taking them up on their offers, but that day he wasn't feeling it.

He cleaned up the room, then sank down onto the desk chair and opened the screen on his desktop. The dark eyes of Nolan Colley stared at him. Goldie had pulled up everything he could find on the douchebag just so he knew who he might be dealing with. To him, Nolan Colley looked like a snot-nosed punk who needed a few fists to the face to teach him a lesson. When Hailey told him Nolan had hit her, anger raced through him. He'd love nothing better than to catch the fucker in Alina and give him a good beating before he sent him packing.

Hailey. What the fuck am I going to do about her? He hadn't been able to get her out of his mind since she'd come to the shop the previous week. The last thing he wanted to do was rebuff and embarrass her, but that was exactly what he did when he'd spurned her. The feel of her body so close to his, her hand scorching his skin, it was all he could do to keep from kissing her and pushing her on the table to give her a good fucking. Then he'd thought of Ryan, how his friend had trusted *him* to take care of Hailey.

For the past week, he'd kept an eye on her without her knowing it, and each time he saw her, he wanted her more. She was on his mind all the damn time, and he had Ryan to blame for it. Several times, he'd thought about having a prospect watch her, but he knew Steel wouldn't go for that; she wasn't his old lady, so he couldn't justify asking his president to assign a prospect to do non-club work.

Glancing at the clock, he wondered if his appointment had flaked on him. He rolled his shoulders back and a forth a few times to work out some of the tightness. For the last six hours, he'd been hunched over working on tattoos. He wondered how Hailey's ink job looked, and hoped he'd get a chance to check it out.

Minimizing the page on the screen, he leaned back in the chair. He had to stop thinking about Hailey and all the dirty things he wanted to do with her. Each time his dick reacted to his thoughts of her, anger would shoot through him. He'd never been in such a predicament with any of the women he'd dated and screwed over the years.

Maybe it was because she was into him and had been ever since they were kids. It'd been so obvious that she'd had a crush on him, and the way she looked at him now told him she still did. There was no way he was off on the signals she'd been sending him since the first night she came into the tattoo parlor. And even though she knew he was Garth, she had still come in to see him the previous week. *But you're the older one. You're the one Ryan trusts. You can't fuck this up.*

The phone rang and he saw it was his younger brother, Dylan. His parents had loved Garth Brooks and Bob Dylan, hence his and his brother's names.

"Hey. When did you get back in town?" Goldie asked. Dylan worked for a marketing company that helped businesses with opening and closing their stores. Most months, he was gone for two or three weeks, traveling all over the country.

"Last night. It's good to be home."

"For a week. Then you'll probably go out again." Goldie leaned way back in his chair and rested his feet on the desk.

"I think I'm here for a few weeks, and then I have to go to Tennessee. I'm not looking forward to the heat and humidity. How's Grandma?"

"Good and bad days, but I think the bad days are getting more frequent. Chad hasn't been out to see her in a while. I'm gonna have to call and chew his ass out. Monica comes by but all she does is cry, and it upsets the shit out of Grandma."

Dylan cleared his throat. "I get what Monica's going through. It's hard to see Grandma like that."

"Yeah, but fuck, the whole visit? Anyway, we have to appreciate what Grandma is now with Alzheimer's and spend that time with her, not sobbing about the past. I mean, of course it fuckin' sucks, but save it for when you get home. Maybe you can talk to her. She doesn't listen to me."

"I'm going to go over later today. Did you want to meet me there?"

"I've got work. I can meet you later for some wings and a beer. Say about nine?"

"Sounds good. I may bring Skyla with me. Is that cool?" Dylan said.

"Sure. You guys getting serious?"

"We're moving in that direction. What about you? Still partying with all the women who can't resist a biker?"

Goldie laughed. "You know me well. Wouldn't want it any other way. Let's meet up at Bulldog Pub at nine."

After hanging up and slipping the phone in his pocket, Goldie meandered to the reception area. "Did my five o'clock call in?" he asked Liberty.

The blue-haired woman looked up from her phone. "Nope, but your six thirty rescheduled to tomorrow night. She said she was having extreme anxiety and couldn't leave the house."

"About getting another tattoo?"

Liberty shrugged. "She didn't say. Just said she'll be in tomorrow for sure."

With the no-show and cancellation, he had some free time. "I'll be back for my seven forty-five. Jimmy and Tattoo Mike are here, so we should be good. If it gets crazy, call me."

Looking back down at her phone, Liberty bobbed her head. He went outside and jumped on his Harley, roaring out of the parking lot.

When he arrived at Sweet Stems, Hailey was arranging a floral display in the storefront window. The aroma of flowers hit him in the face like a wall when he entered the shop. There were quite a few people at the counter and milling around the mcdium-sized store, and he went over by a large topiary near the front window. From his vantage point, he could see Hailey's nice ass encased in yoga pants. Her long yellow shirt had crept up past her behind as she bent over and arranged some teacups on a small table.

Straightening up, she gathered her messy tresses in a high ponytail and secured them with some sort of rubber band. Watching her, he pictured his fist tangled in her hair, pulling it back forcefully as he entered from behind, her pretty ass red from his handprints. As his dick twitched, he shifted his position and smiled when she looked at him, red streaks running up her neck.

"Hailey. Nice job with the window."

"What are you doing here?" she asked as she brushed away some stray hairs on her face.

"Just passing by. I thought I'd stop by and see how you're doing."

She shoved some ribbons and lace in a plastic bin, picked it up, and stepped down from the display window. "I'm fine. I've been real busy.

How've you been?"

"Good. Have you seen your ex-asshole around?"

She tilted her chin down and frowned. "Oh… so that's the reason you came by?"

The way her blue eyes dulled touched him. "No. I wanted to see you and see if you want to grab some food and a beer after I get off work."

The spark he loved seeing in her gaze came back. "Really? I mean, sure, I'd love to, but just as friends, okay?"

"No kissing or touching?" he asked in a low voice as he took a step toward her, sniffing her intoxicating scent.

She stepped back. "Right. Just friends. Like old times."

"We weren't exactly friends. You were Ryan's little sister." He curled his finger around one of the tendrils that had escaped from her ponytail.

Blinking, she pulled away slightly. "You know what I mean."

As he leaned in, his head tilted down, she fixed her gaze on his and parted her lips.

"Miss?" a voice from behind him interrupted them.

Hailey cleared her throat and glided past him. "May I help you?" she asked a middle-aged woman.

She and the woman walked to the coolers as Goldie watched her hips sway, imagining his fingers digging into them as he spread her legs wide and dipped his tongue into her wet folds, tasting her juices. *I bet she tastes fucking sweet. I wonder if her pussy is as pink as her lips. And her nipples. Fuck.* His dick jabbed against his zipper.

"I'll pick you up at eight thirty," he said over his shoulder as he walked toward the exit. There was no way he was going to let Hailey see him sporting a boner.

"Wait. You don't have my address," she said as came from behind the counter.

"I remember where your aunt lives. See you."

"How do you know I'm staying at my aunt's?"

She should've been a damn lawyer with all her questions. "'Cause I got a brain. I gotta go." He was on his Harley before she reached the front of the store and down the street by the time she yelled out his name. His shaft throbbed like hell as he rode out of town. He needed a ride through the desert to calm down. He'd have to do a better job controlling his excitement. There was something about Hailey that stirred him way up. It was like she'd invaded his mind, his senses, and his dick.

Turning down the old highway, he hit the accelerator and sped into the landscape.

As GOLDIE PULLED up to the Victorian, the streetlight on the corner clicked on as the last light of day gave way to the velvety dark of night. Only the faintest of light shined through the leaves as the moonlight danced across the darkened sidewalks and streets.

Amber light flooded over him as the porch light switched on and a chain slid off the door. Through the mesh of the screen door, he saw Hailey's smiling face, the light bouncing off it. From where he stood, her amazing scent filtered through the screen to curl around him. She unlatched the door and opened it wide. "Come on in."

Seeing her in her scoop-neck, hip-hugging dress with her shoulders bared took his breath away. Her chestnut hair spilled around her, the highlights shimmering like threads of gold, and the creamy swells of her breasts tempted his restraint in the worst way. *She's stunning.* In the night, her blue eyes seemed endless, like the ocean under a full moon. All he wanted to do was tug her into his arms and smother her throat with kisses, then dip his tongue down to the hollow between her breasts.

He glimpsed the pink tip of her tongue nestled between her teeth. Grasping her hand, he kissed it, then leaned in to her. "You look real pretty," he said, his lips grazing her earlobe. He felt her shiver and he pressed her closer against him. "And you smell so fuckin' sexy. Your perfume is doing a number on me, but you already know that, don't you?" He rubbed against her and chuckled when her eyes widened.

"I thought we were going out as friends," she breathed, her warm breath proving to be an aphrodisiac to him.

"We are."

"Do you always act like this with your female friends?" She tilted her head back and her enticing lips beckoned him.

"I'm new to this. You're my only friend who's a chick." He ran his thumb under her bottom lip.

"FYI, friends of the opposite sex don't really act like we are."

"I'll try and remember that." Then he crushed his mouth on hers and pushed his tongue through the seams of her lips, delving deep inside the recesses of her mouth. Instead of backing away from him, she clung to him as she shivered in his arms. Ramming his tongue deeper into her mouth, he slid his hand over her soft curves down to the ass he knew well. With all the women he'd held and kissed in his lifetime, none of them affected him the way Hailey did. His body and mind were on high alert, and even though he knew what he was doing was wrong, he didn't give a shit. Hailey fit into his arms so perfectly, and he'd never met a woman who magnetized him the way she did. And she didn't even know the affect she had on him.

The wild tones of "Girls, Girls, Girls" broke their connection as Goldie grabbed for his phone. Hailey stepped back and smoothed down her hair, then went over to an oval mirror hanging on the foyer's wall.

"Yo," he said as he watched her reapply her lipstick.

"Are you still planning on coming?" Dylan asked. The din of chatter, music, and glasses roared in the background.

"Yeah. Just running a bit late. On my way." Goldie stepped onto the porch. "We have to get going. Dylan's waiting for us."

"Dylan's going to be there? You didn't tell me that." She tugged at the hem of her dress, then stepped on the porch and locked the door. "We went to school together."

"Yeah, that's right. I didn't tell him you were coming, so it'll be a surprise."

"Is he married?"

"Not yet, but he's got a woman he's interested in. Her name's Skyla and she's going to be there too." He grasped her hand and led her to his Harley.

"Are you serious? I've never been on a motorcycle, and I can't go on one with this short dress. I'll be flashing my butt to everyone."

His gaze lingered on her backside, and then he nodded. "You got a point there. I don't want anyone seeing your ass but me." He popped open his saddlebags, pulled out a small blanket, and handed it to her. "You can put this on the seat and wrap it around you."

"I'm not doing that. It's hotter than hell, and I don't want to worry about balancing on the bike and keeping myself covered. We can just go in my car."

"I don't like cages."

"Cages? You mean cars?"

"Cars, trucks, or anything else that keeps you enclosed."

"So you don't have a car?"

"I have a pickup for hauling stuff and for the winters. Sometimes it's too damn icy for the bike. But I basically ride everywhere."

"Well, I'm not going to ride tonight in this dress. I'll take my car and meet you at the restaurant."

Goldie stood staring at her, amazed that she was turning down the chance to press her body against him as the wind rushed around her. He'd never had a woman turn down a ride on his Harley. For that matter, he rarely had women not go along with what he said. Hailey was driving him crazy, and a part deep inside him loved the challenge of her.

"Are you just going to stand there staring while Dylan's waiting for us?" She opened her purse and took out her keys. "Do you want to drive over with me or meet me there?"

From the way she lifted her chin and held her keys, he was pretty sure she wasn't going to change her mind. He'd concede, but he wasn't going to make a damn habit out of it. He grabbed the keys from her hands. "Let's go."

"I can drive."

"I'll drive. I'm not into chicks driving me around."

"You're impossible. And slow down. It's not easy to walk on an uneven sidewalk in five-inch heels."

He held the door open for her, then slipped into the driver seat.

Soon they were pulling into the lot at Bulldog Pub. The place heaved with people, and Goldie wrapped his arm around Hailey as they passed by a group of guys. The way some of them checked her out made his blood boil. *If any of them say something or even make a sound, I'm gonna slam my fist into their fucking faces.*

Inside the rustic-styled bar, pints of beer were being drawn for thirsty patrons as they crowded around the long mahogany bar. In the middle of the room, diners filled many of the wooden tables and chairs, as well as the red-leather booths that lined the walls of the establishment. There was an elemental feel to the décor, with lots of wood and exposed stone. It seemed as though it had been transported from a small village in England.

The hum of conversation, punctuated by sudden squalls of laughter, surrounded Goldie and Hailey as he guided her to a large booth. Dylan's beaming face greeted them.

"I thought you'd never get here. It's crowded for a weeknight," Dylan said, his gaze directed on Hailey as she scooted toward the wall.

"I got tied up." He slid in next to her. "Did you order?"

"Just drinks."

"Hi, Goldie," the cute woman next to Dylan said.

"Skyla." Goldie tipped his head. He placed his arm around Hailey. "This is Hailey. You remember Hailey Shilley."

Dylan's mouth opened as he stared at her. "Wow, you grew up." He quickly kissed Skyla's cheek when she punched him in the arm. "No. I mean, it's been a long time. I haven't seen you since we started high school. What're you doing back in Alina?"

As Hailey told her story, Goldie picked up the draft the waitress had brought and watched her use her hands as she spoke. She was so animated and, for a reason he couldn't understand, it was turning him way the hell on. Then again, it seemed like everything about Hailey turned him on. Never had a woman captivated him the way she had. Her laughter sparkled like drops of water in the sunlight, and it hit him right in the groin. But when she looked up at him through her thick lashes, his pants grew tight. Shifting, he tried to get comfortable, and when Hailey asked him if he could let her out of the booth, he grabbed his napkin and stood up. Skyla followed Hailey as they went to the ladies' room. Sliding back into the booth, Goldie threw his napkin on the table and shook his head.

"How long have you been going out with Hailey?" Dylan asked.

Goldie jerked his head. "I'm not going out with her. We're just friends."

Setting his beer down, he laughed. "You could've fooled me. The two of you got something going on between you. I can see it in both of your eyes and by your hard-on."

"What can I say? She's fuckin' hot. I always get a boner for a hot woman, but that's where it ends. Ryan's my best bud, and he asked me to keep an eye on her. She's got some fucked-up ex-boyfriend in her past and Ryan's afraid he may come to Alina and try some shit with her." Goldie took a long drink, avoiding Dylan's gaze.

"I've seen you with other hot women, and you don't act the way you are with Hailey. And she is damn hot. I couldn't believe it when you told me it was her. I mean, I always thought she was cute, but now she's definitely a grown woman." Dylan laughed.

"You and Skyla seem good together." Goldie wanted to turn the conversation away from Hailey. The more they talked about her, the harder he grew, and he needed to calm way the hell down before she came back to the table.

"We are. I think she's the one, bro. I want to spend all my time with her. I'm thinking of asking her to move in with me. Maybe even marry me."

"That's cool. I always thought Skyla was good for you."

"Are you guys done talking about us?" Skyla said as she slipped back into the booth.

Goldie stood up and let Hailey in. As she skimmed against him, his jeans grew tight again. *Fuck!* He sat down and retrieved his napkin, placing it over his bulge. The waitress came over with their burgers, wings, and salads, and he was grateful for the distraction.

Throughout dinner, they laughed and talked, and everything about her sent him into overdrive: her soft laughter, her scent, her eyes, and her leg pressed against his. She had no clue what her nearness did to him, and he kept reminding himself that she was Ryan's sister. Over and over the words "She's Ryan's sister" played in his head like a mantra; he wished his dick would pay attention to it.

"We should get going. I've got an early meeting in the morning," Dylan said.

"Me too. There are so many weddings this summer. I had a couple come in from Tula to order flowers for their September wedding. Anyway, I have a long day tomorrow." Hailey turned to Goldie. "We should go."

"Sure." He stood and helped her out of the booth.

After saying their goodbyes, Goldie drove Hailey home.

"I had a real nice time tonight. It was so much fun seeing Dylan again. And Skyla is so nice. They seemed really into each other. Maybe he'll be the first of your siblings to tie the knot."

"Maybe."

"I bet you're the last. You don't seem like the marrying type." She climbed out of the car and quickly closed the door behind her.

"I'm not." Before he could capture her in his arms, she'd sprinted up the porch steps and unlocked the door. He tugged her to him, his arms looping around her waist, her back pressed to his chest. Nuzzling her neck, he said, "You drove me wild all night."

"I'm sorry. I didn't mean to." She cocked her head to the side.

"I loved it," he said against her soft skin. "Are you going to invite me in?"

Stiffening, she placed her hands on his and tilted her head back. "I don't think that's a good idea. I have to get up early, and we're trying to just be friends, remember?"

"Bad ideas are usually the most fun. And we are friends."

She laughed dryly. "I don't want a friendship with benefits. Anyway, what would Ryan say?"

The mention of Ryan's name was a sure cockblocker. He released his hold on Hailey and stepped away. "I lost my head. I think you're a damn hot woman, and sometimes I forget it's you. I gotta go."

She turned around. "Where are you going?"

"For a ride, then back to the clubhouse."

"I'd like to ride on your Harley sometime." Her gaze caught his and the sexual tension between them crackled.

"I'll remember that." He jumped off the porch and hopped on his bike. He needed to go for a fast, hard ride to clear his head. For him, riding his bike was better than a cold shower. He'd have to ride extra fast to rid himself of the image of Hailey's soft body fused to his, sweat glistening off them as he fucked her hard while watching her come.

The night sky sparkled with thousands of bright specks, the blacked-out rock formations now flat shapes dissolving into the desert ground. As Goldie roared down the desolate road, the darkness swallowed him up.

Chapter Twelve

HAILEY WATCHED GOLDIE ride away before she closed and locked the door. Sadness enveloped her as she trudged upstairs to her bedroom. Every ounce of strength she possessed fought hard to keep her from inviting Goldie in and letting him have his way with her. From the first time she'd seen him at the tattoo shop, she was smitten. There was no denying the electrifying sizzle between them, and she knew he experienced it too. And when she found out he was Garth, she took it as a sign.

But you ran away scared. Pushed him away. And it wasn't because of Ryan. The truth was she was scared out of her mind. When Goldie wasn't around, she thought about him a lot—and her panties dampened, her nipples ached, and her sex throbbed like hell. It was unbelievable. And when she was with him, her whole body was in a frenzy.

She slipped into the cool sheets and turned off the lamp. Lying on her back, she looked up at the custom ceiling with ornate floral patterns and tried to imagine what it would feel like to have a fling with Goldie. *It would be awesome and devastating.* Since she was a young girl, she'd had a crush on the blond, blue-eyed Garth, and if they came together now, she knew she'd flip completely for him. *Look how worked up I get just* being *with him. Imagine having sex with him.* No, it would be a disaster because he was nothing but a womanizer. For him, it would be just a wild night of sex while for her it would mean everything.

No, it would never work. She didn't actively seek getting a broken heart. And he would break her heart terribly; she was sure of that.

Closing her eyes, she hoped sleep would stop the twirling of her thoughts.

★ ★ ★

RORY PICKED UP her piña colada margarita—it was the summer special at Alfonso's—and ran her tongue over the rim. "This is the best margarita I've ever had. Good choice for dinner, Hay."

"I know we all like Mexican food, and the first time I came here I almost died the food and drinks were so good." Hailey took a sip of her pineapple margarita.

"I can't believe you're just having your usual white wine when there are so many yummy drinks on the menu," Rory said to Claudia.

"A glass of stellar chardonnay suits me just fine."

The waiter came over with three steaming dishes. "Will there be anything else?" he asked.

"I ordered corn tortillas," Claudia said.

"I'll be right back with them." The server rushed away.

"Are you going to be able to eat all of those?" Rory said, pointing to the pile of clams on Claudia's plate.

Picking up the salt shaker and a lemon wedge, she nodded. "You bet. I love this dish so much."

Hailey laughed and picked up her fork, digging into her *chile relleno con camarones*—a large poblano pepper lightly fried and stuffed with cheese and shrimp. Popping a piece in her mouth, she leaned back and savored the burst of fresh flavors from the cilantro and peppers. "This is so damn good. I'm officially hooked."

"Mine's to die for too. How's your chicken enchilada?" she asked Rory.

"Good, but I'd be just as happy to drink my dinner and forgo the eating. I've got to have another one of these margaritas."

As the women ate their food, drank, and talked, a loud rumble traveled through the restaurant. "Is that thunder?" Claudia said.

Craning her neck, Rory looked up. "It can't be. There isn't a cloud in the sky."

"You're right, and it's clear over the mountains too. I wonder what it is."

Before Hailey could voice a guess, eight motorcycles roared by the eatery. Several diners covered their ears and many more directed their attention to the street, clearly annoyed. A shiver climbed up Hailey's spine as her stomach fluttered. *I'm turned on over a motorcycle? How stupid is that?* The truth was her body was reacting to the possibility of seeing Goldie again. It hadn't even been twenty-four hours since she'd seen him and she already missed him. Earlier that day, she'd hoped he would've called her, but she wasn't all that surprised he didn't because the bad boys always wanted the women to chase them.

"Did you see all those motorcycles? I bet the guys are in the Night Rebels," Rory said as she gestured to the waiter for another round of drinks.

"Probably. I've seen some of them and they're damn good-looking. Real buffed and firm." Claudia giggled.

Rory's eyes widened. "Oh shit. They're coming in here."

Hailey's stomach turned over, and she slowly looked over her shoulder. Amid all the people, her gaze found his penetrating one—the one that was striking yet soft and made her insides dance. Goldie turned to a guy next to him and said something, then approached her, his shimmering gaze fixed on her. Mesmerized by his powerful legs encased in blue denim and his toned arms in a sleeveless T-shirt, she gawked at him as he came closer. The way his biceps bulged as he walked made her clench her legs together. A long silver earring dangled in his left ear, picking up the sun's rays, gleaming against his tanned skin. She'd never seen him wear an earring and she found it incredibly sexy, even more so than the colorful ink that moved with him across the room. Every muscle in his body rippled, and her body ached for his touch. His raw maleness didn't go unnoticed by several of the female patrons, who ogled him as he passed their tables.

"Hey, isn't that the guy who gave you the tattoo on your butt?" Claudia said, breaking the spell. Hailey turned around and nodded. "He's coming over here. He must've remembered us."

"Great. Why can't a good-looking guy in something other than denim and leather come over here?" Rory hiccupped loudly.

"Hey, Hailey." His baritone voice landed right between her legs.

"Hi," she mumbled before reaching for her drink.

"You're the tattoo guy," Claudia said.

He nodded. "How're you ladies doing?"

"Just great!" Rory replied. "These margaritas are damn good. Are you a Night Rebel? You got the bike, the body, and the leather vest. If you're not, you're impersonating them and they're going to kick your ass." A peal of laughter burst from her mouth.

"She's liking the margaritas a little too much," Hailey said softly.

"That's cool. And I am a member of the Night Rebels." He pulled a chair over and sat down next to her. Claudia and Rory lowered their heads. "I guess that was a conversation killer." Grasping her hand, he brought it to his lips and kissed it. "It looks like you survived your day."

All of a sudden, Hailey's mouth went as dry as the summer heat and all she could do was nod.

"Did you get the contract for the couple's wedding? The ones from Tula."

Wow... he was actually listening to me last night. A huge plus. "Yeah, I did. How was your day?"

"Busy."

"Goldie! What the fuck do you wanna eat? This sweet babe wants to take our order," a man with long red hair yelled out.

"Is that your friend?" Hailey asked as she turned to look at the table of bikers.

"Yeah. That's Sangre. I better get over there." He rose to his feet, then reached out and stroked her cheek as he locked his gaze on hers. For several heartbeats, he stood transfixed, and she thought he was going to kiss her. Her body tingled and pulsed in anticipation of it, but a half smile curled on his face and he sauntered away.

"Oh my God. What the fuck was that about?" Claudia said.

Rory grimaced. "Don't tell us you've got a thing for the biker tattoo guy. Not when you had a chance with Brent."

Hailey took a big gulp of water. "The tattoo guy is Goldie, who used to be Garth. I found that out when I bumped into him in Mrs. Humphries's room at the rehab center. She's at Cherry Vale just like my aunt. Isn't it a small world?" She smiled weakly.

Claudia looked over at the biker table. "Holy fuck. That gorgeous guy used to be Garth Saner?"

"And you still have a crush on him, don't you, Hay?" Rory held up her hand before Hailey could answer. "Don't say it. I know you do. I could tell by the way you were looking at him. And he's into you too. Don't let this happen, Hay. Brent really likes you, and he's a nice guy. A sure bet. Garth will be a disaster."

Grinding her teeth, Hailey raised her chin. "For who? Anyway, we're not dating, but if we were, it would be my decision. And since you're so hot for Brent, why don't you go out with him?"

"Because he likes you. I wish he liked me that way. Anyway, it's just a matter of time before you start up something with Garth. Remember, he's a player. Ryan's best friends with him, and he told you that. He was such a jerk in high school too. He went out with all the easy girls. Do you really want a guy who's been with most of Alina?"

"Fuck, Rory. Lighten up. If Hay wants to screw Garth-turned-biker-turned-Goldie's nuts off, it's her business. I'm still reeling about what a hunk he is. And you had a crush on him too back in high school." Claudia brought her wineglass to her lips.

"You did?" Hailey said to Rory.

"I don't want to talk about him anymore. Let's just forget about him being here, have some more drinks, and let me tell you about the vacation I have planned for me and Troy next month."

While Rory went over every detail of her travel itinerary, Hailey was acutely aware of Goldie's presence in the room. She felt his eyes on her, and the connection they had pulled hard at her. Pretending to look for their waiter, she turned around, catching his piercing gaze that held a mixture of emotions: lust, irritation, tenderness, and impatience.

"Are you listening, Hay?" Rory's thin voice broke through her heated haze.

"Uh… yeah. I'm trying to find our waiter. I could use another drink." She glanced back in Goldie's direction, and even though he was talking to the guys at his table, the pull was still there. Lingering on his rugged face, she chided her foolishness, but just when she was about to focus back on Rory's travelogue, his heated look grounded her. *Oh, Garth. I still have a massive crush on you.* But this time around she was a woman and he was a man, and her body ached for him in the worst way.

After sharing dessert, Rory placed her elbow on the table, rested her chin on her hand, and drooped her head. "I'm so sleepy," she mumbled.

"Then we better go. It looks like she'll be crashing with me," Claudia said as she stood.

"Do you need me to follow you home to help you with her?" Hailey picked up her purse.

"She's not that smashed. I've seen her worse. I'll be good." Claudia helped Rory up from the chair.

"I'll at least help you get her to the car." Hailey came over and placed her hand around Rory's arm.

"You guys, I'm good. Quit making a fuss over me," Rory said as she swayed.

On the way out, Hailey glanced over at the biker table, disappointment twisting inside her when she saw it empty. *He didn't even come over and say goodbye. It doesn't matter. I don't give a shit.* But she really did. She wanted to keep in contact with Goldie, yet she was afraid of her feelings for him. She was afraid he'd treat her like just another one of his women. *I'm so damn mixed up. I never should've gone to the tattoo parlor.* She pressed her lips together. *I should've stayed in Albuquerque.*

After strapping the seat belt over Rory and waving goodbye to Claudia, Hailey went to her car, pressing the remote to unlock the doors. Before she could open her door, she heard the crunch of footsteps behind her. Darting her eyes around, she realized she was the only one in the parking lot. Hurriedly, she pulled open her door, only to have a hand slam it shut. She screamed out, trying to turn around, but someone pinned her against her car.

"There's money in my purse. Take it," she said hoarsely.

"That's not what I want," a deep voice replied.

Goldie! Pushing backward, she shoved him away, then spun around. "You scared the shit out of me!"

He chuckled and drew her close to him. "I didn't mean to. I thought you saw me by my bike."

"I didn't. I thought you left. What do you want?" The pounding in her ears began to dissipate.

Without saying a word, he grasped her shoulders and yanked her to him. She couldn't help but notice his strength, the way his biceps bulged as he held her, and the bulk of his shoulders. Before she could say anything, he slammed his mouth on hers and kissed her with such passion her knees buckled. Holding her up, he cupped her ass cheeks while he continued to devour her mouth. His tongue invaded her mouth, flicking across her teeth, entwining with hers, and she looped her hands around his corded neck. She'd never been kissed like that; it was wild, consuming, and addictive all at once, making her senses come to life.

"Oh, Hailey," he murmured on her lips.

Hearing him say her name between kisses sent chills from her pulsing lips into the opening between her legs. She never wanted him to stop kissing her. Moaning, she ran her fingers through his hair, her nipples hardening as his hard dick rubbed against her. At that moment, she wanted nothing more than to have him inside her; it didn't matter that they were in a public place. His scent of soap and leather filled her senses, and her arousal screamed for his touch. Pressing closer, she ground against him, loving the low growls he emitted.

"What're they doing, Dad?" a small voice rang out in the parking lot.

"Nothing. Come over here, Scotty," a man's voice replied.

"I can't believe this," a woman's shrill voice added.

The voices pierced the sexual veil engulfing her and she pushed

Goldie back, immediately missing the warmth of his body. She glanced sideways at the couple and their child, noticing other diners walking to their vehicles.

"We need to go somewhere and get this thing we have going between us out of our system," Goldie said as he traced her jawline with his finger.

His words were like a bucket of cold water thrown at her. "What does that mean?" Her voice dripped ice.

He raised his eyebrows, then smiled. "I think you know. We both hunger and crave each other, and that's standing in the way of everything. I need to watch over you, but all I can think about is fucking you."

"How romantically put." She crossed her arms.

"I don't go in for romance." He cocked his head back.

"That doesn't surprise me. So you're proposing that we have sex so you can get it out of your system?"

"Yours too."

"My system's just fine." *I'm such a liar, but he's worse. He just wants to screw and move on. Treat me like a piece of ass like he does all the other women. He's such a player.*

Goldie stepped back, his smile gone and his lips forming a thin line. "Guess I misread you." He shoved his hands into his pockets. "I'll wait until you take off. You haven't heard from your ex-douchebag, right?"

He's pissed at me. He has a lot of nerve. "No. Ryan's overreacting on this. He usually does when it comes to me." Her glare held his.

"He just wants to make sure you're safe. Go on now."

Sexual tension sparked between them, and then she opened her car door and slid in. Pulling out of the parking lot, she watched him as he stood by his bike watching her. Her body was wound tightly from unquenched desire, her lips red from his ardent kissing. Part of her regretted not taking him up on his offer to "get it out of our system." But she didn't want to be like all the women he'd had in his life. She'd had a crush on him for so long that if they were going to come together, she wanted it to be special, to *mean* something to her—and to him.

I was doing just fine before I bumped into him. She'd have to go back to her life pre-Goldie. She could do it. After all, they hadn't really had much between them except a few kisses. *But his kisses are mind-blowing.* She shook her head. *I've got to stop thinking like that.* She'd just have to forget about him. When she spoke to Ryan, she'd tell him to call off his watchdog. The whole thing was wearing thin.

She was done.

End of story.

Chapter Thirteen

LINDA SALINAS TRUDGED up the porch stairs to her house, swaying slightly as she held grocery bags in both hands. From the shadow of the bushes, he watched her. He knew her routine and her every move. For weeks, he'd been watching her, and Tuesday night was grocery night. He smiled as she dropped a bag to grab onto the railing so she wouldn't fall. When she bent over to pick up her groceries, he glimpsed the backside of her tanned thighs. His breath quickened as his eyes fixed on her movements.

Tuesday night was the one night she was alone. There were no children or grandchildren who came over, no friends, and she had nowhere to be. After learning her schedule, he'd marked Tuesday as the day he would pay her a visit. Many Tuesdays had come and gone, but that night he was in predator mode. That night he would attack, and afterward, he'd find another target. There were a couple women he'd been staking out, but nothing as intense as Linda Salinas. At least not yet.

The excitement of surprising her, of seeing the fear in her eyes, of smelling it oozing from her body was what he loved. Fear and dominance were what drove him to seek, stalk, and attack his victims. A lot of his time was spent fantasizing and hunting, and once he decided to give in to his craving, he was past the point of no return.

That night, as he watched Linda Salinas close and lock her door, he was beyond fantasizing. The rush of adrenaline surging through his body reminded him how badly he needed this. He would wait for the next several hours until she went to bed. He'd broken into her house earlier that day and unlatched a window in the family room. She never checked her windows before she went to bed.

In all his hunting, it never ceased to amaze him how many women left their windows and door unlocked, or never checked them when they arrived home. He wasn't complaining because it made what he did so much easier. It just surprised him how trusting people were in general. Maybe some would reason that the women felt safe in a small town, but he'd seen it when he was hunting in the city before he moved to Alina. He chuckled. Predators such as he relied on women's naiveté to feed their hunger.

With a backdrop of crickets in the long grass, nighttime erased all remnants of twilight. The predator's gaze fixed on his prey's lighted bedroom window. Very soon now it would go out. Licking his lips, he shoved his hands in his pockets and waited. Darkness brought the primal nature to the front, an invigorating state for those who craved fear and dominance.

Then the light went out. Jittering a foot against the ground, his heart pounded as he imagined the look of fear on Linda Salinas's face. *Slow down. Keep cool. You've got time. You want to make sure the bitch is fast asleep.* Waking up a woman from sleep when she thought she was safe hit him below the belt each and every time. He doubted that he'd ever tire of the rush of excitement the woman's fear brought to him. And it only got better as he threatened her and told her all the awfully nasty things he was going to do to her. There was really nothing like it.

A little less than two hours later, he was in Linda Salinas's bedroom doorway. In the glow from the moonlight, he saw her form encased in a blanket. The air conditioning made the room cool, and it reminded him of a tomb. He smiled at his analogy, then pulled the knife out of his pocket. The blade gleamed as he slowly approached the bed, his heart beating, his excitement through the roof. And still she slept, oblivious to how drastically her life would forever change.

Standing over her, he saw her black hair curled around her forehead and her body moving up and down as she breathed. *Showtime, my sweet lamb.* Grasping her shoulders, he shook her firmly, loving the way her eyes flew open and confusion masked her face. When her sleepy gaze became clear, it fixed on his ski mask, then on his brown eyes. Her gaze was terrified. *Perfect. You didn't disappoint me, darling.*

"Don't move or I'll kill you," he gritted as he held the blade against her quivering neck. Her fear kept growing and his desire pushed him on.

He threw off her bed coverings, and the small whimpers and ever-present fear etched on her face fed him and pushed him on. He cut off her clothes with the knife, his eyes feasting on her breasts. *I'm going to have fun with those.* Out of instinct, her hands flew to her breasts in an attempt to cover them from his piercing gaze. He shoved them off and leaned close to her ear.

"You're going to do everything I tell you to do. If you don't, I'll fucking kill you. If you scream, I'll cut you bad, then fucking kill you. And if you *ever* try to cover yourself, I'll fuck you with the knife. You got it?" She nodded, her face pained with terror. "Then we understand each other."

For the next four hours, he brutally raped her. She was compliant, not even daring to cry out. The only evidence of her grief, fear, and shame was the tears that kept rolling down her cheeks. Of course, he fed off those wet streams just like he did with her fright.

When he was fully sated, he took out a camera and snapped a slew of pictures of her in various poses, and then he dragged her to the bathroom and made her sit in the tub. Turning on the cold water, he ordered her to stay there until he came back. He returned to the bedroom and stripped the bed of all coverings, shoved her clothes in a large plastic bag, and carefully cleaned anything that could have any trace of his DNA. He went back to the bathroom and ordered his victim to wash herself while he watched, grabbing the soap from her and roughly cleaning her vagina and rear end. Throwing the soap into the bathwater, he said, "Don't move. If you call the police, I'll put all the pictures I took of you on the Internet. Be smart, not stupid. Remember, I know where you live."

Past experience taught him that, fearful he may still be in the house, Linda Salinas would most probably stay in the cold bathwater for at least an hour before her courage allowed her to venture out. By then, he'd be long gone.

He disposed of the bedsheets and clothes, then headed to his house. After checking on his children, he slid between the sheets and tugged his wife to him. She moaned slightly and snuggled close to him. In a matter of seconds, his exhaustion overtook him and he fell into a deep, restful sleep.

Chapter Fourteen

WEXLER TOOK A big sip of day-old coffee and thumbed through the report Deputy Miles Carmody had given him concerning his inquiries at Cherry Vale. In the report, the number six stood out like a beacon. *Six deaths in four months. That doesn't sound right.* Either Cherry Vale had a slew of very sick, unlucky patients, or something sinister was going on beneath the surface.

He scrubbed his face and leaned back in his chair. *I need a damn vacation.* There was nothing he'd rather be doing at that moment than sitting on his boat on La Plata River, fishing with his son and throwing back a few beers. Instead, he was sitting in a stuffy office, dripping in sweat thanks to the air conditioner breaking down again, and waiting to get a verbal chewing out by Mrs. Heller's daughter for the umpteenth time. *Shit.* He grabbed the handkerchief out of his pocket and mopped his face.

"Rhoades!" he yelled.

A tall, lanky deputy stuck his head in the doorway. "Yes, sir?"

"Call the goddamn town council and tell them we're on day three of a heat wave and our AC is still broken."

"Yes, sir." The young deputy went over to his desk.

Taking out the autopsy report, Wexler reread it. Under the heading "Immediate Cause of Death," the medical examiner indicated "Congestive Heart Failure." Even though the report indicated that there seemed to be an unusually large amount of digoxin in the deceased's body, the coroner noted that Mrs. Heller was taking digoxin intravenously as part of her treatment for heart problems. Then under the heading "Manner of Death," the coroner wrote "Natural Causes." *Then why was there so much of this heart drug in her body? Where the hell did that come from?*

After reading it several more times, he couldn't find a place where the medical examiner addressed the reason for the surplus of digoxin in the deceased's body. A stab to his gut told him something wasn't copacetic at Cherry Vale.

As he picked up the phone to call Terri Crews to share with her the autopsy finding, Rhoades stood in the doorway. Wexler put the phone back in its cradle and raised his eyebrows.

Rhoades cleared his throat. "Our air conditioner is next in line for repair. The guy should be here within the hour. A call came in that there's been another rape."

The sheriff pounded his fist on the desk. "Fuck! When?"

"Seems like it started last night and ended sometime this morning. I was going to head over there, but I knew you'd want to know."

Wexler pushed up from his chair and pulled at his pants that were sticking to him. "Let's go."

When they arrived at Linda Salinas's house, all the curtains were pulled, and she sat on one of the straight-backed dining room chairs staring at the floor. Since Mesa County was small, and Alina even smaller, there was no provision for a victim advocate program; it was up to him and Rhoades to try their best in helping her out with the aftermath of a rape.

After giving the victim some names of local counselors and a program St. Joseph Hospital offered for coping with violent crime, the sheriff left the other two deputies to finish investigating the crime scene. Even though the perpetrator had her bathe, Wexler held out hope that the rape kit would turn up some DNA. He knew it was a long shot, but he had to explore all the possibilities.

This is the third one in two months. The last one was only ten days ago. Shit. We're in over our heads.

Knowing when to call for experienced detectives who could help find the guy responsible for the attacks was part of the sheriff's strength. Taking out his phone, he dialed Detective Contreras to see if he could offer any help. He knew the detective worked in the homicide division of the Durango police department, but he hoped he could offer some insight, or at least recommend someone to help him and his deputies.

"How're you doing, Doug?" Contreras said.

"Shitty. It's hotter than hell and the AC's been out for a few days. Typical county bullshit. And we got what seems like a serial rapist in our town. How're you?" Wexler walked over to the oak tree and stood under its leafy branches for some much-needed shade.

The detective chuckled. "Cool in our air-conditioned office, but up to my neck in shootings. The hot weather brings out the worst in people. The homicide rate always goes up in the summer. So all the rapes have the same markings?"

"Yeah. The bastard enters late at night, wears a ski mask, brutalizes the women for several hours, takes pictures of them, makes them bathe, and takes all the bedsheets and clothes before leaving. It's the same fucker. We haven't had a rape in Alina in years, and not any for the last year in the county. I don't have the manpower and my deputies don't have the expertise to handle this one. You got someone who can help us out?"

"Sounds like you have an experienced perpetrator. Jack Barnard is the one you want. He's in our Sex Crimes Unit, and he never gives up until he gets a case solved. He's been with the department for about six years. Before coming on-board, he lived in Los Angeles and did eleven years with LAPD. Jack knows his stuff. I'll e-mail you his chief's number and you can talk to him to see if he can spare him. It sounds like your perp isn't going to stop."

"Fuck no. He's actually kicking it up. We haven't released anything to the media because I don't want to cause a panic." Wexler leaned against the tree.

"You need to. Even though the town council will be up your ass daily, the women need to know there's a sexual predator out there. Maybe someone saw or heard something. You never know."

The sheriff's stomach churned. "You're right. I'll give the chief a call when I get back to the office. You got any plans to take your family on vacation?"

Contreras laughed. "I always have plans. The trouble is they always change. I want to take the family to Disneyland, but I haven't let them know in case it doesn't materialize. What about you?"

"Not any time soon. With these rapes and some other problems, I'll be lucky if I can take a day off."

"I hear you, man. Let me know how things go. If you need my help with anything, give me a call."

Before going to the office, Wexler decided to stop by the office of the *Alina Post*. He'd have to brace himself for the pressure his department would experience from the town council and the residents. His life would soon be hell after the evening paper came out.

He shoved a stick of gum into his mouth, cranked up the patrol car's AC, and headed to the newspaper office.

Chapter Fifteen

GOLDIE SAT IN the recliner, his eyes fixed on the hallway in front of him as his grandma slept. For the past half hour, he'd hoped to catch a glimpse of Hailey. Earlier he'd gone to Patty's room to check in on her and find out whether Hailey was coming by for a visit. Patty had told him Hailey said she'd be by around three o'clock. It was now four o'clock. He had no intention of leaving until he saw her.

Each time the nurse came in, he seemed surprised to find Goldie still in the room. Goldie's habit was to leave once his grandmother fell asleep, but he couldn't risk not seeing Hailey. As he waited, sparks of anger zapped his nerves. Why the hell did she have to be so damn hot? The way she looked at him with her innocent eyes and the way she brushed against him drove him wild. What was it with her? The only woman who'd ever messed with his head happened to be his best friend's little sister. *Is that ever fucked.* He was supposed to be watching over her. He'd promised Ryan he would, and all he could think about was kissing, touching, and licking her. He wanted to make her beg him to let her come, then watch her as she did. *Fuck!*

Blue orbs caught his and Hailey smiled weakly before darting her eyes away as she walked past the door. Like a jack-in-the-box, he sprang up and dashed to the door. "Hailey," he said to her departing back.

Stopping, she looked over her shoulder. "Goldie. I didn't know you were here."

Bullshit, but if that's how you want to play it, I'm in. "Yeah. I looked in on Patty when my grandma went down for her nap. Come on in. I want to talk to you."

Frowning slightly, she shook her head. "I have to see my aunt. I'll come by later. How late are you staying?"

He shrugged. "What about you?"

"An hour or so. I have to get back to the shop. I'll be by in a bit. If you're there, I'll stop in."

Goldie went back into the room and debated about leaving. If it were any other chick, he never would've hung around hoping to run into her, and then she acted like it was no big fucking deal. *I should go now and show her I don't give a shit.* But the problem was he did give a shit, and he didn't know why. There was something about her that gnawed at him, made him do silly stuff like wait around for her. He shook his head; he was going to go.

"Is she still sleeping?" Dan, the nurse, asked.

Goldie nodded. He looked at the medium-built man as he leaned over his grandmother. Even though he'd been thrown into the medical arena by his grandma's illness, he still couldn't get used to men being nurses. "I noticed one of my grandma's eyes is a little red and crusty. It's the right one."

Dan turned on the overhead light, then bent over and looked at Helen. "You're right. There's a lot of crustiness there. I'll let Dr. Rudman know. We need to get her up. Dinner is ready and she really needs to try and eat something."

"Okay. I'm here, so I can coax her."

Dan smiled. "She always eats so much better when you or your sister are with her. I'll have the CNAs help her up and see if I can find Dr. Rudman."

Goldie tensed as Dan left the room. He was not a fan of Dr. Rudman. His feeling was that the doctor decided who should be treated and who shouldn't based on the quality of their lives. At Cherry Vale, there were three doctors who treated the patients: Dr. Tyrell was the head physician, Dr. Rudman was part-time, and Dr. Daniels, also part-time, had his own practice. Goldie had tried to have another doctor assigned to his grandma, but so far Dr. Rudman was still her physician.

After the CNAs had his grandmother up and seated in her recliner,

Kevin, a part-time CNA, came into the room with a dinner tray. He placed it on the hospital table and stared at the older woman. "Are you gonna eat good tonight, sweetheart?"

"What the fuck?" Goldie pushed away from the windowsill.

Kevin shifted his cold gaze to him. "Did you say something to me?"

"Yeah. You don't fuckin' call my grandma 'sweetheart.' That's just fuckin' weird."

"I was only trying to be nice. Sometimes when I talk like that she'll eat better. Won't you, sweetheart?" He stroked her cheek.

Goldie grabbed his hand and squeezed it hard until Kevin cried out. "Don't ever call my grandma anything but her name. Give her the respect she deserves. And never touch her like that again. Next time, I'll break your goddamn hand."

"Garth! Don't take the Lord's name in vain." Her voice was strong and clear.

As mad as Goldie was, he laughed aloud and stroked her cheek. "You always catch me, Grandma." He bent down and kissed the top of her head.

"And don't you forget it. I'm hungry."

Looping his foot under a stool, he dragged it over and sat down, then took off the plate covers. From his peripheral view, he saw Kevin still standing and watching them. "You're done here. Get out." Goldie glared at him.

"So you're going to help her eat? I usually do."

"You're pretty dense. I'm fucking here so I'll help her."

Kevin's gaze was fixed on her as he slowly walked backward until he exited the room.

"Does he act weird like that all the time?" he asked as he put a towel around her neck.

While nodding, she picked up her fork. "He's a strange man. I really don't like him."

Goldie's jaw tightened as he helped her cut her chicken. "I'm gonna make sure he doesn't come into your room. I don't like the sonofabitch."

She broke out in a string of laughter. "You're on a roll tonight."

He loved it when the clarity came back and his grandmother was the person he'd known since he was born.

"Hi, Mrs. Humphries. It looks like you're enjoying your dinner with Garth." Hailey's voice was bright and warm, as if a beam of sunshine had been melted into sound. Goldie watched her as she came into the room and stood before his grandmother. "I'm Hailey Shilley. I'm not sure you remember me."

Helen peered at her as she chewed her food. After swallowing, she grinned. "You're Garth's girlfriend. It's about time." She clapped her hands.

"She's not my woman, Grandma. She's Ryan's sister." Goldie scowled at Hailey as she giggled.

"I know Ryan. Where is he? Is he coming over for dinner tonight?"

"I hope I'm not confusing her," Hailey whispered.

"You're not. She has moments of clarity and then they slip away," he said flatly as he saw the vacant gaze he was too familiar with creeping into his grandmother's eyes.

"What seems to be the trouble here? The nurse told me your grand-mother's left eye is having a problem?" Dr. Rudman, a man in his late thirties, walked into the room, a stethoscope around his neck and a clipboard in his hand.

"My grandma's got an infection. I noticed it when I came in. It's all crusty and red."

Dr. Rudman went over to Helen's side and bent down low. "The eye looks fine to me," he said straightening up.

"Are you fuckin' serious? It's all crusted over, and no matter how many times I wipe and clean it, the crud comes back."

The doctor smiled thinly. "Stuff like this happens all the time to old people."

"My grandma was old yesterday and her eye was fine. She's got a damn infection, and I want you to treat it."

"It's hard to see a loved one slip away. We want our loved ones to never get old, to never be sick, and to never start the process of dying. Your grandmother is a very sick woman who has a serious illness that will only progress. Her quality of life is very much compromised. You need to consider that. A lot of families have a hard time letting their loved one go, but it's liberating for a sick patient to let go and move on to another level. Some call it heaven, but I like to think of it as—"

"Shut the fuck up before I bust your face! My grandma has a god-damn eye infection and you're spewing all this shit about not letting her go and the quality of life? I want her comfortable. Get the damn medicine now or you'll live to regret you walked into this room." Goldie was inches away from the startled physician, who whirled around, mumbled something inaudible, and left the room.

"Unbelievable! What a jerk," Hailey said. "I'm going to find Dr. Daniels. He's great and compassionate. He's my aunt's doctor here. I know he's here." She bounced out of the room and disappeared.

Goldie grabbed one of the many pillows on his grandmother's bed and pounded his fist into it over and over. If he were alone, the room would be trashed, but he'd have to appease his rage with the synthetic pillow. With his bare hands, he grasped it hard and tore it open, the stuffing spilling onto the floor.

A hand on his shoulder interrupted the rage, and he jerked his head up and saw Hailey. Standing behind her was a man about thirty-six years old in a solid shirt with a paisley tie. "Are you okay?" Hailey asked in a soft voice near his ear. The tips of her hair tickled his arms and the scent of the ocean swirled around him, calming him.

Letting out a deep breath he didn't know he'd been holding, he nodded. Jerking his head at the man behind her, he asked, "Who's he?"

"That's Dr. Daniels. I asked him to come in." Hailey gently took the mangled pillow out of his hands.

"I heard your grandmother has a problem with her eye." He walked over, traipsing through the synthetic chunks from the destroyed pillow.

"I just told Dr. Fuckman there was something jacked up with her eyes and he gives me all this shit about having to let go." The anger still smoldered inside him. Hailey sat next to him and took his hand in hers.

Dr. Daniels glanced at him quickly, then looked at Helen's eye. "You've got quite an infection there, Helen. I'm going to put some ointment on your eye to give you some relief for now. Are you okay with me doing that?" Helen stared at the blank TV screen. The physician put on gloves, took out a tube, and applied the ointment over her eyelid.

"So why the fuck didn't the other doc do anything?" Goldie asked.

Dr. Daniels shook his head slightly. "I'm not sure. Helen's eye definitely has an infection. I'll prescribe eye drops four times a day, an ointment twice a day, and in a few days you should see an improvement. After a couple of weeks, she should be good as new. The ointment I just applied will give her some relief. I'm glad you're vigilant in watching your grandmother. It's important that families are like that, especially when the patients can no long communicate for themselves. I'll come back in and check on her during the next several days to make sure she's doing okay."

Goldie lifted his chin, his face stony. The doctor cleared his voice, then smiled at Hailey. "Patty is doing great. This time around she's following all instructions to a tee."

"It may take a while, but when she finds out her way isn't exactly the best, my aunt ends up coming around. Thanks for coming to see Mrs. Humphries."

"Of course. And you need to take some time for yourself. Your aunt's been telling me that you're on overload. It won't help if you end up getting sick. You should take a couple days off to reboot. Just some unsolicited advice." He smiled and walked out of the room.

Hailey stood up but Goldie tugged her back down and she tumbled into him. He hugged her close and nuzzled her neck. "Thanks," he breathed into her ear, then kissed her soft neck. The scent of the ocean mingled with the aroma of papaya as he breathed in deeply. "You smell like a tropical island. I'd like to see you in a bikini, then strip it off and suck your tits as I fuck you under the sun."

A small moan vibrated against her throat, and he put his finger in his mouth before trailing it down her throat. "I need a drink, and I want you to join me."

"Are you done with your tray, sweetheart?" Kevin's voice shattered the heated haze between Hailey and Goldie.

Without a word, Goldie gently moved Hailey away from him, leapt up, grabbed Kevin by the shirt, and dragged him into the bathroom. After closing the door, he said in a low, dangerous voice, "You were fuckin' warned about giving respect to my grandma." He slammed his fist right into Kevin's face, and the man threw his hands in front of it as if to ward off another punch. "Next time I'll make sure you'll have to go to the hospital."

Goldie came out of the bathroom, ignoring the question on Hailey's lips. Soon Kevin came out, a towel pressed against his nose. Without a glance or a word, he left the room.

"Did you just hit him?" Hailey asked.

"I warned him not to disrespect my grandma. He did. He knew the consequences."

"What if he tells the police? I mean, that's assault. You could get in trouble."

Goldie shrugged and picked up Helen's tray. "I'm going to take this to the kitchen." When he returned from the kitchen, he bumped into Dan.

"Dr. Daniels told me your grandma does have an eye infection. In no time, we'll make sure it's all cleared up. Oh… Kevin told me he slipped and fell in the bathroom in Helen's room. He said you were there and heard him fall."

"Yeah. Must've had some water on the floor. Slammed his face on the sink."

"I think he broke his nose. Anyway, I sent him home."

"Is the administrator in?"

"Yes. I'm going to check on Helen. She's probably ready to go back to bed."

After Goldie told the administrator that he didn't want Kevin any-where near his grandmother or he'd pull her out, he gave Helen a kiss on her cheek, grabbed Hailey's hand, and headed out to the parking lot. In less than fifteen minutes he had a shot of whiskey in his hand and she had a bottle of beer in hers as they sat at a small table at Cuervos.

"How long have you been with the Night Rebels?" she asked.

"Since I got out of high school. I'd started hanging around their bike repair shop ever since I heard they had a used Harley for sale. I put a small down payment on it and would turn over most of my paycheck every two months to get it paid off. I got friendly with some of the guys and they invited me to a couple of their parties, and I ended up prospecting for them. I really liked the feeling of brotherhood among the members. I don't know. It was like for the first time in my life, I belonged. I fit in." He placed his empty shot glass down and gestured for another one.

"You didn't like high school much, did you?"

He laughed. "I liked the parties and the chicks, but that was about all. There were so many pompous assholes. I see some of them in town in their suits acting so important. They glance at me and I see hints of respect and fear in their eyes when they pass me and my brothers on the street."

"It must've been hard not having your dad around."

"Yeah, well, that's not why I joined the Night Rebels. Don't try to psychoanalyze me. My mom bailed when we were young, then came back and tried to make us a family. The truth was my parents never should've been together. They fought all the time and we were caught in the middle. My grandparents saved us. If it wasn't for them, I don't know where we would've ended up."

"I can't imagine how hard it must've been with your mom and dad going back and forth like that."

"Yeah. There'd be periods when they were all lovey-dovey, but then they'd start fighting and throwing punches and shit at each other. They'd be separated for a while and we'd end up at my grandparents.

When they'd reconcile, we'd move back in with them and the shit would start up all over again. It was fucking insane. But it was still better than them not being there anymore."

"I can't even imagine losing my parents, especially at the same time. It must've been real hard."

Goldie's jaw tightened. "Life happens. The good is great, the bad sucks, and you just have to deal with it. I take life as the moments come. How the fuck are you getting me to talk about all this shit?"

She smiled. "We've known each other a long time. I thought you were the coolest kid in the neighborhood. I used to wonder how you and Ryan got together. You guys seemed to be the opposite."

"For the record, I *was* the coolest kid in the neighborhood. And I met Ryan when he was on the ground and three older kids were using him as a punching bag. I jumped in and we became close friends. He was the rational one and I was hot-tempered. We had a balance to our friendship. We still do."

"And you're still hot-tempered. I can't believe you punched Kevin in the nose in your grandmother's bathroom."

He shrugged. "I didn't like the way he treated my grandma."

"Do you usually resolve your conflicts that way?"

"Pretty much. It works for me. End of story."

"Aren't you gonna introduce us to your pretty chick?" Army asked as he pulled out a chair and joined them.

"Move on, dude. She's my best friend's little sister."

"And who is *she?*"

The lustful sheen in Army's eyes pissed the hell out of Goldie, but before he could say anything, Hailey smiled and held out her hand. "I'm Hailey."

Army grasped it and held onto it a bit too long for Goldie's liking. "I'm Army." His gaze slipped down to her ample bust.

"Let go of her hand," Goldie said.

Army raised his eyebrows and grinned as he released her. That grin told Goldie he was going to have a good time ribbing him later on after he told all the brothers that Hailey had Goldie's balls.

"Hey, who's your lady?" Sangre said as he and Paco came over to the table. The vulture-like attitude around a pretty, stacked woman was one aspect of the brotherhood he didn't like, especially since their hungry eyes were fixed on Hailey's tits. Although, he couldn't blame them—Hailey was a biker's wet dream. Hell, she was most men's wet dreams. And he'd be acting just like his brothers if he'd spotted one of them with a woman like her. But since she was someone he knew and respected, he didn't like the way they were looking at her.

"Back the fuck off. She's a good friend of mine. Show some respect."

And just like that, they backed off. Pride in his brothers' loyalty spread through him as puzzlement fanned out across Hailey's face. They chatted for a few minutes about Harleys and the upcoming rally, then left Goldie and Hailey alone, drifting toward some other brothers who leaned against the jukebox in the far-left corner of the room.

"Were those some of the other guys in your club?" she asked as she watched them move away.

"Yeah. They can come on strong. They're always looking for a pretty woman to score with."

"Do they find them?"

"Most of the time. Women are crazy about bikers. The more tats and patches we have, the more they want to fuck us." Goldie turned away and watched as Paco approached a table with two big-busted blondes. He sniggered.

"Are you always looking for a woman to score with?"

He jerked his head around. "Not always."

"But a lot of the time?"

"I guess it depends on how you define 'a lot.' I don't walk around with my tongue hanging out, wanting to jump every chick's bones, if that's what you mean."

Hailey glanced around the bar. "No, I didn't mean that. It's just that I heard your club likes to have parties, and women go to them just for the sex."

"And the booze, the drugs, and the thrill of partying with a bunch of outlaws. Some of the women are professionals who wear suits with a prim, high-collar blouse to work. For them, it feels good to let loose without being judged."

"So it's anything goes at these parties?"

"Pretty much. We don't let hard drugs into them. We try and keep that shit out of the county period. We also don't let anyone under eighteen in, and if someone gets rough with one of the women, we stop it. But other than that, we let everyone party the way they want."

"How do you like to party?" Hailey had moved her chair closer and her arm rested against his.

"You don't want to know, Hailey. If you're trying to find out if I've fucked a lot of women, the answer is yes. Don't ask me how many because I couldn't tell you. But you should know that I've never had a serious relationship with any woman. Our fucking is for fun, and it's a mutual thing."

"You've never been in love?"

He shook his head. "Enough about me. What about you? Besides that asshole Nolan, has there been anyone else in your life?"

"Not really. I mean, dates here and there, but nothing meaningful or satisfying. I wasn't in love with Nolan. I thought I was because in the beginning, we had a good time together and hung out a lot, but after we had sex, he got all weird and possessive. I just wanted to run away from him. I know Ryan thinks he's going to come to Alina, but I doubt that."

"You never know what a person will do. You can't ever underestimate them. You gotta always be on guard."

"Is that how you live your life?"

"Fuck yeah. In my world, you never know who's gunning for you."

Their gazes locked, and he was pulled in by her. Everything about her made him want her more. The whole loyalty thing to Ryan was waning so thin that it was fading into obscurity. The music, the chatter, and the clinking glasses disappeared. The only thing he was acutely aware of was Hailey: her arm touching his, the bar's red lights falling softly over her face, her hair spilling around her shoulders, and her mesmerizing gaze. Desire, lust, and sweet electricity ran through him. He'd experienced desire and lust with a woman more times than he could count, but the circuit of emotional feeling was alien to him. He didn't know how to process it, and he wasn't sure he wanted to. Before Hailey entered his life, things were simple: lust after an attractive chick, let her know, and then fuck her. His sex life was on autopilot, and he liked it that way. Until now. *Fuck.*

He moved away from her. "We better get going. I have to get back to the ink shop." He stood up, ignoring the confusion etched on her face. Without arguing, they left the bar.

As she drove away, he took out a joint and lit it, his gaze plastered on the red lights of her car fading into the darkness. He wanted to go after her and hold her in his arms, smothering her with kisses. Instead, he stubbed out his joint, went over to his Harley, and headed to Get Inked. He hoped he'd be busy as hell; he needed something to block her from his mind and his dick. She was slipping dangerously close to his heart, and he couldn't have that. He was a bastard with women, and he knew he'd end up hurting her. And he didn't want to do that.

For the first time in his adult life, he cared about a woman and how she felt. It was both an unsettling and exhilarating feeling.

And for the first time in his life, Goldie was scared shitless.

Chapter Sixteen

HAILEY TURNED OFF the lights and locked the door to the flower shop. She'd stayed way past closing hour, trying desperately to stop thinking about Goldie. The way he'd practically dragged her out of Cuervos still made her cheeks burn. *He still thinks of me as Ryan's little sister. I need to just forget about him. He's not interested.*

But he *did* keep giving her mixed signals. Sometimes she'd catch him staring at her, desire heating his gaze, and then once in a while, she'd see something mixed with the desire. Affection? *Stop it. You're making too much of this. Anyway, he just wants to screw women, not date them.* At times she'd tell herself that she was fine with them being friends with benefits, but she knew she wasn't that type of woman. Though she wasn't exactly the waiting-for-your-prince type either. She'd hoped to find something in-between. Goldie was the extreme all-male type of guy. And it surprised her how attractive she found his take-charge personality. It gave her a charge the way he took care of business, not apologizing for his actions. Like the way he handled that creepy Kevin. Her aunt had complained about him to her. She'd hated the way he'd look at her, try and brush against her, and make excuses for having to be in her room. Laughing, she slung her tote over her shoulder. *Aunt Patty's going to laugh her ass off tomorrow when I tell her what Goldie did to Kevin.*

The clack of her heels echoed in the empty street. Hailey had forgotten how quickly life folded up on a weeknight in the town, especially when it was past ten o'clock. That night, the street was quieter and darker than usual. The amber streetlights were dimmer and the town lights ebbed to a mere twinkling. Looking up, she noticed the clouds were blackened shadows that shifted with the wind that had kicked up.

They blotted out the stars and the moon, making the street like an old-fashioned photograph—everything a shade of gray. She clutched her tote tighter and made her way to her car.

When she'd returned to the store that evening, the only parking space she could find was by the small park. The white iron benches and bright green leaves appeared ominous amid the blackness of the night. In the shadows, the trees' branches resembled grotesque caricatures of arms and fingers as they swayed and moaned. As she fumbled in her bag for her keys, a rustling behind the thick bushes made the hairs on the back of her neck stand on end. *Where the hell are my car keys?* She swore under her breath that she'd bought the tote without any compartments as her fingers kept grabbing at everything but her keys.

Rustling. Silence. The wind groaning. More rustling.

Where the fuck *are my keys?* Someone was behind the bushes. She could feel him. *Nolan? Oh God. I hope not.* Glancing around, there wasn't a person in sight.

A crunch on the dirt. A snap of a twig. Rustling.

Hailey normally liked the quiet and darkness of night, but at that moment, it seemed to press on her like an awful weight. *Someone is here. I can feel him watching me. I hear him.* Heart pounding, she pasted her body to her car as if that would offer her any protection. Balancing the tote on her upraised knee, she clawed and shoved the items aside until her fingers curled around her remote entry. Pushing the button, the car's headlights were two beacons offering her some comfort.

The rustling grew louder. She pulled at the door, flung herself onto the driver seat, slammed the door, and locked it. Rushing blood to her temples made her head feel like it was about to explode.

A burst of movement frightened her, and she cried out just before she saw the white tip of a tail peeking out from the bushes. Glowing honey-colored eyes stared at her as the fox scurried across the street, disappearing into the darkness in a flash. Nervous giggles erupted from her as she loosened her grip on the steering wheel. *It was only a fox. It must be the wind that's spooking me.* Gulping in and releasing a couple of deep breaths, she turned on the ignition and pulled away from the curb. As she made a U-turn, a smudgy outline of a man stepping from the bushes filled her peripheral vision.

After clearing the turn, she stopped her car and looked at the bushes across the street. No one was there. *Were my eyes playing tricks on me? I could've sworn I saw someone coming out of the bushes.* Icy chills spread through her as she slowly drove away. Someone *was* there; her gut told her as much. *But who? Nolan? The guy was shorter than Nolan. Why was he there watching me? He was probably a perv.* The thought of a stranger staring at her from behind the greenery made her stomach twist.

When she reached the house, the wind had picked up substantially, howling around the darkened neighborhood. Shadows she never noticed before at night loomed everywhere, taunting, teasing, and scaring the hell out of her. Even the Victorian, which she loved, appeared gloomy and foreboding that night.

Taking out her phone, she dialed Goldie's number.

"Hey." He sounded surprised it was her; detachment laced his voice.

She didn't care. "I'm like super spooked right now."

Immediately his tone changed to concern. "What's going on?"

"I don't know. Nothing, probably, but I'm in my car in front of my house, and I'm petrified to get out and walk to the front door. I wish my aunt would've added a garage."

"Okay. Is it the wind that's freaking you out?"

"Maybe. But that man watching me from the bushes started all of this."

"Whoa. What man? What bushes? I'm on my way. Keep talking."

"I was super busy at the floral shop and ended up staying later than I normally would. When I was trying to find my car keys, I heard a lot of noise and stuff from the park. I had a real strong sense someone was watching me. It creeped me out. As I was getting ready to leave, this fox ran out from the bushes, and I thought that was the end of it. I hung a U and then I saw a man standing by the bushes as I passed the park. It totally freaked me out. When I turned to get a better look, he wasn't there, but I know I didn't imagine it."

"Did it look like your ex-asshole?"

"No. Nolan is really tall, like over six feet. This guy looked about five nine or so." The rumble of his motorcycle broke through the groaning wind and washed over her, bringing comfort. She jumped from the car and rushed over to Goldie, throwing herself into his waiting arms.

He rubbed her back and held her close. "Fuck. You're shaking like a leaf. Did you get a good luck at the fucker?" She shook her head and buried it into his chest. "Let's go inside. I felt a couple of drops on me." He led her up the stairs and she opened the door.

Sitting on the couch, she watched him as he walked around the main floor, tugging at the windows. "What're you doing?"

"Making sure everything's locked up." When he pulled at the side window in the dining room, she gasped as it flew open. He turned around. "You left this one unlocked."

"I didn't. I always check before I leave. I kind of got in that habit when I lived alone in Albuquerque. I could swear the window was locked this morning." Her mind reeled backward to that morning. She'd been in a big rush since she'd overslept and had to meet a bride-to-be and her mother. *Did I check the windows this morning?* She couldn't remember. Stretching out her legs on the couch, she said, "Maybe I forgot to do it this morning. I was in a hurry. But even so, I never open that window, and I know it's been locked every time I check it."

"Do you know how easy it is to break into this old house? I could get in here in less than a minute. I'll send Army, Skull, and Chains over in the morning to help me change all the locks on the windows and doors. You really need an alarm, but I know that's your aunt's call. Talk to her about it. In the meantime, we'll make it hard to break in here. I bet the windows in the basement are for shit. I'll run down and check."

"Don't go down there," she said, goose bumps carpeting her skin.

He jerked his head back. "Why not?"

She pulled at a loose thread on the couch. "I don't know. I guess I watch too many horror movies, but whenever someone goes in the basement on a windy, dark night, something always happens."

He came over to her and leaned down, tipping her head back with his finger. "You're too damn cute. Nothing's gonna happen to me. If the bogeyman's down there, he better be scared of me." He brushed his lips across hers. "I'll be right back."

She watched him go, nervousness and fear crackling around her. After what seemed like a very long time, Goldie came back into the living room. "All secure in the basement and here. I'll check upstairs." He rushed up, then came back about ten minutes later. "Seems like the only one unlocked was the window in the dining room. You feeling better?" He went over to the window and glanced out.

"Do you see something?" she whispered.

"No. The rain's coming down hard. You got any beer?"

"I'll get you one."

When she came back into the living room, Goldie had a fire sparking in the fireplace. She smiled and handed him the beer. "I love a good fire. And tonight I'm chilled to the bone. I'll be right back. Make yourself comfortable."

"I haven't been in here since you guys moved to New Mexico." He went over to the couch, kicked off his boots, and plopped his feet on the coffee table.

Aunt Patty would freak out if she saw him. She went upstairs, peeled off her clothes, and took a quick shower. She slipped a long fuzzy nightshirt on and padded down the stairs. She loved seeing him in her space. He made her feel comfortable, safe, and breathless all at the same time. Hailey sat on the couch and tucked her feet underneath her.

"Feeling better?" he asked.

She nodded. "I really did think I saw someone. Though the street-lights were so dim that it was hard to see much."

"There's been power outages all over town. Every time we get a bad storm, the streetlights start acting up. It's so weird. And I'm positive you saw someone. One thing I've learned over the years is that you gotta listen to your gut. You know, that inner voice that tells you when things aren't right. The question is who was it? Was it just some damn perv who gets off on watching women, was it someone who was going to harm you, or was it someone you know?"

She rubbed her arms up and down. "I only know one thing—it wasn't Nolan. Whoever it was made my blood run cold. I got a real bad vibe about him. I don't know." She shuddered.

He grasped her arm and tugged her to him. She willingly went, and he cocooned her in his embrace. She nestled into him, inhaling the scent of leather, wind, and antiseptic. Her hand fell loosely around his waist. She couldn't believe how taut his muscles were. "Were you working when I called?"

"Yeah." He kissed the top of her head.

"I'm sorry if I interrupted you."

"You don't need to ever apologize for my help. I told Ryan I'd watch out for you."

See? You're making his kindness to be much more than it is. Again. When are you going to learn? Him being here is all about Ryan and their friendship.

"What's wrong?" he asked.

She froze. There was no way he could read her thoughts. "Nothing. Why?"

"You stiffened up on me."

"Oh. I was just thinking that it's probably a drag for you to keep watch over me. I mean, I don't hold you to your agreement with Ryan."

"Did I say it was a drag?"

"No… but I'm sure there are women you'd rather be with right now. You don't have to stay. I'll be fine."

"I want to be with you. I'll stay with you until you fall asleep."

"Just to make sure I'm safe, right? Of course. That's why you're here."

He tangled his fingers in her hair and pulled her head back so she was looking straight into his smoldering gaze. "You know that's not the whole reason."

The intensity of his stare sent shock waves straight to her core. "It isn't?" she breathed.

An intense heat sizzled between them. "No. It isn't." He pressed his mouth on hers, his kiss searing her lips. Letting go, she fell into the kiss, parting her lips, coaxing his tongue to invade. Whimpering in anticipation, she trailed her hands around his body, feeling each line, each ripple of his perfect physique. He delved his tongue inside her mouth, tangling it with hers in a fiery, passionate, and demanding dance. Running her fingers down his spine, she drew him closer until there was no space left between them.

"Hailey," he said against her mouth, the sound of her name on his lips unfurling a desire deep inside her. She savored every letter as he rasped her name over and over, her heart fluttering and the ache between her legs throbbing.

It was magical the way his lips connected with hers. Even though they'd kissed before, she hadn't known who he really was then. At that moment, the world fell away. The way he held and kissed her was comforting in a way words never would be. Amid the hunger, the lust, and the desire, there was softness and understanding, and it was that naughty and nice combination that drove her insane with want for him.

The phone ringing pierced through their desire, and Hailey cursed its interruption. By the frown on Goldie's face, she suspected some choice words were running through his head. Glancing at the screen, she sucked in her breath: it was Ryan. Not wanting to break the connection she and Goldie were sharing, she decided not to tell him who it was.

"Hello?"

"Hailey. How're you doing?"

"Fine. You?"

"Okay. Did I interrupt something?"

"No, not really." *Just an awesome kiss.* She glanced at Goldie, who stared at the fire.

"Have you seen Garth? I asked him to keep an eye on you. I worry about you. When I heard that ex-creep may be in Alina, I called Garth right away."

"Things are fine. They really are."

"Have you seen Garth?"

"Yeah. I've been so busy running the floral shop. Most of the time I'm either there or at home." She wanted to get him off the subject of her and Goldie.

"How's Aunt Patty doing?"

"Good."

"Watch out for Garth. Even though he's my best buddy and he's doing me a favor, I wouldn't put it past him to make a play for you. He's a womanizer at heart. Make sure you keep him at a distance. Speaking of guys, have you met anyone worth talking about?"

"No. Like I said, I'm super busy. When am I going to see you?"

"Working on it. I'll let you know. I gotta go. Take care of yourself."

"I will."

When silence replaced Ryan's voice, an emptiness filled her. She missed him and wished he'd be sent stateside so they could see each other and talk more often.

"That was Ryan on the phone." It was a statement, not a question. She nodded, her heart sinking when he sighed and stood up. "I should go. You gonna be okay?"

"Of course. You secured everything."

"I'll be back in the morning with my brothers. If you need or want anything, call me. I could stretch out on the couch and crash if you want me to."

"It's pouring out there."

"I have my rain jacket in my saddlebags. I've ridden in worse. If you're worried about me, don't be. If you want me to stay, I can do that."

She wanted him to stay so she could be back in his arms, kissing his warm, smooth lips. "You don't have to. I'll be fine."

Nodding, he walked over to the door and unlocked it. Without another word, he slipped out into the darkness and headed to his bike. She closed the door and heard the rumble of his Harley.

And just like that, he was gone.

Chapter Seventeen

"**F**UCK!" HE SCREAMED as he hit the steering wheel over and over. His fury matched the howling wind and sheets of rain as he drove away from Hailey's house. The damn biker had to screw everything up. He'd planned the execution so carefully. He'd broken into her house a half hour after he'd seen her leave that morning. He wanted to get the feel of the layout and know which room was hers so when he came back later that night, he'd know right where to go. He'd unlocked the side window and spent the rest of the day anticipating what was to come.

By the time the day had ended, his whole body was tense with sexual current. Not daring to go home, he went to the diner for some dinner, but his heightened state dulled his appetite. Instead, he sat staring at the clock as it painfully edged toward seven: the time the flower shop closed.

Parked a few cars away, he waited patiently for her to close the shop and come out. Part of the fun in his game was to watch his prey before he pounced. He'd spotted her car by the park, and when it appeared that she was finally finishing up, he'd quickly headed that way and positioned himself behind the bushes. Then he'd waited until he heard the solitary echo of her shoes on the pavement. When she'd come into sight, he'd almost jumped her and dragged her into the safety of the bushes to have his way with her; he'd been that wound up. When her headlights turned out and he saw her terrified face, he almost lost it in his pants. The only thing stopping him was the anticipation of taking his time and torturing her for the rest of the night.

When he'd arrived at her house, he'd been surprised to see her still in her car. A short time later, *he* appeared, ruining everything. Hoping the biker had just come by for a visit, his craving for Hailey turned to pure rage when he'd seen the leather-clad man locking the window.

Weeks of stalking, fantasizing, and planning had disappeared. His body shook with anger and his hard-on throbbed painfully. Some would say he could just grab a random woman to work out his anger and sexual frustration on, but if he did that, it would only be worse. What made him tick before he attacked was the planning and stalking of his victim, and he'd invested quite a bit of time in Hailey Shilley.

I'm not letting all that go to waste. I know you're going to be delicious. His lips turned up in a snarl as he turned onto his street. He was positive the biker would secure the house; he had that look of concern and determination on his face as he went from room to room. *I'll have to find another way to get to you. And I* will *get to you and enjoy every ounce of fear that'll course through your body.*

The garage door closed as he entered the kitchen. The house was dark and quiet. He opened the refrigerator and took out a small bottle of orange juice, downing it in one large gulp before throwing the empty container in the recycle bin. He ambled up the stairs and headed to the bedroom.

Pulling back the comforter, he slid between the cool sheets. He breathed in and out a few times, trying to relax so he could get some sleep. All his senses were still on high alert, and the frustration of a plan thwarted so completely chocked his nerves.

"You're home early," Trisha, his wife, said as she turned over on her side, her hand sliding down his bare arm.

"Change in shifts." He scooted closer to the edge of the bed.

"The thunder's been awful. It took me almost an hour to calm Kyle. You know how he is about rainstorms." She moved closer to him, then pressed her lips against his shoulder. "Kyle's fast asleep now, and Jade's been in bed for over an hour. Let's take advantage of it."

"I'm not really feeling it." His jaw tightened.

"You could've fooled me." She laughed as she placed her hand on his semi-hard shaft.

That was for Hailey. "It doesn't mean anything."

"I'll let you use the handcuffs and spank me the way you like to. We just can't be too loud on account of the kids." She kissed him firmly on the lips.

He knew she'd keep bugging him about it. The truth was he couldn't really get off with his wife. Even when she let him spank her and occasionally flog her ass, he knew she wasn't scared of him even though she tried to fake it real well. He needed the rush of real fear: terror at its best for him and at its worst for the victims.

Turning toward her, he decided to play along. He watched as she pulled open the nightstand and took out the handcuffs. "Fuck me from behind. I like that." She handed him the cuffs and went down on all fours. He restrained her arms behind her back, shoved her head and torso down on the mattress, and smiled when she pushed up on her knees, making her butt rise higher.

Staring at her, he no longer saw his wife's blonde hair and lithe body. Instead he saw Hailey's long, chestnut hair and rounded hips. In his mind, he pictured his knife skimming across her shivering flesh, fear etched in her face. Her striking blue eyes filled with terror.

"Not so hard!" Trisha gritted as he pummeled into her.

Before he could answer, he'd come hard. Panting heavily, he took off the cuffs, tossed them on the floor, then flopped on his back.

"What the hell was *that* all about?" Trisha sat on the edge of the bed, rubbing her wrists.

"You wanted to get fucked so I fucked you." The coldness in his voice even surprised him.

"You bastard." She got up and went into the bathroom.

He rolled over and fell asleep.

Chapter Eighteen

GOLDIE'S CHAIR LEANED against the back wall as he listened to his brothers rant and rave about the Satan's Pistons. It seemed the surviving members hadn't taken too kindly to the Night Rebels' tactics in showing them who's boss in the southwestern territory of Colorado. Normally, Goldie would've jumped into the discussion, but his mind was on Hailey. She'd taken such a hold of him, and he didn't know how the hell it'd happened.

He'd always been careful not to get too emotionally involved with any of the women he knew because he never had any plans to settle down. It wasn't that he was afraid of commitment like a lot of women had told him over the years. If he had to be honest, it was that he just loved women too much. The thought of settling down with just one woman for the rest of his life didn't make sense to him. There were so many women to experience, and his style was to indulge, give them a damn good time, and move on to the next. He never looked back, let alone *thought* about them. "Out of pussy, out of mind" was the way it worked for him, yet he couldn't get Hailey off his mind. And he hadn't even had a taste of her.

What the fuck is up with me? She's just a chick.

He'd said that often enough to himself hoping it'd convince his damn dick and mind, but so far, it'd been a bust. Even though he shouldn't even think of Hailey as someone he'd fuck, that was all he'd been thinking about since she'd come into the tattoo parlor.

"Are you zoning out on us, Goldie?" Paco's voice broke into his thoughts.

"Yeah. Sorry. Are we still talking about the asshole Pistons?"

131

"Don't start that up again," Army said as Crow jumped up and started cussing up a storm about his nemesis.

Steel pounded the gavel on the wooden block. "Come to order. We know the Pistons are a bunch of whiny pussies, and I don't give a shit what they're saying. If they come back into our territory, it's all-out war, and the Insurgents will be by our side. Banger and Hawk are sick as shit of these assholes coming into Colorado and acting like they own it." The brothers erupted in cheers and whistles as Steel pounded harder on the block. "We got shit to discuss about the upcoming rally."

"Which brings us back to you, Goldie. What's going on with the charity poker run?" Paco asked.

"It's great. I have the whole route and itinerary firmed up, and we have a hundred bikers signed up. I've been busy with Chains running backgrounds on them. I don't want any fuckin' Satan's Pistons, Skull Crushers, or Deadly Demons to slip in. Plus we don't want any shit from the wannabe gangsters who think they can pretend to be bikers for the rally."

"Good work. Have all the dudes who signed up cleared the background checks?" Paco asked.

Goldie nodded. "So far. I'll keep you posted if something turns up."

After discussing the financials for the rally, Steel adjourned church and the brothers shuffled out to the main room. The club girls greeted the men and immediately molded themselves into the ones who were looking for some intimacy. Goldie, Army, Sangre, and Muerto went over to the bar and picked up their waiting drinks.

"How you making out with your best bud's sister? What's her name again?" Army asked as he brought the beer bottle to his lips.

"She was fuckin' hot. Does your friend know you're fuckin' his sis?" Sangre laughed.

"Damn, dude. If one of you assholes were messin' with one of my sisters, I'd go ballistic," Muerto said.

Nodding, Goldie threw back his shot. "Are you all done?"

"We haven't even started, bro." Army clasped him on his shoulder.

Turning to Muerto, Sangre said, "You shoulda seen him at Cuervos a few nights ago. He's got that pussy-whipped look in his eyes. Like the one you had when you kept telling us nothing was going on with you and Raven."

Muerto shook his head. "You've got a hard-on for your friend's sister. This is gonna be interesting."

"Fuck interesting. It's gonna be damn fun to watch." Army guffawed and Sangre and Muerto joined him.

"I'm just waiting until you've got this shit outta your system. And if it's not out soon, I'm going to have to bash some heads. Get me another shot," he said to Ruger, who promptly placed one in front of him while he mumbled his apologies for not having done it before being asked.

"What's going on here?" Paco asked as he scooped up a handful of pretzels.

"Just asking Goldie about his best friend's sister. The one whose pants he's dying to get into," Army said.

"Maybe he already has," Sangre added.

"That cutie with the sweet ass? I heard you tattooed it," Paco said.

Goldie gritted his teeth. He should've known that Skull and Tattoo Mike would've told the brothers about that. Or it could've been Kelly. *No, my bets are on the them. The brothers gossip way more than the club girls.* "I didn't know it was Hailey when I gave her the tattoo."

The men burst out laughing. "But since you found out, you've been running around with a boner for her," Army said between snickers.

"I can't say I blame him. She's hot," Paco replied.

"But your friend's sister? Can't you find another chick?" Muerto said.

"There're plenty of hot pieces of ass every weekend. It's fuckin' awesome. You haven't been to a party in a while. This weekend you should get someone to cover for you at the tattoo shop and have some fun. You'll forget Hailey in a flash," Army said.

He's right. I should just lose myself between a stacked woman's legs. "I'll keep that in mind," Goldie answered as he looked over at Skull and

Chains screwing Angel on the couch.

Muerto placed his empty beer bottle on the counter. "I have to get to work." Leaning toward Goldie, he said, "Dude, when you got a woman on your mind, there's no pussy in the world good enough to take your mind off her. The fact that this one's your friend's sister sucks, but she's in your blood. I know the fuckin' look, and you've got it all over your face."

Goldie watched as Muerto walked out, his jaw tight, his muscles tense, and his temples pounding. "I have an appointment in an hour. I'm out of here." He gave his bothers a chin lift and went out into the bright sunshine.

IT WAS A warm, drizzly Saturday night, and the bars at Saguro Street were packed, as usual. Tucked between the trendy brewery and the newly opened club, the High Dive had been around for four decades. The bar had undergone several renovations over the years, and the latest one had transformed the dive into a wannabe trendy bar. The scratched wooden floors and wraparound oak wood bar survived the previous transformations. A small dance floor had been one of the recent additions.

Goldie had just finished his last appointment and wasn't ready to go back to the clubhouse. Restlessness had curled around him all night, and when his last appointment left, he'd told Liberty that he was taking off for the rest of the night. It'd been a while since he'd taken off early on a Saturday.

He'd been going to the High Dive since he'd turned eighteen. Elmer, the owner, was a crusty old man who always had an unlit cigar in his mouth. He'd chew on it furiously, especially when he was mad about something. He'd hired Goldie to sweep up and break down boxes when he'd been in high school and needed a part-time job. After he'd graduated, Goldie just started hanging out, helping as needed until he'd begun prospecting for the Night Rebels. Elmer still tended bar, but he mostly let his son, Carl, run the place.

Walking inside, the jangle of voices competed with the rock music as Goldie brushed against warm bodies on his way to the bar. The sallow light of the streetlamps trickled through the rectangles of colored lead-paned windows. Tilting his head at Elmer, who sat on a stool behind the bar, Goldie leaned on the bar, his eyes scanning the room and resting on a group of women in sequined dresses. One of the women caught his gaze and pushed out her red lips just a little. His eyes dropped only momentarily to her low-cut neckline, then away from her.

"The usual?" Carl's voice resonated behind him.

Glancing over his shoulder, he nodded, then resumed his stance. The place was packed, and each time he came in on a weekend, the patrons looked trendier. He missed the dive-like feel the place used to have. Many of the old-timers hung out at the bar during the week, and if he had a chance, he'd sneak over for a couple of shots and to talk bullshit with Elmer and a few of the gruffy old guys from back in the day.

Picking up his shot, he let it slide down his throat, the scorching effect of the whiskey landing in his belly. He wrapped his fingers around the cold bottle of Coors and watched the crowd. A few women tried to get his attention, but he wasn't interested. His mind was on Hailey, something that had become a habit for him. The way they'd kissed a few nights back blew him away. If Ryan hadn't called, Goldie knew they would've ended up screwing.

"You having a good time?" a cute woman asked as she wedged her way between him and another guy leaning against the bar.

"Sure." He turned away. He wasn't interested in conversation, and he wasn't on the make for any women—which was against the norm. Normally, he'd have already picked one out and been at her table charming the hell out of her.

"I've seen you before. You're a tattoo artist at that shop down the street, right?" He nodded. "My name's Nikki." She held out her hand. He glanced at it and turned away. She giggled nervously. "I bet you meet all sorts of people, huh?" Again, another nod. "I've been thinking about getting a tattoo but I'm afraid it'll hurt. But so many people I know have them so it can't hurt that bad. Does it?"

She was getting on his nerves. "Ask the people you know."

"I have, and some say yes and some say no. So what is it?"

"I guess it's yes and no. I didn't come here to talk, okay?" He gave her a hard look.

"So you're telling me to stop talking to you?"

"You got it."

"That's rude."

"No, you talking to me when you know I don't want to is fuckin' rude."

She ordered her drink and walked away without a backward glance, which suited him just fine. He only came in to have a few drinks before he headed back to the clubhouse. He knew the club would be crazy and he didn't want to deal with it that night, which surprised him. Never one to forgo a clubhouse party before, he just hadn't been feeling it for a while. *Since I kissed Hailey that night at Cuervos.*

He didn't want to go there, so he ordered another shot and a beer. If he ended up getting drunk, he'd crash at Get Inked. It seemed the only way he could get her out of his mind was to get smashed and pass out.

As he drank his beer, he saw Nikki sitting at a table filled with men and women. She was laughing about something, then leaned over and said something to a woman next to her. The woman turned to her and he stiffened. *Hailey.* She sparkled in a low-cut, lightly beaded, green top, and the way her face lit up when she smiled made him chuckle. *Each time I see her she's more beautiful than the last.* Suddenly, all he could see in the bar was her; everything else was a meaningless backdrop. Then the sparks of excitement and desire snapped to anger as he saw the man's arm, the one seated next to her, curved around her shoulders. *Fuck that!*

Pushing away from the bar, he shoved a few people as he made a beeline for her table. When he approached it, he saw her usual cohorts, Rory and Claudia. Nikki smiled smugly at him, smoothing down her silver sequined top, her eyes shining with anticipation. He went directly to Hailey, who had her head down.

"Let's dance," he said, ignoring the guy's annoyed face.

Hailey glanced at the goon beside her, then back at Goldie. "No, thank you."

Grasping her hand, he tugged her up. "I wasn't asking, I was telling." Placing his hand on her waist, he whisked her onto the dance floor.

The goon rushed up to them. "You can't be dancing with Hailey. She's my date."

Goldie glared at him. "If you know what's up, you'll back the fuck off. Way off."

The guy ran his eyes over Goldie as if he were sizing him up, and then with shoulders slumped, he mumbled, "I'll let you have this one dance," and shuffled back to the table.

Tossing her head back, Hailey's eyes flashed. "What the hell do you think you're doing? He's my date. You're not."

"Ryan told me to keep an eye on you."

"What the hell does that have to do with this? Ryan's concerned about Nolan, not all men."

"I know he wouldn't want you going out with a wimp-ass like him."

Red blotches mottled her skin as she pierced him with her eyes. "You're impossible!"

"And you're fuckin' cute when you're mad." His lips curled in amusement.

"You think this is funny? You've just ruined my date and you're smiling?"

"I didn't like the fucker."

"Guess what? I don't care if you like him or not. I'm the one out with him not you."

"Why the fuck are you on a date anyway?" He drew her closer to him.

"Rory fixed me up. She's worried about me not having a boyfriend. She thinks I'm still wallowing in my breakup with Nolan."

"Are you?"

"No. It's the opposite of that. I'm elated he's out of my life. I've told Rory that, but she doesn't believe me. It's easier to play along than to have her on my ass about it all the time. At least this one is more fun than the last one." Her body relaxed in his arms.

"You still big into eighties hair metal?" he asked.

She laughed. "Yeah. I can't believe you remembered that."

"I remember a lot about you, like how I noticed you weren't a little kid anymore when you started high school."

"I thought you always saw me as a kid."

"No way. And a lot of guys noticed you. You were stacked back then, and I had to fight the urge not to bash the guys' faces when they talked about you."

"The guys talked about me? I never knew that. I mean, I noticed how they all stared at my bust. I used to hate that."

"You can't blame them. You had a great pair of tits. You still do."

She cast her eyes downward, the light picking up the tinge of red streaking across her cheeks. He laughed and held her close, swaying to Poison's "Every Rose Has Its Thorn." As they danced, he sang the lyrics softly into her ear as he ran his hands down her back, stopping just before her ass. The scent of her surrounded him, and the more they moved, the harder he got until he had a full-blown hard-on. She tilted her head, her heated gaze met his, and then his lips hungrily covered hers as he kissed her frantically and deeply for the rest of the song.

After the song ended, she pulled away, smoothing down her hair. "I have to get back to the table," she said.

"Why?" He grasped her hands again and started moving to the next song.

"Because it's rude. I agreed to the blind date."

"You don't owe him shit."

"Common courtesy. But I don't owe you anything."

"I don't want you to 'owe' me. I want to be with you."

Goldie watched her face as sadness crept in.

"Me too, but each time we try to start something, you freak out and bolt. I can't keep turning my feelings and desires on and off at your whim. I get the whole thing with Ryan, but I'm a woman now, and neither you nor Ryan get that."

"I totally get that you're a woman. That's the fuckin' problem."

"I don't mean it in a sexual way. I mean that I'm grown and can choose who I want to go out with and who I don't, and Ryan doesn't have the right to tell me otherwise. I'd like to get to know you, but you won't let me. We always end up kissing and touching each other, but then you let Ryan invade your mind and you're gone, leaving me feeling empty and shitty." Her voice quivered, and she pulled away.

"We need to talk. I know I'm acting like a fucked-up shit, but loyalty goes deep with me." Goldie scrubbed his face with his fist.

"Then move on. Forget about me. Leave me the hell alone." She spun around and walked off the dance floor, joining her table of friends.

At first he wanted to follow her, yank her to him, and cart her off to the tattoo shop so they could talk, but he let her go. She was right, he wasn't being fair to her. He wanted to play it in the middle: touch and screw her, and maintain his loyalty and friendship with Ryan. He knew better. *Life can never be played that way. It's either all or nothing.* The way he'd been acting, he wasn't playing it straight with Ryan, Hailey, or himself.

Giving her table a sidelong glance, he wanted to rearrange the smug look the goon had on his face as he walked by, but he didn't. He gave Elmer and Carl a chin lift, then walked out into the drizzling rain.

Chapter Nineteen

SUSAN O' BRIEN had worked hard to become the administrator of Cherry Vale. Hailing from Ireland, she'd grown up poor. With her nine siblings and a father who liked to play the big shot in the village at the local pubs, her family barely survived on the meager government assistance her mother had to collect each month.

Coming to America was like a dream come true, and she promised herself she wouldn't fuck it up like she did most everything in her life. Each month, like a dutiful daughter, she sent money home to her mother. Sometimes she felt guilty about not visiting, but she rationalized it away each time she wired the money to her mother.

Glancing down at the stats, she groaned inwardly. She'd hoped she could've kept the recent surge in dead patients internal, but that gum-cracking sheriff had to shove his nose in it. How she hated it when people chewed gum. It always reminded her of cows chewing grass. And when the people cracked their gum, well, it was like nails on a chalkboard for her. Sheriff Wexler *loved* cracking his damn gum.

Corporate had become aware of all the deaths and now the situation had blown up into a proper maelstrom. She groaned again and grabbed a small key from her coin purse. Unlocking the bottom drawer in her desk, she took out a bottle of vodka. She'd only have a few nips. God knew she deserved it after the hellacious week she'd had.

Pouring her medicine into the Dixie cup, she leaned back in her office chair and sipped it. The smoothness from the clear liquor calmed her as it made its way down her throat, spreading warmth in her chest, and finally in her stomach.

"What's the big deal anyway?" she muttered out loud. "It wasn't like the patients were young, healthy people." She took another sip. The truth was that the four patients who'd died in the last few weeks—Rose Higgins, Lucille Heller, Albert Swartz, and Henny Simpson—were all old, frail, and in poor health. She saw it as a blessing that those patients left the world to enter another one where disease didn't exist. If one of the deceased patients would've been her parent or grandparent, she would've thanked God for sparing them more years of pain.

Another long pour in her cup. "That stupid sheriff's saying it's murder. Now I got all the attention on me." She couldn't screw this up. Her job paid well, and, for the most part, she loved it.

The buzzer on her phone made her jump, spilling her drink all over her desk. "Shit!" She quickly grabbed some paper towels and soaked up the liquid.

Pushing the buzzer, she said, "Yes?"

"Sheriff Wexler's here to see you."

"Thanks. Give me a minute." She wrapped the paper towels in several plastic bags, sprayed air freshener on her desk and around the room, and popped in two mints. She went over to the door, plastered a smile on her face, and opened it.

"Sheriff Wexler. How good to see you. Won't you come in?"

The tall man sank down into one of the chairs. "You got a problem at your facility," he said without any pleasantries. How she hated boorish men.

"Do I?"

"You've got patients dying way more than any other facility in town or the county. Hell, you've got a higher deaths-per-patient ratio than any facility in Durango. Something's going on here."

She forced out a chuckle. "We deal in very sick patients. They die. Sometimes it happens that we have a rash of deaths, depending on how many terminally ill patients we have at one time. Sometimes we may only have one or none. I don't know what more I can say."

"There're people a lot sicker than the ones who've died. Some of them weren't that sick, like Mrs. Heller or Mrs. Higgins. I talked to their doctor."

She smiled. "Dr. Daniels was their doctor. Out of the three doctors here, he's the most optimistic. Dr. Rudman is definitely more realistic about the patients and what the quality of their life is. I would say Dr. Daniels probably held out a lot of hope in his assessment of the two women you mentioned. They were both quite ill."

"But you got sicker ones here. I've been talking with all three of the doctors and they all told me that."

"Of course we do, but I can't play God and decide who lives and dies. In life, things don't work logically a lot of the times."

Wexler leaned forward and propped his elbows on her desk. "Well, someone's playing God around here, and I aim to find out who." He took out a document and handed it to her. It was a subpoena asking for all written records for patients and employees.

When he cracked his gum, it was like a bullwhip snapping in the air. She jumped up, her nerves on edge, her fingers trembling slightly. She needed a drink.

"Of course, it'll take some time to gather all the records you're requesting." *Get the fuck out of my office, you inconsequential man.*

"Of course. I took that into account when I put the date in the subpoena that we need them produced by." He walked over to the door, opened it, and walked out.

She dashed over, locked it, then scurried over to her desk and took out the bottle of vodka again.

"Just a few nips," she said to no one as she brought the bottle to her lips.

Chapter Twenty

"I BLEW IT with Goldie," Hailey said as she picked at her dinner.

"You mean Garth, right?" Rory said as she took a bite of her barbecued ribs.

"He goes by Goldie now. I've told you that before." Hailey pushed her plate away. She shouldn't have gone out with Rory and Claudia. They had a standing girls' night out every Tuesday, and they usually went out to dinner. Sometimes they'd go to a new club or bar, but mostly they tried out different restaurants.

Since the night she'd danced with Goldie at High Dive, she hadn't seen or heard from him. She hadn't even bumped into him at Cherry Vale, even though she'd purposely stay later in the hope she'd see him. It was like he was avoiding her.

"I did tell him to leave me alone," Hailey said.

"And he is, so all is good. He was so not your type. You were just taken in by his looks. I'll admit that he's got a totally drool-worthy body, but when he gets older he'll probably get the middle-age spread that seems to hit most men, and his tats will fade and look ridiculous on crepey skin."

For a brief instant, Hailey imagined herself stuffing Rory's mouth with her napkin to get her to shut the fuck up. *I shouldn't have come out tonight.*

"Stop it, Rory. You're not helping. Hailey obviously likes Goldie." Holding her hand up to stave off yet another quip from Rory, Claudia shook her head. "And it doesn't matter if you get it or not. The point is you like him. Right, Hailey?"

She nodded. And boy, did she like him. Never had she been so taken with any man. At first she'd thought it was because she'd known him, but as time went on, she realized they had a real connection apart from their background. And whenever she was with him, her whole body responded. His touch, his voice, his scent, his body, and his taste combined wonderfully, making her mind swim with a heady intoxication. And now she'd blown it with him.

"I think if a man wants you, he'll chase you. Since he's not, I think you have to accept that he still thinks of you as your brother's little sister and move on. What was wrong with Palmer? I mean, he handled the whole thing with Garth like a gentleman. Garth acted like an arrogant rogue, but Palmer held his own."

"He came back to the table with his tail between his legs. He was scared shitless of Goldie," Claudia said.

"I was talking to Hailey, not to you." Rory put a forkful of mashed potatoes into her mouth.

"Goldie would never chase a woman. I don't think it's in his biker lifestyle," Hailey said.

"If a guy wants you, it shouldn't matter if he's a biker or a lawyer or a welder. A guy should chase a woman. I hope you're not thinking of calling him or anything like that," Rory replied.

Hailey shook her head. "No, I'm not. I know he won't come after me, and it's probably not all because of the biker thing. The whole thing with Ryan is complicated for them. It's not for me, but it seems to freak them both out."

"You should go out with another biker," Claudia clapped her hands and squealed. "He'd totally deserve that. He shouldn't have played with your emotions if he was fucked up about who you were."

Hailey nodded. *But we were attracted to each other before either of us knew the truth. I was drawn to him the moment I saw him, and he was to me. I don't care what anyone says. Goldie and I shared something that night. Some damn connection that kept pulling us together.*

"I'm serious about going out with another biker," Claudia invaded Hailey's thoughts. "Oh shit. One of them is coming over to our table. I can't believe it."

Hailey turned around and saw a tall, good-looking guy covered in tats and wearing the same type of vest Goldie wore. "He's Goldie's friend. I've met him before. His name is Army. I wonder why he's coming over here."

"Because they're all wolves looking to score." Rory's eyes were glued on him as he came over to the table.

Army went over to Hailey and bent down on his haunches. "Goldie's brother is getting married and he wants to pay for the flowers."

"Dylan asked Skyla to marry him. How wonderful," she said.

"Dylan's got a great job, and he's good-looking. He's a catch. He's the one you should've been looking over," Rory said.

"Dylan's cool. I see him all the time when he comes into the pet store. He's got the cutest dog. It's a mutt he got at the pound, but he's super friendly and just a sweetie," Claudia added.

Army fixed his gaze on the two women. "That's great. Enough about Dylan. Goldie wants to buy the flowers for the wedding."

"So? He can come to the shop and place an order. Or if he'd rather not see me, then he can go to Rambling Rose. It doesn't concern me what he does."

He shook his head. "You're just as fuckin' stubborn as he is." He rose to his feet and swaggered away.

"That was strange," Rory said, her gaze fixed on him. "He's got a nice butt."

Nodding, Claudia let out a loud laugh. "I totally agree."

"Goldie's such a jerk. Sending his friend to tell me to call him. Screw that. If he wants to talk to me, he can call me."

"Maybe he came on his own. He's sitting at a table with a bunch of guys, and they're all wearing leather vests." Rory craned her neck. "I don't see Garth in the group."

"Why would he come over here and tell me that? I hardly know him. Besides, he's a biker, and I can't picture bikers doing that."

"Are you kidding? Men can be way worse than women with gossiping and getting involved with the petty crap." Claudia squinted. "There're some hot men over at that table."

"Maybe Goldie's been acting like an insufferable pain in the ass since High Dive and his buddy's sick of it." Rory placed her napkin on the table.

Hailey darted her eyes from Rory to Claudia. "Have I been an insufferable pain in the ass?"

"Not insufferable, but a bit mopey and whiny. I mean, we understand, but you have to admit it's been the topic of all our conversations," Claudia said as Rory bobbed her head.

"Wow. I didn't realize it. Sorry, guys. Now let's talk about something totally unrelated to bikers, Goldie, or Ryan."

They laughed and talked well into the night, and when Hailey came home, she was in a better mood than she had been all week. After unlocking the four locks Goldie had installed on her front door several weeks before, she turned to lock her screen door when she saw the outline of a man standing across the street, his white shirt having caught her eye in the darkness. It seemed like he was looking at her. Slamming the door, she quickly locked it, then went around the house closing the curtains. Goldie and his buddies had secured all her windows and made her basement into Fort Knox, so she felt relatively safe in her home. But the mere fact that a stranger had been watching her made her legs buckle.

Stumbling to the couch, she sank down and called the police. She told them about the man, then about the man she'd seen a few weeks before coming out of the bushes. The deputy assured her it was probably nothing, that all the women living alone had been jumpy since news broke about the series of rapes in town. He promised he'd send over a patrol car to canvass her neighborhood.

For a long time, Hailey stayed on the couch, staring ahead of her at nothingness. *Was the guy the same one who'd been watching me that night I was spooked? The one tonight looked like he was the same height, but I can't be sure.* Over and over her thoughts turned topsy-turvy in her head until she wanted to scream. With a tissue, she dabbed her damp hairline, then stood up. All she wanted to do was forget everything unpleasant.

After she switched off the lamps, she went over to the picture window and peeked out into the blackness. A police car cruised slowly by, then disappeared around the corner. Nothing seemed out of the ordinary. Exhausted to the core, her legs like lead, she slowly climbed the stairs, wishing she were already tucked under the cool sheets.

VASES FULL OF flowers, Mylar balloons, and a volume of "get well" cards taped haphazardly on the wall facing the metal bed distracted Hailey while she waited for her aunt to return from physical therapy. A soft knock on the door made her heart leap in anticipation as she jerked her head toward it. Kevin stood there with a tray in his hands.

"It's dinnertime," he said as he came into the room and set the tray on the swivel table. "Where's that pretty aunt of yours?"

The guy's so weird. "At physical therapy. She loves burgers, so I was going to get some for her and me."

Kevin frowned. "You didn't tell the kitchen. You're supposed to tell the kitchen so they don't make a tray for her. It's been that way since Patty has been here. You should know this."

What the hell's the big deal? "I do know the rule but I forgot. Sorry."

For several seconds, he glared at her, and then he went over and picked up the tray. "You're so flippant about it. None of you know what goes into caring for your loved one."

"Here we go," Nadine said as she walked into the room with Patty. She smiled at Hailey. "Your aunt did very well today. She keeps getting stronger all the time."

"That's good." Hailey went over and gave Patty a quick hug, then helped her into a cushy chair. Kevin still hung by the door with the tray in his hands. "That's all we need, Kevin. Thanks." He smiled at Patty and glowered at Hailey, then left the room with Nadine on his heels. "That guy's a creep," Hailey said as she turned her attention back on her aunt.

"He is strange. Did he bring me a tray? I always build up an appetite after physical therapy."

"I'm going to get us some burgers. I just wanted to wait for you to get back so they didn't get cold. I saw the sheriff's car here when I came in. It's like the third time I've seen the cops here in the last couple of weeks. What's up with that?"

"I'm not sure. No one around here is talking, but there's been a flurry of activity the last few days. I think it has something to do with how many patients have died in a relatively short period of time."

"Do they think something's suspicious with the deaths?"

Patty shrugged. "Who knows, but it seems kind of suspicious to me that there've been so many deaths. I mean, Albert died last week, and he told me he was feeling so much better and looking forward to going home. He didn't look like a dying man."

"How old was he?"

"Eighty-three. I know that's old, but the point I'm making is that he was feeling better. I even heard Dr. Rudman tell him that when I was taking one of my night strolls down the hall. And if Dr. Rudman says anything positive, you have to take him up on his word. Then Albert died the next night." Patty pulled her cardigan tighter around her. "It gives me the chills thinking about how he died just like that." She snapped her fingers to emphasize her point.

"That does seem odd, but he was older. The cops must be looking into something. I'll go get our dinner. Be back in a flash."

After they'd eaten their dinner and watched a bit of TV, Hailey said goodbye to her aunt and walked down the hallway. She stopped at Mrs. Humphries's doorway and saw her form on the bed, a blue blanket covering her.

"Looking for Goldie?" Shelly asked her from behind.

Hailey spun around. "No. I was just looking in on Mrs. Humphries. How's she doing?"

"I can't discuss her health with you. You're not family. Goldie was here for a little over two hours. He just left fifteen minutes ago." Shelly smirked.

Hailey knew the nurse was enjoying the fact that Goldie never went down to her aunt's room to see her. Holding her head high, she said, "I'm glad he's able to come often to visit his grandmother. I have to go." She walked out to the parking lot, the realization that Goldie didn't even walk the fifteen yards down the hall to see her crushing her heart.

He had to have seen my car. He knew I was visiting Aunt Patty. Just face it. He doesn't want anything to do with you. He's probably already hooked up with a woman. I hate him! But she didn't; she couldn't. Garth had been a part of her life for as long as she could remember, and she couldn't just turn off any feelings she had for him as easily as he apparently could with her.

Texting everyone she knew, she sighed in frustration: no one could hang that night. Gripping the steering wheel, she drove back to the flower shop. There was no way she could go home and spend the night in that big house, all alone and obsessing over him. Elated that there was a space right in front of the shop, she pulled in and took out the keys before she left the car.

Magenta and amethyst streaks painted the sky as the first twinkle of lights appeared in the eastern sky. The scent of sweet honeysuckle drifted in the air, and in the distance, she heard the lone wail of a train's whistle. She breathed in deeply the sweetness of a summer night, wishing she were wrapped in Goldie's arms, watching the sunset from Dolores Canyon. That was where the boys and girls used to make out when they were in the early stages of romance. She wondered if it was still the go-to place for teenagers.

With a sigh, she unlocked the door and stepped inside the shop, locking the door behind her. In the still quiet of the store, Hailey spruced up the arrangements slotted for the following morning's deliveries. Rubbing her sore neck, she glanced up and saw a shadow by the front door. It looked like someone was standing against the brick wall next to the entrance as if to avoid detection, but the recently lit streetlight cast the person's shadow. Hailey cursed under her breath for forgetting to pull down the blinds so she would be obscured. Sitting in the shop with the lights on suddenly made her feel like she was in a fishbowl.

Standing up, she crept slowly to the front of the store, her heart pounding a mile a minute. She tapped in 911 in case she had to call the cops in a hurry, then picked up one of the heavier vases in case the person broke through the window. She figured she could always clobber him over the head with the vase. Keeping as close to the wall as she could without toppling everything off the shelves, she approached the front door. Then she saw the tips of the person's shoes. *If I can just grab the chain and pull down the shade without him seeing me.* Then she froze. *What if it's the same guy who was watching me across the street a few nights ago? Oh no. It can't be him. What if it's the serial rapist? Why am I thinking like this? I'm scaring the shit out of myself.*

Leaning over, she reached for the chain, her hand wildly trying to grasp it, and then the man came out of the shadows to face her full-on.

And she screamed.

Chapter Twenty-One

THROUGH HER PIERCING yells, a baritone voice broke through and her eyes flew open. Instead of the bogeyman who'd been lurking in her thoughts, the man at the door was blond, gorgeous, and pissed.

She flung open the door. "Why in the hell are you lurking around scaring the shit out of me?"

Goldie walked into the shop. "Why the fuck are you at the shop so late?"

"How's that your damn business? You still haven't answered why you were lurking outside."

"I wasn't 'lurking,' I was watching out for you. Remember the last time you stayed late? I didn't want you to have any problems."

"How did you know I was even here?"

"I was headed to Get Inked and I came down this street. I was surprised to see your lights on. I just wanted to check to see if you're good. From your frown and pouting lips, I'd guess you're not."

"I'm fine. Thanks for looking out for me. Wait, that's your job, right?"

"You going to start in on that shit already? And it's not my job anymore. I talked to Ryan and told him that I found out Nolan's stalking another woman in Albuquerque. So Ryan's let go of the leash."

"Oh. Was Nolan ever in Alina?"

He shook his head. "Never. That's the problem with the grapevine, it's rarely accurate. I had one of my brothers check him out. You don't need to worry about him anymore."

"Why're you still looking out for me?" Standing next to him in a small space brought an influx of butterflies dancing inside her.

"Because I care about you." His gaze melted over her.

"You do? You could've fooled me. I mean, I haven't heard from you. You were at Cherry Vale tonight and I know you saw my car, but you never came down to my aunt's room."

"I know," he said softly as he ran his hand down her arm.

Tingles shivered through her as she watched his fingers against her skin. "Why have you been dissing me?"

"Because you asked me to. You told me to leave you alone." He grasped her wrist and pulled her closer. "But I can't. I want you, Hailey. You were right. You're a grown woman and I'm a man, and if we want to be together it's our damn decision."

"I've had a crush on you since forever, but I felt something pull me to you when I first saw you the night I got the tattoo."

"Me too. I wondered if you felt it. It was a jolt and it made me take notice. When I found out it was you, it was so fucked up. But now it's clear. I want to be with you."

"For tonight? I'm not into one-night stands. I like being with someone and having a relationship. I'm afraid of getting hurt."

"There's always a risk in getting hurt, but it's worth it. I'm gonna be honest with you. I can't promise you forever. Hell, I don't even know what the fuck to do in a relationship because I've never been in one. All I know is that you're in my head all the time, my dick's been hard for too fuckin' long, and I want to spend time with you. I want to get to know all of you—inside and out. I've never wanted that with a woman, so I'm pretty sure this is more than just lust."

"What about all the women you have?"

"Are you hearing me, woman? I want to be with you. You. Only you. I don't want any other women. Let's just see where this takes us. We don't have to figure it all out tonight."

She smiled. "First thing for you to learn about me—I'm an obsessive planner. I cringe at spontaneity and don't do so well with a change in plans."

"I know that. Remember how you'd make a fuss when Ryan and I would take you to the fair instead of swimming when the carnival was in town? You always could go swimming the next day, but you'd carry on like it was the end of the world. And you always ended up having a good time at the fair."

Shaking her head, she laughed. "I think it's going to be dangerous to go out with you. You remember too much."

He drew her into his arms and kissed her hard on the mouth. "I don't know what it is, but you do something to me." Kissing her again, his hand roamed down her back, landing on her ass.

"You do something to me too. I've never had a man make me feel things the way you do."

"You haven't seen anything yet." In one fluid movement, he picked her up and set her down on the front counter, his lips never leaving hers. He slipped his hand under her blouse and teased his fingers up to her breasts.

Pushing his hand away, she whispered, "Let me pull the blinds. I don't want anyone passing by to see us." Ignoring his protests, she jumped off the counter and pulled down the shades, then dimmed the lights. As she walked back to Goldie, his gaze tracked up her body, then locked on hers. Desire heated his eyes. The look sent a bolt of fire between her legs.

Licking her lips, she slowed her pace, his low growl fanning the lust inside her. Without warning, he reached out and jerked her into his arms, crushing his mouth on hers. His kiss was hot, hungry. Her mind reeled out of control as he thrust into her mouth, touching her body and making it burn. She clawed at his shirt in a desperate attempt to rip it from him so she could run her tongue over his taut muscles.

"Need some help with that?" he said in a low, deep voice that made her panties damp with want. He tugged his T-shirt over his head and threw it on the floor.

She pushed him away and stepped back far enough so she could take him in. Seeing him shirtless for the first time made her knees shake as her gaze traveled up and down. He was magnificent. Every muscle was taut, lean, and so wickedly delicious. He had a smattering of blond hair on his chest that trailed down and disappeared into the waistband of his jeans. She couldn't wait to see how far down it went.

"You're gorgeous," she murmured as she ran her fingertips across his chest and then lower on his stomach. A small groan ripped through his throat and she glanced up and met his lust-filled gaze. As her fingertips slipped into his waistband, he shook his head and yanked her to him.

"I want to see your body first. All of it." He feathered kisses up her neck and across her throat as she tilted her head back and moaned. "Fuck," he said. His warm breath on her skin sent tingles up her spine. Pulling away slightly, he grasped her blouse and ripped it open, buttons pinging everywhere. He bent his head and lavished a trail of kisses over the tops of her breasts as his hands traveled up to cup them. His thumb grazed over her nipples, then flicked them teasingly until they ached for his mouth. He jerked her bra down, the straps capturing her arms at her sides. The cool air from the AC suddenly felt icy against her hardening nipples. Leaning back on the heels of his boots, his gaze devoured her, stroking her with dark intent.

"Your tits are fuckin' beautiful," he rasped as he dipped his head.

Embarrassed by his gaze and words, she closed her eyes.

"Open your eyes. I want you to watch what I'm doing to you."

Fluttering them open, she met his and watched as he slowly licked the tip of her nipple. It was exquisite and tormenting at the same time. Arching her back, she thrust her breasts closer, hoping he'd take them in his mouth. He leaned back again. *Damn!* He chuckled.

"Do you want more?"

"You know I do. Touch them."

With a wicked glint in his eye, he slid his tongue around her nipple before sucking it between his lips. Heat flooded between her legs and she pressed closer to him, humping his leg. Harder and faster he sucked, and her low moans turned into cries. When he slipped his hand into her jeans and placed his palm on her damp panties, sparks rushed up her spine.

"That's so good," she muttered as she ground against his hand.

"What do you want me to do?"

Swallowing hard, she looked into his eyes. "I want your cock deep inside my pussy," she said in a naughty voice. Hearing her voice saying the words shocked her a bit. She'd never said anything like that to a man, but she'd been practicing how to talk dirty ever since she'd read several articles on the subject.

Silence. Goldie stopped playing with her breasts. His hand came out from her jeans. Embarrassment flooded her and she closed her eyes. *What the hell was I thinking? Why did I say it?*

Her eyes flew open when Goldie lifted her and then slammed her down on the front counter. Her legs hung off the side and her sandals fell to the floor. There was a feral, predatory look in his eyes as he pushed her down on the counter and stripped off her jeans, leaving her just in panties. Mesmerized by the hunger she saw reflected in his blue orbs, she lifted herself up on her elbows and watched as he grasped one side of her panties and ripped them at the seam. A wicked smile spread across his lips and he ripped the other side easily.

After kicking off his boots and shedding his jeans and boxers, Goldie's fingers dug into her soft flesh, spreading her bent knees wide until she felt a small stretch down the insides of her thighs. Goldie stared at her pussy, and instead of feeling shy about being so completely exposed, excitement filled her. She could feel her juices dampening the small strip of blonde hair on her engorged lips.

"Fuck," he said in a low voice as he slid his hands under her and cupped her ass cheeks. His shoulders kept her opened wide as he lifted her. She raised her head and flattened her hands on the counter as she captured his piercing gaze. Holding her breath, she watched as he slowly licked the length of her, his lips soon glistening from her arousal.

Her body jolted from the sheer pleasure of it, and her synapses sparked and sizzled as he shoved his tongue into her slippery slit. Over and over, he licked, nipped, and feasted on her until her insides were mush and she was half-crazed with frenzied desire. As he shoved his fingers in and out of her, he steadily licked her hardened nub while his penetrating gaze watched her. Never in her life had she been so aroused. Everything around them blurred; the only thing she was aware of was the tangy scent of their arousal, the sound of his tongue swishing in and out of her, the feel of his warm, soft tongue coaxing her to orgasm. And then the tight coil deep inside her unfurled with such ferocity that she didn't recognize the guttural screams coming from her. Thrashing on the counter, she came hard, raw, and completely.

"That was incredible," she panted, the blowing air cooling her sweaty body.

Goldie leaned over and kissed her passionately. "That was just for starters."

As she watched him slip on a condom, she wondered if it'd hurt to have him inside her. He was pretty big; much bigger than any man she'd been with, although there hadn't been that many. He pulled her off the counter and turned her around so her ass was to him. Placing his hand on the small of her back, he pushed down. She bent over and put her hands flat against the side of the counter. With his leg, he spread her wide, then pushed her head down more so her ass was sticking high in the air. He cupped her wet pussy and smeared her juices over her ass.

"Your tat looks good. Real sexy and such a turn-on."

"You're the first one to see it," she said.

"And the last."

Then he pummeled into her, his hand on the small of her back, pinning her in place so she was completely at his mercy. And she loved it. With each thrust, her body jerked back and forth until they were going at it at such a frenzied pace that Hailey thought for sure the counter would break. Grunts, moans, and skin slapping on skin were the only sounds in the shop. When he reached under her and tugged at her swaying breasts, sparks went off behind her eyelids and she exploded with a yell. One last, hard thrust and feral sounds came from Goldie as he stiffened and yanked her ass closer to his soaked skin.

For several minutes, they stood there panting until he pulled out and helped her straighten up. She fell into his arms and he held her close, running his fingers through her disheveled hair. "Fuck, babe. Just… fuck," he said as she put her lips against his neck.

Hailey was so overcome with emotion she almost cried, but she didn't think Goldie went in for crying women. Most men didn't.

"You want to grab some food? I'm starving," he said in her ear.

"Me too. Is there anything open this late around here?"

"The diner's open until midnight. We better hustle."

Pointing at her ripped blouse on the floor, she said, "I don't have shirt."

"No worries, I got one in my saddlebags. I always carry spares. I'll go grab one."

After she donned his T-shirt and locked up, she followed him to the diner. *I can't believe how wonderful it was with him. Now don't go and make what happened into a bigger deal than it is.* She had to watch herself because if she didn't, she could easily fall head over heels in love with him. *You can't lose your head. Remember, he doesn't even date. He even told you he's never had a relationship.* She pulled up behind his Harley and smiled when he came over and opened her door.

Inside, a few people sat on the stools at the counter and some of the tables were occupied. The waitress led them to a booth by the window and handed them two menus. After taking their dinner order, she walked away.

"I totally forgot about Leroy's. I used to come here with my parents when I was in grade school. Wait a sec… you used to come with my family for dinner sometimes. Do you remember?"

"Yeah." He tilted his head back and looked up at the ceiling. "I'd have the chicken fried steak, Ryan the smothered pork chops, and you'd always have the chop suey." He looked back at her and smiled.

"That's right. How in the hell did I eat chop suey? Do they even have it on the menu?" She scanned the menu. "I don't see it."

"I think they got rid of it after you moved to New Mexico. You were the only one who ever ordered it." He laughed. She made a face at him and that made him laugh harder.

"I hear Dylan's getting married. I don't really know Skyla but they seemed like they were a good fit the night we hung out with them."

"Yeah. She's good for him. He's always needed that structure more than any of us. He was real young when our parents died, and I think it affected him the most. I used to think Monica was the one who had the hardest time with all of it, but I don't think that anymore."

"How's she doing? I'm surprised I haven't bumped into her in all these months."

"She's good. She works for a wholesale company and does a shitload of traveling all over the world. When she's home, she's so busy catching up with everything and everyone that I don't see her that much."

"Next time she's in town, we should get together for drinks or something. I always liked her."

At that moment, the waitress set down a plate of chicken fried steak and mashed potatoes in front of Goldie and a pastrami on rye with fries in front of Hailey. "Did you want anything else?" she asked. When they both shook their heads, she scurried away.

"I'm sure she'd like that. How'd you find out about Dylan getting married? Are you guys talking?"

Shaking pepper on her fries, she shook her head. "No. Your buddy Army told me a few nights ago when I was out at Big Brothers Barbecue for dinner with Rory and Claudia. He said you were going to take care of the flowers. I'm pretty sure he was hinting that I call you." She picked up a fry and dunked it in ketchup.

"What the fuck? Dylan's not getting married until next summer. I didn't say shit about buying the flowers. I'm gonna punch Army in the face when I see him."

"Don't do that. I think he was trying to get us to talk again. I think it was kind of sweet."

"Fuck that. 'Sweet' and 'Army' don't ever go together in the same sentence. He was putting his goddamn nose where it doesn't belong. He's got a real knack for that." He sawed into his meat.

Hailey reached over and put her hand on his. "Don't be mad at him. I think he meant well. Rory said if you were acting anything like I was, she could see why he said it."

After chewing, he grinned. "How were you acting?"

She shrugged. "All whiny and pathetic. You?"

He laughed. "Pissed as fuck. I must've started at least four fights at the clubhouse and a couple at Iron Rose Saloon." Leaning across the table, he put his arm around her neck and pulled her toward him, kissing her deeply. Settling back against the seat, he smiled.

She licked her lips. "I guess everyone will be glad we're talking again."

"And I'm glad we're fucking. Damn, woman, you know how to get me off."

Glancing around, she said softly, "You just say whatever comes into your head, don't you?"

"Why not? I was blown away by our screwing. When I first saw your ass, I thought it was the most perfect one I'd seen, and I still do. But damn, your tits are something else."

"Goldie! This is stuff we say in private, or at least in a lower voice. You're so bad." She slipped out of her sandal and rubbed her foot over his leg.

"You keep doing that and I'm going to spread you out across this table and eat you out."

Not having any reason to doubt him, she jerked her foot away and picked up her sandwich while he guffawed. For the next hour, they reminisced about growing up in Alina. He told her about life in the brotherhood, she told him her dreams of owning her own store one day, and they spoke about their families and how sad it was to see people you love grow old and sick. Even though she still had her parents, she'd lost her beloved grandmother a few years before, so she could understand how Goldie felt at that point in his life.

When they left the restaurant, the waitress locked the door and turned off the neon sign. Darkness engulfed them. He circled his arms around her, folding her to him. She bent her head back and her body tingled in anticipation of his kiss. Gently, his lips touched hers and they exchange a tender moment.

"I need to get you on the back of my Harley. What about this Sunday?"

"I think I'll be too scared." *He's making plans with me. This isn't a one-time thing.*

"I'm not gonna let anything happen to you. Riding on my Harley is required."

"Is it?" She licked his Adam's apple, loving the way his groan vibrated against her tongue.

"Damn straight." He cupped her behind and squeezed.

"Then I guess I'll have to try it out with you. Sunday works."

Smiling, he leaned down and seized her lips again. They stood under the dark sky kissing well after the diner's employees left.

"I better get going," she whispered against his mouth.

"I want to fuck you on my bike. Right here. Right now."

Her eyes widened and he laughed. "If I said yes, I bet you would do it."

"Damn straight."

"I don't think I'm that adventuresome."

"We can leave it for another time." He winked at her.

She opened her car door and kissed him again. "Maybe I'll see you at Cherry Vale tomorrow night. I usually go there around five or so."

"Maybe. I'm never sure how my day goes at the ink shop. I'm going to follow you home. I want to make sure you get in all right."

"Thanks. I appreciate it."

After Goldie walked her safely to her porch and kissed her for several minutes, she watched him until the red taillights disappeared into the night. Locking the door, Hailey went into the family room and turned on one of her favorite Whitesnake CDs. When the music filled the room, she danced up a storm, her body an explosion of sensations. She had so much pent-up emotion from the most wonderful night of her life that she wanted to dance, sing, run up to the roof, and shout out that she was the happiest person alive.

And it was all because of Goldie.

Knowing she was letting her emotions get the better of her, she didn't care. For that one moment, she wanted to feel all the loving, raunchy, and happy emotions until she tried to talk herself out of getting too involved with him.

That night, she would let herself be ecstatic.

Chapter Twenty-Two

T HE BROWN-HAIRED MAN stood in Nadine Bretoux's family room, waiting for his eyes to adjust to the darkness. He'd been in the room earlier that day, but at night, everything looked different. He'd had his eye on the physical therapist ever since he'd seen her at Cherry Vale. She was his type: long blonde hair, big breasts, and rounded hips. She sort of reminded him of Hailey in that they shared some of the physical attributes he preferred. He hadn't given up on Hailey, of course; he was just waiting for the right opportunity to present itself. Securing all the locks on her windows and doors had thwarted him, but it hadn't defeated him. In his mind, it just made the pursuit more challenging and exhilarating. He wanted to take his time with her, to savor each moment of her terror as he did terrible things to her.

The tightness in his pants brought him out of his reverie, reminding him that he had an unsuspecting victim at the end of the hallway. Anticipating her fear overwhelmed him, and he quickly made his way to her room.

From the hallway, he could hear the deep breaths of sleep, and he slowly entered her room. The full moon shone in through the sheer curtains, covering her body in a white glow. To him, she looked as though she were made of alabaster. It reminded him of the time he and his wife had gone to New Orleans. It was before the kids were born, and he remembered how frightened his wife was when he took her to the cemetery after dark. All the graves were above ground and many had ornate carvings and statues of angels, gargoyles, and human forms. His wife's fear had been so great, he'd pushed her against a tomb and fucked her, loving every moment of her cries and protests. The louder she pleaded for him to stop, the harder he hammered into her until he was spent. It was the best sex he'd had with Trisha in the twelve years they'd been married.

He glanced at Nadine and smiled, thinking she looked like one of the white marble forms on the tombs. It was funny how something as inconsequential as moonlight basking over his prey could inspire such comparisons.

Then she bolted up. It was like she'd sensed him. All thoughts flew from his head. He was in predator mode.

"What do you want?" Nadine asked. The slight tremor in her voice hit him in the groin. He slowly walked to her, his gaze locked on her. As if trying to disappear, she pressed closer to the headboard, her fingers gripping the sheet she held up in front of her.

"Do as I say and I won't kill you," he hissed.

"Please don't do anything to me. I have money in my purse. I have some jewelry. You can take whatever you want, but please don't hurt me." Her voice shook and fright spread across her face. She was exactly where he wanted her to be.

Grabbing her ankles, he pulled her down toward the edge of the bed. The blade of the knife caught the moonlight and gleamed in the dark.

"Please don't do anything to me. Please," she whispered as he cut her nightgown off. Her begging was an aphrodisiac to him, and the more she pleaded, the harder he became until he couldn't stand it anymore. At that point, the monster was unleashed.

A few hours later, he removed her panties from her mouth. "Get up," he ordered.

Groaning, she pushed her naked and bruised body up. Tangles of her hair covered her face as she stared vacantly. Grasping her arms, he dragged her to the bathroom and turned on the shower. "Get in and wash up." He shoved her inside the stall and then leaned against the wall, watching her wash away all evidence of him. When she was done, he dragged her back into the bedroom. As he picked up her nightgown and shoved it in a black bag, she went over to the bed and lay down.

"Get up."

For a brief second, determination burned in her eyes, but then she stood up and he gathered the sheets, placing them in the plastic bag. The way she stood, shoulders slumped, defeated, made him sloppy— something he would berate himself about later. Without warning, she rushed over to him; he caught it in his peripheral vision, but before he could react, she'd grabbed his ski mask and pulled it off.

Shock mixed with contempt and disgust washed over her face. "You? Why did you do this to me?" Without a word, he pulled her to him. "No, oh no, please. I won't say anything. I promise."

She struggled a bit, but it was hard to do when he was squeezing her trachea. It sounded a bit like Styrofoam peanuts crunching. Letting go, he took out his knife from his back pocket. Nadine didn't scream, only yelped like a whipped dog. With one movement he slid the knife across her neck, watching the blood gush out, his penis harder than it had ever been. As he ejaculated, he watched her blood seep into the carpet, taking her life with it.

Throwing his head back, he breathed in and out as he tried to regain his composure. After several minutes, he went into the bathroom and took a quick shower, then stuffed his clothes and shoes in the plastic bag with the soiled bedsheets. Making sure to steer clear of Nadine's bloody body, he stuffed whatever he thought could be used to trace him into the bag and took another look around the room.

Satisfied that he'd cleaned everything up, he went down the stairs and left the house. He'd burn everything he'd taken in one of the ash pits at an abandoned farm he'd discovered the year before. The farm was about thirty miles from Alina, and the inspectors never bothered to check out all the illegal burning of trash that was rampant in the rural area of the county. As he drove home, he replayed the scenario over and over in his mind, mad at himself for being sloppy and not securing his victim before he gathered the evidence.

The house was dark when he arrived home and entered the garage. That night, he had blood on his clothes. It felt funny driving home naked. He chuckled when he thought about what would've happened had he had a flat tire or been stopped by a cop. He slipped into the house and crept up the stairs, positive his wife would be fast asleep.

As he gazed up at the ceiling, he came to a startling revelation: the fear in his victim's eyes right before he snuffed out her life had given him the biggest thrill of his life.

He was hooked.

Chapter Twenty-Three

G OLDIE SAT AT the bar watching two guys play pool at Balls and Holes pool hall. He'd had an hour to kill between appointments, and with Skull, Tattoo Mike, and Jimmy all at the shop, he figured they could handle any walk-ins. Weekdays could be slow, so an hour shooting the shit with Muerto and Crow seemed like a good way to break up his day.

"I heard you're looking to get a new bike," Goldie said as Muerto came over to him.

"Yeah. Ever since you got your new Road Glide Special, it's been on my mind."

"You gotta do it. My new bike just hums when I ride her. Just like a fine-tuned woman."

"Damn. I gotta check them out. I wanted to wait for the rally and check out some of the bikes."

Goldie felt his phone vibrate against him. A smile spread across his face when he saw Hailey's name pop up.

Hailey: *R u going 2 see ur grandma tonite?*

Goldie: *Ya. Probably bout 6.*

Hailey: *I missed u last nite.*

Goldie: *Had work. What u doing now?*

Hailey: *At the shop. Working.*

Goldie: *Send me a pic of ur nipple.*

Hailey: *R u serious?*

Goldie: *Ya. Want 2 see it up close.*

Hailey: *I'll think about it. Customers. Gotta go.*

Goldie laughed as he set his phone on the bar counter. "What?" he said to Muerto, who stared at him.

"That was a chick who was texting you."

"So?"

"Chicks don't text you. Remember your rule?" Muerto smiled.

"Are you trying to piss me off? I came in here for a beer and to relax, not to discuss my fuckin' rules and chicks texting me."

"Which chick's texting you?" Crow asked as he came from the back room.

"None," Goldie said.

"I just mentioned his rule about chicks texting him and he went apeshit," Muerto said to Crow.

"Why're you pissed about that?" Crow asked.

"Why the fuck are we still talking about this?" Goldie gulped down the last of his beer and slammed the bottle on the counter. "Later." He marched out, anger pricking his skin as he heard the guffaws behind him. "Fuckin' assholes," he muttered under his breath as he headed back to the tattoo parlor.

The brothers were having a real heyday with him ever since they'd seen him and Hailey together at Cuervos a couple of months before. He couldn't blame them; he'd done the same shit to Muerto, Diablo, and Steel when they were hung up on the women in their lives. *Is that what I am? Hung up on Hailey?* Never being serious about a woman, he was at a loss as to what the hell was going on with him in regard to Hailey. They'd been wanting to tear each other's clothes off from the moment they'd seen each other, and they'd finally done it two nights before, but was that something more than just lust?

Over the years, there were plenty of women he lusted after, but he didn't consider their hookup as anything more than two people pleasuring each other. After it was done, he'd fuck 'em a couple of more times and then move on. Sometimes he was with a couple of women in the same day. It was a lot of fun, but it was no big deal.

Until now.

Hailey was something entirely different. If it was just lust between them, then why couldn't he get her out of his mind? Why couldn't he stop replaying their awesome coupling? Being with her wasn't the same as being with the others; he wanted her all the damn time. Instead of being sated by their fucking, he just wanted more and more.

Liberty waved at him as he entered the tattoo shop, and he gave her a chin lift as he went to his office in the back. He sat down and pulled out his phone. Hailey had texted him but he hadn't heard it. When he opened it, a shot of desire went straight to his dick. A picture of Hailey's pink, round nipple teased him. It was hard to understand what happened to him when he saw her perfect buds, but something deep within him yearned to take them in his mouth, lavishing them with soft attention, and then bite, squeeze, and suck them until she cried out from pain and pleasure.

A loud ping.

Hailey: *Is that what u wanted?*

Goldie: *Ya. Got a damn hard-on. Can u come over & fix it?*

Hailey: *Shop's too busy. U're the one who wanted the pic. ;)*

Goldie: *Smartass. That ass of urs needs a spanking.*

Hailey: *I've never been spanked.*

Goldie: *I'll fix that.*

The buzzer filled the room and Goldie pushed the intercom button. "What's up?"

"We have a walk-in and all the other guys are busy. Can you take him?" Liberty asked.

Glancing at his stiff dick, he said, "Yeah, give me ten minutes." He clicked off and opened Hailey's text.

Hailey: *That sounds wicked.*

If I keep texting with her, I'll never get rid of my boner.

Goldie: *It is. I gotta go. I have a tat to do.*

Hailey: *K. See u later at Cherry Vale.*

Goldie pulled out a technical book from the bookshelf and perused it, concentrating on the sentences and willing himself not to think about the delectable picture Hailey had sent him. After a while, the buzzer sounded again.

"The guy wants to know if you can do this. It's been over fifteen minutes.

"Sure. I lost track of time. I'm coming out."

The technical reading did the trick, and Goldie headed to the lobby to meet the client. Once he got to designing and coloring the tattoo, he'd have laser focus. He walked up to a man in his early twenties and led him to one of the rooms.

AT SIX O'CLOCK, Goldie went down the hallway to Patty's room in search of Hailey. When he arrived, the only person he saw was Patty sitting by the window staring. He knocked softly on the door. Patty turned around, and he noticed her eyes were puffy and red, wet trails glistening on her cheeks. Tissue was balled up in her hand, and taking a corner of it, she wiped the corners of her eyes.

"Are you okay?" he asked. Shaking her head, she looked down at her hands in her lap. "Do you want me to call anyone?"

"No. I'm just upset over Nadine. I just heard about it a little while ago. Why would anyone do something like that to such a sweet young woman?" The tears spilled down her face before she covered it with her hands.

Goldie shifted in place. "I don't know who Nadine is. What happened to her?"

Patty lifted her head and wiped her cheeks with the palm of her hand. "You don't know her? She's one of the physical therapists here. I loved working with her. She was such a nice girl."

"I may have seen her around. My grandma doesn't do physical therapy. What happened to her?"

"She was brutally raped and murdered in her home last night. Isn't that awful? How can someone do that? I never thought something like this could ever happen in our town. Now I've found out there've been several of these rapes. Another victim worked in the laundry here. It's terrible. Something's going on around here. There've been four deaths of patients and now this. I saw the sheriff and his deputies here last week. Something's not right."

Goldie walked in and sat on a straight-backed chair. "You may have something there. I thought something was fucked when the second person died. Now you're saying it's been four?"

"Yes. And Hailey thinks I'm being paranoid. I mean, she didn't say that, but I could tell she was trying to humor me. And now this latest with the rapes. Nadine's the only one he killed. Why did he have to kill her?"

"Maybe she figured out who he was."

"Are you guys talking about poor Nadine? I read it in the paper an hour ago. How awful," Hailey said as she rushed into the room, going over and giving her aunt a quick kiss on the cheek. She looked at Goldie through her lashes and smiled.

"Hey," he said as his gaze slowly raked over her.

"Hey," she whispered as she ran her fingers over the back of his neck.

"Garth agrees with me that something funny's going on around here," Patty said.

"Like what?"

"Like the patients dying, the rapes, and now Nadine's murder." Patty's voice quivered.

Hailey glanced back at Goldie. "Do you really think they're connected?"

"I'm always suspicious when there are too many coincidences. That's just me and my world."

"Knock, knock," Dan said from the doorway. "I'm here to give you your pain pills, Patty. Do you think you need them?"

"I could use one for my nerves. I'm so upset about Nadine."

"I know. It's terrible. The staff is still in shock. She was so good with the patients. A real nice and sweet woman who loved her job."

"I think everyone loved her," Patty said as she dabbed her eyes with a tissue.

"Pretty much." He held out his hand with a cup of water.

"Who didn't?" Goldie asked.

Startled, Dan shook his head. "I don't know."

"Then why did you say it?"

"I meant sometimes we have run-ins with the doctors because we may not agree with some of their advice. It can be like that sometimes because we spend a lot more time with the patients than the doctors or the administrators do."

"Which doctor are we talking about here?" Goldie narrowed his eyes.

"I don't like talking about the staff."

"I'm not gonna tell anyone what you say. I don't work that way."

Dan stood for several seconds in the middle of the room as if trying to decide whether or not to say anything. Glancing at the door, he lowered his voice. "It's really all of the doctors. They don't like it when we ask questions. I know Nadine had a run-in with Dr. Rudman a couple of times, and Dr. Tyrell and Dr. Daniels can be bad about sharing information with physical therapy. Nadine and Thelma, the woman who works in the laundry who got raped, had run-ins with some of the CNAs, especially Kingsley, Hendricks, and Kevin. Nadine even wrote them up a few times. She found Hendricks smoking pot in one of the patient's bathroom. He tried to disguise the smell with some strong pine air freshener, but it only made it worse."

"Hendricks and Kingsley are usually my grandma's CNAs. Did Hendricks ever smoke in her room?"

Dan chuckled. "No way. Everyone's a bit afraid of you. They know you're a member of the Night Rebels. They don't want any problems."

Goldie stood up. "You tell me if any shit goes down with my

grandma. If I find out someone did something and you didn't tell me, I'm gonna make sure you end up as a patient here." He loomed over Dan, who quickly walked to the doorway.

"Enjoy the rest of your visit," he mumbled, then scampered away.

"You love doing that shit, don't you?" Hailey asked.

"What?"

"Scaring the hell out of people." She grazed his fingers with hers.

"Scaring means to frighten someone into doing something or make them worry. I just tell people how it's going to go down. When I say something, it happens." His jaw muscles twitched.

"You always were direct, Garth," Patty said.

Goldie stayed for a while longer in Patty's room, then went down to his grandma's room and sat on the chair watching her as she slept in the bed. An hour later, Hailey came down and said she was taking off. He kissed his grandmother on her soft hair, then walked out with Hailey.

Intertwining his fingers with hers, he breathed the night air in deeply. It'd been so hot for the past week that the coolness of the breeze was a welcomed relief. Above, a carpet of stars glittered against the dark blue background. A sudden chill inched up his spine and he drew Hailey close to him, cocooning her in his arms. Lowering his head, he kissed her silky hair, the tropical scent filling his nostrils.

"You need to take care of yourself. There's a real crazy fuck out there hurting women. I hate that you don't have a garage."

"I'm not going to lie to you and say I'm cool, because I hate that I don't have a garage either. I have the feeling I'm being watched, or at least was being watched. It started when that guy came out of the bushes over a month ago. Then my window was unlocked. Remember?"

"Yeah. Have you seen anyone since we fixed all the locks?"

She nodded. "Last week a guy was watching me from across the street. I'm pretty sure he was the same one from before based on his height and build, but I couldn't make out his face or any other identifying features. I called the cops and they patrolled the neighborhood for a while. I haven't seen him since, and I haven't had the vibe he's watching me."

"You didn't tell me about the second incidence. Why didn't you call me?"

"We weren't talking."

"Fuck, Hailey. That shit doesn't matter when something like that happens."

"I know. Anyway, it's over and done, and we're good, so all is fine."

"Except for your fuckin' garage. You're gonna have to call me when you come and go. I'll make sure you're safe. I just don't have a good vibe about all this."

"Each time? You've got to be kidding. I'm in and out a lot."

"Just call me when you're on your way home or leaving in the morning. If I can't make it, one of the prospects or brothers will be there. It's just temporary until they catch the fucker."

"Okay. I'll admit, I'll feel safer."

"And if you stay late at the shop, call me. I don't want you walking alone on the street either."

"Isn't this going to get old for you?"

He smiled. "Nah. Most of this is moot anyway because I'm planning on spending a lot of nights with you. Like tonight."

She giggled. "Oh really."

Slipping his hands under her ass, he cupped her cheeks and pressed her close. "Yeah. Really." Then they lost themselves in a heated kiss.

When they arrived at the Victorian, Hailey bounced up the steps while Goldie walked behind her, loving the way her cute ass wiggled. Inside the house, he yanked her to him and kissed her passionately as his fingers pushed up the hem of her top. He'd been craving her nipple inside his mouth since she'd sent him the picture. Tugging her top over her head, he grabbed her bra straps and shoved them down past her arms. Her breasts tumbled out, and her delicate pink nipples, hardening nicely, beckoned him. He cupped her tits and squeezed them while he took one perfect bud into his mouth and sucked, licked, and bit at it. When he tweaked her other nipple with his fingers, she cried out and placed her arms behind her, arching her back and pushing her tits further into his face.

He sucked the delicate flesh of her breasts hard, knowing she'd have a trail of love bites all over her skin in the morning. He wanted to mark her, to have her think of him each time she saw the red marks decorating her tits. Then he felt her palming his painful bulge and he reached down and unzipped his jeans, his dick springing free. With her hands on his chest, she pushed back and looked down, a devilish smile dancing on her lips.

Hailey dropped to her knees and unbuckled his belt, then pulled his pants down past his knees, his gray boxers going with them. When she looked up at him with lowered eyelids and slightly parted lips, he thought he was going to lose it. Digging her fingers into the soft flesh of his inner thighs, she pushed his legs and he immediately spread them for her. She licked his inner thighs slowly, never quite touching his balls or his straining cock. Her fingers tickled his lower abdomen, behind his knees, and even his ass, but she kept them away from where he wanted them the most.

Goldie grabbed her hair, but she shooed his hand away and kept licking and touching him until he thought he'd have to hold her head tight and fuck her face hard. At that moment, she grabbed the base of his cock and licked up and down his shaft, rolling her tongue around all sides. Her heated gaze held his and he leaned back against the wall, enjoying the burst of sensations rushing through him as she worked his dick.

She gently kissed and licked the tip before she slowly drew it into her mouth, then a little more, until she had his whole cock inside her mouth, her lips tight around it as she swirled her tongue.

"Fuck yeah. That feels so good," he rasped as they continue to hold each other's gaze.

As she went up and down on his hardness, wet and sloppy, she gently cupped and caressed his balls. The small whimpers, moans, and "mmmmms" drove him wild. He watched as his cock disappeared between her lips over and over again.

"Don't stop," he said unevenly.

His breathing was rapid and ragged, and he was ready to explode. His balls tightened. The tension built until it broke, and he grabbed her hair, pulling her to him to meet his final thrust. Then a surge pushed through him and he exploded in her mouth, grinding against her.

"Fuck!" he yelled as he threw his head back, his hand fisted in her hair. He stayed like that for a while, then slowly pulled out of her.

She wiped her shiny chin and grinned at him. All at once, he kicked his pants off and shoved her onto the floor, tearing off her skirt and panties. Throwing one leg over his shoulder, he bent over and made a trail of love marks from the tops of her tits down to her belly. Scooting down, he dipped his tongue between her puffy folds, loving how wet she was.

"I love tasting you," he said between licks.

"It feels so good. So damn good," she murmured.

After several minutes of licking, soft nipping, and light sucking, he dropped her leg and slid up to kiss her. When he dipped his tongue into her mouth, he tasted the brine of his cum and the sweetness of her juices as they mingled together, making an intoxicating elixir of raw desire.

"Do you like the way you taste on my tongue?" he said as he plunged two fingers into her wetness.

"Oh…," she moaned against his lips.

Then he kissed her as he fingerfucked her and rubbed his thumb against the side of her engorged button. Each whimper she muttered, he swallowed, each moan filling his mouth until he felt her warm walls clamping around his fingers. He held her tight as she deafened his ear, her body quivering and shaking as she rode the wave of her orgasm.

"Goldie! It's so good," she chanted over and over as more quivers rocked her. And all the while he held her, loving the sight of her climax so completely.

They lay on the floor of the foyer for a long time, their sweat-drenched bodies soon dried and cold from the AC blowing over them.

Hailey stirred, then tilted her head back and kissed his chin. "That was amazing. I've never experienced sex like this before. Were you this good in high school?"

He laughed and squeezed her close. "You bring out my primal desires." He kissed her forehead, then pushed up. "Let's get off this hard floor." She giggled as he pulled her up.

"Do you want to spend the night?" she asked.

He detected apprehension in her voice. "I'd planned to. I'm fuckin' starved. Do you want to order a pizza?"

"Okay. I could eat a slice or two."

Thirty minutes later, they were snuggled on the couch, chomping on pizza and watching TV. If he were at the club, he'd be downing shots, watching his brothers fuck, and getting hit on by scantily clad women. *I'll take a night of pizza and Hailey next to me any day.*

And that surprised the hell out of him.

Chapter Twenty-Four

DETECTIVE JACK BARNARD perused the crime scene photos for the umpteenth time, trying to pick up something he may have missed. His chief had loaned him out to help Sheriff Wexler and his department to find and stop the serial rapist who'd just been elevated to a murderer.

"Pick up any new clues?" Wexler said as he placed a cup of coffee on Barnard's desk, then slumped in the chair in front of it.

Shaking his head, he picked up the coffee and took a sip. "Something happened that night that made the perp change his MO."

"Maybe she recognized him," Wexler said.

"I agree. Killing her became necessary to avoid being caught, but now that he's done it, he has a taste for it. I'll bet he experienced the ultimate high. From what the previous victims told us, this bastard gets off on control, but more importantly, the terror he inflicts. Knowing you're about to die is the ultimate fear, and he's not going to stop."

"Shit. Now we got a rapist and murderer? Where the fuck did this one come from? We've never had something like this in our county."

"He could be a newcomer, or perpetrated his crimes elsewhere. He's meticulous in making sure he doesn't leave any evidence, but he fucked up this time. Two types of blood were found on the carpet. My guess is he cut himself while killing the victim."

"Did DNA come back?"

"Not yet. They're backlogged, but once we get it, we'll put it in the national database and hope we get a hit. There's a connection to Cherry Vale. Two out of six of his victims came from there. Aren't there a string of suspicious patient deaths from there?"

Wexler nodded. "Three of the patients had above normal doses of a heart medicine in their system, and one of them had an abnormally high level of insulin. But these people were old, and there were no signs of sexual molestation. Besides, this rapist is all over the place with the women he goes after. Some are in their forties and fifties, some young and blonde, some brunette. There doesn't seem to be a pattern."

"I disagree. The pattern is blonde, curvy, in her twenties, and connected to Cherry Vale. I think the others are random to throw us off his pattern. He thinks he's real smart, so he goes after women who aren't his actual type to make us think it's all random. He's attacking in all parts of town rather than one specific area. But the only thing he's been consistent about is the two women who work at Cherry Vale. *That's* his pattern."

"So the old people dying is to throw us off?"

"Could be." Barnard scrubbed his face. "We gotta get this bastard before he strikes again. I can guarantee the next attack will end in murder."

Jack Barnard knew his stuff. He'd seen a lot of horrible things people did to each other, especially when he worked at the Los Angeles Police Department. After years of the rat race, he decided to relocate to a smaller city. When he'd visited the southwestern part of Colorado, he'd fallen in love with it. He'd spent several vacations in the area, so when a position came up with the Durango police department, he applied. When he got the job, he was elated. He packed up the few things he had and never looked back. He loved working for a small department and being able to devote most of his time to his cases.

When his chief sent him to Alina to help out with the rapist case, he'd thought he'd be able to get in there, figure it out, and stop the bastard, but it wasn't playing out that way. Now a woman had been murdered, and that made Barnard madder than hell. This sick bastard thought he was smarter than the cops, but he'd made a mistake and left his DNA at the scene. That's the way it was with serial criminals when they started to feel too cocky. It usually happened that way, and that's when Barnard would zoom in for the kill. He just hoped he'd be able to find the killer before he struck again.

And the only thing certain was that the bastard would strike again.

Barnard would bet his life on it.

Chapter Twenty-Five

FOR THE PAST couple of weeks, Hailey had been on top of the world, and her relationship with Goldie played a big part in her happiness. She'd never been involved with a man who made her feel as special as he did. And the sex was beyond fantastic. She never knew her body could feel so delicious. Since they'd given in to their desire, they'd been at it nonstop, and she didn't dare wear anything low-cut or too revealing because her body was covered with love bites. When she looked at them, her insides would flutter; she loved seeing his mark on her.

"That guy looks kind of suspicious," Ellie, one of her employees, said to her.

Hailey looked up and saw a man standing by the ribbons and bows. He looked familiar, but she couldn't quite place where she knew him from. "I'll take care of it," she replied to Ellie and walked over to him.

"Can I help you?" She racked her brain, trying to remember how she knew him.

"Hi. How're you doing?" he asked as his dark eyes bored into hers.

"Fine. I'm sorry, but you look familiar. Have we met?"

His eyes narrowed. "You don't recognize me? I'm Kingsley. I work at Cherry Vale."

She smiled broadly. "Of course. That's it. You're one of the CNAs. I'm sorry. I don't see you that often."

"I usually work the day shift." His piercing stare moved down to her bust and she quickly crossed her arms over her chest.

"What can I do for you?"

"Uh… I came in here to get some flowers for my wife."

"How nice. What's the occasion?"

180

"Her birthday. She told me that I never give her flowers, so I thought I'd surprise her."

"She'll love it. What's her favorite flower?"

"I don't know. What do you like?"

"I'm all over the place. I love roses, lilies, sunflowers, orchids, and tulips. I could keep going. I can make you a beautiful arrangement. What's your wife's favorite color?"

"Red? Maybe blue. I'm not sure."

"Okay. What's your price range? I can fix up something real nice for you, and I guarantee your wife's going to love it."

Kingsley darted his eyes around, then shoved his hands in his pockets. "I'll come back." He rushed out the door.

That was strange. They have so many wackos working at Cherry Vale. I can't wait until Aunt Patty gets out of there. Hailey went back to the front desk and pulled out a book of arrangements. She'd promised to send over some samples to the couple she'd met with the day before.

"What did that guy want? He was sort of creepy," Ellie said.

"He's thinking about getting his wife some flowers for her birthday. He works at the rehab center where my aunt is."

"Oh. How's Patty?"

"Doing better every day. Her doctor said that if she keeps it up, she'll be able to come home in a month or so. I can't wait."

"Are you going to stay on when she gets back on track?"

"I'm not sure. It'll depend on what my aunt wants to do."

Hailey resumed what she was doing, not stopping until she heard Ellie say, "Damn, he's hot."

Lori, another employee, replied, "I'm waiting on this one."

Hailey looked up and grinned when she saw Goldie. *Damn, he is hot. And he's all mine.* A slight tug at her heart reminded her that she didn't really know where she stood with Goldie. They were having a good time and enjoyed being with each other, but he never talked about them in the future, only the present. She tried so hard to be cool with that and not let herself get caught up in her feelings for him, but the more time they spent together, the stronger her emotional attachment to him grew.

The one thing they never spoke about was Ryan. Of course, they mentioned him when reminiscing about the past, but he was the elephant in the room, and neither of them wanted to face it.

"Hey." He leaned over and kissed her deeply.

She pulled back a bit as all eyes were on her. Ellie's shocked expression was classic, and Lori's frown surprised Hailey. Several people in the shop turned away, pretending to be interested in plants and ribbons they hadn't even been looking at before Goldie appeared. And Goldie just didn't give a damn about what people thought. He was unfiltered, confident, and lived in the moment, and those were the things that made him irresistible—besides his drop-dead-gorgeous body and face.

"I came by to take you for a ride. It's too nice outside to waste it cooped up."

"Don't you have to work?"

"Nope. And you're taking off too. You work too damn much."

Hailey waved her hand over a bunch of notebooks in front of her. "But I have all this work to do."

"You taking one day off isn't gonna close down the business. You can pick it up tomorrow. Let's go."

"Let me get this straight. You're not *asking* me to go with you— you're *telling* me."

"Yeah. We're wasting time. You can put your purse in my saddlebags."

Ellie gently pushed her arm. "Go on. We can handle things in the store."

Giving Goldie a half smile, she shook her head. "All right. You win. I'll go get my purse."

When she came back out, Ellie told her that Goldie was waiting for her outside. His metallic silver bike glimmered in the sunlight, and he looked so badass leaning against it. The flirty smiles from the women who passed by him didn't go unnoticed by Hailey, but he didn't pay any attention to them; his eyes were fixed on her as she approached him.

"You look too sexy with your Harley. All the women want to climb on behind you and wrap their arms around you," she said as she handed him her purse.

He curled his arm around her and drew her to him. "You're the only one I want on the back of my bike," he whispered in her ear, then nibbled her neck.

She chuckled and planted a kiss on his soft lips. She'd never get tired of kissing him. He was hands down the best kisser. The way he held her and the intensity he gave to each kiss blew her mind. She figured he'd had a lot of practice with a bunch of women, but she didn't like to think about them. Especially the women who lived at the clubhouse. Sometimes it gnawed at her, so it was better to push it away and pretend they didn't exist.

"Climb on," he said.

When they'd gone to Dolores Canyon a few weeks back, she'd been petrified of his motorcycle. It was so big and there was nothing around her to make her feel safe. All sorts of graphic scenarios played in her mind as she settled herself behind him. At first it was damn scary, but as they rode, she let her body relax and move with the rhythm of the bike. The feel of the powerful engine vibrating beneath her made her admire the way Goldie maneuvered the bike around the curves. The landscape and the smells of the pines, the earth, and the rippling creek hugged her in a way she'd never experienced before. It was like she was part of the scenery and it was part of her, and it gave her an incredible sense of freedom. And holding on to Goldie, her front pressed against his back, her hands clinging to his tight stomach made her horny, which surprised the hell out of her.

After their outing, all she wanted to do was climb back on his Harley and hold him tight, melding her body with his as he rode into the great expanse.

She eagerly settled behind him outside the flower shop and placed her arms around his waist. When the bike jumped to life, a single shiver of excitement bolted through her, and they took off.

The ride to the Iron Horse Saloon was a short twenty-minute one, but he'd promised a longer ride after they had something to eat. Inside the roadhouse, several older bikers lining the bar checked her out as she followed Goldie to a table on the back patio. They were the only ones on the patio, and Goldie moved the umbrella to shield the sun from their faces. The lush foliage, the random smattering of wildflowers, and the full pine and evergreen trees surrounded them. In the distance, a rush of water echoed.

"It's pretty and so calming up here," she said, watching a few iridescent dragonflies skipping over the bushes.

"I love it up here. It's close to town, but it feels like we're in another place." Goldie dragged her chair closer to him. "Now, give me your lips."

Tingles skated over her skin as she leaned forward and kissed him deeply as she grabbed his hair and pulled it. Moaning softly, her tongue danced with his, her nipples hardening when he brushed his thumb across them over and over. With each swipe over her aching buds, her arousal surged through her senses, landing at the opening between her legs. She slipped his bottom lip between her teeth and sucked it, then bit down as her passion escalated.

"Fuck, Hailey." With his hand tangled in her hair, he yanked her head back and kissed her hard. "You're irresistible," he rasped. Parting her lips, their tongues entwined as he placed his hand over her breast, his finger stroking the very tip of her nipple.

She squirmed and moaned under his touch, his lingering kiss dampening her panties and making her clench her legs together. The firmer and wetter he kissed her, the more it drove her wild with desire. She craved to ride him while his thick cock was deep inside her.

"Do you know how fuckin' sexy you are?" he said against her lips.

"You're driving me crazy," she breathed.

"I like that." His low chuckle rumbled in her ears, and then his lips were back to doing wickedly delicious things to hers. "I can't stop kissing you," he whispered.

Someone clearing his throat made Hailey pull away. A tall, bearded man in a black shirt and jeans held a notepad and a pen. "How's it going, dude?" he said to Goldie.

"Good, bro."

"I'm guessin' you're not gonna start any fights, right?"

Goldie laughed. "Nah. I'm in a good mood." He squeezed Hailey flush to him.

"I can see that. You guys want something to drink and eat?"

"A Coors for me." He looked at Hailey. "What do you want?"

"A peach margarita," she said, to which Goldie and the waiter busted out laughing. "Is it an inside joke?" she asked.

Goldie smoothed her hair back. "This is a biker bar. Margaritas aren't on the list. Beer and hard liquor are what's available."

"Okay. I guess I'll have a White Russian." Goldie and the waiter shook their heads. "You don't have that either," she said out loud. "Bring me a Coke with a couple of slices of lemon."

"That we have," the man said.

"Do you want some nachos?" Goldie asked her.

"Sure. I prefer them without any meat. Are you cool with that?"

"Yeah. Bring me an order of wings with the habanero sauce. You gonna go on the charity poker run?"

"Yeah, put me and Bruiser down. I'll let you know if Lizard's gonna go. Does the lady want anything besides the nachos?"

"No. The nachos are enough for me. Thanks."

When he walked away, Hailey asked, "What's a poker run?"

Goldie explained it and told her about the upcoming rally. He told her what his duties were as the road captain of the club. She loved hearing about his lifestyle and his world; it was different from anything she'd ever known.

When the man came back with their drinks, he gave her a once-over and winked at her, then headed back into the restaurant.

"I can't believe he did that in front of you," she said as she squeezed lemon into her Coke.

"Rusty's a horny bastard. Don't take offense. He thinks you're a hang-around or a one-nighter. I'll set him straight."

"Why would he think that?"

"'Cause he knows me. I don't have women around for long."

"We've been hanging out for a few weeks. Am I your record?"

He laughed. "Yeah, you are." He picked up one of his wings and took a bite. "Fuck, these are good."

"What's a hang-around?"

"Women who come to the clubhouse to party with the brothers. They're there for a good time. Believe it or not, women go crazy for the chance to party with a biker. They all want to be on the back of a Harley. It's crazy."

"A lot of women like the idea of a bad boy, and I'd say a guy in a rough motorcycle club would turn a lot of women on."

"Does it turn you on?"

She shook her head. "*You* turn me on, not your lifestyle or your motorcycle."

Putting his beer down, he leaned over and kissed her hard on the lips. "You're fuckin' incredible."

Licking her lips, she picked up her Coke and took a long drink. "How can you eat that habanero sauce?"

"I like hot and spicy things." He winked at her and picked up another wing.

She snickered, then popped another chip in her mouth. *I'm having the best time with him. It's just so easy and natural between us. I'm really falling for him.*

"What're you thinking about?" he asked.

"About your clubhouse. I heard you guys have some wild parties. I want to go to one of them."

"They're not for you."

"I'll be the judge of that. I want to go."

Pushing back in his chair, he stared at her. "The parties can get out of hand. Fights break out, people are real open, and the whole atmosphere can be crazy. Sometimes we have other guys from other clubs come by, or wannabes who're trying to get in good with the club will come with patched members. It isn't like a regular party."

"I'm just curious. I'll be with you, so nothing's going to happen. Please?" She tipped her head down and looked up at him. She knew the look drove him crazy, and she could get her way when she used it.

Running his hands through his hair, he blew out a long breath. "Damn, woman. I should say no, but for some fucked-up reason I'll go ahead and take you to the party this Saturday. But I don't want to hear any complaints or judgments from you. Got it?"

She nodded and gave him a peck on the mouth. "Thank you. What should I wear?"

"Nothing revealing. Jeans and a T-shirt are good."

"Since we've been together I haven't been able to wear anything revealing," she said.

He chuckled. "Another bonus to sucking your soft skin."

After they finished eating, Goldie took them to Arrow Lake, which was a good hour from town. The day had grown hotter, and there weren't any people at the lake.

"I haven't been here in years. Ryan used to take me to Overland Lake to swim since it's closer to town, but I've only been to Arrow Lake once. I don't remember it being this pretty." Rays of light from the afternoon sun danced across the water. The shore was a mixture of earth, rocks, and grass, and the circle of trees surrounding cast its reflection on the shimmering cyan blue water.

Goldie took out a blanket from his saddlebags. "I prefer to come here. Overland Lake is too crowded, especially in the summer. It's quiet here, and sometimes it's good to get away from the noise of life."

"Is that why you like to ride your Harley?"

"You bet. I love the way it makes me feel. Riding solo gives me freedom and solitude. There's nothing like it."

"I can understand that."

He grasped her hand and led her to a grassy area, spreading open the blanket before kicking off his boots and tugging her down.

She laughed. "I'm sort of freaked because the first and only time I was here, my dad and I were bitten to death by mosquitoes. Someone at work told my dad Arrow Lake was a great place to fish."

"Fishing here sucks."

She nodded. "We found that out the hard way."

"I can't see you going fishing. I'm surprised your dad took you."

"I pleaded with him. He always gave in to that."

"You were always such a princess," he said.

"Still am." She smiled when he playfully poked her in the ribs, his fingers close to the underside of her breast. She sucked in her breath, even the hint of him touching her intimately made her skin tingle.

"Did you catch any fish?"

"Three." They both burst out laughing. Holding her stomach, she lay on her back, her sides aching. He hovered over her and peppered her face with small, feathery kisses, then trailed down her neck to her collarbone. "Hailey."

The vibrations of his lips on her skin sent a direct surge to her pussy. She was still on high alert from the restaurant, so it didn't take much to heighten her arousal again. Under the clear blue sky, the lull of a slight breeze, and the melodic chorus of birds, she wanted him to fuck her hard. The fear of someone watching didn't matter to her. Normally, she'd be squeamish about it, but Goldie brought out a nasty side of her she never knew she had.

"I can't get enough of you," he said as he raised her top, then yanked down her bra and devoured her tits.

"I'm so crazily turned on by you. I always crave your touch," she said as she fumbled with his zipper.

"I want to feel you raw, baby. I'm clean. Are you on birth control?"

"Yeah. I want to really feel you too."

Then he raised up, shrugged off his clothes, peeled hers off, and bent back down, hovering over her once again. The feel of his skin on hers fueled the burn deep inside her.

"I want you inside me. Right now," she whispered against his chest.

Without another word, he grasped her legs, put them over his shoulders, and rubbed the head of his cock over her wet pussy. Lowering his head, he sucked on her breasts, then pulled up and slammed into her. A million sparks flew through her as he pumped in and out, her warm walls clinging to him as he stretched her more and more. Tendrils of wicked pleasure tore through her pussy as she exploded into a million pieces.

Goldie stiffened, then held her gaze as he grunted, "Hailey," before he filled her. His cock kept twitching in her as her pussy walls clamped around him, milking his dick dry. She kissed his head and caressed him as he panted and collapsed on top of her, his chest heaving. *I could get addicted to this.* She sighed contentedly and ran her hands up and down his back.

After a long while, he rolled off her and tucked her in the crook of his arm. The gentle breeze cooled their bodies, and joy coursed through her. After a few minutes, she heard him snoring, and she smiled as she clung to him and watched the ripples in the lake.

Most perfect day ever.

Chapter Twenty-Six

S USAN O'BRIEN RUBBED her eyes and swiveled her office chair to face the window. The street was quiet and most of the windows from the apartment complexes were dark. She glanced at the clock, surprised she'd worked past midnight. Yawning and stretching her tired limbs, she leaned back and closed her eyes. Part of her was too tired to get up and go home, and another part of her wanted to get away from her office and forget the paperwork that kept piling up on her desk daily. Grasping the arms of the chair, she pushed herself up and grabbed for the corner of the desk, steadying herself. Sitting for hours had made her joint stiffen up, and having a few drinks made standing a bit challenging.

She gathered the paperwork she knew she wouldn't look at and placed it in her briefcase, along with the nearly empty bottle of vodka. After switching off the desk lamp and overhead fluorescent lights, she left the room.

The corridors were quiet and dim, with only a small amount of light around the baseboards illuminating the floor. The residents were asleep in their rooms, and she soundlessly walked down the hall to the door leading to the basement. An unopened bottle of vodka in her locker had been on her mind for the past two hours; it would make excellent company for her when she arrived at her empty townhouse.

When she passed Gus Halpern's room, something moved in the dark. Fear seized her as she thought Gus was trying to get out of bed. Whipping around, she rushed to the doorway. The room was so dark, it took a few seconds for her eyes to adjust to it, but when they did, she saw a figure standing over Gus.

"I'm glad you came over, Vera," Gus said hoarsely. The figure didn't answer. "Ow! That hurt. Why did you do it, Vera? Where's my mother?" Gus began to cry softly.

Susan's heart broke when she heard the patient's tears. Gus suffered from vascular dementia, and he obviously thought the person was someone from his past.

"Gus?" she said in a low voice as she walked into the room. Then she saw the figure pulling a needle from his arm. No injections were ordered for Gus. As a matter of fact, he wasn't on any medication at all. The eighty-two-year-old was healthier than a lot of men half his age, which made his dementia that much more tragic. "What are you doing?" she asked as she approached the bed.

The figure stiffened and turned around. Stopping mid-stride, Susan's mind raced as she tried to figure out what was going on. "I thought you requested tonight off. What were you injecting into Gus?" She froze as the realization of what was happening hit her full force like a tidal wave. "You? You've been responsible for these deaths? It can't be."

Without a word, the figure rushed over to her. Something hard hit her head before she could yell out, dazing her, and she stumbled while red spots danced in front of her eyes. Before she could get her bearings, she was being half dragged to the locked door that led to the basement where her vodka bottle awaited her. *I could really use a drink. My head is pounding. What's going on? Why did—*

Then a rough shove had her arms flailing to grab onto the bannister, but she couldn't. Her feet were slipping off the concrete steps, trying desperately to steady themselves. The crash of the bottle in her briefcase sounded like a bomb in the stairwell as her briefcase flew out of her hand and slammed down on the landing. In less than a second, she followed it, her head meeting the floor. The crunch of bones in her skull deafened her before everything went black. From above, she heard the steel door shut, and she knew her mangled body wouldn't survive the fall. After all the years of poverty, adjustment to a new country, and hard work in her career, she'd end up dying on a cold floor that smelled like bleach. If her breathing weren't so ragged, she would've laughed at the irony of it all.

What a bloody silly way to die.

Chapter Twenty-Seven

"**Y**OU'RE GOING TO a lot of trouble with this chick," Paco said.

"Do I have use of the prospects or not?" Goldie replied, ignoring Paco's comment.

"Steel and I are wondering how we can justify taking the prospects away to do personal stuff for a brother who has a hard-on for his best friend's sister."

"I'm just gonna tell you this one time, dude. I don't give a shit that you're the VP of the club. If you say that shit to me again, I'm gonna smash your goddamn face."

"Then we'd have a bloody mess after I kick your ass." Paco's arms flexed when he crossed them over his chest.

"If the club doesn't want to help me out with this, fine. I can figure it out. I was just asking because it didn't seem to be a problem when Muerto and Diablo asked for their women. Just fuckin' forget about it." He pushed away from the bar.

"He's messing with you," Steel said as he walked over.

"You sick fuck," Goldie said.

Paco laughed and handed him a shot of tequila. "You were the one always giving Muerto and Diablo shit about their women, so I thought I'd take over your spot."

A half smile curled Goldie's lips as he shook his head. "So I can use Ruger and Patches if I need to? I'm gonna be doing it most of the time. I just want to make sure she's safe until they catch this fuckin' perv."

"Since Wexler can't find his ass with both hands, I'd say you're gonna be watching your woman for a long time," Paco replied.

"I heard a detective from Durango's manning the case," Army said as he came over.

"Who're you fucking this time at the sheriff's office?" Steel asked.

"A hot redhead. She just loves telling me everything going on after I fuck her good." Army laughed and picked up his beer.

"What do they know about this bastard?" Goldie said.

"They think he may be the one offing the old people at your grandma's place."

"Fuck. I got a bad feeling about all this. I have to figure out how to protect my grandma when I'm not there."

"Why don't you move her out?" Chains asked as he sat on one of the barstools.

"Cherry Vale's the nicest private place in the area. The state-run ones are shitholes, and I don't want to send her to Durango. Besides, moving her now would totally screw her up. I just have to figure it out." Goldie scrubbed his face.

"You know the badges are usually wrong. I can't believe a guy raping women is also offing old people. It doesn't make sense," Paco said.

"If he's trying to avoid detection and throw the badges off, it does," Chains replied.

For a few seconds, silence descended on the group. Then Paco clasped Goldie on the shoulder. "When are you gonna tell your friend about fucking his sister?" The others guffawed.

"I don't know," he grumbled. After he finished his beer, he begged off a game of pool and headed to his room. Paco's question needled him, and he knew it was something he had to do. Since he and Hailey had come together, they'd both acted as though Ryan didn't exist, but he was always in the back of Goldie's mind. Sometimes he'd chastise himself for being so weak or a disloyal, shitty friend, but then the memory of Hailey's kisses and the sunlight in her hair washed the guilt away. How could he give up the way she snuggled close to him when they slept, the way her lower lip jutted out when he annoyed her, or the way her face contorted when she climaxed? He couldn't. It was that simple, yet somehow it wasn't.

Kicking his desk chair, he cursed under his breath. Of all the women he'd ever hooked up with, why the fuck did it have to be Hailey who'd found a way into his heart? *Fuck. I need to tell Ryan. He'll get it. He knows I'd never hurt Hailey. We've been buds since we were five.* And what was Hailey to him? His feelings for her were all scrambled inside him, and the fact that he even *had* feelings for her surprised him. In all his years, he'd never felt anything more for a woman than pleasure. Some of the women had been more fun than others, and he'd liked hanging out with them more, but if they started pressuring him, he'd walk away without a backward glance. And on the rare occasion when a woman decided she wasn't into his no-commitment mentality and left him, he'd usually be with another one within twenty-four hours. That was the way he lived his life, and it had suited him just fine until Hailey came into his shop.

Being with Hailey touched something deep inside him, and it thrilled and angered him at the same time. He loved his easy life in the brotherhood: all the booze and pussy he could ask for, camaraderie, killer parties, and doing whatever the fuck he wanted. He didn't need a woman complicating his life, and he wasn't willing to give it up, but when he wasn't with Hailey, he was thinking about her. He'd skipped the last several club parties, and the only pussy he'd been in for a while was Hailey's. It was the only one he craved.

Fuck, this shit's complicated.

A knock on his door was a welcomed distraction from his dizzying thoughts.

"It's open."

Brutus walked in. "Some of us are going out drinking. You wanna come?"

"Where're you going?"

"Rear End."

"I haven't been there in a long time. Count me in." *It'll be good to just go out with the brothers.*

"We're gonna leave in an hour," Brutus said as he walked out.

Yanking off his T-shirt, Goldie headed to the shower. A night out with his buds was just what he needed. Freshly showered and shaved, Goldie slipped on a clean pair of jeans and a black muscle shirt that molded over his chest. He reached for his phone on the desk and noticed several unopened texts.

Hailey: *Whatcha doing?*

Hailey: *R u busy?*

Hailey: *U must b tatting someone.*

Hailey: *Forgot to ask. U wanna hang tonite? I feel like a drink.*

Hailey: *Text me when u're done.*

Goldie reread the texts, looked out the window, and then replied.

Goldie: *Sorry. Was in the shower. I'm hanging with my buds tonite.*

Hailey: *Where u guys going?*

Goldie: *A biker bar.*

Hailey: *Have I been there?*

Goldie: *Doubt it. It's raunchy & a hottie like u wouldn't survive ten secs before the wolves started circling.*

Hailey: *hehe. Have a good time.*

Goldie: *Thx. I'll call u tomorrow.*

Hailey: *:)*

Goldie put the phone in his pocket and went over to the window. Down below, he saw Brutus, Jigger, Sangre, Army, Eagle, and Skull walking toward their bikes. The encroaching darkness slowly swallowed the last light of day. The shadows from the oak tree fell over the brothers' heads and shoulders like a web. *I almost canceled going to Rear End to be with Hailey.* But he didn't. He had to prove to himself that he could go out with his brothers and have a good time without her on his mind. She'd been totally cool with it, and he kind of wished she would've given him an attitude to prove that she was just like all the women he'd known. But she wasn't. She wasn't like anyone he'd ever known. Grabbing his keys, he went down to meet his brothers.

Rear End had been around since the 1960s and had a longtime reputation as a biker's haven. Framed posters of naked women in leather boots posed in various positions on motorcycles hung on the dirty gray walls. Beer kegs shot up by the patrons in the desert were part of the dive's decorations. Old neon beer signs blinked intermittently behind the bar and in the small windows facing the street. The back wall was known as the "Memorial Wall" where broken bits and pieces of motorcycles shared space with photos of longtime regulars—both dead and alive. Bullet holes marked the walls, and a canopy of women's bras decorated the ceiling. Brawling was the norm, and sometimes violence would erupt among the customers over something as simple as a lost pool or dart game. Most nights Rear End was packed with bikers and women who wanted to be near them.

Goldie and his brothers entered the dive, jerking their heads at some of the men in leather standing by the bar. Zito, the owner and bartender, grinned at the Night Rebels, his top gold teeth flashing under the flickering neon signs. "It's been too fuckin long," he said as he set down seven shot glasses. Zito inherited the bar after his dad had passed away ten years before. He was built like a linebacker and didn't put up with shit from anyone. If one of the patrons justly pissed off another, he'd let them fight it out, but if someone started bullshit for no reason, he'd find himself kissing the pavement or staring into Zito's double-barrel shotgun.

"On the house," he said as he filled the shot glasses with Jack.

"Thanks, man," the brothers said as they lifted their glasses and threw them back.

Goldie panned the room and saw a woman he'd hooked up with eight months before. He'd met her at Rear End, and she seemed like a good time. They got drunk and he ended up at her place for a couple of days. All they did was smoke weed, drink, and fuck. When he'd taken off, she'd been madder than hell that he hadn't wanted her number. He'd been sorry that he hadn't just given it to her so he could've avoided the scene, but he'd been too high and hadn't thought it through.

Goldie turned his head, but she'd already spotted him and was headed his way. He ordered a double Jack and braced himself. Her long nails dug into his bicep at the same time a nauseatingly sweet citrus scent roped around him.

"It's been a long time, Goldie. How've you been?"

Turning slightly, he lifted his chin. "Been good."

White, crooked teeth shone between dark lips. With her jet-black hair and pasty complexion, she looked like a vampire. *Did she look like that when we hooked up? And what the fuck's her name?*

"I haven't seen you around here. I hope you weren't avoiding it because of me." Her nails dug in deeper.

"Hardly." He jerked his arm away and gave her a warning glance.

"Not in the mood to be friendly?" She leaned in close but he pushed her away.

"Nah. Go on and circulate." He turned his back to her.

"What's the story with Vampirella?" Eagle asked.

Goldie chuckled. "I was drunker than shit the last time I was here and ended up crashing a couple of days with her. We fucked like crazy, and then I left. She got pissed."

"The usual story. Damn. I was hoping for some real blood sucking, not the hickey shit."

"She'd probably do it now. I don't remember her looking like the undead."

"Was she a good fuck?"

"Yeah. I mean, I stayed for two days, so she must've done something right."

"Whoa, bro. Look at her now. She's giving you the evil eye, and the dude with her is acting all tough." Eagle laughed.

"What a couple of losers. If he wants to start shit, I'm right in. It's been too long since I had a good bar fight."

"Vampirella would probably love to see you crush him. Bitches like that love to have a man fight for them. Makes 'em feel special. Maybe he's her Igor." Goldie and Eagle laughed.

"Some dudes from the Jagged Aces challenged us to a pool game. Are you guys in?" Army asked.

"I'm out, but I'll watch," Goldie said.

Army jerked his head back. "I thought you'd be all over this."

"I'm in," Eagle said.

Soon, Brutus, Army, Eagle, and Skull were lined up to play a few rounds of pool with four Jagged Aces. The club was not a one-percenter, but they had their hands in several smaller illegal activities around the county. Their main claim to fame was stealing cars and motorcycles in and around the county. The Night Rebels never had any run-ins with them, and they normally got along at rallies, with several of the Jagged Aces members participating in the charity poker runs the Night Rebels organized. The Aces respected the Night Rebels and never laid claim to any territory in southwestern Colorado.

Eagle sat next to Goldie, waiting for his game to come up. "Vampirella's Igor is a Jagged Ace."

Goldie glanced over and she smirked at him, then wrapped her arm around her man's waist. Goldie turned away. "She's a biker slut."

"Aren't all the women we meet?"

Not Hailey. Never Hailey. She doesn't give a damn that I'm a biker. She knew me before the Night Rebels. He chuckled when he remembered she'd told him she'd had a crush on him since she was thirteen. All of a sudden, the women in the club looked like pathetic barflies, and the pool game didn't interest him. All he could think about was Hailey, wishing she were seated in his lap, or riding behind him on his bike.

Eagle whistled and Sangre, Skull, and Jigger hooted. Brutus was wiping the Jagged Aces' ass in the game. Goldie tried to concentrate on it. He was out with his brothers, so why wasn't he having a good time? Something was gnawing deep inside him. While Brutus hit the winning shot, Goldie took out his phone.

Goldie: *R u home?*

Hailey: *Ya. Y?*

Goldie: *I need 2 see u.*

Hailey: *Is everything ok?*

Goldie: *I need to be inside u.*

A few seconds passed.

Hailey: *I miss u 2. Come fast.* ♥♥

Goldie read her text several times. That was it: he missed her too. Standing up, he clasped Eagle's shoulder. "I'm fuckin' beat. I'm outta here. Good luck on the game."

"This is a first."

"What can I say? Not enough sleep, no food, and too much booze." He sauntered away before Army started up with all the questions.

Even though the sun had gone down, it was still like an inferno, the hot air wrapping around him like a down blanket. With his cams screaming, he exited the parking lot and drove by the front of the bar. Vampirella and Igor stood on the sidewalk watching him. He sped away.

Hailey ran down the stairs right when he set his kickstand. Opening his arms, she flew into them, laughing and kissing him like she hadn't seen him in years. He tangled his fingers in her silky hair and pulled her head back, crushing his lips to hers. *This is exactly where I want to be.* When he scooped her up, she yelled and then laughed as he carried her into the house, up the stairs, and laid her on the mattress.

"I have a surprise for you," she said with a wicked glint in her eyes.

"Oh yeah?" he replied while he stripped off his clothes.

She jumped up from the bed and pulled him toward it, shoving him backward. His ass hit the mattress and he looked up at her. "What's going on in your pretty little head?"

"Don't move."

She went over to her computer and the pulsing beats of "Girls, Girls, Girls" filled the room. As she slowly pulled her sundress over her head, she wiggled around. Then she placed her hands over her breasts and he thought he'd lose it. Dressed in a black, cutout, sheer teddy, she looked luscious with her pink pussy peeking out. When she whirled around, the lingerie opened just enough to show her bitable ass. Before the song went into the chorus, he had her on the bed, sucking her tits as he buried his fingers between her damp folds.

After a few hours, they held each other as he twirled strands of her hair around his finger.

"I'm so happy you came over," she whispered in the darkness.

"Me too."

"I was surprised when I got your text. At first I was worried something happened."

Something did.

She kissed his chest. "I feel so good right now."

"Yeah." He wanted to tell her he was feeling shit he never had before, but how could he explain it when he didn't even understand it. Instead, he held her tighter, never wanting to let the moment slip away from them.

"You're pretty special to me," she said softly.

"You too." And she was, but there were complications, like his lifestyle and Ryan. But earlier that night, none of it had mattered when he'd entered her, their bodies crashing together, smacking and sliding against each other. They'd fucked over and over until the sheets were wet from their frenzied passion.

After they'd both calmed down, he'd kissed her sweetly, and she'd whimpered and curled around his body. And that's when he'd made love to her. Long, slow strokes fueled their passion, and when they'd come together, he knew he'd experienced something he'd never had with any other woman. The smell of her hair, the taste of her mouth, the feel of her skin seemed to course through him, electrifying him and everything around him. Her essence gripped him; she captivated him.

And he could never let her go.

Chapter Twenty-Eight

HAILEY STOOD IN the doorway as a man in his late forties in a crumpled sports jacket ambled down the hall. His shoulders were slumped, and it looked like he'd never polished his shoes. A tall, young deputy followed after him as they disappeared around the corner.

"I wonder what's going on," Hailey said as Shelly approached the room. Hailey stood back and let the nurse walk in.

"How're you doing, Patty? Are you sore from your physical therapy? Mica said you did great today."

"I'm very sore. Mica worked me hard." Patty smiled.

"What's going on here? I see a couple of cops around." Hailey glanced down the corridor again.

"There was an accident late last night," Shelly said as she handed Patty a pain pill.

"What sort of accident?" Hailey asked.

"Susan tripped and fell down the stairs. Kingsley found her in the stairwell when he went downstairs to take his break. He said it was awful."

"Is she all right?" Patty asked.

"She died. Must've broken her neck. Kingsley said she was dead when he found her."

Patty's hands flew to her mouth. "Dead! Oh my God. How dreadful."

"I just spoke to her the day before. I can't believe it," Hailey said.

"We're all shocked by it. Corporate will send a replacement, of course, but it's always hard to get used to a new person in charge. Well, let me know if you need anything." Shelly whirled around and left the room.

"She didn't seem too broken up over it," Hailey remarked as she watched the nurse go into another room.

"I don't think she and Susan got along that well. Shelly's very good friends with Dee, and Dee and Susan didn't see eye-to-eye on many issues of patient care," Patty said.

"I know you've told me this before, but refresh my memory. Who's Dee?"

"The DON—director of nursing. She's a lovely woman whose poor husband was just diagnosed with cancer."

"Why didn't Dee like Susan? I thought Susan was real nice, and I loved her accent."

Darting her eyes around the room, then back at the hallway, Patty said in a low voice, "She didn't like the way Susan drank on the job."

"Susan was an alcoholic?" Hailey asked, wide-eyed.

Patty nodded. "I felt so bad for her. I think it was all the stress of running this place. She was constantly pressured by corporate to show increases in earnings, but she also had to provide quality care. It was a hard juggling act. I bet she was drunk when she fell down the stairs. A few months back, she slipped and fell, but she only got bruised up. Poor, poor, Susan."

"Wow… I didn't know. When you get out of here, you should write a book."

"How's one of my favorite patients doing?" Dr. Daniels asked as he walked into the room.

Patty beamed. She always did when she saw the handsome doctor. Hailey was convinced she had a crush on him and wished she were twenty-five years younger.

"I'm doing great. Mica gave me quite a workout," Patty said.

"She's also upset about learning that Susan died in a fall last night. Is that why the cops are here?" Hailey asked.

Dr. Daniels turned to her, a sad smile on his lips. "I'm sure it's more about Mr. Halpern. He died last night."

"Gus died? Oh no. You know, he was a brilliant trial attorney before he retired. How sad," Patty said.

"It is. I didn't know he used to be a lawyer," Dr. Daniels replied.

"What was wrong with him?" Hailey asked.

"He had dementia, dear. An old friend and colleague of his came to see him, and then he sat down in the lobby, tears streaming down his face. We got to talking and he told me all about Gus. A brilliant man before the disease."

"That is sad. Isn't he like the fifth one to die around here? Don't you find that more than a coincidence, Doctor?" Hailey said.

Clearing his throat, he popped his head out the door, then turned to look at her. "Actually, I do, and apparently, so do the police. I shouldn't have said what I did, so please don't tell anyone you heard about Mr. Halpern from me."

"Was he your patient?" Hailey asked.

Shaking his head, he said, "Dr. Tyrell's. Sometimes I'd stop in if I was the only doctor on the floor. It's a shame. And now we've lost Susan. She was a wonderful person. Once in a while, we used to go to Bulldog Pub and have a pint. She told me it reminded her of Ireland." He stared vacantly at the wall.

"I didn't know her that well, but she was always nice and cheerful whenever I went in to talk with her," Hailey said.

He smiled. "I have to finish my rounds. I'm glad to see how well you're progressing, Patty. Keep it up and I may release you sooner than two months."

"I can't wait to get home. It seems that every week or so someone's dying around here." Patty grasped her arms and shuddered.

"I know. It must be awful being here. Seven months is more than enough." Hailey sat at the edge of the bed.

"What are you doing this weekend?" Patty asked.

"Goldie and I are going to a party."

"I can't get used to calling him Goldie. Why did he change his name? Garth is so much nicer."

"It has something to do with the club he's in. All the guys have road names. It's just what they do. He told me that his mom and dad were obsessed with Garth Brooks and Bob Dylan, so they named him Garth and his younger brother Dylan."

"You like him, don't you?"

"I always liked Goldie."

"I mean *really* like him."

Hailey shrugged. "I guess. I mean, we have a good time." *I'm crazy about him, but I'm scared to think about it.*

Patty patted her hand. "If he's the right guy for you, your heart will tell you. Does Ryan know you two have been dating?"

She grimaced. "No. I'm not sure how he'll react." *Yes I do. He's going to be so pissed because he warned me to not get involved with Goldie.*

"I would think he'd be happy for you and Garth. After all, he's known Garth most of his life, and they're still friends. You should tell him. By keeping it secret, it'll make him feel like he can't trust you."

"I know, you're right. I'll tell him." *Someday.*

"So where's the party you're going to?"

"At Goldie's clubhouse."

"Is it a dinner party?"

"Not exactly."

"What kind of party is it?"

"Uh, you know… just hanging out and stuff. Did you want me to bring you a pizza tomorrow night? I thought we could watch *Some Like It Hot*. It's playing on TCM."

Patty laughed. "I've seen that movie so many times, and each time I see it, I laugh my head off. That sounds wonderful." She yawned.

"Getting sleepy?"

"It's the pain pills. They knock me out."

"I'll take off and let you take a nap. I'm going out with Rory and Claudia for dinner. We've missed our girls' nights out for the last few weeks, but we're all available tonight, so we're going for it."

As Hailey walked through the parking lot, she noticed the cop in the rumpled jacket heading to a dark blue sedan. He glanced at her briefly, then turned away. She wanted to ask him what the hell was going on, but she knew he wouldn't tell her squat. Maybe she could get some more information from one of the CNAs.

The sedan turned out of the lot as she slipped into her car. Glancing at the digital clock, she pushed down on the accelerator and sped off to the restaurant to meet up with her friends.

Thai Garden House was a newer addition on Saguro Street. Nestled between a wine bar and a boutique specializing in handmade items, the restaurant catered to a more adventuresome palate. Large windows brought in a lot of sunlight while hand-painted silk fans on the walls and brightly colored umbrellas suspended from the ceilings added to the exotic feel of the eatery.

A sleek brushed silver bar lined the side wall, and the lighted glass shelves hosted a colorful array of bottles housing an assortment of alcohol from liqueurs to bourbon. Bronze tables and chairs were filled most of the time, and reservations were recommended in order to avoid an hour or two wait.

Besides the excellent food, the gem of the restaurant was its outdoor dining on the back patio. Replete with bamboo pergola, reflecting pool with fountain and moss-covered rocks, wind chimes, and vibrant plants and flowers, the back area was like an oasis in the desert.

"I just love it here," Hailey said as she bit into her spring roll.

"It doesn't feel like we're in Alina. It's like we're on vacation," Claudia said.

"Exactly, that's why I love it back here. Speaking of vacations, what's going on with yours, Rory? I thought you and Troy planned to get away."

Rory slumped back against the chair's thick cushion. "I did. You guys know I've been planning this damn trip since the beginning of summer. Each time we get ready to go, something comes up with him. I'm beginning to think he doesn't want to go."

"Duh, he doesn't," Claudia said.

"Why? I would think he'd be dying to get away. Alina can be stifling in the summer. I have the whole seaside trip planned. I'm tempted to go without him. I'll show him he's not going to ruin my plans."

"You should," Hailey said.

"Do you guys want to go on the trip with me?" Rory asked.

Hailey picked up her passion fruit daiquiri. "I'd love to go, but I can't leave the flower shop or my aunt alone."

"I'm going to my cousin's wedding in Houston, but Hay's right. You should go alone."

"I know, but I think I'd be too depressed to be there alone knowing Troy and I were supposed to go. I don't know. Maybe we can plan a fall trip." Rory took a bite of her pad thai noodles.

"How's it going with you and Garth?" Claudia asked.

"Good. He's actually really sweet." Hailey dipped her beef satay into a spicy peanut sauce.

"What does that mean? Details." Claudia snickered.

"Like, he's always texting or calling me, he waits for me when he goes to visit his grandma, and he's been making sure I come in and out of my house without a problem. Remember I told you about that creepy guy who'd been watching me?"

"Yeah, I remember. Have you seen him again?" Rory asked.

Hailey shook her head. "Not since Goldie implemented his 'Safe Hailey' plan." She giggled.

"How in the hell can you remember to call Garth 'Goldie'?" Claudia mixed some hot sauce on her rice.

"At first I didn't think I'd be able to, but Goldie is so different from the Garth I knew when I left that it isn't that hard."

"To me, he'll always be Garth," Rory said, a finality to her tone.

"So, have you guys fucked?" Claudia asked.

Hailey laughed. "You've always gotten straight to the point. Yes, we have."

"Oh shit! I knew you'd been lusting after him." Claudia laughed.

"I can't believe you slept with an outlaw biker." Rory wrinkled her nose.

"He's more than his label, Rory," Hailey countered.

"Who cares about that anyway? How was he? I'm dying to know. He's so attractive and well-built." Claudia placed her elbow on the table and leaned forward.

Scooting her chair in closer to the table, Hailey said in a low voice, "He's freaking amazing. I've never had a man touch me and make me come the way he does. I can't believe how great he is."

Claudia clapped her hands softly while giggling, and Rory shook her head. "There's a reason why he's a womanizer, Hay. Of course he's good, but is he loyal? Have some fun with him, but don't give him your heart. He's probably doing you and a few other women."

Claudia reached out and patted Hailey's hand. "Don't listen to her. Go for it all the way if that's what you want."

"I'm the only one here who's practical," Rory said.

"You're in a pissed mood today because Troy canceled your trip. Hay and Garth are steaming up the sheets and I love it." Claudia settled back and took a gulp of her peach daiquiri.

"Give me some damn credit. I'm not saying this because I'm disappointed about my trip with Troy. I'm saying this because I care about Hay. I don't want her to get hurt, and I know Garth's going to shred her heart if she falls for him."

Hailey sipped her drink as she watched her two good friends banter back and forth over what she should do about Goldie. It was interesting to hear each one's advice. The funny thing was they were both saying what she'd been telling herself for weeks. Part of her was over the moon about him like she'd always been, but the other part was scared he'd break her heart. She didn't even know how he felt about her in a deep sense. They had a great time hanging out, and the sex was beyond fantastic, but if he felt more or wanted more, he never said. And she couldn't read him. She didn't want to ask him and be one of those women who made him feel pressure. He'd told her often enough that he hated that, so for the time being, she'd just keep having fun with him and enjoy their sexual times together.

"Earth to Hay." Claudia's voice brought her out of her thoughts.

"Sorry," she said.

"How do you feel about him?" Rory asked.

She lifted one shoulder. "He's nice, we have fun together, and the sex is the best. I'm having a good time, that's all."

"Is it?" Rory's penetrating gaze made her uncomfortable.

"Yeah. I mean, I somewhat agree with you, Rory. He's had a lot of women, so there's always that fear that he'll grow tired of me. But then, when we're together, he's so attentive, so sincere that I think maybe he's just never found the right woman and that's why he played the field. I don't know. Why do I have to decide now? I don't have to put a label on what we have."

"You just don't want to fall for him. You have to be careful, so knowing how you feel helps you to decide if you want to keep seeing him. I'm just trying to be helpful," Rory said.

"I get it. I guess I don't really know how I feel about him, but I do know I want to keep seeing him."

Silence descended on the trio for several seconds, and then Claudia smiled. "Now for the real important stuff. Does he lick your twat like a real man's supposed to?" A peal of laughter burst out from all three of them.

Dabbing at her eyes with the corner of her napkin, Rory said, "Well... does he?"

Hailey grinned. "You can't believe what he can do with his tongue." And for the next twenty minutes, Goldie's sexual prowess was the focus of their conversation. Of course, she left out a lot of things that were too private, but after she was finished and they moved on to another topic, her nipples ached for his touch. She couldn't wait to have him back inside her.

If she were being totally honest, she'd have admitted to her friends that, in addition to liking him, there was also an addictive quality to it all. She craved him, she got her fix, and then she always wanted more.

Her insatiable appetite was not just for the sex but for the whole confusing mix of physical and emotional feelings. Needing and wanting him had quickly become a huge part of her life.

And she wasn't sure if that was a good or a bad thing. All she knew was she was in deep.

Real deep.

Chapter Twenty-Nine

SATURDAY NIGHT HAD come and Hailey was a mess of nerves. She'd been reading and watching so many documentaries about outlaw motorcycle clubs that she now questioned her sanity in wanting to go to one of the club parties. She'd almost backed out, but when Goldie came by to pick her up, she pushed aside her nerves and fears and decided to embrace it. After all, it was only one night.

When she arrived at the clubhouse on the back of his bike, a sea of leather-clad men crowded around the front yard, the floodlights bouncing off the chrome of their bikes. She'd never seen such an array of bikes, leather, and denim congregated in one place. Several groups of men shared pulls off bottles of whiskey that were being passed around.

Glad to have Goldie's arm wrapped around her, she walked toward the entrance, ignoring the men's lustful looks.

"Remember what I told you about sticking with me. It looks like there're a lot of bikers from different clubs here. They're not gonna know you're with me if you go off on your own. Since you're not wearing my patch, they're gonna think you're here for fucking."

"I can't even go to the bathroom without you escorting me? That's crazy."

"That's the way it is. You're the one who wanted to come. You're in the biker world now and have to play by its rules or there are dire consequences. You're glued to me tonight." He smiled and kissed her gently on the lips. "That's not a bad thing, is it?" He winked at her and opened the front door.

With her stomach twisting, she stepped into the large room. The heat from all the bodies hit her full-on and the scent of sweat, weed, and booze snarled around her. They pushed their way through the hazy labyrinth of bodies until they reached the bar. Goldie said something to one of the men seated on a barstool. The loud pulse of music made it impossible for her to hear what he'd said, but the man nodded, got up, and walked away. Goldie helped her onto the barstool, then ordered her a Jack and Coke and a double Jack for him. While she waited for her drink, she looked around the room, her eyes now adjusted to the subdued lighting and the smoky veil.

Men in leather vests were everywhere, a lot of them standing in small groups drinking, talking, and smoking weed and cigarettes. The men far outnumbered the women in the room, and most of the women were dressed quite provocatively in their short shorts, barely there tops, skintight dresses, and five-inch stilettos. Hailey's black jean skirt, white cold-shoulder top, and three-inch wedge sandals made her stick out like a sore thumb. Several of the women smiled at Goldie, then threw her a dirty look as they disappeared in the crowd.

"You have a stripper pole in your clubhouse?" she asked as Goldie handed her the Jack and Coke. The pole, to the left side of the jukebox, gleamed under the red and blue lights.

"Not always, just for tonight. The guys put it up when we have a big party or if they're in the mood to watch the women strip. A couple of the club girls used to work in strip bars, and you'd be surprised how many citizen women like to take their clothes off in front of a roomful of bikers."

"So not all the women here tonight are club girls? Are some of them the men's girlfriends or wives?"

He took a sip of his shot. "Fuck, that's good stuff. All the women here wanna party with the guys. They're here for the booze, sex, and drugs. Old ladies aren't allowed at the club parties."

"So if a wife wanted to come tonight, she couldn't?"

"No. Anyway, the old ladies don't want to come."

"But what if they did?"

"They couldn't. It's one of the rules."

"Why can't they come?"

"Some of the guys want to party hard, and they don't want an old lady cramping their style. Some of the married brothers like to have fun on the side with the club girls or some of the hang-arounds. They don't want an old lady running back and telling *their* old lady what they were doing. Besides, we respect the old ladies, and sometimes when a party gets real wild, it can be real raunchy."

"It sounds very one-sided to me."

"An MC is a man's world. That's the way it is. Remember, you wanted to come even though I warned you how it was."

"I know. And I'm not judging even though it sounds like I am. I'm just really trying to understand your world."

Lowering his head, he kissed her deeply. "I know, and I love that you're doing that."

"Did you party hard with the women?" The minute the question left her mouth, she wished she could've taken it back. She didn't want him to think she was a petty, jealous woman, but looking at the all the pretty women in their revealing outfits made her a little insecure.

"I'm not gonna lie to you. I love club parties. I love the drinking, the bullshitting, talking about Harleys, and all the fucking. But I haven't really been into them for the last few months. I was restless as hell for quite a while. Then I saw you at Get Inked, and you've been the only one I want to fuck ever since." He trailed kisses from her collarbone to her earlobe. "Why would I want any other pussy when I've got the tastiest and sweetest one around?"

Hailey smiled, but she couldn't help but wonder how many of the women at the party he'd been with before. She bet it was many of them, and she couldn't help the stab of jealousy as one buxom redhead blew him a kiss as she walked by, her underbutt wiggling in her super short Daisy Dukes. Even though she knew bikers enjoyed the attention they received from women who wanted to party on the wild side, it still made her feel funny about how easily accessible they were to the men—to Goldie.

Is he going to get bored with me? These women embrace the wild, crazy side of his world. They throw caution to the wind. I'm not like that.

"You want another drink? We've got food out back. Do you wanna check it out?" he asked.

"I could use another drink, and I am kind of hungry." He brushed his lips across hers and leaned over to talk to the bartender.

I'm being silly. Goldie's here with me. He could be with any of the women in here, but he chose to be with me. And we've been hanging together a lot. He's practically living at the house.

"Ready to go?" He helped her down from the stool and they wound through the droves of people until they went outside. The cool, late summer air felt good after being inside the smoky, stuffy clubhouse. Strings of white lights hung around the tall chain-link fence that surrounded the back of the property. Four bronze tiki torches in each corner of the yard, brought a natural flame ambience to the area. Under a canopy, men swarmed around two large tables loaded with Mexican food. A makeshift bar with skull lights strung around it was on the other side of the yard.

"Who catered the party?" Hailey asked as she spooned some rice onto her plate.

"Lena and the club girls prepared the food. Lena's our cook, and she makes sure we're well fed." Goldie chuckled as he placed a beef burrito on his plate.

"It smells delicious."

"Wait until you taste it."

After filling their plates, Goldie led her to one of the many aluminum picnic tables set up outside. Biting into her cheese enchilada, Hailey savored the flavors, and in a short time, she'd cleaned her plate. "I guess I was hungry," she joked to Goldie as he smiled at her.

"Do you want me to get you something more?" he asked.

"I was thinking about getting another cheese enchilada. I can tell your cook makes the corn tortillas herself. They totally rock. Stay seated and finish your dinner, I can get it." She started to get up but he pulled her down.

"I'll get it. I don't want to have to fight any of the brothers."

"The table is right behind us. This is ridiculous."

"It's not. They're gonna think you're a biker slut and you wanna fuck. I'll be right back." He jumped up and went to the buffet table. While she waited, she noticed several men stop in front of her and gawk at her breasts. Waves of heat ran through her like wild internal blushes as her skin tingled from the back of her neck and across her face. Looking down, she swirled her fingertip in the condensation pooling under her glass, trying to ignore the men who still stood there staring at her.

"Fuck off. She's with me," Goldie growled.

"Sorry, dude. I didn't know," one of the men said as he instantly diverted his eyes.

The other men mumbled their apologies, clasped Goldie on the arm as if to show there were no hard feelings, and swaggered away. She leaned against his shoulder, then looked up at him. Looping her hand around his neck, she drew him close and kissed him. Goldie wrapped his arm around her waist, pulled her closer, and touched her thigh. Several of the men at the table watched them, and when Goldie pulled away and went back to eating, she noticed they kept their eyes off her. *It's amazing how fast they switch gears once they know I'm with Goldie.*

While they were eating, Army and Crow came over. "I'm glad to see your ass here," Army said to Goldie.

"Yeah. I haven't seen you at a party in quite a while. Is this what's been keeping you away?" Crow glanced at Hailey. "Can't say I blame you." He wiggled his eyebrows and laughed.

"She's not a hang-around. Hailey, this asshole is Crow, and you already know Army."

"Are you liking the way we party?" Army asked Hailey.

"I love the food. I'll just say that I'm glad I'm with Goldie. You all put frat parties to shame."

The guys laughed and Goldie squeezed her close to him. "I don't think I like knowing that you went to frat parties," he whispered in her ear.

"That was in college. I can guarantee I didn't party as hard as you. Not even close."

"Tonight's party is the best one because you're here with me."

His words helped melt the images of him screwing the club girls out of her mind. She figured out early on which of the women at the shindig were club girls because they wore the "Night Rebels MC Property" patch. Goldie had explained what all that meant. She was hoping the club women would look worn and strung out but, to her chagrin, they didn't. The girls were pretty, had nice bodies, and looked like they took care of themselves. The men seemed to treat them decently, unlike how some of the outlaw clubs she'd read about. She wondered if any of the brothers ever fell in love with one of the women or vice versa. For a split second, she felt sorry for them, but then one of them strutted by and opened her leather vest, showing her big boobs to Goldie.

"See what you've been missing, sweetheart?" She beamed and kept going until she curled herself around a tall, good-looking man. He immediately kissed her and slipped his hands under her tiny shorts, squeezing her ass cheek.

"Who was that?" she asked.

"That's Ruby. She's hooked up with Roughneck. He's prez of the Fallen Slayers, a club we're friendly with. They came down from Silverado to party with us."

"Have you been with Ruby?" Hailey hated that she was asking, but she couldn't help herself.

"Yeah. Hailey, you can't get obsessed with this. You know I've fucked a lot of women. It was just for good times. They didn't mean anything to me."

She nodded. "I know, but I can't help thinking about it. I mean, did you screw all the club girls? Are there women here tonight that you've been with who aren't the club girls?"

"Why does this shit matter? It was in the past. I'm not gonna ask who you fucked."

"Well, I could count them on one hand. You'd need hundreds of hands." *Stop it! But I want to know. This is stupid.*

Goldie looked at her for a few seconds, then took a pull from his beer. "I've fucked all the club girls, and there're several women here that I've fucked. You want the details?"

She shook her head. "No. I'm sorry. It's just that when I think you have all these women available to you—"

He placed his hands on each side of her face and made her look at him. "I've already told you that none of these women meant anything to me. I'm with you tonight, and I don't see anyone but you. You mean something to me, Hailey. I've never had any woman touch me, but you're all over me. You're in my head, my blood, my skin, and even my heart. So don't think for one second that I'm spending time with you and fucking up a storm when we're not together. You need to trust me. Now no more questions about sluts. I have a past. You have a past. But we're each other's present, so let's live in the now. Got it?" Then he kissed her hard and demanding, and her body responded in kind. His kisses, his touch, and his words affected her in a cozy yet passionate way.

He's right. The past is the past.

She squeezed his inner thigh and he threw her a hard look. "Keep that up and I'm gonna have to fuck you on this table." He chuckled when her eyes widened.

"I heard you customized the fuck outta your new Harley," a man seated across the table said to Goldie.

Soon the two were talking Harleys, and a few others joined in on the conversation. While the men talked, Hailey observed the scene around her. A naked woman lay on her back in the middle of the table across from theirs, serving as a human dinner tray as the men licked and scooped up food from her body. On the grassy area behind the tables, several women were on their knees giving blowjobs while a few couples tangled together in hard sex, oblivious to the people around them. Drunk women swayed to the tunes of Whitesnake, Metallica, and Avenged Sevenfold that blasted from the speakers perched on the top of the fence. It seemed that the drunker the crowd became, the less clothing the women wore and the more the men hauled them over their shoulders to an empty space on the grass. Hailey had never seen such debauchery live before, and it shocked and titillated her at the same time. There was something about giving in with abandonment that intrigued her.

Standing up, Goldie pulled her with him, then pressed her close. He bent down and kissed her, sticking his tongue halfway down her throat as he slipped his hand under her skirt. When he touched her exposed ass cheeks, he grunted and squeezed them. Her eyes fluttered open and she saw several men watching them, as well as a few women. Some of them were touching each other as they gazed at her and Goldie. Without thinking, she pulled away and pushed Goldie back. "That's enough," she said in a low voice.

Goldie yanked her to him, his eyes glowering. "What the fuck does that mean, woman?" Some of the spectators snickered. Her face and neck were impossibly hot, like a blanket of steam had covered her. "I want to kiss you. Now kiss me."

Her skin prickled and anger rapidly replaced embarrassment as she stiffened under his touch. "Is this how you get respect from your brothers?"

Without answering, he kissed her again, but that time he didn't touch her butt, keeping his hands on her hips. After a few seconds, he pulled away and cheers and whistles deafened her ear. *This is so unreal.* Goldie guffawed, then led her over to the bar. They had a few more rounds, and the crowd grew wilder. Several fights had broken out, and from the screams, lewd comments, and whistles coming from inside, Hailey concluded that some of the women were making good use of the stripper pole.

"You want to find a spot and have some fun?" he asked.

"Out here? I mean, in front of all these people?" The idea of it aroused her, but actually doing it was another thing.

"No one's looking. They're all bombed off their asses."

"Plenty of people are watching us. I'm surprised so many are. Don't you live at the club? Let's go to your room." She ran her fingers over his bare arms. "I do want to have fun with you, just not in front of everyone."

"That's cool. I just thought you wanted the full adventure. We can go to my room." He grabbed her hand and placed it on his crotch. His hardness strained against his jeans. "Feel what you do to me, babe. It's like you got this fucker trained."

Giggling, she pressed her palm against his erection. "I can't wait to feel this inside my mouth and then inside me." She licked his lips.

"Fuck, woman. Let's go."

With a hard pull, he was dragging her past the multitude of men and women engaging in all variations of sex. They blitzed by the people in the main room, and the two women fondling each other on the stripper pole blurred past her. In the stairwell, he abruptly stopped, and she slammed into him.

"What's wro—"

His mouth consumed her question as he kissed her hungrily, his hands slipping under her skirt. That time, he pushed her legs open a bit with his knee, then swiped his finger over her damp sex. "So good, woman," he said against her lips as he slipped his finger inside, moving it in and out slowly. Moaning, she gripped his shoulders to balance herself on the stairs.

"Can you guys move over a bit? I gotta get something in my room," Sangre said as his heavy footsteps clumped behind her.

Goldie pulled away and grabbed her hand. "We're going up too." He pulled her to the top of the stairs and down to a room. Opening the door, he shoved her in, then kicked it shut. With his mouth on her neck, his hand squeezing her tit, he pushed her toward the bed. Clutching his hair, she pulled at it until her mouth found his. Her tongue pushed against his teeth, coaxing him to let her in. When he opened his mouth, their tongues twisted together as she pressed closer to him, grinding against his hardness.

"Fuck, woman. You need it real bad, don't you? It's fuckin' hot," he whispered against her lips.

"I want you. It's that simple," she breathed.

Shoving her on the bed, he went down with her, his lips still glued to hers. "I want to undress you. Then I'm gonna play with your sweet pussy and your ass."

Sliding out from under him, she swiveled around and pushed him down on the bed. "I want to undress you first. I want to see your hard cock." She threw him a sultry look.

"I fuckin' love it when you talk dirty," he rasped as he grabbed her top. "Take this off. I wanna see your beautiful tits."

Lying on top of him, she slowly rubbed her body down to his feet, then pulled off his boots and socks and yanked her top over her head. Lust filled his eyes as they feasted on her breasts filling a lacy bra. Tracing the contours of her lip with the tip of her tongue, she shimmied out of her skirt, kicked off her sandals, and climbed back onto the bed. Bending down, her hair spilled around him as she ran her mouth over his denim-clad bulge.

"You like that?" she said as she slowly unzipped his jeans. His hardness popped out and smacked her in the face. She giggled and tugged his jeans off, then unhooked her bra. Her tits bounced out, and he sucked in his breath. Gliding her hands under his T-shirt, she flicked his nipples with her fingernail, then shoved his shirt up and licked and sucked them.

"Fuck, woman, that feels good. Rub your tits against my skin," he said huskily. He grabbed her breasts and fondled them, pulling the nipples.

Moaning, she pushed his hand away and stroked her hard beads across his firm chest. His cock pressing against the small fabric covering her aching mound, she gripped it and squeezed the base.

After shucking his T-shirt, he pushed her head toward his pulsing dick. "Suck me," he ordered.

Smiling at him, she opened her mouth and slowly took him in, her gaze locked on his. Catching her hair, he yanked it. "You look so fuckin' sexy with my cock in your mouth."

As she pleasured him, she slid her hand down and pressed it against her throbbing clit, loving the way he groaned as she picked up her speed. Soon he yanked her head up.

"Why're you stopping me?"

"You're gonna make me blow and I don't want to just yet. I want to play with you and suck your sweet pussy. Get up here," he said as he gripped her wrists and jerked her up. Kneading her tits, he played with her nipples as she threw her head back and arched forward.

"I love the way you touch my boobs. You make me feel things I've never felt."

"I love your tits. I could suck on them all night."

Reaching behind her, she grasped his shaft and ran her thumb over its smooth head, then put her thumb between her lips and sucked off his precome. "Mmmm… salty with a tang. Reminds me of the ocean." The way he stared at her made her insides quiver, and she bent down and kissed him passionately.

Hooking his fingers on each side of her thong, he pushed it down. She wriggled out of it and tossed it on the floor.

"Open your pussy up for me." He pinched her nipples and she yelped, opening for him. "So pink and glistening. You're sopping wet and aching for my touch."

She moaned in answer.

"Get closer and feed me."

A surge of heat flushed through her; Goldie always pushed her to do new things. She'd never had a guy lick her the way he did, and now he wanted her to straddle him and put her wet-as-hell sex on his mouth. At the height of her arousal, she planted her knees on each side of him and lowered her swollen lips to his mouth. With his fingers digging into her hips, he pulled her down more, and then he kissed her engorged folds with open lips and protruding tongue. Excitement coursed through her as his fervent kisses and gentle nips drove her mad with desire. The sounds of her guttural moans and his sucking filled the room as his tongue explored.

"I love the sounds you make when I'm eating you," he said, the vibration of his lips driving her arousal even higher.

"And I love what you're doing to me right now. It feels so good."

"You taste so good." His fingers stretched her puffy lips even further as he sucked her clit. She arched into his face, losing herself in the moment and the flood of sensations scorching her body.

Then he pushed two fingers into her wetness and she gasped; they were cool in her tight heat as he shoved them higher inside her. Looking down, seeing his tongue lap her sensitive folds while his fingers pushed in, curled forward, and touched her sweet spot pushed her over the edge. Spasms and a million sparks exploded within her, and she was lost in a haze of sexual fireworks.

Flushed and panting, she rested her forehead against the wall as she started to come down from her orgasmic high.

"I love the way you look when you come," Goldie said as he gripped her waist and rolled her onto her back. Stroking the hair away from her eyes, he peppered her face and throat with small kisses as she lay beside him.

Hailey put her arm around his neck and pulled him down. "I'm crazy about you," she whispered in his ear. The glow of her orgasm still resonated within her, and she wanted to tell him that she loved him because she did. She wanted to shout it to him, to the partygoers one floor below them, and to the world. Ever since she could remember, she'd been crazy about him, but she kept denying it. Now she welcomed it, but she was afraid to tell him. She wasn't sure how he felt beyond the good times and comfort in shared memories. Her biggest fear was that he'd run away from her, and she wouldn't be able to deal with losing him. Not after she'd finally found him.

"I'm crazy about you too. You do shit to me that I don't understand but I like." Smoothing out the line in her forehead, he said, "What're you thinking about? Don't tell me nothing because that line on your forehead always gives you away when you're overthinking something."

"Just thinking how you need some pleasing." Throwing him a wicked smile, she rubbed his semi-hard dick. "Just relax. Now it's my turn to taste you."

For the next hour, they took turns pleasuring each other until they both lay sated and spent. They didn't talk, just held each other tightly, enjoying being together. After several minutes, Goldie's deep breathing washed over her. After kissing his neck, her eyes slowly sealed shut as she drifted off to sleep.

Chapter Thirty

T HE KILLER WATCHED the gray-haired woman as her eyes pleaded with him, her arms and legs secured to the bedposts. *She's probably thinking about her grandkids and wondering if she'll ever see them again.* The several times he'd broken into her house when she'd gone to her book club, he'd seen the framed pictures of her grandchildren on the top of the piano in the living room. Hanging on the wall, in a large gold picture frame, was an old black-and-white photograph of a younger version of her and a young man in uniform on their wedding day. He'd stare at the picture each time he broke in; it reminded him of his grandparents' wedding photograph.

A small whimper brought him back to the bedroom and his victim. When he'd awakened her, she hadn't yelled. It was funny how some women wouldn't say anything; they'd just do as he said, hoping it would end soon. The look of regret, desperation, and terror was the same in all the women he'd attacked, but whether they spoke to him or not, or screamed out, was always different. The fear was predictable but the reaction was not.

Placing the knife flat on her breasts, he ran it across the tops of them as she whimpered like a wounded dog. Watching sadness and terror sink into the lines of her face, his pants grew tighter and his arousal began to escalate.

"I saw your wedding picture on the wall. You were a pretty lady. Your husband was lucky." He continued to caress her skin with the knife and smiled when he saw two tears slip out of the corner of her eyes. "Are you scared, pretty lady?" When she nodded, a rush of desire flooded him, and he placed the knife on the nightstand.

Bending down low, he whispered in her ear. "I'm going to fuck every hole you have, and I'm not going to be gentle. I bet your husband was, but I'm a bastard. But first I'm going to bite your tits real hard. After that, it's up to you to guess what I'm going to do." He pulled back and grabbed her underpants. Balling them in his fist, he commanded her to open her mouth, then stuffed them inside. He knew what he was going to do to her would be painful, and he wanted to make sure no one would hear her cries. And she *would* scream out. It would be instinct.

With narrowed eyes, he lowered his head and sucked one of her nipples. His tongue flicked and played with it until he bit down hard. Very hard. Eyes on hers, he kept biting as he pulled and twisted her other nipple. Her muffled screams, streaking tears, and horror-filled eyes pushed his brutality further until he was hard as granite. Heavy panting, gagged yells, and her body thrashing against the sheets pierced the stillness of the quiet neighborhood.

After several hours, her abused body lay still on the saturated bed sheet. He straightened up and swatted her ass. "Get up," he ordered.

She groaned as she pushed off the mattress, and he grabbed her roughly and took her into the en suite bathroom. A yellow toothbrush rested on the shelf in the medicine cabinet.

"Here. Brush your teeth, tongue, sides, and roof of your mouth. Now." He glanced out the window. The blackness in the east was beginning to fade; he needed to be finished and out of the house before the sun rose. He'd been so worked up that night, he'd taken much longer with her than he'd intended.

When she handed the toothbrush back to him, he shoved it in his pocket and pushed her toward the shower. Checking the water, he made sure it was warm before he shoved her in. He watched as she scrubbed her body. Some of his women scrubbed themselves raw, as if trying to wash away what had happened, and others did a crappy-ass job and he'd have to help them out. This one was scrubbing hard—he wouldn't have to get wet.

After she patted herself dry, he took the towel and shoved it into a plastic bag, then told her to go back into the bedroom. He collected all evidence that may have any of his DNA, then stared at her. The rush of exhilaration that normally surged through him as he prepared to leave was missing. That rush was what he craved and needed until the monster resurfaced and he went hunting again.

Slipping the knife out of his pocket, he came up behind her and yanked her head back, forcing her to look at him.

"You promised you wouldn't kill me. You told me if I did everything you said, you'd leave. I did everything you said." Her voice hitched before soft sobs filled the air around him.

Without a word, he sliced her throat, then let her drop to the floor with a thud. Gasping breaths and gargling blood through her severed windpipe were the only sounds in the room as he watched blood squirt out of her carotid artery while she lost consciousness.

As he left the room, he laughed out loud. *Someone's going to have a real mess to clean up.*

On his way home, his body was still vibrating from the high he'd had when he'd cut her throat. In that one swipe, all the tension, all the pressure, had just vanished, dissipated. He was on top of the world. He switched on the radio and sang along loudly.

Pulling into his garage, he decided to hold on to his euphoria for as long as he could until the monster came back and overtook him.

Humming, he opened the back door and went inside.

Chapter Thirty-One

THE STAIRS GROANED as Detective Barnard and Sheriff Wexler slowly walked up to Joyce Gillen's bedroom. A couple of deputies stepped aside as the two men walked into the room. The lifeless body of the seventy-five-year-old victim was on top of a red-stained carpet. The gap in her throat told Barnard that her death had been quick. Running his hand through his short hair, he bent down and shook his head: her right nipple looked as though it'd been chewed off, and her body was covered in bruises.

"The fucking bastard has escalated his violence. I was afraid this was going to happen," he said to Wexler, who'd turned away.

"I knew Joyce. She was a great lady. My grandkids and hers are friends. Shit, I can't believe she died like this. Such an upstanding woman. She'd do anything to help someone out. We gotta find this fucker." His voice shook with anger.

Barnard straightened up, then put a hand on Wexler's shoulder briefly. "We have a monster on our hands and no solid clues. If only we could get a damn break."

The CSI team from Durango came into the room then, ready to begin their systematic search for any incriminating evidence. Barnard went up to the supervisor, Carlos Torres. He'd worked with Carlos on many rapes and homicide cases in the past; he knew if the sick bastard left any evidence, Carlos and his team would find it.

"I hope we get something," he said.

Carlos nodded. "We'll work the scene hard. What kind of a sick person is he?"

"Who the hell knows. I just want to find him before he does this again. To think she went through the ups and downs of life, raised her kids, helped out with the grandkids, and survived the heartache of losing her husband only to end up on the floor, naked, raped, and killed. There's no fucking rhyme or reason in this goddamn universe."

"Seems that way in our line of work. I'll let you know if I find anything," Carlos said.

"Thanks," Jack replied as he walked out of the room.

He found Wexler talking to a middle-aged man in the living room. A woman in her early fifties sat on the couch, wiping her nose and cheeks as her gaze fixed on the sheriff. The detective went over to Wexler and the man.

"It looked to be a dark SUV, parked across the street and several houses down. I didn't get a license number, but when it passed, I noticed a shiny hood ornament. The way the streetlight hit it, I could see it pretty well. It was an American eagle. The wings were spread wide. I've seen a lot of cars around here that have the same ornament."

"Did you see who was driving the vehicle?" Wexler asked.

The man shook his head. "I didn't get a good look at him. It looked like he had a hood or something over his face."

"Like a ski mask?" Barnard interjected.

The guy nodded. "Yes! It was a ski mask. I didn't really see anything else. I was captivated by the hood ornament. I guess I should've paid more attention, but it was dark. There was some light in the sky, but it was still too dark to make out anything more."

As the sheriff talked to the witness, Barnard went over to the woman on the couch. "I'm Detective Barnard." He extended his hand.

The woman placed her hands in her lap. "Jeannie Bennell. My mom is… was Joyce Gillen." She placed her fingers on her trembling lips.

"I'm very sorry for your loss. I'll do everything I can to apprehend the person responsible for your mother's murder. Did she have any strange incidents that she mentioned to you? Like in the past few weeks or even months?"

Shaking her head, she stared at the floor. "No. She never mentioned anything. If something were amiss or if she was worried about anything, she would've told me or my brother. This is just so terrible. Why would anyone want to hurt my mom?"

"That's what I'm going to find out."

After several hours at the crime scene, Barnard walked out into the bright sunshine. It was always surreal for him to leave a brutal crime scene and enter back into the ordinariness of life. It seemed as if there should be something different to mark the passing of a life, but there never was. Trees swayed in the breeze, birds chirped, and butterflies flitted around in the garden in front of the house.

Wexler came out, his jaw tight, his eyes narrowed; a couple of his deputies followed him. Silent with slumped shoulders, Barnard followed them to the patrol car as the body of Joyce Gillen, bagged and on a gurney, trailed behind.

Chapter Thirty-Two

T HE SMILING FACE of Joyce Gillen graced the front page of the *Alina Post*, mesmerizing Goldie. The woman looked very familiar, and he racked his brain trying to figure out where he'd seen her before. As he perused the article, he read that the charity she'd done a lot of volunteer work for was the same one his grandmother had devoted so much time to after he and his siblings were grown and out of the house.

"What's going on?" Eagle asked as he sat down by Goldie, a coffee cup in his hand.

"I knew this woman." Goldie tapped Joyce's picture.

Eagle took the paper. "Fuck. That sucks what happened to her. How did you know her?"

"She worked on a lot of committees my grandma did for Volunteers Helping Native Americans. I remember bumping into her at some of the fundraising events."

"When did the fuckin' psycho go from raping to murder?" Eagle put the paper down.

"He offed another victim before this one. She worked at the rehab center. Now the fucker's got the taste for blood."

Eagle nodded. "When you take that plunge, there's no going back. They get some rush out of it. It's pretty sick."

Goldie nodded as he took out his phone. He wanted to make sure Hailey was safe.

Goldie: *Hey. U good?*

Hailey: *Ya. Good 2 hear from u so early in the am.* ☺

Goldie: *Thinking bout u. Want 2 make sure ur safe.*

Hailey: *Safe n sound. Something came up. I'm going 2 Albuquerque.*

Goldie jerked back. "What the fuck?" he muttered.

"Bad news?" Eagle asked as he stared at the TV.

"No. Just something I need more info on."

Goldie: *WTF?*

Hailey: *My best friend's having a bday party. Wants me 2 come. Miss my parents, so can see both at the same time. Win-win.*

Goldie: *I don't wanna talk bout this by text. I'll pick u up @ 7:30 for dinner.*

Hailey: *Sounds good.*

Goldie: *Remember 2 text when u leave shop. Ruger will watch out 4 u tonite.*

Hailey: *K. Gotta go. Shop is crazy today.*

"I'm outta here," Goldie said to Eagle.

"Are you going to the ink shop?"

"Not yet. My bike's making a funny noise, so I'm headed to Skid Marks to see what's up. What're you doing?"

"I was going to check out one of the new dancers at Lust, but I think I'll head over to Skid Marks to see what's going on with your bike."

"You're passing up a new stripper?" Goldie chuckled.

"I can see a stripper any day, but I wanna see what's up with your bike and what Diablo and Shotgun can do. Anytime we can learn something about our Harleys takes precedence over everything."

"Damn straight," Goldie said as he walked out to the parking lot.

The familiar scent of motor oil filled their nostrils while cool air encased them when they entered Skid Marks. Diablo sat on the stool behind the counter, a scowl on his face. When he saw Goldie and Eagle, he lifted his chin.

"It's fuckin' hot out there," Goldie said as he went behind the counter and pulled out a cold bottle of water. He tossed one to Eagle.

"You guys bored or have a bike problem?" Diablo asked.

"My bike's making a funny noise. I'm not sure what's up with it. I wanted you or Shotgun to check it out."

Shotgun came out of a small office, wiping his grease-stained hands with a rag. "Your new Harley's acting up? What the fuck's up with that?"

"I dunno, bro. I just noticed the noise last night. I want to check it out."

Throwing the rag in a bin, Shotgun said, "Let's go out and take a listen."

The four of them stood out in the blazing heat and listened to the engine. "Sounds like something in the valve train," Diablo said.

"I totally agree. It doesn't sound bad. I'll have Cal check it out and see if he can fix it now or if you'll have to leave your bike," Shotgun said.

"I was hoping you or Diablo could fix it. Is Cal good?" Goldie ran his hand over his bike's leather seat.

Shotgun quirked his lips. "Yeah. You think I'd hire a shitty mechanic to work here?"

"He's just nervous. I get it," Eagle added.

"We all fuckin' get it, but Cal definitely knows his way around bikes and cars," Shotgun replied.

"Drive it around back. I'll meet you there," Diablo said.

Soon the four brothers were inside the shop and talking about bikes while Cal made the necessary repairs to Goldie's Harley. They reminisced about past antics at various runs and rallies, and Eagle busted out laughing.

"What's so funny, bro?" Diablo asked.

"I was just thinking 'bout Army and all the women he fucks. Each rally he's got his dick in new pussy," Eagle answered.

"Correction—pussies," Goldie said, and the others laughed.

"Did you hear how he fucked up and met up with three women at the same place?" Eagle said.

"No shit. I didn't hear that one," Goldie said.

Diablo shook his head. "Me neither, but it sounds like something he'd do."

"The chicks were all pissed off, and he ended up fucking one of the club women." Eagle laughed harder.

"He better juggle his bitches better, 'cause one day he's gonna meet the wrong woman and she's gonna chop his cock right off," Shotgun said.

Diablo sniggered. "Army just needs to meet the right woman. Once that happens, he'll settle his ass down."

"Not sure he's gonna meet his ideal woman unless she's a nymphomaniac who owns a liquor store and has a brother who works at a Harley dealership," Goldie said.

The brothers guffawed, but when Wexler and a man in a crumpled suit walked in, they all went stone-faced. Wexler went up to the bikers right away, but the man with him paused and mopped his face with a handkerchief before approaching.

"A couple of the department's bikes need a tune-up and an oil change," the sheriff said. Shotgun nodded and pulled out a service slip. "It's a scorcher today. Are you getting ready for the bike rally? You're having it over at Helmstad's place, aren't you?"

"Is that all you're gonna need?" Shotgun asked as he wrote some things on the service form while the other brothers remained stoic and silent.

Wexler nodded, and then the man, who was sweating profusely, said, "Have you sold an American eagle hood ornament for a dark-colored SUV, maybe burgundy or brown?"

"Why the fuck are you asking?" Diablo said.

"And who the hell are you?" Goldie added.

Wexler cleared his throat. "This is Jack Barnard. He's helping out with an investigation in our town."

"I'm a detective with the Durango police. We received some information we're just following up on."

The brothers just stared at him; they didn't give information to badges. Ever.

Shotgun shook his head. "I don't recall selling any American eagles. We don't really carry them."

"That's funny because the bottom shelf behind you has two American eagle ornaments. I've also seen several around town, and people tell me they bought it at this store," Jack said.

"All we want to know is who you sold them to and the dates. We're not asking for anything more."

They didn't say anything.

Jack pounded his fist on the counter. "Fuck! The bastard who raped and murdered the older woman on the front page of the paper had an American eagle hood ornament. Chances are high he got it at this shop. We just need to know who you've sold them to."

"That ornament is common as hell and all shops carry it. It can be bought online. There's nothing sayin' we sold it to the killer," Diablo said.

"I'm not saying you did, and even if you did, you had no way of knowing who he was. I'm just trying to cover all the bases. I want to catch this fucking bastard and put him away for life. If any of you have sisters, mothers, girlfriends, wives, or know and care about any woman, I'd think you'd want this sick bastard caught."

Hailey flashed through Goldie's mind, as did the man who'd scared her. The muscle in his jaw twitched. *I'll be on the lookout for the eagle. And if the fucker bought it from us, I'll tear him apart.* Their lifestyle dictated that he and his brothers would take care of business in their own way. And in their world, a person was guilty until they thought he was innocent.

Wexler fixed his gaze on each of the brothers and a tacit agreement passed between them. Smiling weakly, he turned to Jack. "Let's get out of here. We've got work to do."

"We'll be back with a subpoena for those records," Barnard said.

"Do what you need to do," Shotgun said. "When do you need the bikes back by?"

The sheriff spun around. "In a couple of days. Does that work?"

Shotgun nodded. "Works fine. I'll call you."

"Sounds good. And thanks."

When the two cops drove off, Goldie leaned against the counter. "Check to see if this fuckin' asshole bought the hood ornament here."

"Yeah. We'll take care of him," Diablo growled.

"The fucker's gonna find out what a fucked-up pussy he is when we get through with him," Eagle said.

"It's gonna take time to go through all the records 'cause we sell a shitload of those eagles in the store and online. I'd bet money he got it at our store. It'll take some time, but I'll find the bastard."

"You better talk to Steel about having Chains dummy up the records. There's no way that Durango badge isn't coming back with a damn subpoena," Goldie said.

"I'm gonna call him now." Shotgun went into the small office and closed the door.

"Bike's ready," Cal said as he walked into the store. "Did you want me to pull around in front, or do you want to pick it up in the back?"

"Was it in the valve train?" Diablo asked.

"Yep, but it wasn't anything major."

"I'll get it out back," Goldie said to Cal. Bumping fists with Diablo and Eagle, he left the shop and retrieved his bike. He had a few appointments at the ink shop, and then he'd pick Hailey up for dinner. *I can't wait to see her. I'm so damn into her. I don't like that she's going to Albuquerque by herself.* He'd talk to her about it that night at dinner.

As he rode to Get Inked, he checked out all the ornaments he saw on all vehicles. Most new cars didn't have hood ornaments, so he figured it couldn't be too hard to track down the fucker. He'd find him, and when he did, he'd rip him from limb to limb.

"I DON'T LIKE you driving to Albuquerque by yourself," Goldie said as he cut his porterhouse steak.

"I'm a big girl. I've driven that route hundreds of times. The drive is a little more than three hours. It's no big deal."

"Yeah, well, we weren't hanging when you were doing all that damn driving. I'll pay for an airline ticket for you."

She laughed. "By the time I wait through the long lines at security, transfer in Denver, and land in Albuquerque, it'll be six hours if I'm lucky. I'll be fine. Don't obsess over this." She brought the glass of white wine to her lips.

"You need to call or text me while you're on the road and when you get to your parents'."

Hailey saluted him. "Yes, sir."

Goldie scowled. "I'm not fuckin' around here. Shit happens when you think it won't."

Taking his hand, she kissed it, tenderness shimmering in her gaze. "I know, and I think it's sweet that you're concerned for me. I know the biker lifestyle isn't all roses and puppy dogs so I do understand your apprehension. I guess I don't think that there's danger lurking around every corner like you do. We just have different mindsets."

Leaning over the table, he drew her to meet him halfway, then kissed her. With his forehead pressed against hers, he whispered, "I don't want anything to happen to you. A person's obliviousness to danger is what sick fuckers use to hurt them. I'm always aware that danger is just under the surface and may strike at any time. I'm always on guard. I'm just asking you to be super careful and keep in touch with me." He brushed his lips across hers.

"I promise," she whispered back.

"How long are you going to be gone?" He pulled away and resumed cutting his steak.

"Only four nights. I'll be back Monday morning."

"Are there gonna be guys at this birthday party?"

"I don't think so. It's more of a girls' night out thing, and we're going to have a cake and presents."

I hate all her fuckin' girls' night out shit. Just thinking of a guy hitting on her makes my blood boil. "Is it at your friend's house?" Hailey shook her head, then glanced out the window. *She doesn't want to tell me. I don't want her to be afraid to tell me shit.* "I'm not gonna freak out, babe. Just tell me where it's at."

"A club."

"Why didn't you want me to know that?"

She shrugged. "I just thought you'd be mad, although we never discussed not dancing with other people."

The vein in his temple twitched as he tensed. "What the fuck does that mean?"

Blinking rapidly, she took a big gulp of water. "Nothing, really."

"Then why the fuck did you say it? Do you wanna dance with other guys?"

"No. It's just that I'm not sure if you'd be mad if I did."

"I'd be fuckin' pissed if you danced with a guy and he had his hands all over your body. Do I really have to tell you that? I haven't looked at another woman since we've been hanging out."

"I'm sorry. I definitely don't want to dance with anyone but you. It's just that I'm confused as to what we are."

"We're two people who enjoy being together and are having a helluva good time. You mean something to me, Hailey. I don't hang with a chick more than a couple days."

"I'm just being silly. Forget what I said. I love hanging with you, and as long as we're together, we'll be exclusive, okay?"

"I've been exclusive. I don't need an agreement for that, but it seems like you do. So yeah, I'm just with you."

"And I'm just with you, so I won't be dancing with anyone at the club but my friends."

Goldie nodded and a silence settled between them. *I know she wants to pin me down on every aspect of our relationship. Fuck. I can't believe I'm even in a relationship.*

"Are we good?" she asked, breaking the silence.

"Yeah."

"You're not mad at me?"

"Nah."

When the slice of strawberry cheesecake came, Goldie scooped up some of the whipped cream with his finger and placed it in her eager mouth. Mesmerized by the desire in her eyes as she sucked on his finger, he slowly moved it in and out. Low moans and her tongue swirling around his digit drove him crazy.

"You keep doing that and you're gonna get yourself fucked."

"Maybe that's what I want," she rasped.

Then her bare foot pressed hard on his bulge and excitement rushed full force into it, making it feel tight and full. When her toes wiggled against his hardness, a frantic desire for it to be absorbed into her heated wetness consumed him.

"Does that feel good?"

"It feels like my cock wants to rip out of my jeans and be crammed into your tight pussy." He put his hand on her foot. "Let's get out of here," he said huskily.

The ride back to her house was miserable, his erection aching to be freed. When they came into the house, he chased her up the stairs and, after catching her, threw her on the bed. Discarding both their clothes in record time, they were all over each other, kissing, biting, scratching, smacking, and licking. He loved how she moaned when he spanked her ass cheeks, and the deep scratches and bites she'd given him turned him way on. He liked that she wanted to mark and claim. Running his hands over her skin, he noticed she was hot to the touch with primal need. Begging him to enter her, she grabbed his hard dick and rubbed it between her juicy folds. The head of his cock was sensitive and tingling, and he wasn't able to hold out any longer. Pushing it against her wet slit, he plunged inside her, grunting as the muscles of her walls hugged him tightly.

As he pummeled her, she thrashed and moaned, and their primal desire pushed them harder and higher until it overwhelmed and consumed them, ending in a shared burst of euphoria.

Breathing heavily, he pulled her close. She snuggled into him and they lay holding each other, their breathing filling the room until sleep took them.

Chapter Thirty-Three

PARKED SEVERAL HOUSES down from the Victorian, he saw the biker place Hailey's small suitcase in the trunk of her car. A surge of energy bolted through him as he realized how fortunate he was to have come by that morning to watch her. He almost hadn't due to his job, but he'd made up an excuse and switched his shift, and now he had the whole morning free. Free to follow Hailey and find an opportunity to finally claim and devour her. He'd been waiting too long to capture his prey.

The man's gut twisted when she looped her arms around the biker and kissed him. Watching his hands run down her back and land on the ass he'd hoped to ravage in about an hour's time made him sick. What did she see in him? Hailey was much too pretty and sophisticated to waste her body on a dirty biker whose name escaped him.

The man chuckled. *The lowlife is so inconsequential that I don't even remember his name.* For the past six weeks, he'd seen the outlaw's motorcycle in the rehab's parking lot at the same time as Hailey's car, and every time he noticed it, he'd wanted to take a razor blade to the Harley and scratch it up. But he didn't dare. Acting out of impulse was sloppy and stupid, and could only lead to getting caught.

He smiled when Hailey waved goodbye to the biker. The thrill of the hunt and the image of what he'd do to Hailey had his senses and arousal on overdrive. He knew she'd planned a trip to Albuquerque; he'd overheard her tell her aunt when he walked past the room. That stretch of highway was usually pretty quiet, and he knew she'd have to stop for gas. That's when he'd make his move. The excitement tingled and flushed his skin, and he willed himself to calm down.

Forty-five minutes into the drive, his phone went off for the fourth time. Again it was from his wife. Tempted to ignore it like he had the last three times, he reluctantly answered.

"Why haven't you picked up my calls?" Trisha asked. Panic laced her voice.

"I didn't hear them. What's wrong?" He smiled when he saw Hailey veer off the highway, taking the exit for gas and restaurants.

"Kyle's in the hospital! He was eating and then just started screaming. I freaked out. I didn't know what was wrong with him. I called 911. He's in the emergency room. I need you to be here."

He pulled into the gas station and parked at a distance. *She looks so sexy in her shorts.*

"Are you listening to me?"

"Uh… yeah. You said Kyle's in the hospital. Do they know what's wrong with him?"

"Not yet. He's getting X-rays. I need you here. I don't want any bullshit excuses either. I don't want to hear about having to go to work. Our son is sick! You need to get here fast. I can't do this alone."

A flash of his hands around Trisha's neck ran across his mind. *Shut the fuck up, bitch!* Hailey went inside the convenience store as the nozzle pumped gas into her car. *This is my chance to get inside her car. This is the opportunity I've been waiting for. I'm so close that—*

"When will you be at St. Joseph's Hospital?" Trisha's voice buzzed in his ear, annoying him like a swarm of gnats.

Then he watched Hailey place the nozzle in its holder and go inside the car. In a few seconds, she pulled out of the station and drove in the direction of the highway ramp. His eyes focused on her car until it disappeared.

"Soon. I'm on my way," he gritted. He hung up before Trisha could answer, then pounded his hands on the steering wheel and the dashboard over and over in an attempt to disperse his built-up excitement and now anger.

Turning left out of the parking lot, he made his way to the ramp that would take him back to Alina. Hailey had alluded him yet again, and his determination to have her grew to a dangerous obsession.

I will have you, bitch. All of you. And I'm going to take all the time in the world to enjoy you. You fucking owe me!

Chapter Thirty-Four

GOLDIE LOOKED AT Hailey's text for the umpteenth time while Sangre went over the club's treasury reports. As he scrolled through a series of pictures of her taking off a sexy-as-hell purple bra, he shifted in his seat. *She knows how to push my buttons.* The final picture was her glossy puckered lips with the words "Miss U" captioned under it.

It'd only been two days since she'd left, but he missed her like crazy. Some of the brothers ribbed him about it, and he got into a couple of fistfights over it, but at the end of the day, he still missed her like hell. The feeling was new for him, but he was getting used to feeling a lot of things he never had before. Hailey was definitely someone very important in his life.

"Chains, did you fix the records at Skid Marks?" Steel asked.

Goldie diverted his attention back to the meeting.

"Yep. When the badges come by with their subpoena, it'll show only a few of the American eagle ornaments have been sold."

"We don't need to worry 'bout that now. For the past few days, I've been going through all the online and in-store purchases until I couldn't see shit anymore. There're a lot of fuckin' cars out there sporting our ornament," Shotgun said while the members chortled.

"Did you find out if the fucker bought it through us?" Goldie asked.

"He didn't. I wish to hell he had, because then we would've taken care of business, but he didn't. Me and Diablo already checked out the SUVs who bought from us in Alina and the county. He's not among them."

"How do you know?" Paco asked.

"The color of the SUVs didn't match, or if it did, the ones driving it or had access to it didn't match. We looked at a bunch of shit and ruled everyone out. Maybe he's in Durango or somewhere else. A lot of the online sales came from all over, but I doubt the fucker's commuting." More snickers.

"He knows the area too well. He's either from here or lived here for a while," Goldie said.

"Damn! I wish we could've nailed him. When Shotgun first told me about it, I thought for sure we had this fucker. Disappointing as hell." Steel crossed his arms.

"Most of the people who bought the eagle from the store were older, like in their sixties and seventies," Diablo said.

"I'm pretty sure this fuck's younger," Muerto replied.

"Let's pay attention to what we see on the streets. Also, if an SUV comes in for repairs with the eagle, check it out. Now, let's go on to some other business. The arms deal went down without a hitch, and Roughneck is pleased as shit. It should help him out with the punk gang that's been making too much noise in Silverado. And it seems like everything's set for the rally. I asked Banger if he wouldn't mind if Rock and Jax helped Diablo with the security. He agreed, and Roughneck said Brick would be willing to help too."

"I already talked with them and we're all ready to go," Diablo said.

After another half hour of club business discussions, the gavel signaled church was over. Goldie tucked his phone in his pocket, deciding to take another look at Hailey's bra-teasing photos when he was in his room and could relieve the ache they gave him.

"You going over to Cuervos?" Brutus asked.

"We got a group going?" Goldie said.

"Yeah. You in?"

Goldie nodded. It was just what he needed for a Saturday night. If he stayed in, he'd probably imagine all kinds of shit about Hailey in the club. It wasn't that he didn't trust her; he didn't trust other men.

When Brutus, Skull, and Goldie arrived at Cuervos, Steel, Muerto, Army, Diablo, and Eagle were already there, drinking beer and wolfing down baskets of spicy wings. Jorge ran over and pushed another table together, and they sat down.

Eagle laughed and elbowed Goldie. "Is Vampirella stalking you?"

Goldie looked behind him and saw her staring, the Jagged Ace from Rear End next to her giving him a hard glare.

"Fuckin' pathetic," Goldie said as he picked up his beer.

"What?" Diablo asked.

"The Jagged Aces need to clean up their club. They got some real pussies in it." Goldie put four wings on his plate.

"And they need to screen the bitches who hang with them," Eagle added.

"You talking 'bout Dog? He's cool," Diablo said as he craned his neck.

"No. Talking about that fucker at the bar with the queen of the undead," Goldie replied. Several members sniggered and looked toward the bar.

"I don't know him," Diablo said, turning back to his food.

"That's Rusty. He and a few of the other members have become a real pain in the ass in the club. Dog's thinking of throwing their asses out." Steel motioned for the waitress.

"The sooner the better. That asshole doesn't deserve any patch. If he keeps up with the looks, I'm gonna have to beat his ass." Goldie rose from his chair.

"More wings?" Jill asked as she came over to the table.

Steel nodded. "Yeah, and bring four macho nachos. What's the chick's name with Rusty?"

"I can't fuckin' remember," Goldie answered.

"And you didn't have nightmares?" Muerto joked.

"When I hooked up with her, she looked alive. I'm gonna straighten out that sonofabitch she's with." As he made his way through the crowd, he saw Rusty grab Vampirella's hand and bolt out the door. "Fuckin' pansy-ass," Goldie muttered. Returning to the table with a beer in each hand, he sank into the chair.

"Did you beat his ass already?" Diablo asked between chews.

"The pussy took off. Good thing too." Goldie scooped up a bunch of chips. As he munched on his food, he watched various men trying to pick up different women, and his mind went to Hailey. He took out his phone.

Goldie: *U better not be having 2 much fun.*

Immediately his phone pinged.

Hailey: *How can I be when ur not here?*

Goldie: *I miss u.*

Hailey: *Me 2. What r u doing?*

Goldie: *Hanging with my brothers @ Cuervos.*

Hailey: *U being good?*

Goldie: *Ya. U?*

Hailey: *Yes. Always good 4 u. ;)*

Goldie: *I can't stop looking @ the bra pics u sent me. Want to suck ur tits real bad.*

Hailey: *U know I'm still sore from a few nights ago. Deliciously sore.*

Shaking his head, he laughed out loud. *She's turning me on, just like that. Damn. She gets to me real good.*

Goldie: *Fuck, I wish u were here. I got a real itch for u.*

Hailey: *When I get back, I'll make up for lost time.*

Goldie: *Damn straight.*

Hailey: *My friends r trying 2 take my phone away. Better go.* ♥♥

He stared at the screen, wanting their conversation to go on until she came back. He missed falling asleep and waking up next to her. For someone who never spent the night with women, he didn't think he would miss her in his bed as much as he did.

Taking another gulp of beer, he focused his attention on the conversation at the table. He couldn't keep mooning over her. *I'm acting like a damn pussy.*

"I heard *Easyriders* contacted you to have your bike on the cover of their magazine," Army said.

"Yeah. I was blown away," Goldie said.

"Fuckin' awesome!" Muerto said.

"A rep from the magazine saw my bike at the rally in Laughlin. He was drooling over it. All the custom chrome and hand-painted zombie apocalypse stuff on the body gave him a hard-on. If it were a woman, he would've fucked her until the end of the rally."

The brothers guffawed, and the conversation settled on Harleys, Sturgis, and poker runs that netted the best money and women.

After a few hours of motorcycle talk, drinking, and playing pool, Goldie walked out with Army, Muerto, and Diablo. "What the fuck?" Goldie said as he scanned the lot. "Where the hell's my bike?"

"You lost your bike? I didn't think you were such a lightweight with booze," Army said.

"Maybe you parked it down the street," Muerto joked.

"I'm not that drunk. I know where the fuck I parked my bike."

Diablo dashed around the parking lot, alley, and the dirt lot down the block. "No sign of it," he said grimly.

"Someone with a death wish stole my bike."

"There's no way it was a citizen unless he was fucked in the head," Muerto said.

"I bet it's that Jagged Aces asshole. He's fuckin' dead!"

"Does he know your bike?" Army asked.

"Yeah. He was in front of Rear End when I left that night. That sonofabitch asshole!" Goldie kicked the metal trash can until it was full of dents. "Does anyone know where he hangs out? I'm pretty sure he didn't take my Harley to their clubhouse." He leaned against the concrete wall, breathing heavily.

The brothers shook their heads before Diablo offered, "I can find out from Dog. We're good with each other. We'll get your bike back."

The brothers stood on the pavement, fury etched in their faces, jaws clenched, and fists balled up, ready to smash their anger out of their systems. Stealing a Night Rebels' bike was the worst crime someone could commit. A Night Rebel protected his motorcycle as if it were part of his body. No one messed with his Harley.

Looking at Diablo, Goldie gritted, "Find out where that fucker hangs and let me know right away. I want my bike back, and I want the asshole to pay for what he did."

"I'll get the info. We're with you on this, bro," Diablo said as Muerto and Army nodded.

"Jump on back and I'll give you a ride," Army said.

The ride back to the clubhouse fueled Goldie's fire even more, so by the time he arrived he was a seething ball of fury. He grabbed a bottle of Jack and rushed up to his room. As he stared out into the darkness, the whiskey scorching his throat, a fear like he'd never felt grabbed hold of him. *What the hell?* A sinking feeling invaded him as a chill shrouded his body. A foreboding darkness crept into his veins, twisting around his nerves, and he was seized with an overwhelming urge to go see his grandma. Not one to ignore his gut, he jumped up and dashed down the stairs.

"Chains, my truck's in the shop so I need to borrow your SUV," he said while extending his hand. Without questioning him, Chains placed the keys into his opened palm. Goldie ran out of the club, headed to Cherry Vale.

When he arrived at the rehab center, it was quiet and all the lights in the rooms were off as it was nearly one thirty in the morning. Knowing the only way to come in through the front door after ten at night was to ring the bell, he went around back, not wanting to draw attention to himself. He tried a couple of doors but they were locked. Behind the kitchen, he spotted the glow of a joint and approached the smoker cautiously. Hendricks looked up.

"Hey, man. What're you doing here so late?" the CNA asked.

"I was in the neighborhood and thought I'd check up on my grandma. How's she been?"

"Good, I guess. I'm upstairs tonight." He pulled out a joint from his pocket. "Want one?"

Goldie shook his head. "I need for you to let me in. Something's wrong with the bell in front."

"Sure. Don't tell anyone you saw me smoking," Hendricks said as he pulled open the employees' entrance.

"No worries. Thanks, dude." Goldie went in, then quietly walked through the darkened kitchen and dining room. He cut through the lobby and looked down the hallways on either side. Nothing seemed amiss. Pressing his lips together, he went to his grandmother's room, stopping short in the doorway. Ice ran through his veins as the dark outline of a person looming over his grandmother came into focus. Goldie switched on the light and white brightness momentarily blinded him as fluorescent lights flooded the room.

The person, dressed in scrubs, turned around quickly, shock covering his face. In his right hand, he had a syringe.

"What the fuck are you giving my grandma?" Goldie demanded.

"Something to help her sleep better. Dr. Rudman ordered it," Dan said.

"You fuckin' liar! You're trying to inject some shit in her. You're fuckin' trying to kill her." Goldie rushed over to the nurse and slammed his fist into his stomach. Dan groaned and bent over, the syringe falling from his gloved hand. Goldie brought his knee up and slammed it against Dan's face. The crunch of bone and ping of teeth falling on linoleum gave Goldie a surge of satisfaction as he crashed his steel-toed boot into the nurse's groin.

A rush of footsteps sounded behind him and then hands clasped his shoulders, pulling him away from the crumpled man on the floor, enraging him. "Leave me alone. I'm gonna kill his fuckin' ass!"

"Goldie! Stop!" Shelly's voice broke through his fury-filled haze.

When he relaxed, Kingsley and Kevin pulled him farther away from Dan.

"What's going on here?" Shelly asked, her voice unnaturally high.

"I came in and this fucker was standing over my grandma, ready to inject some shit into her arm." He rushed over to Dan, who still lay on the floor, and kicked him hard in the ribs. A low grunt came from the battered man's parted lips.

"Goldie. Please, calm down." Shelly placed a hand on his shoulder and tugged him back. "I don't even know why Dan's here. He wasn't on the calendar for tonight."

Hendricks came in, redness rimming his off-focused eyes. "You came here to beat Dan, dude?"

Shelly sighed loudly. "Kevin, call the police. I'll call corporate."

Kevin rushed out of the room, his voice echoing in the hallway.

In less than ten minutes, blue and red flashing lights blinked through the curtains. Kingsley and Shelly left the room and spoke to Wexler, who stood in the hallway. Inaudible voices filled Goldie's ears, but the thought of his grandma almost dying at the hands of someone who was supposed to care for her stuffed his mind.

Wexler and Barnard walked into the small room. One of the deputies came in and helped Dan to his feet and gave him a handful of tissues; he put them to his nose.

"What the hell happened here, Goldie?" Wexler asked.

"This fucker tried to kill my grandma, and he would've succeeded if I hadn't caught him." He pointed to the syringe under the bed. "He was trying to put that shit in her arm."

Barnard went down on his knees, picked up the syringe, and bagged it. "Do you want to tell me what's in it?" he asked Dan.

"Medicine. I'm a nurse, and my job is to make sure the patients are comfortable. Dr. Rudman told me to give her some if she's restless. She was. Then this crazed biker attacked me. I want to press charges."

Goldie lunged at him, his arm pulled back, ready to punch him again. "You lying sack of shit. You're lucky the badges showed up."

The deputy and Wexler held him back. "We've got this, Goldie," the sheriff said.

Barnard turned to Shelly, who was standing in the doorway. "Do you know anything about the doctor ordering anything for this patient?"

She shook her head. "Dr. Rudman's never ordered any sleeping aid for Mrs. Humphries. I don't even know why Dan's here. We only have one night nurse on the first and second floors. I'm the first-floor nurse tonight, and Janet is working the second floor. He's supposed to be home with his wife and kids."

"Mr. Krutcher, you're under arrest for attempted murder," Barnard said as he placed the handcuffs on the nurse's wrists. "Anything you say may be used against you in a...."

Goldie stood by his grandmother's bed as they led Dan out of the building and to the waiting squad car. Kevin came back in with a mop and bucket and started cleaning up Dan's blood. Goldie glanced at Wexler, who nodded at him and then walked out of the room.

After the room was cleaned and Goldie had turned the light back off, he sat by his grandmother and held her hand. He kissed her soft, wrinkled cheeks and his gut twisted. "I almost lost you tonight, Grandma. That would've killed me. You'll go when you're ready."

Helen lay still, her eyes closed, oblivious to the drama that unfolded in her room. For a long time, he sat holding her hand, and then he stood up and walked to the door.

"Garth," a voice said behind him.

He spun around and saw his grandmother looking right at him with clear blue eyes. "Grandma."

"Thank you." Then her eyes closed.

"You're welcome," he said to the darkness, then stepped into the hallway.

Chapter Thirty-Five

W EXLER STOOD ON the other side of the two-way mirror, looking at Dan Krutcher's battered face as Barnard sat opposite the suspect on a metal folding chair in the interrogation room.

"We know about the deaths that occurred at each place you worked. St. Clare's Hospital in Topeka had seven suspicious deaths, Pinehurst Nursing Home in Omaha had five, Mesa Clinic in Tucson had four, and now we have six at Cherry Vale. And you know what the common denominator is? You. When you get to a place, patients die, and when you leave, the dying stops. What do you say to that?"

"I'd say it's a pretty big coincidence." Dan smiled and leaned back in the chair.

"I don't think coincidences work out like that so many times. And you were caught with the syringe trying to murder Helen Humphries. And before you lie to me again, we checked with Dr. Rudman. He never ordered any sleeping medication for Mrs. Humphries."

"She was living in darkness. I needed to bring her back to the light."

"And how were you going to do that, Dan?" Barnard leaned forward.

"By ending her darkness. I was trained to care for people. Letting them linger when they are so ill, when they have no quality of life left, is not caring for them. I'm their angel of mercy, and they always smile at me when I help them on their journey to the next world. The world of light and peace."

"Did Susan O'Brien need your mercy?"

Dan scrunched his face. "She was just a nosy drunk. She tried to stop me from helping Gus. By being a drunk, she put all the patients' lives in jeopardy. She got what she deserved."

"You pushed her, didn't you? Our crime scene team tells me her fall isn't consistent with tripping."

"Detective, I'm not going to do all the work for you." Dan smiled.

Barnard wanted to finish what the biker started, but he just smiled and leaned back. "You're going to make me work for Susan. What about Nadine and Doris? They both worked at Cherry Vale."

"What about them?"

"You raped them, but you killed Nadine. Did she tell you your dick was too short?"

Dan shifted in his chair. "I didn't kill Nadine or rape Doris. I liked them. Doris worked hard in the laundry room. Do you know how hot it gets in that room?"

"Then why did you rape her? She didn't want to have an affair with you?"

"Can I have an aspirin? My head is pounding. The doctor ordered it when I got my stiches. That Goldie's one crazy biker, attacking me like that."

"I'll get you an aspirin when you tell me about Nadine, Doris, and all the others."

"Are you trying to pin those rapes that have been on the news and in the paper on me? I don't rape women. I'm the angel of mercy for sick people. I've known that since I was a child. That's why I went into the medical field."

"What did you do with the American eagle ornament on your SUV?"

"I don't know what you're talking about."

"We know you have a dark brown SUV."

"A lot of people have that color." Dan squirmed in his chair.

"But they aren't rapists." Barnard pounded on the table.

Dan shook his head. "I want a lawyer," he said, then looked down at the table.

Barnard stood up and walked out of the room. "I pushed too fucking hard," he said to Wexler, who met him in the hallway.

"We got him on the murders at Cherry Vale. While he's stewing for those, we'll have time to get more evidence on the rapes. I know he's the one doing them. He's a sick bastard."

"Yeah. I'm going to interview a few more witnesses. I'll catch up with you later."

When the detective walked into the sunlight, he squinted. Sitting in the interrogation room made a person lose track of everything. Putting his sunglasses on, he ambled to his car.

Chapter Thirty-Six

AFTER DAN'S ARREST, Goldie breathed a little easier knowing a killer had been put out of commission. If he hadn't had any interruption from the staff that night, he would've saved the taxpayers a helluva lot of money. But the badges got him, and now the criminal process would go on for months, maybe years.

"They're saying that fucker who tried to kill your grandma is the serial rapist. They should give you a fuckin' medal," Paco said.

"I shoulda killed the bastard. I was ready to, but the citizens interfered," Goldie replied.

A blast of heat surged in, and Goldie turned around just as Diablo entered the club. He gave Goldie and Paco a chin lift.

"Any news on my bike? I don't want those fuckers to dismantle it for parts. And *Easyriders* is coming to the rally next week."

"I got an address for their mechanic shop. Dog says Rusty hangs there most days."

"Does Dog know anything about my bike?"

"He says no, but we know that's a crock of shit. I'm positive it wasn't his idea, but he's not gonna sell out a brother, even a shitty one."

"Let's get the bike. Then we can decide how to handle Dog and his fuckin' club."

"You need some help?" Paco asked.

"If you've got nothing else to do," Goldie replied.

"Hell no. Stealing a Harley's a capital fuckin' offense. When do we roll?" Paco motioned to Ruger to bring him a shot.

"As soon as we assemble a posse." Diablo grinned.

Army, Diablo, Paco, Muerto, Brutus, Eagle, and Goldie took off on the old highway to find the stolen Harley. After forty minutes, at Diablo's direction, the group of riders turned down a small road that led to a makeshift shop surrounded by a broken-down wooden fence. Tires, auto and bike parts lined the dirt lot. Switching off their engines, the bikers entered the shop, guns drawn, startling Rusty and four other Jagged Aces members. Rusty jumped up from the chair.

"What the fuck is this?" he said as he stared at Goldie.

"Don't fuck with me. Where's my bike?" Goldie went up to him and shoved him back into the chair.

"I don't know." He looked at his fellow members. "Do any of you guys know where his bike is?" They shook their heads. "Guess you should be better at keeping track of your shit." The four men sniggered.

"Guess you'll be finding out what happens to pussies who steal a Night Rebels' Harley," Goldie gritted.

"We're not gonna waste time on this shit. Tell us where the fuck the bike is and no one dies. It's pretty simple," Paco said.

The Jagged Aces were mute.

While his brothers talked shit to the losers, Goldie spotted a drill on the worktable. Before anyone could react, he grabbed it and switched it on, then lifted Rusty's leg. "Hold this fucker down!" Goldie yelled while he pulled off the asshole's boot and sock. Army and Diablo stood behind the wide-eyed Rusty, pressing down hard on his shoulders.

Then Goldie drilled right through the thief's instep and back out. Rusty was screaming and wailing as skin, blood, and bone flew around them. In the end, Goldie's tactic served a purpose: Rusty's memory came back, and he gave up the location of the bike.

"It better be in one piece, fucker, or I'm gonna come back and give you some extra holes." The Night Rebels laughed while they wiped the bloody spatters off their faces and arms. As they were leaving, Goldie spotted several American eagle hood ornaments on a shelf.

"You sell these?" he asked as he took one down. One of the Jagged Aces nodded. "You got the sales receipts?"

"Dog takes care of that," he said.

Turning to his brothers, he pointed to the door. "Let's go get my bike."

When they arrived at the chop shop, Goldie spotted his bike in the corner of the yard. Several pit bulls and German shepherds snarled and barked as he and his brothers approached. A large, burly man covered in tattoos came out. On the side of his mouth, between his lips, he chewed on a toothpick. As he eyed the bikers, he spit it out.

"What can I do for you?" he asked.

"Call off the fuckin' dogs or we'll shoot them," Army said.

The man nodded and closed a gate that contained the dogs. "Now, what can I do for you?" He stepped back as they came up to him. "I don't have any problems with you."

Goldie leaned in so close he could smell the fear on the man. Pointing to his Harley, he said, "The fuck you don't. That's my bike, and it looks like it's ready to be dismantled."

The man's eyes widened and he blew out a fetid breath from his opened mouth. "I had no idea the bike belonged to a Night Rebel. Fuck, man, I'm not stupid. I never would've touched it if I'd known."

"Who sold it to you?" Paco asked.

"A couple of Jagged Aces. I do business with them all the time. I never had no problems. I don't want no trouble. Take your bike. I'll deal with them later."

Goldie punched the man's soft belly, and he gasped for breath. "Please, man. I didn't know. I swear on my grandmother's grave. I wouldn't do that shit to you guys."

The brothers watched as the owner of the dilapidated chop shop begged to be spared. Goldie could tell his brothers believed what he was saying; they knew this guy's reputation, and he'd never messed with them. With one last blow to the guy's jaw, Goldie retrieved his Harley and they took off down the old highway. The desert sky was ablaze in deep shades of orange and magenta, and the warm air hugged Goldie as he embraced the rush of wind around him. It was so good to be back on his bike. He'd felt like a part of him had been amputated for the past week. Now everything was back on track—Hailey had returned, and so had his Harley. *It can't get any better than that.*

When they came back to the clubhouse, Goldie went over to Steel.

"From the way you look, I'm gonna guess you got your bike back in one piece," Steel said.

"Dusty as hell but intact. Good thing for that fuckin' Rusty too."

"He was planning to go back and make a watering can outta the asshole if even one part was dismantled." Paco laughed. Sitting down, he picked up his shot of tequila and winked at Angel, who ran over and sat on his lap.

Several of the other club girls went up to the returning brothers and wrapped their arms around them, rubbing their tits against them. Before too long, a few of the women were on their knees, taking and sucking dick.

Goldie and Steel turned to the bar. "The Jagged Aces sell the eagle ornament. I saw them in the shop."

"Why're you telling me this?" Steel asked.

"Because I wanna make sure that fucker who almost killed my grandma never gets off. If I can give the info to the damn badges, it'll be harder for this asshole to plead insanity."

"Okay. I'll ask Dog if he can run the names of people who bought them. He definitely owes you since one of his asshole brothers stole your bike."

"Tell him if he does this, he won't have to always be looking behind his back. He knew that asshole had taken my Harley."

"Of course he did. I'll tell him. I'm gonna bet Rusty and the others will be thrown out of the club."

"Let me know when Dog gives us the info."

Before going upstairs to take a quick shower, Goldie called over one of the prospects.

"Go wash and shine my bike. I'll be leaving in a half hour." The prospect rushed out and Goldie trudged up the stairs to his room.

A little while later, Goldie walked to his bike, which gleamed under the last light of day. The first buzz of mosquitoes came as the last slivers of day gave way to the velvety dark of night. Goldie straddled his bike and sped toward Hailey's house. Even though she'd been home for a little over a week, she'd been so busy at the flower shop with all the weddings and he'd been so swamped at the ink shop that they'd only had time for sex. Not that he was complaining, but he missed spending time with her.

When she opened the door in a sexy bra, thong, and garter belt, he decided to forgo his plans. *There's always tomorrow.*

He yanked her to him and squeezed her perfect ass as he kicked the front door shut.

Chapter Thirty-Seven

O N WEDNESDAY NIGHT, the bikes and RVs started arriving to the campgrounds for the Night Rebels' biker rally. The area was awash with black leather and denim, worn by men and women alike. Several vendor booths selling motorcycle gear and trinkets butted up against the tall evergreens, and the scent of smoky wood chips from the barbecue shacks permeated the grounds.

Steel stood by the area designated for the rally races, a smile spread over his face. "You did a good job with getting everything together," he said to Goldie.

"Thanks. A lot of the brothers helped out. The poker run is kicking ass." Goldie slipped his hands in his pockets.

"We're gonna raise a shitload of dough for Bikers Against Child Abuse." Paco brought his beer can to his mouth.

As the brothers watched the motorcycles get ready for the race, Hawk, the vice president of the Insurgents MC, came over with his fellow brother Throttle.

"You guys did a fuckin' good job with this rally," Hawk said.

"This is way bigger than your usual rally," Throttle said.

"Yeah, we've been planning this for the last few years. How're things in Pinewood Springs?" Goldie asked.

"Same, which in our world is fuckin' good." Hawk laughed.

"When are the races gonna start?" Banger asked as he walked toward the group.

"In about five minutes. Any Insurgents racing?" Steel asked the Insurgents president.

"Axe, Chas, and Wheelie. Jax wanted to but he's working with Rock and Diablo. It seems there haven't been any major problems yet. That's fuckin' good," Banger replied.

"That's because the only outlaws here are us and you." Paco laughed.

"None of the Satan's Pistons have made an appearance?" Hawk winked.

"Those fuckers know better," Goldie said.

"If they start shit again, let us know and we'll help you destroy them like the fuckin' Demon Riders," Throttle said.

"That would give us a damn good time," Steel replied.

"How did the arms deal with Liam go down with the Fallen Slayers?" Hawk asked.

"Good. They got all the shit they need to stop the punk gang from taking over their turf. We offered our help if needed," Paco said.

"They're pretty good guys. We have an issue on how they treat women, but we can count on them if need be," Goldie added.

"That's what's important," Banger said, and the group nodded in agreement.

Several women passed by, checking them out as they headed to the races. Most of them were scantily dressed or had elaborate body paint on their exposed breasts. Paco laughed and pointed at a curvy woman who kept looking over her shoulder at him. "Besides the bikes, that's the next best thing about rallies. I'd love to ride that sweet bitch."

"Go for it, dude," Throttle said.

"You guys down for some fun?" Paco asked.

The Insurgents shook their heads. "We got old ladies," Banger said.

"Kimber would crush my balls, and I'm not even fuckin' kidding." Throttle looked at Banger and Hawk. "You know she would."

Hawk laughed. "And with one of her favorite wrenches. Cara would borrow it for me." The guys laughed.

"I'm not hitched, so I'm gonna have a helluva good time. I'm gonna see if that hottie likes biker cock as much as I think she might. You coming, Goldie?" Paco started to walk away.

"I'll go with you to watch the races, but I'm waiting for Hailey. She's coming with a few of her friends." Goldie tossed his beer can in a recycle bin.

"I might want to meet her friends," Paco said.

"You would." Goldie chuckled as he walked toward the racing area with Paco. Banger, Steel, Hawk, and Throttle followed behind.

As they watched the races, arms wrapped around Goldie's waist and the scent of the ocean swirled around him. *Hailey.* The familiar aroma was all he smelled amid the oil and exhaust fumes from the bikes. He craned his neck and saw her smiling face.

"I'm here," she said.

He turned around and pressed her close. "I can see that, babe." Dipping his head down, he kissed her passionately, loving the small noises she made. "I'm glad you were able to come today since it's Saturday."

"I put Ellie in charge of the shop. I wanted to support your event. The charity you're raising money for is a great one. I also wanted to see you in a tight muscle shirt, showing off your tats and biceps. You know I'm crazy for your biceps, right?" She trailed her tongue around one of them.

"I wanted to share the rally with you. And what you're doing right now is gonna get you dragged to my tent."

"That sounds like it could be fun. I missed you these past two days… and nights."

"Me too. I had to stay here, but maybe we can go to your place tonight."

"The tent isn't big enough for two?"

"You don't want to stay here. It gets real raunchy at night. Anyway, I don't want anyone looking and coming on to you. There'd be a fight for sure."

"Okay, but at some point before dark, I want to check out your tent." Hailey's lips curled into a wicked smile as she patted his behind.

"You should enter the tattoo contest. I bet you'd win," he whispered in her ear.

"I love your confidence in your work."

"I wasn't thinking of the tat, only your sweet ass. You'd win hands down."

She giggled. "A couple of my friends and I were thinking about entering the wet T-shirt contest. The prize money is big. Do you think I have a chance at winning?" She rubbed her breasts against his chest.

Goldie stiffened. "There's no way in hell I'm going to let you parade your tits in front of a bunch of men." Anger pricked his skin as he glared at her. He jerked his head back when she tried to kiss him.

"Don't be pissed. I was only joking. You should know that I wouldn't be comfortable doing something like that. My friends and I were joking about it when we saw the signs."

"I should've known better. Fuck, woman, you get me all mixed up."

"In a good way?" She looked up at him through her lashes and he thought he was going to lose it.

He kissed her forehead. "Yeah, in a good way. Having you in my life makes me happy, makes me feel shit I never felt before."

"That goes for me too," she whispered against his throat.

A series of cheers and boos swirled around them and Goldie laughed. "I missed the fuckin' race." Gazing into her eyes, he saw tenderness, desire, and love. Brushing his lips against hers, he crushed her tighter to him.

"I'm sorry I distracted you."

"It doesn't matter. I'd rather look at you."

"Wasn't that a damn good race?" Diablo said as he and Rock approached.

"Didn't see it. I was looking at my woman," Goldie said.

Rock and Diablo nodded. "I get that," Diablo remarked.

"Who won, anyway?" Goldie asked.

"Some dude who had a wicked Sportster. It looked like the Indian Scout was gonna take it, but right at the end, the Sportster blasted through. It fuckin' ruled," Rock said.

Hawk, Banger, Steel, Paco, Axe, Chas, and Throttle joined Rock, Goldie, and Diablo as they chatted about the race. Goldie saw several of the Insurgents dart their eyes back and forth at Hailey. Putting his arm around her, he broke into one of the conversations. "This is Hailey. She's my woman," he said.

The Insurgents nodded at her, but Wheelie, who'd just joined the group, said, "You got yourself a woman? Damn, what's happening to all of you? It seems like most of my brothers are hitched and now the Night Rebels?"

Paco laughed. "I'm still on the market. And since you are too, I gotta tell you. I hooked up with this chick, and she and her friend really like to party."

"Count me in," Wheelie replied as he went over to Paco.

"I don't know 'bout anyone else, but I'm craving a rack of ribs," Banger said.

For the rest of the afternoon, Goldie hung out with Hailey, showing her all the bikes, introducing her to his friends, and buying her tons of biker purses, scarves, sunglasses, and T-shirts. He even bought her a pair of short Daisy dukes for her to wear just for him. The rally was the best one he'd ever attended; it even beat out Sturgis. And he knew why—Hailey. She just made everything in his life seem better. It was like they were meant for each other, but they had to grow up and become the people they were before they could come together. In the past few months, she'd become his everything, and he was fine with it.

Love had never entered the equation of his life, but after spending time with and getting to know Hailey, he guessed the strong feelings were love. They had a shared past, and when they reminisced, it made him feel like he was Garth again. They laughed at silly stuff, and he loved that they didn't have to fill the gaps with words all the time. What blew him away was the way she sensed his moods. Like when he was pissed at everything, she'd sit and listen to his rants without offering advice or any opinion. Or when sadness about his grandma over-whelmed him, she'd place his head in her lap and run her fingers through his hair over and over. Hailey *knew* him; she was the only woman who did. And he loved getting to know the adult Hailey.

Long after the sun had dipped behind the San Juan Mountains and the heat of the day had melted into the cool night air, Goldie wrapped his arms around Hailey. The glow from the flames sparking in the fire pit danced across her face, and he never thought she looked more beautiful.

Snuggled in the crook of his arm, she rested her head against his shoulder. "This was a perfect day," she said softly. Lacing her fingers with his, she stared into the fire. "I loved getting to see you among your friends, your brothers, and in such a relaxed situation. It was a nice glimpse into your world."

"Not like the club party?" he teased.

She giggled. "That was an eye-opener, but today provided the balance to that craziness. And I loved meeting Breanna, Raven, and Fallon. I was beginning to wonder if there were any normal women associated with this club. I'm surprised I didn't meet them before."

"I meant to have you meet them, but you're so busy at the shop and with your aunt, and with me—" He tilted her chin up and kissed her quickly. "—that there never seemed to be any time."

"I know. I've been so greedy and wanted to spend any spare moment I had with you, especially since I've been working so much at the flower shop."

"That's okay. I like it when you're greedy, especially with my cock."

"Is your mind always on sex and your dick?" She chortled.

"Only with you. I'm like a goddamn addict and you're my sweet, sexy fix." His mouth swallowed her next words. When he released her lips, he ran his finger over her face. "Do you want to head back?"

"I want to be with you. Are you sure you don't want to stay in the tent? I think it could be romantic."

Goldie guffawed. "With a bunch of guys belching and farting all night? If you want romance in a tent, we'll go camping at the national park in September. Come on." He stood and held out his hand to help her up.

Under the full moon, Goldie rode back to Alina, loving the way

Hailey circled her arms around him and rested her head against his back. If he had it his way, he'd keep riding into the darkness under the carpet of sparkling stars until they were too tired. He'd love nothing better than to head to California with Hailey tucked behind him. Riding up the coastline with the Pacific Ocean as a perpetual backdrop was something he'd always wanted to do, and having Hailey with him would be the dream vacation.

The cluster of lights ahead let him know they were close to Alina, so he slowed to make the sharp turn that would take him behind the downtown area and into Hailey's neighborhood. When he pulled up to the curb, Hailey kissed the back of his neck.

"That was such a beautiful ride. It felt like we were the only two people in the world. The stars were humungous. When we moved to Albuquerque, I missed the star-filled sky. In the city, the lights from office buildings and streets make the stars and the Milky Way invisible." She tipped her head back.

Goldie planted gentle kisses down her throat, feathering up and down until his mouth captured hers. "You're gorgeous in the moonlight," he murmured against her lips, then looped his arm around her waist and led her up the sidewalk to the porch.

Once inside, they climbed the stairs and went into the bedroom. She opened the window, and a light breeze blew in.

"Let's leave the curtains open. I want to see the stars and moonlight," she said softly as she ran her fingers over his broad shoulders.

"Whatever you say." He watched her slender hands tug and yank off his boots and clothing. His erection stood stiff and waiting as she skimmed her tongue over his legs, slowly inching her way up. When she got dangerously close, he pulled her up. "My turn," he rasped. With gentle, soft hands, he unwrapped her, kissing each part he revealed and relishing the silkiness of her skin.

He eased her onto the bed, the desire beating fiercely in his veins fueled by her nakedness encased in moonlight. Hovering over her, their noses only a whisper apart, he gazed deeply into her eyes. "You're everything to me," he said in a low voice. "You're my heart. You're the air."

He grazed his fingers over her breasts and a low moan slipped through her parted lips. They held each other's gaze, and every movement, every ounce of longing was reflected between their eyes. Goldie's hands caressed her skin and pulled her hips tightly to his. Hailey met his passion with her own as she kissed him deeply. He slid deep into her and she moaned, wrapping her arms tightly around his neck.

Goldie began to move within her, and she moved with him. Nuzzling her neck with his nose, he whispered, "I love you," then increased his pace.

"I love you too," she panted.

He reached down to catch her mouth as he thrust faster and faster, driving them both to a shattering climax.

Wrapped in each other's arms, sated and spent, his hand drifted slowly over her back. After a long while, Hailey asked softly, "Did you mean what you said, or was it just the heat of the moment?"

Goldie paused. He felt so many emotions for her: passion, love, adoration, joy, comfort. "I meant it. I love you." He never thought he'd utter those words to a woman.

"I love you too. I feel like I have for a long time, but now it's a grown-up love."

Kissing her temple, he pulled her closer until there was no space between them. *Everything makes sense now. Fuck. It's so easy and simple.* He'd tell his grandma about it the following day before he headed back to the rally. He knew she'd be happy. All she ever wanted for him was to find a wonderful woman to love and for her to love him.

Mission accomplished, Grandma.

THUNDEROUS POUNDING WOKE Goldie and he immediately looked over at Hailey. She was sitting up in bed, rubbing the sleep from her eyes. "I think I forgot that I made an appointment today," she said as she threw her robe on.

"On a Sunday?" Goldie pushed up.

"I'm doing that just for the summer, but not every Sunday. You stay here, I'll be right back." She gave him a peck on the mouth and rushed out of the room.

Goldie glanced at the clock: eight thirty. *Too fuckin' early for a Sunday.* He scrubbed his face with his fist and went to the window. Behind his Harley was a dark blue sedan. He yanked his jeans on and padded out of the room. As he descended the stairway, he heard voices in the living room.

When he entered the room, he saw Hailey sitting rigidly, her smile tight and her eyes pleading with him. He had no idea what they were pleading for until the man sitting with his back to Goldie turned around. *Ryan. Fuck!*

Ryan leapt up, his eyes darting from Hailey to Goldie. He scanned over Goldie's bare chest and feet, then Hailey's short robe, realization spreading across his face. "You bastard! You're screwing my sister?"

"Ryan, it's not what it seems," Goldie said as he took a couple of steps toward Ryan.

"There are a ton of women to fuck and you chose Hailey? You asshole!" Ryan swung and belted Goldie in the jaw.

"Ryan! Stop!" Hailey cried.

Goldie stepped back. When Ryan came for another punch, Goldie caught his fist. "I deserved the first one." Ryan slammed his other fist into Goldie's side. "Fuckin' stop, bro, or we're gonna do shit to each other we'll regret."

"I'm not going to regret anything. I'm going to beat your ass for touching Hailey." Ryan went for another punch, but that time Goldie blocked it.

Hailey ran over and tried to pull her brother away. "Ryan, stop it. Please. Stop. Goldie didn't do anything I didn't want."

Ryan stopped and turned to her. "You don't know what you want. He took advantage of you. I'm not blaming you. He should've known better."

"I'm not a child anymore. I hate when you treat me like one. How do you know what I want? You've been away for the last four years. Give me some credit for making my own decisions."

"I warned you to stay away from him. He fucks anyone with boobs. Do you really think you're special to him? There are women at the clubhouse who are only there to service the men. Is *that* the type of guy you want? Is that how Mom and Dad raised you? What do you think they'd say?"

"That they're happy for me. I told them when I went home for a visit last week. They were cool with it. You're overreacting."

Goldie came over to Hailey and grasped her hand. "I didn't mean for this to happen. I fought it for a while, and so did Hailey, but what we have is too strong. I'll treat Hailey right. I love her."

"Love?" Ryan laughed dryly. "You don't even know what that means. I *know* you. Don't forget that."

"I love him too," Hailey said.

A strained silence stretched between the three of them. Ryan went to the door. "You're still my sister, and I love you, but that doesn't mean I'm going to accept this. And you," he said, pointing at Goldie, "are dead to me." Then he marched out of the house, slamming the door behind him.

Goldie and Hailey stared at the closed door, and then he pulled her to him and kissed her. "Fuck, I'm sorry I messed up your relationship with Ryan."

"Don't take the blame for this, and don't run away from me." Tears rolled down her sun-kissed cheeks.

Wiping the wet streaks with his thumb, he shook his head. "I'd never run away from you. I'm sorry I didn't keep my ass upstairs, but it was a matter of time before something like this happened. I should've told him. This will be hard for you, but I'm staying for the long haul. I've never told a woman I loved her."

"It'll be okay between Ryan and me. He's just really pissed. I hope he comes around with you. I didn't want to break up your friendship."

"You didn't. We both knew what we were doing, and we wanted it. I don't have any regrets except that we didn't handle it right from the get-go. But that's in the past and we can't change it. I hope you're strong enough to see this through."

She squeezed him hard. "Of course I am. I'm not leaving you. I've wanted you my whole life, and I'm not walking away from that. Finding a person who fits with you, gets you, loves you, and a million other things is rare. We were meant to be together."

"Then let's do it. You should spend some time with Ryan. I'll hang at the clubhouse for a few days. You need to be good with him before he goes back to Afghanistan."

She nodded and glanced down at her phone. "I got a text. I didn't hear it." She read the message and grimaced.

"Who's it from?"

"My aunt Patty. She sent it twenty minutes before Ryan came, telling me Ryan's in town and wanted to surprise me."

"He fuckin' did that," Goldie said.

"No shit. She wanted to give me a heads-up in case you were with me."

"Would've helped if we hadn't slept through the text."

"Yeah. I guess it was just meant to be. I'm going to see my aunt. I want to find out where Ryan's staying. I'm sure he was expecting to stay here."

"Let him. We can meet somewhere else."

Hailey smiled. "You're the best. Are you going back to the rally?"

He nodded. "I'll text you later. If you need something, let me know."

"I love you, Goldie."

"And I fuckin' love you, Hailey." They kissed, then went upstairs to get ready for the day.

As Goldie rode to the rally, his gut was all twisted in knots. He and Ryan had been friends for almost twenty-five years. The man was like a brother to him, and when Ryan told him their friendship was over, it had stabbed him in the gut. He acted cool about it because of Hailey, but he hoped that once Ryan cooled off and saw that he was sincere with Hailey, his anger would dissipate. If it didn't, then it was over. But one thing he was certain of: he'd never leave Hailey.

She was his heart, his blood, his bones. She was his life.

Chapter Thirty-Eight

T HE FLOWER SHOP was bustling with people when Hailey rushed in with an iced chai in one hand and a bag of ribbons in the other. Her hectic life hadn't let up for one moment, even with Ryan back in Afghanistan. He'd been in the States for a ten-day leave, and she was happy that they had mended things before he left. Of course, he hadn't come around all of a sudden and embraced her and Goldie's relationship—that was the stuff of romance movies. Basically they just ignored the whole thing. She went along with it because his time at home was too short, and if something happened to him overseas, she'd die from guilt and grief.

Unfortunately, he didn't reach out to Goldie, and even though Goldie told her it was the way life went, she knew he was hurt by the loss of the friendship. The only hope she had was that, in time, Ryan would see what a wonderful boyfriend Goldie was and that he'd changed. Only time would tell.

"Hailey, I'm glad you're here. We're slammed. And we're out of the rose-patterned tea cups. Some lady wants six dozen for a charity luncheon she's chairing."

"Okay. Did you write all of that down, because I probably won't remember that by the end of the day."

"Yes. Is your brother still in town?"

"He left a few days ago. I miss him already. He said he's going to take the rest of his leave at Christmas. I hope it works out. The last few years it's been canceled."

As Hailey waited on customers, Sheriff Wexler walked in. He smiled and nodded at her and she waved at him.

"Carol, can you finish with this customer, please?" Hailey asked as she made her way over to the lawman. "What brings you into the shop?"

"I need some flowers for a dinner party," he replied.

"Is it a formal or informal dinner party?"

"Actually it's just me and this lady friend of mine. I wanted to bring a nice arrangement to her." Wexler gave a half smile.

"Is this someone you're very interested in? The beginning of something, perhaps, or just a friend? And before you think I'm being nosy, all of that matters when picking the right flowers."

He shuffled his feet a bit. "I didn't realize it was that complicated."

"Flowers hold messages. The wrong flower, the wrong message. Like if you gave red roses to a woman you only liked as a friend. Wrong message."

Nodding, he looked inside the case of premade floral arrangements. "I'd say it's someone I want to get to know a lot better."

"Perfect. First date?"

"Fourth."

"Great. We'll start with what flowers she has in her garden and what her favorite color is. By getting something specific, you'll show her that you remember things about her, and she'll love the flowers since she has them in her own garden. Providing she has one, of course."

"Sounds good. I know purple is her favorite color, and she loves tulips and hydrangeas."

"Excellent. Do you know how many men don't know that about the women they're with?" She laughed and went to the cooler to gather the flowers and some greens. As she started putting flowers into a vase, she said, "The paper's been printing that Dan Krutcher is also the serial rapist. I can't believe I was in the same room with him all those times. You never know what goes on in a person's mind."

"That's the truth. We've officially charged him with the murders at Cherry Vale and, once the DNA results come back, probably the rapes as well."

"I wonder what his poor wife is going through. Can you imagine finding that out about your husband?"

"I heard she's taking the kids and moving back to her hometown in Illinois."

"I just can't imagine it." She added one last sprig of greenery and turned the arrangement to face the sheriff. "How do you like it?" The vase contained a beautiful and colorful assortment of flowers, greens, and ribbons.

A wide smile spread over Wexler's face. "She'll like that a lot. It's very nice."

After she rang him up and gave him his change, she said, "When you have a chance, pop in and let me know how she liked it."

"Will do."

The rest of the day was a blur as Hailey and the other employees worked relentlessly. When six o'clock came, Ellie quickly flipped the "Open" sign to "Closed" and pulled down the shades. "My feet are killing me," she said as she came behind the counter.

"I never thought the day would end," Carol added.

"I can't believe how busy we were. It was too crazy. Let's hope to-morrow isn't as bad," Hailey said.

"Aren't you taking off?" Ellie asked as Hailey settled on the stool in front of the computer.

"Not yet. I didn't have any time today to order all the stuff we're out of, including the tea cups for Mrs. Spencer's charity luncheon. And I have to go through dozens of e-mails and sift out the urgent ones from the not-so-urgent."

"Do you need any help?" Ellie asked in a small voice.

Hailey smiled; she knew Ellie would be crushed if she said yes. "Go. I'm good."

The two women left and Hailey began punching in the inventory numbers. When she was halfway through, her phone pinged. When she saw Goldie's name, her stomach fluttered. *I hope I'll always be this excited when I see or hear from him.*

Goldie: *Let's get dinner.*

Hailey: *I can go @ 10.*

Goldie: *WTF? U still at shop?*

Hailey: *Ya. Crazy day. Have 2 finish some work. Maybe 9:30?*

Goldie: *9:30's better. U want me 2 pick u up?*

Hailey: *Ur sweet, but I'm good. Feel like Mexican. Alfonso's?*

Goldie: *It closes @ 9. Leroy's the best bet.*

Hailey: *K. See u @ 9:30. ♥ u.*

Goldie: *Me too.*

Happy that she'd see Goldie in a couple of hours, she rubbed her shoulders, stretched out her neck, and returned to the computer.

★ ★ ★

GOLDIE WASHED UP, glad his last appointment of the day was over. He shook out his hands and clenched and unclenched his fingers many times. *I need a good workout.* Sitting for hours at a time, hunched over while tattooing someone made his muscles stiffer than a board. He normally worked out five to six times a week, but he'd gotten off his schedule since he started seeing Hailey. Deciding he had to get back to his routine, he chose to go to the clubhouse before meeting up with her for dinner.

The clubhouse had a full gym in the basement, including a small boxing rink. Most of the brothers took advantage of it, and sometimes they would stage fights between themselves. He loved getting into the rink and punching a worthy opponent, especially after a stress-filled day.

Ryan had left without a word to him. He hadn't seen him since that fateful day when his friend found out about his relationship with Hailey. Goldie had hoped that at least they could've talked, but Ryan never returned his texts or his phone calls. He'd let it go, but the sting of Ryan giving up their friendship started to anger him. Ryan acted like Goldie wasn't good enough for Hailey, like he was a piece of shit. He supposed that's what hurt the most, the way Ryan abhorred the idea of Hailey with him. *Fuck it.* As long as he and Hailey were good with each other, nothing else mattered.

Walking into the clubhouse, he shook his head at Patches, who had started filling a shot glass. Then he went downstairs and began his workout.

An hour later, he came out of the shower and put on a clean T-shirt and pair of jeans. He glanced at his phone to check if he missed any texts from Hailey. Seeing that he had a little bit of time before he met up with her, he went to the main room and took the shot Patches poured for him. The smokiness of the smooth whiskey tasted good, and it warmed his belly. He motioned for another.

"We're getting a poker game together. You in?" Brutus asked.

"No, I'm meeting Hailey soon. Another time."

"You're never around here, dude," Skull said.

Goldie smirked. "Do you miss me?

Skull punched his arm and sat on one of the barstools.

"We miss you," Ruby said from the couch. "All of you." She placed her finger in her mouth and pushed it in and out.

Goldie laughed. "You got plenty of that with the brothers. One less cock doesn't mean that much."

"It does when it's yours," Fina said as she pressed her breasts together and bent down low.

"Fuck!" Brutus said as the brothers in the main room whistled.

"Give us a dance and show us your big tits, sweet butt." Army said as he laid down his pool cue and came over to Goldie and the others.

In a flash, the TV was muted and the jukebox blared out "Pour Some Sugar On Me" as Fina started moving seductively. Not to be outshined, Ruby jumped up and joined her, and the men hooted and whistled. Goldie watched as the women ran their hands over their bodies. From the corner of his eye, he saw Diablo come in. The sergeant-at-arms glanced over at the women, then back at Goldie as he came over to the bar.

"I got the list of names from Dog. You wanna see them?"

Goldie looked away from Fina and Ruby playing with their tits. "For the eagle ornament?" Diablo nodded. "Yeah. Let's go to the church room."

Inside the meeting room, Diablo handed him ten pages. "I looked through them, but I'm not sure what I'm looking for."

"Any name we recognize, the vehicle, and whatever shit they have in their records. That chick Army's fucking at the sheriff's office said they hardly have any evidence in the rape cases. They know it's that fuckin' Krutcher, but they don't have much to convict him. She said his car matched a witness's description, but they didn't find any hood ornament."

"He probably took it off," Diablo said.

"That's what I'm thinking. If we can get proof he bought one, it'll help put him away without any shit about being a nutcase. I just want to nail his ass any way I can."

"I can see that. Helping the badges with their case isn't like you."

"If the fucker wasn't in custody, he'd already be in a grave." Goldie picked up the document and started going through the names. On the last page, he paused.

"See something?"

Unblinking, he nodded slowly. *Fuck!* "I gotta go, and I need you, Army, Skull, Brutus, and Eagle with me. Fuck!"

"I'm in. I'll go round up the others."

Goldie called Hailey, but it went straight to voice mail. "Shit!" He sent her a text but nothing came back. Then he called the floral shop, but once again voice mail picked up. Cursing under his breath, he ran out to the main room and saw his brothers waiting. A gamut of feelings flashed through him as he saw the five brothers staring at him, in their cuts and packing their Glocks staring at him. *This is why I fuckin' love the brotherhood.* Jerking his chin at them, Diablo opened the door and they all went outside.

Soon the Night Rebels were flying out of the parking lot. *I gotta make sure she's safe. I got a bad feeling. Shit! I let my damn guard down.* As the wind stung his eyes, he pressed on, all his thoughts on Hailey.

He couldn't lose her.

Chapter Thirty-Nine

HAILEY STRETCHED HER arms and turned off the computer, having called it quits when black spots floated on her screen. Glancing at the clock, she knew she'd be a little early for dinner, so she'd take the time to stretch out her legs and stare idly at nothing until Goldie came. She looked at her dark screen and cursed her stupidity at forgetting to bring her charger. *Maybe it's a good thing. That damn phone's attached to my hip. I need the break.* Her brain was mush. All she wanted was to relax, talk to Goldie, then snuggle next to him and sleep. She was so exhausted.

After she locked the shop, she walked over to her car that was near the park. She laughed as she remembered how freaked out she was that night when she saw that man coming out of the bushes. *I'm positive it was Dan. I still can't believe what a psycho he turned out to be. I'm so glad Goldie caught him.*

She opened the trunk of her car and put her briefcase in it. When she shut the trunk, she thought she saw something.

A dark shadow disappearing behind the trees.

Silly. She had to stop parking by the park.

Shaking her head, she went to her car door.

Still….

Something made her uneasy, and waves of cold washed over her. She pushed on the remote and her door unlocked, her headlights beaming.

She stopped dead, the remote slipping from her fingers and clanking on the asphalt.

There, right before her, not fifteen feet away, stood a man. He was shadowed by the large branches of the trees. He didn't move. Petrified to bend down to pick up her key, she stood glued to the spot.

Then he came slowly out of the darkness.

The car's headlights turned off. Hypnotized by fear, she watched him come closer and closer.

Opening her mouth, ready to scream, she breathed a sigh of relief as the streetlight lit his face.

"It's you," she said. She giggled, giddy with relief. "You startled me."

"I didn't mean to. Working late?"

"Yeah. I'm beat though. You're working late too. Are you on your way home?"

He shook his head. "No, I was waiting for you. I've been waiting for you for a long time, Hailey. Too long."

"What? Is something going on with my aunt? You can—" Hailey took a step backward. His friendly eyes had evaporated into cold, hard ones. His lethal stare pierced her. Her heart hammered erratically as the blood drained from her face. With widened eyes, she took another step backward, but as he grabbed her wrists, his fingers digging into her skin painfully, her suspicions were confirmed.

He was going to kill her.

GOLDIE POUNDED ON the flower shop door even though it was dark inside, then took out a bump key he always carried in his wallet. Unlocking the door, he walked inside. Nothing seemed amiss. After checking everything, he joined his brothers on the pavement.

"Find anything?" Diablo asked.

"No. I'm going to see if I can find her car. It's a white Mustang. Brutus and Skull, check across the street, and Diablo and Eagle, check behind the shop and the alley. I'm gonna check this side of the street."

The brothers dispersed and Goldie walked toward the park. As he approached the area, chills scurried up his spine. *Something happened here.* Glancing around, he went to the bushes and rifled through them. Nothing but a few scared raccoons. Walking back to the sidewalk, the streetlight bounced off an object in the road. He walked to the curb and picked it up, his blood running cold. A silver charm of a ram and the word "Aries" etched on it shimmered in his palm. *This is from Hailey's charm bracelet.* Jaw clenched, he rushed back to the shop and whistled loudly. The brothers came over and Goldie told them what he found.

"The charm may have come off without her knowing it," Skull said.

"If that's the case, then she'd be waiting for me at the diner. Brutus, Skull, you guys go over to Leroy's and see if she's there. Let me know. Diablo, Eagle, and I will go to her house."

The brothers revved their bikes and left in a plume of dust.

Chapter Forty

I CAN'T MOVE! *What the hell's going on?* Hailey blinked several times, trying to clear her bleary eyes as she regained consciousness. Her nose tingled and she went to scratch it, but her wrist was secured to something. She craned her neck. *I'm tied to the bedpost!* She tried moving her other arm and legs, but they were secured tightly. Goose bumps pebbled her skin as she raised her head and saw that her clothes had been cut down the middle. Eyes bulging, she looked around the room.

Her mind was in a fog as she tried to remember the series of events that brought her to being tied spread-eagle on her bed. Then he walked in.

Dr. Daniels! That's right. He came over and then he... struck me with a hard object. When he did it the second time, I blacked out. This doesn't make sense. Why is he—

"I'm glad you finally came to. It's no fun when the woman's knocked out."

"Why are you doing this, Dr. Daniels? I don't understand."

He came over and trailed the tip of the knife gently over her forehead, then down to the base of her throat. "I love the way fear is creeping into your eyes. You have no idea what I'm going to do to you. The unknown is your enemy, but it's my best friend." He leaned over and tried to kiss her, but she thrust her head against his face and he jerked back. Surprise replaced cockiness.

"Don't touch me. Untie me and stop this right now!"

Taken aback, he stepped away, his wide gaze beginning to narrow.

I'm supposed to meet Goldie. When I'm not there, he's going to freak. He'll come here. I just know he will. I have to stall.

"You've caused me many sleepless nights, Hailey. I'd planned to take you a couple of months ago, but Goldie butted his low-life nose into your life and my plans had to go on hold. But now you and I have all the time in the world. I checked Goldie's schedule at the tattoo place and he's busy all night, so it's just you and me."

"Are you the one who's been raping all the women? Did you murder Nadine?" She couldn't stop the icy shivers strangling her nerves. When he smiled wide, she knew he was getting off on her fear. *I have to try and calm down. Goldie will be here. I'm going to be fine. It's all good. I can't act afraid. But I am. I'm scared to death.* She forced herself to think of the sun setting over the mountains.

"She pulled off my mask. I didn't want to kill her, but I'll let you in on a secret." His dead eyes stared at her as he leaned down close to her ear. "When I slit her throat while she looked at me, I fucking *loved* it. And then I was hooked." He bit down hard on her earlobe and she yelled out, but he wouldn't let go. Afraid he was going to bite it off, she raised her head again and hit him in the jaw.

Whack! Her head turned from the force of his slap. Tears rolled down her stinging face as he leaned close once more, watching her intently. "Yes, we're going to have a lot of fun," he muttered under his breath.

Keep talking. Stall! "Everyone thought Dan Krutcher did the rapes."

Sitting on the side of the bed, he smirked. "That was just luck. I was surprised at the ineptness of the police department, but then we're in a small town. I can't believe Dan killed the patients. He was supposed to care for them. They trusted him. When it occurred to me that someone might be killing the patients, I was horrified. The medical staff is there to care for, comfort, and prolong life, not destroy it." He shook his head.

He's fucking nuts! "Why do you hurt women?" she asked in a soft voice.

"I have a monster in me that needs to be fed. And you have been tempting me for a long time." He ran his hands over her breasts and she bit her inner cheek hard.

"If you're a real good girl, I'll let you live."

"No you won't. You didn't even try and conceal your face. You decided to kill me when you drove over to Main Street and hid in the bushes waiting for me."

He laughed without mirth. "You got me. Such a smart, pretty one." He trailed his fingers down her body and she closed her eyes, bracing for his touch in her most private parts.

"Keep your fucking eyes open, bitch. I want to see them. Now!"

Her eyelids flew open and the man she saw before her wasn't the Dr. Daniels she knew—he was a menacing, evil man. His features had darkened, his eyebrows were narrowed, and his lips were tightly closed, forming a thin line. She arched her body and pulled on her ties in a vain attempt to get away from him. He stood and unzipped his pants, and she turned her head away.

Pop! Pop! The killer's eyes bulged and his mouth gaped open. With the sound of her heartbeat thrashing in her ears, she screamed as red soaked Dr. Daniels's T-shirt, then splattered over her. His face froze and he fell over, his head hitting the nightstand. She shut her watering eyes tight, flinching when fingers touched her wrists.

"Hailey, it's okay. You're safe." Goldie's voice filtered through her brain.

"Is that you, Goldie?"

"It's me, babe." He pulled her sore body to him and held her tight. The fear she'd been holding back broke through and tears flowed freely down her face.

"It was Dr. Daniels all along. I can't believe it. He wanted to kill me. I can't believe it," she said over and over again like a mantra.

"You're safe now. I'm here."

Sirens wailing in the distance eerily filled the room. Still clinging to him, she moved her head up and down in rhythm with his deep breathing.

"You guys better get out of here. I'll handle it with the damn badges."

Low grunts, shuffling feet, and then quiet except for the sirens, which sounded closer now. Goldie pulled on the sheet, yanking it from the mattress as she still clung to him, moving with him as though they were glued together. Pushing her back a little, he wrapped the sheet around her exposed body, then pressed her close again and waited. When the blue and red flashing bounced off the bedroom walls, she knew what he was waiting for.

Heavy clumping up the stairs unnerved her and she whimpered, but his soothing hand on her hair calmed her as the footsteps came closer. Peeking through her semi-shut eyelids, she saw Sheriff Wexler walk into the room. *I bet I spoiled his date. I wonder how she liked the flowers.* That was all she could think of: Wexler's date.

"What happened here?" the sheriff asked as his glance went from her to Goldie to Dr. Daniels's dead body.

"He's your rapist and murderer. He came after my woman. The fucker had a knife in his hand, ready to cut her, so I shot him."

"Did you yell out to him?" Barnard asked, coming closer to the body.

"Yeah."

Barnard looked at Hailey. "Do you have anything to add about what happened?"

She shook her head. "It was awful. He'd unzipped his pants, and he had a knife in his hand. I was petrified. He'd tied me up and cut open my clothes. I heard Goldie tell him to stop but he didn't. He just kept coming closer to me." When she glanced at Goldie, pride shone in his gaze. She rested her head against his shoulder.

"We'll need your full statement, Ms. Shilley. You can do it downstairs or at the station. It looks like a justified shooting," the sheriff said, nodding at Goldie.

"We're going to have to investigate a little further before we can rule it justified. How'd you know he was here with Ms. Shilley?" Barnard asked Goldie.

"I didn't. I went to meet her for dinner, and when she didn't show and I couldn't get her on the phone, I got worried and came over to her house."

"So you had no idea the rapist was here?"

Stone-faced, Goldie said, "I just answered that."

"Do you always bring a weapon when you come over to your girl-friend's?" Barnard folded his arms over his chest.

"Yeah."

Wexler cleared his throat. "I issued the permit for it. It's all good. We got the DNA results a few days ago ruling out Dan Krutcher as the rapist-murderer. We'll do a DNA comparison on Daniels, then wrap up the case. Do you want to come down with Ms. Shilley and give your statement?" Wexler asked Goldie.

He grasped Hailey's hand and went out into the hallway. Wexler's voice drifted over the low murmurings of the deputies. "We've got a handle on it, Jack. Thanks for helping us out."

"You believe the load of shit that outlaw told us?"

"I do. You can head back to Durango tomorrow morning. I'll wrap this one up."

Hailey and Goldie walked down the stairs and waited for the law-men in the family room. Goldie stroked her hair. "You're gonna need to talk with someone about all this shit that went down. Breanna can get you in touch with some counselors."

"I'll be fine," she said, but Daniels's face jumped into her mind and she shuddered.

"Just talk to whoever Breanna recommends. Do it for me, okay?"

"Okay." Wetness coated her eyelashes, cheeks, and chin.

The two lawmen came into the room then and sat down. She sat up straight and waited for the questions to begin.

This is going to be a long night.

Chapter Forty-One

T RISHA DANIELS STARED at Sheriff Wexler as he shuffled through his paperwork. Cold anger mixed with anguish coursed through her as she tried to come to terms with what her husband had done.

"I just need you to sign here," Wexler said pointing at the paper he handed her.

"Then I can bury him?" she asked while signing her name.

"Yes. Once again, I'm sorry for the way this all turned out for you." The sheriff leaned back in his chair and watched her.

"You never really know a person. I mean, at times, Seth was a loving and caring husband. And he was a good father to our kids. But at other times, he was a mean, vindictive bastard. For the most part, we got along real well. I met him at the hospital when I lived in Chicago. I'd just been hired as a nurse. He was so charming...." She wiped the corners of her eyes. The images of her husband's smiling face filling her mind. "I just can't believe it," she said softly.

Wexler shifted in his chair. "You're right in that we never know a person a hundred percent. There are a lot of dark areas inside some people and they keep them well hidden."

She shook her head. "The only area we weren't compatible in was sex. He needed me to be afraid of him when we'd make love. It was the oddest thing, but I ignored it and played along with him, but I knew I wasn't really satisfying him in the way he wanted. Our sex life had dwindled down to just once or twice a month." She laughed dryly. "To be honest, I thought he was having an affair. He spent so much time away from home, especially at night. And to think that he was stalking, raping, and killing women instead. I could never have imagined he'd do something like that." Her voice broke and she covered her face with her hands. *What's wrong with me that I couldn't see what he really was?*

"I hope you don't blame yourself for this. Are you going to stay in Alina?"

"No. I'm moving back to Chicago. My whole family's there. We came to Alina because Seth thought a small town would be a good place to raise our kids."

The sheriff nodded. "Do you need help in finding a transport company to send Dr. Daniels's body to Illinois?"

"No. I found one in Denver. They're just waiting for the release of the body." The sound of her voice saying those words felt so alien to her. She mourned the loss of her husband, the father of her kids, and the good memories they shared. Whenever she thought of him now, she couldn't get the images of his victims out of her mind. The good times they'd had would be forever tainted with the blood he shed.

Pushing up from the chair, she said, "I should get going. I have a lot of packing to do. Thank you for everything." Her eye caught the headline of the *Alina Post* that was on the desk—"Maniac Rapist-Murderer Gunned Down During Attack." On the left side of the page she saw her husband's face, his brown eyes penetrating and brooding. She remembered when he'd taken the picture at a medical convention they'd attended in Denver the previous year. She averted her eyes as she thought how much had changed in just one year.

Pulling open the doors of the police station, she walked out into the bright August sunshine.

Chapter Forty-Two

One month later

THE NIGHT BEFORE was the first time Hailey hadn't woken up drenched in sweat, screaming, and it felt wonderful. The therapist had told her it would take time, but soon the nightmares of that terrifying night would begin to disappear. She couldn't wait to meet with her therapist and let her know that she'd slept through the night unscathed.

"You ready to go?" Goldie asked.

"In a minute. I want to make sure Aunt Patty has everything she needs." Her aunt had been released from Cherry Vale by Dr. Rudman just a few days before. Even though Patty was getting around well and had a nurse staying with her for another few weeks, Hailey still worried that she'd fall or need something and Hailey wouldn't be around.

"You sure you'll be okay without me here?" Hailey asked as she went into the bedroom.

Propped against the headboard with five pillows cushioning her, Patty laughed. "Yes, go. I'm good, and if I need anything at all, Lisa's here. Have a good time."

"All right. You have my number if anything comes up. I'll see you later."

Hailey bounced down the stairs and flew out the front door. As she walked toward Goldie, who straddled his bike, a fluttery feeling swirled inside her, as it usually did when she looked at him. He'd been her strength during the long month since Dr. Daniels had attacked her. Even though she loved Goldie madly, she also really *liked* him. When she'd told Rory that, her friend didn't know what she was talking about, but Claudia had squeezed her hand and whispered, "That's a rarity. He's a keeper." And he was. She had no intention of letting him slip away.

"Aunt Patty's doing great," she said as she climbed behind him. Clutching him tightly, they pulled away from the curb. The first rush of air, the wind whirling around her, and the scent of oil and leather always hit her hard, and she loved it. She wanted so badly to tell Ryan how freeing it was to ride on a motorcycle, but they didn't talk about bikes or Goldie. After she'd told Ryan how Goldie had saved her life, she'd hoped it would fix what was broken between her brother and his best friend, but it didn't. Ryan had sent a quick e-mail thanking Goldie, but that was all. Goldie was never mentioned in their conversations, and when she'd bring him up or gush about him, Ryan would feign bad interference and end the call.

At the stoplight, Goldie looked at her over his shoulder, and she stretched forward and kissed him tenderly. He'd been so patient with her when she didn't want to do anything except have him hold her. The past few days, she'd finally been able to make love to him again, and it thrilled her beyond belief.

They went for a ride through the desert landscape, ending up at a small bright pink restaurant set atop a hill on the edge of the county line. Floor-to-ceiling windows all around made for a spectacular view of the desert and the mountains.

The hostess seated them at a table for two next to the window, where the red rock formations glowed under the setting sun's rays. Hailey looked up from her menu, meeting Goldie's intense eyes.

"What're you staring at? Do I have dust all over my face?"

"No dust. You're perfect."

"That's nice to hear, but I wouldn't say perfect," she replied.

"You're so beautiful, Hailey. You've been so strong since that fuckin' night. In my world, strength is admired."

"I couldn't have done it without you," she said softly.

"We complement each other. We have each other's backs. We have a helluva good time. And we fuck real good together."

"Anything else?" she said winking.

"That about covers it. I never thought I'd settle down with a woman. You ground me, and it feels fuckin' fantastic." He reached out and clutched her hand.

"I can't believe how fate brought you back into my life."

"And it was all because you wanted a tat on your sexy ass. I wanna give you another tattoo. I'd love to cover you in them."

Shaking her head, she said, "I don't know about *covered*, but I'd love to have another tattoo. I was thinking either on the back of my neck or on my ankle."

"Why not both?"

"You're right. Why not? My parents won't like it, but parents aren't supposed to like stuff like that, right?"

"I don't know. My mom had some ink, and my dad had a ton of it. Anyway, if you want to do it, it's your skin. I think you'd look wicked sexy in more tattoos." He leaned across the table and kissed her deeply.

"I love the way you kiss me," she murmured.

He reclined back in the chair. "We gotta get our own place," he said.

Excitement flooded through her as she sat up straight. "You want us to live together?"

"Yeah. Now that your aunt's home, I'm not that comfortable being there all the time, and you got too many purses, shoes, clothes and other stuff to live at the clubhouse, so I thought we should get a house. They have some nice ones over by Las Cruces Road. You wanna check them out this weekend?"

"Definitely."

"So you're down with it?"

"I'd love to live with you," she answered.

"That's good. Do you want to take it one step further and be my old lady?" He brought her hand to his mouth and kissed it, gazing into her eyes.

"Is that like going steady?" Hailey had read up on the term in her research about the biker clubs, but she didn't quite see herself as someone else's "property." She saw wearing the cut in the same way as wearing a promise ring.

"It's way more than that. It means you belong to me and I belong to you, through all the good and bad times in life. I'll always have your back and you mine. We're entwined and will be until our last ride."

It sounds like a proposal. "I don't really understand everything about your world, but I'm willing to try. If wearing a leather vest means we're bound to each other, I'm down for it. I'll wear it proudly."

"I love you," he said, leaning over and planting a big kiss on her lips.

"Me too," she said, kissing him back.

After a delicious meal of steaks and baked potatoes, they walked hand-in-hand into the night. When they arrived at his Harley, he opened the saddlebags and took out a black vest, handing it to her. "This is your cut that has my patch. I never thought I'd give a woman my patch, but I've never loved a woman before you."

Turning it around, she saw the words "Property of Goldie" in white embroidery. A grin spread across her lips. "Pretty sure of yourself, aren't you?"

"Fuck yeah."

He helped her slip it on over her halter top. The buttery softness of the leather was cool against her skin. A shiver skated down her spine as she folded the cut around her. The pride in Goldie's eyes almost had her bawling, but she blinked rapidly as she looked down at the ground to ward off her tears.

"You wanna go to Arrow Lake?" he said thickly.

"I'd love to." Making love to him under the stars seemed like the perfect way to end their evening.

"I want you naked except for my cut, babe." He swung his leg over his bike and she climbed on.

As they left the lights and noise of the town behind, Hailey tilted her head back, smiling at the cluster of stars that speckled the inky sky. The wind rushed around and darkness surrounded them, and she was on top of the world. She'd been there since that night she walked into his ink shop.

Life was funny. She had been rambling along, doing what she was supposed to do, and then in came Goldie, turning her life upside down. And ordinary was no longer enough.

Goldie, her first real crush when she was a kid, and now her grown-up love.

When they arrived at the lake, Goldie's desire-filled eyes held hers as he eased her down on the blanket. When he slowly moved his lips down her body, kissing and biting her skin, she looped her arms around his neck and held on tight.

He was her rock, her love, her life. And they'd hold onto each other no matter how rough the ride got.

She was finally where she'd always wanted to be, and she was never letting go.

Epilogue

Five weeks later

H AILEY WAVED AT Fallon as she entered the restaurant. Pulling out a chair, she said, "Sorry I'm late. I got tied up at the shop."

"No worries. Breanna and Raven are running behind as well. I just got a text from them. How've you been?"

"Better. I still can't believe Dr. Daniels was the psycho. He was so different at the rehab center."

Fallon nodded. "I know what you mean. People can be so deceiving."

"He sure was, but then I only knew him through small snippets of time at the center. I just can't even begin to imagine what his wife thought when she found out."

"Would you like anything to drink?" the waitress asked just as Breanna and Raven came over to the table.

"A glass of merlot would be awesome," Hailey said.

"A double Jack. Neat," Raven said. Turning to the women, she shrugged. "I've had a shitty day."

Breanna laughed. "I'll have a glass of merlot as well."

Fallon picked up her glass of white wine and shook her head. "I'm good, thanks."

"I'm so glad I had an excuse to get away from the house. I've re-worked this lady's necklace like a hundred times. She keeps changing her mind on what charms she wants on it and she's driving me up a fuckin' wall." Raven leaned back in her chair, a scowl wrinkling her brow.

"It's like that at the flower shop. A lot of people tell you what they want and when you give it to them, they've already changed their minds on the colors or the flowers. Drives me nuts." Hailey smiled when the waitress put a glass of merlot in front of her.

"How're the plans for your California trip going?" Fallon asked.

"Goldie and I are leaving next week. It'll be so good to get away for a while, especially for him."

"How's his grandmother doing?" Breanna asked softly.

"Getting worse. It just rips him up. It's so hard to see someone you love die slowly. I don't know how to help him," Hailey answered.

"Just be there for him," Breanna said. Fallon and Raven nodded.

"I am, but I wish I could take away the pain." Hailey tore off a piece of bread and dipped it into the oil and balsamic vinegar.

"You being there means more than anything for him," Raven said.

Before Hailey could answer, her phone rang. She glanced at the screen and saw it was Ryan. "It's my brother. I'll be right back," she said as she pushed up from the chair. Standing outside the restaurant, she tapped the button. "Ryan! How are you?"

"Good. How're you doing?"

"Better than okay. I'm out with some of the old ladies having dinner. A new Italian restaurant opened in town and it's really good. When you come for Christmas, I'll take you here. You're coming, right?"

"That's the plan. I put in for my leave, but you know how that goes."

Hailey inhaled deeply then slowly blew out. "When are you going to talk to Goldie?" she asked.

"Hailey, let's not go there," Ryan replied.

"We have to. Goldie doesn't say much, but I know he's hurt about the way you're acting. He saved my life, Ryan. You guys have been friends for years. This has become ridiculous. If it weren't for Goldie, I would've been killed by that wacko."

"I know," he said in a low voice.

"Then…?"

"I texted him and told him I was grateful that he saved your life. But it doesn't take away from the fact that he betrayed me."

"Because he fell in love with me? So, he had to deny all feelings just to keep you happy? What about me? I have to walk away from a great guy who treats me like I'm the best thing that's ever happened to him? I know you're hung up about his past, but that's just what it is—*his past.* Goldie and I are making our memories in the present. If he were such a horrible guy, why in the hell were you best friends with him all these years?"

"I didn't say he was a horrible person. He's just not the best bet for a woman. I don't want to see you get hurt."

"He's not hurting me. As a matter of fact, he's the only guy who hasn't hurt me. Give me some credit for knowing what I want. Life can't give us guarantees against being hurt, you know that."

Ryan's sigh crackled over the phone. "Let's see how things go. That's the best I can give you."

"I'll take it. I can't wait until you're stateside. I miss you a lot."

"Me too. I'm really pushing hard for the Christmas leave. They've canceled me the last three years, so I figure they owe me."

"All of us being together for the holidays would be awesome. Mom and Dad would be ecstatic."

"I'll let you get back to your dinner. I gotta go. Just wanted to hear your voice. I was missing home."

When they hung up, an emptiness filled her as it always did after they spoke. She took several deep breaths before going back into the restaurant.

"How's your brother?" Fallon asked.

"Okay. I wish he'd come back home. I hate thinking of him over there." Hailey motioned the waitress for another merlot.

"Is he still pissed at Goldie?" Raven asked.

Hailey nodded. "But he didn't pretend we had a bad connection like he always does when I bring up Goldie. This time he said he'd see how things go. That's something, isn't it?"

Breanna smiled. "It is. Your brother's just concerned about you getting hurt, but he's opening the door for reconciliation. It'll come in time, when your relationship with Goldie is stronger."

"I think that too. I figure when he comes for Christmas and sees that we're still together and even closer, then he and Goldie will make amends."

"It'll happen for sure," Fallon said while Raven bobbed her head in agreement.

After a few hours, Hailey waved goodbye to her friends and headed home. She and Goldie had found a beautiful home and had been living in it for a little over a month. Each time she walked into the house, a shiver of excitement would course through her. She still couldn't believe that she and Goldie were sharing their lives together. It was like a dream come true for her.

Muscles deep inside her tightened when she saw his Harley parked in the garage. After reapplying her lipstick, she walked into the kitchen. She saw Goldie sprawled on the couch watching the motorcycle races on the sixty-four inch TV screen he insisted they had to have. He hadn't heard her come in. She quickly shrugged off her skirt and blouse so she only wore her ivory lace bra, thong, and stiletto heels. Slipping her jacket back on, she walked into the family room then bent over the couch and kissed him.

Immediately, he pulled her down to him and wrapped his arms around her. "Did you have a good time?" he asked huskily.

"It was good. Did you miss me?"

"Yeah. I always do. Now give me your lips."

She pressed her lips to his and they kissed deeply. When his hand slipped under her jacket and his eyebrows raised in surprise, she giggled against his lips.

"What the fuck, babe?" he rasped as his hand squeezed her butt.

"You didn't hear me come in, so I thought I'd surprise you."

A devilish grin spread across his face. "I love it when you surprise me." He yanked off her jacket and feasted his eyes on her round tits encased in delicate lace. Within seconds, he had her bra off and his mouth on her erect nipples, sucking them. She had his jeans unzipped and her fingers wrapped around his stiff dick. And with the sound of cams screeching on the television, they fucked each other fast and hard.

Lying on top of Goldie, Hailey swept her fingers over his chest slowly. "That was incredible," she murmured.

He kissed her forehead and squeezed her tighter to him. Reaching over, he grabbed the remote and muted the television. "I can't wait for us to hit the road next week. Riding up the California coast has always been something I've wanted to do, and having you pressed behind me will be fuckin' awesome."

"And we have almost a month to take it easy. I can't wait to make love to you on the beach. We'll have to bring a big blanket because a roommate of mine in college told me that everyone gets gum in their hair when they make love on the beach. She was from Santa Cruz, and she told me she was always cutting gum out of her hair as a teenager." Hailey sniggered.

"I'll make sure the only sticky stuff you have on you will come from me," he said as he cupped her chin. Dipping his head down, he kissed her while he ran his hand up and down her bare back.

"I've always wanted to go to California. I was supposed to visit Amber, my old roommate, in Santa Cruz, but life happened, and after college, we drifted apart. Maybe I'll look her up if we're in her area. It'd be fun to reconnect."

They lay together in a comfortable quietness. After a long while, she said softly, "Ryan called me today."

"I know. He texted me," Goldie replied.

She lifted up and stared at him. "He did? Why didn't you tell me?"

"Because when you came over all sexy, I wasn't thinking about it." He winked at her.

She brushed her lips across his. "What did he say?"

"That he talked to you, and he thanked me again for saving your life. Then he said he'd call me if he got leave at Christmas. I was surprised as fuck that he reached out to me. I just figured we were done."

Elation zipped through her, and she hugged him tightly. "I'm so happy. All I want is for the two most important men in my life to get along. By the time Christmas comes, Ryan will see that what we have isn't a pit stop for you…or for me."

Goldie pressed her closer to him until there wasn't any space between them. "What he's gonna see is how fuckin' crazy in love I am with you. I'd like us to be buds again, but if he can't accept *us*, so be it. There's no damn way I'm letting you out of my life. We're together, no matter what."

Warmth radiated through her, and her heart felt as though it would burst. Loving and being loved by Goldie completed her, and even though she suspected Ryan's anger would eventually dissipate, there was no way in hell she'd ever consider leaving Goldie. He was the piece of the puzzle that made her life perfect. She knew no matter what happened, they'd stand by each other.

"Anyway, once we have some kids, there's no way Ryan's gonna miss out on being an uncle," Goldie said into her hair.

She swallowed. "You're ready to have kids?"

His baritone laugh rumbled from his chest. "Not yet. I was talking about down the road. Like in a few years."

"Whew…I was starting to sweat. I want kids too, but not for a while. We've got time. Anyway, Aunt Patty's officially handing the store over to me after the holidays. She's feeling great and has booked a small villa in Tuscany. She's planning to stay at least six months. My mom's planning to go over and visit her."

"I'm happy for her. She had a rough year. You'll be a kickass business owner."

"It's what I always wanted. I'm so happy, and you're a huge reason why."

Goldie kissed her. "You make my world rock, woman. We're meant to be together."

And they were. She was just glad that they'd given each other a chance.

As they lay together, holding each other, she realized that there was no other place on earth she'd rather be than with Goldie in their new home.

It doesn't get any better than this. She nuzzled her head against his neck, brushing her lips across his collarbone.

And it didn't. After all the dates and failed relationships, she was where she always wanted to be—with Goldie.

"I love you," she whispered against his taut skin.

"And I love you too, babe. I always will." Goldie stroked her cheek with his finger.

With a contented sigh, she closed her eyes and let the comfort and warmth of him wrap around her as she slowly drifted off to sleep.

Make sure you sign up for my newsletter so you can keep up with my new releases, special sales, free short stories, and other treats only available to newsletter readers. When you sign up, you will receive a FREE hot and steamy novella. Sign up at:
http://eepurl.com/bACCL1

Visit me on Facebook
facebook.com/AuthorChiahWilder

Check out my other books at my Author Page
amazon.com/author/chiahwilder

Notes from Chiah

As always, I have a team behind me making sure I shine and continue on my writing journey. It is their support, encouragement, and dedication that pushes me further in my writing journey. And then, it is my wonderful readers who have supported me, laughed, cried, and understood how these outlaw men live and love in their dark and gritty world. Without you—the readers—an author's words are just letters on a page. The emotions you take away from the words breathe life into the story.

Thank you to my amazing Personal Assistant Amanda Faulkner. I don't know what I'd do without you. I value your suggestions and opinions, and my world is so much saner with you in it. You keep the non-writing part of my indie publishing world running smoothly. I so appreciate it. You are always ready to jump in and fix everything when I'm pulling my hair out. You are so cheerful, and when I hear your bubbling voice, it instantly uplifts me. So happy YOU are on my team!

Thank you to my editor, Kristin, for all your insightful edits, excitement with my new series, Night Rebels MC, and encouragement during the writing and editing process. I truly value your editorial eyes and suggestions as well as the time you spend. You're the best!

Thank you to my wonderful beta readers, Jessica, Paula, and Barbara. Your enthusiasm and suggestions for GOLDIE: Night Rebels MC were spot on and helped me to put out a stronger, cleaner novel. Your insight and attention to detail were awesome.

Thank you to the bloggers for your support in reading my book, sharing it, reviewing it, and getting my name out there. I so appreciate all your efforts. You all are so invaluable. I hope you know that. Without you, the indie author would be lost. And thank you to the bloggers who have been with me from my very first book, "Hawk's Property: Insurgents Motorcycle Club." Your continued support for my books is beyond awesome!

Thank you ARC readers you have helped make all my books so much stronger. I appreciate the effort and time you put in to reading, reviewing, and getting the word out about the books. I don't know what I'd do without you. I feel so lucky to have you behind me.

Thank you to my Street Team. Thanks for your input, your support, and your hard work. I appreciate you more than you know. A HUGE hug to all of you!

Thank you to Carrie from Cheeky Covers. You are amazing! I can always count on you. You are the calm to my storm. You totally rock, and I love your artistic vision.

Thank you to my proofreader, Daryl, whose last set of eyes before the last once over I do, is invaluable. I appreciate the time and attention to detail you always give to my books. You ALWAYS deliver, and I love that I can count on you.

Thank you to Ena and Amanda with Enticing Journeys Promotions who have helped garner attention for and visibility to the Night Rebels MC series. Couldn't do it without you! Also a big thank you to Book Club Gone Wrong Blog.

Thank you to the readers who continue to support me and read my books. Without you, none of this would be possible. I appreciate your comments and reviews on my books, and I'm dedicated to giving you the best story that I can. I'm always thrilled when you enjoy a book as much as I have in writing it. You definitely make the hours of typing on the computer and the frustrations that come with the territory of writing books so worth it.

And a special thanks to every reader who has been with me since "Hawk's Property." Your support, loyalty, and dedication to my stories touch me in so many ways. You enable me to tell my stories, and I am forever grateful to you.

You all make it possible for writers to write because without you reading the books, we wouldn't exist. Thank you, thank you! ♥

GOLDIE: Night Rebels Motorcycle Club (Book 4)

Dear Readers,

Thank you for reading my book. I hope you enjoyed the fourth book in my new Night Rebels MC series as much as I enjoyed writing Goldie and Hailey's story. This gritty and rough motorcycle club has a lot more to say, so I hope you will look for the upcoming books in the series. Romance makes life so much more colorful, and a rough, sexy bad boy makes life a whole lot more interesting.

If you enjoyed the book, please consider leaving a review on Amazon. I read all of them and appreciate the time taken out of busy schedules to do that.

I love hearing from my fans, so if you have any comments or questions, please email me at chiahwilder@gmail.com or visit my facebook page.

To receive a **free copy of my novella**, *Summer Heat*, and to hear of **new releases, special sales, free short stories**, and **ARC opportunities**, please sign up for my **Newsletter** at http://eepurl.com/bACCL1.

Happy Reading,

Chiah

Upcoming Books:
Beautiful Boss
Coming October, 2017

A sexy standalone romance novel.

The first time I'd seen Trace Prescott since he broke my BFF's heart was at a nightclub.

He had the audacity to check me out and flirt with me while I was getting another drink for my heartbroken friend.

Well, I went ballistic. I didn't hold back and I told him exactly what I thought of his arrogant, cheating ways.

The jerk made my friend think she was a queen with all the expensive gifts, dinners, and weekend getaways, but he forgot to tell her he had a princess he was boinking on the side.

Unbelievable!

And all the tall, gorgeous, sexy ass did was smirk as I ranted. I almost threw my glass of champagne in his face, but he wasn't worth the fifteen dollars it cost me.

Feeling good, I stormed off. But I did sneak peeks at him for the rest of the night and hated that he caught me each time.

Who cares? I won't ever see him again.

Imagine my surprise the following morning when my new boss turned out to be arrogant, sexy-as-hell Trace Prescott.

If I didn't need the job, I'd quit, but I'm stuck, and that might turn out not to be such a bad thing.

Insurgents Christmas Story
Insurgents Motorcycle Club Series
Coming in November, 2017

As the snow quietly falls over Pinewood Springs, a shadow lurks among the evergreen trees, watching and waiting to strike.

The holiday season is the time for the Insurgents MC's big toy drive, and each year the club strives to give out more toys to the needy children of Pinewood Springs. But this season, the toys go missing, Christmas trees are destroyed, and the inflatables swaying in the wind deflate with the spray of BB gun pellets. Someone is trying to ruin Christmas.

Hawk, VP of the club, has his hands full with his family and some brewing problems with a rival club, the Deadly Demons. The president, Banger along with the sergeant-at-arms, Rock, Throttle, Jax, Chas, Axe, Jerry, Wheelie, and Rags are trying to figure out who keeps stealing all the donations at the charity center.

Amid all the chaos and danger crackling around the club, the Insurgent men make time to show their old ladies all the loving that they need.

But when Hawk's and Banger's children are put in danger, there is nothing like the fury of an outlaw biker.

Time is ticking and the crazed Scrooge must be stopped at all costs.

Will the Insurgents save Christmas for their families and the town?

PACO
Book 5 in the Night Rebels MC Series
Coming in December, 2017

Paco, the rugged VP of the Night Rebels MC, only stopped for some chow at the diner. He was headed back to Alina. He never intended on staying. But then he saw her sitting alone at the booth next to his. She had on too much makeup and too little clothing for the cold winter night.

Then she looked at him. Her eyes were dark like an endless stretch of midnight sky. In their inky depths, he saw sorrow and pain and threads of fierceness. They drew him in.

He, the man who never looked past one night with a woman, wanted to know about this small woman sitting across from him.

Sensing she was in trouble, he wanted to help her. He knew he should just pay his bill, hop on his Harley, and head home, but he couldn't. She grounded him, and in that one instant, he knew she'd be his. The urge to possess her consumed him.

Misty Sullivan hated the cold nights when she'd have to haul her ass from truck to truck to make enough to satisfy her boyfriend, Bobby. She used to have another name, but that was a long time ago when she was normal and life was good. She tried not to think about it anymore—it just made her life worse.

The stranger who stared at her didn't look like a trucker. He was decked out in leather and denim, and he looked at her like she was a person not a piece of ass. But life experience told her he was probably just as bad as all the other men who came into her world.

Men couldn't be trusted. They acted nice to get a woman where they wanted her, and then they turned mean and ugly.

But the stranger's piercing stare doesn't frighten her, and that surprises her. A good-looking, sexy man like him could have any woman he wanted, so why was he wasting his time with her?

Then events throw them together and Misty must decide if she should trust the man who is playing havoc with her heart.

Paco knows that the only way Misty can trust him is to face her past and deal with it. Will she let him help her before her past crashes with her present and destroys her? Can he let her slip away from him?

This is the fifth book in the Night Rebels MC Romance series. This is Paco's story. It is a standalone. This book contains violence, sexual assault (not graphic), strong language, and steamy/graphic sexual scenes. It describes the life and actions of an outlaw motorcycle club. If any of these issues offend you, please do not read the book. HEA. No cliffhangers! The book is intended for readers over the age of 18.

Other Books by Chiah Wilder

Insurgent MC Series:

Hawk's Property

Jax's Dilemma

Chas's Fervor

Axe's Fall

Banger's Ride

Jerry's Passion

Throttle's Seduction

Rock's Redemption

An Insurgent's Wedding

Insurgents MC Romance Series: Insurgents Motorcycle Club
Box Set (Books 1 – 4)

Night Rebels MC Series:

STEEL

MUERTO

DIABLO

Find all my books at: amazon.com/author/chiahwilder

I love hearing from my readers. You can email me at
chiahwilder@gmail.com.

Sign up for my newsletter to receive a FREE Novella, updates on new
books, special sales, free short stories, and ARC opportunities at
http://eepurl.com/bACCL1.

Visit me on facebook at facebook.com/AuthorChiahWilder.

Made in the USA
Middletown, DE
03 May 2018